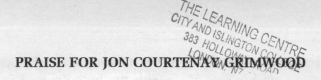

PRAISE FOR JON COURTENAY GRIMWOOD

'. . . vivid gore, sex and high-octane adventure. This is terrific stuff'

THE BOOKSELLER

'Grimwood's depiction of the underbelly of a fragmented future has a memorable bite'

Paul J. McAuley, INTERZONE

'This book is written for people who know what *reMix* means, who know it with their hearts . . .'

Jeff Noon

'The plot gains in interest and complexity as it goes along. Grimwood's eye for the telling detail . . . is getting sharper than ever . . . Grimwood is rapidly developing into a novelist worth watching'

LOCUS

'Grimwood's Napoleonic alternate history gives him a jump cut to a future that could be ours sooner than we'd like to think . . . you'd need a heart of stone not to laugh'

Ken MacLeod

'. . . sordid, vile and vice-ridden'

VECTOR

'Sporadic, y . . . highly charged, acts of violence are hammered out with chillingly forensic detail'

STARBURST

'Some authors recycle . . . A few introduce genuine originality. With *reMix*, Jon Courtenay Grimwood consolidates his place in the latter category – a compulsive, labyrinthine tale'

TIME OUT

'The intelligent absurdities of his plotting, a vein of perverse eroticism, and his love affair with the brand-named impedimenta of an improbable high-tech future, add up to superior brain candy'

Roz Kaveney, amazon.co.uk

'Grimwood gives plenty plot'

SCOTLAND ON SUNDAY

'Darkly witty, violent and weird . . . A futuristic thriller that will not only keep you on the edge of your seat, it'll probably nick the seat as well'

LINEONE ENTERTAINMENT

Other books by Jon Courtenay Grimwood

neoAddix

Lucifer's Dragon

reMix

About the author . . .

Born in Malta and christened in the upturned bell of a ship, Jon Courtenay Grimwood grew up in Britain, the Far East and Scandinavia. He currently works as a freelance journalist and lives in North London. He writes for a number of newspapers and magazines, including the *Guardian* and *SFX*.

Jon is also the author of *neoAddix*, *Lucifer's Dragon* and *reMix* and is now working on a new series of SF novels.

The *redRobe* website is at http://www.j-cg.co.uk

redRobe

Jon Courtenay Grimwood

EARTHLIGHT

LONDON · SYDNEY · NEW YORK · TOKYO · SINGAPORE · TORONTO

www.earthlight.co.uk

First published in Great Britain by Earthlight, 2000
An imprint of Simon & Schuster UK Ltd
A Viacom Company

1 3 5 7 9 10 8 6 4 2

Simon & Schuster UK Ltd
Africa House
64–78 Kingsway
London WC2 6AH

Simon & Schuster Australia
Sydney

A CIP catalogue record for this book is available
from the British Library

ISBN 0-671-02260-1

Typeset in Melior by Palimpsest Book Production Limited,
Polmont, Stirlingshire
Printed and bound in Great Britain by
Caledonian International
Book Manufacturing, Glasgow

F GRI
MO4057

For Jammer, who gets on and off trains
without complaint (well, mostly).
And for Sam, once again with thanks . . .
I owe you both.

'Give me six sentences written by the most innocent man and I will find something in them to hang him . . .'
Cardinal Richelieu

Prologue

Tunic by Issuki Marino

'That one,' said Father Sylvester, pointing to a Japanese whore with tiny breasts and soft legs, her legs wrapped in crepe bandages so fine as to be almost transparent, 'she's perfect . . .'

She was, too. Young enough to pass for his daughter if needs be, not so young that she'd cry at being forced to do things she didn't want to do. Spit at him maybe from that down-turned bee sting of a mouth or lash out with black-lacquered nails, but not cry. This one was long since cried-out. That was, if the emptiness in her dark brown eyes was anything to go by.

No expectations.

Nothing left that resembled hope.

Hollow.

Father Sylvester realised that probably made them equal. The bearded, black-robed priest nodded at Madame Sotto who smiled as if she expected no less, and levered her vast bulk from an ornate and over-gilded chair. Fake Louis Napoleon from the look of it, and not a good fake either.

At Madame Sotto's shoulder stood a Megrib bodyguard dressed in a silver posing pouch, silver body paint and heavy brass bracelets. Behind her, red velvet rose to the ceiling, swathes of it covering all four walls. The whole brothel was one giant fire risk.

'You told me you wanted young,' Madame Sotto said with a short laugh, 'maybe you should have mentioned you also wanted Chink.' The fat woman made it sound like a joke but Father Sylvester knew it wasn't. She was upset. He'd watched the edginess rise in her puffy face as he rejected one after another of her whores. Running first through the beautiful ones, then the sullen, sultry and obviously under-age. After that, she'd tried podgy and then out-and-out odalisque, just in case he was chubby-chasing, but he'd waved them all away until they got to this one.

And now he was interested. Really interested.

The girl was round hipped. Soft from lack of proper exercise. She wore a weird high-collared top of grey canvas that stretched like a restraint-jacket from under her chin down to her thighs. Her legs were bound from the ankle upwards with those crepe bandages and only her arms and feet were bare, each toenail decorated with a tiny henna spiral.

Father Sylvester knew high fashion when he saw it. And though he couldn't put a price on the clothes he recognised expensive.

The Madame had been saving her. That was the reason he hadn't been shown Mai before. This girl was earmarked for someone else but the priest didn't waste his time wondering who. He wasn't interested in anything except leaving with the girl in front of him – and soon.

'Japanese,' he told Madame Sotto, looking at the girl's sullen mouth and heavy cheeks, so rouged they looked like she'd been slapped hard. 'She's Japanese, not Chinese.'

'Nip, chink . . .' Madame Sotto shrugged. She was going to say they all looked the same to her, but then she caught Father Sylvester's eye and swallowed the words. There weren't many Korean priests working for the Jesuits, but she was looking at one of them.

Half Japanese, that's what the girl was. Not full . . . Father Sylvester amended the words in his head, without bothering to tell Madame Sotto. Not that she'd have understood the difference anyway. A bit of Father Sylvester, the dark bit that always burnt at the back of his mind, wanted to tell the brothel keeper that, actually, when it came to Occidentals he couldn't tell one raddled Madame from another either. But as a priest he didn't allow himself the indulgence.

'You . . .' Father Sylvester jerked his chin rudely at the girl. 'Strip.'

He caught it then, inside her head, a faint flare of anger that never quite reached her face. The priest smiled and Mai's eyes widened.

She knew who he was then. Or at least what he was . . .

Psi. Sucking her thoughts like a cerebral vanpyre. And she'd thought it was her body he'd wanted.

'Strip,' Madame Sotto ordered crossly and the girl did, blank-faced as she began to undo her canvas jacket, starting at the left hip, her childish fingers fumbling at tiny hooks. The huge swirl of dark hair wound up on her skull like a headdress shuddered as the girl lent forward to get a clearer view of what she was doing.

Madame Sotto snapped something in Spanish and Mai stopped, fingers frozen over the hooks. Then she nodded and ran one finger quickly down the other side seam of her jacket, waiting impassively as the canvas parted neatly and the grey jacket slid to the marble floor.

Smartcloth. Father Sylvester had read about it. Ate sweat, adjusted its TOG rating according to ambient temperature and kept itself dirt free. Also changed colour by adjusting its refractive index and provided invisible uplift to most of Hollywood, if the *Enquirer* was to be believed. And Father Sylvester made a warped point of believing the *Enquirer*.

The girl was beautiful. In a sulking, pouting, '5 a.m. in the morning, what the fuck am I doing up being gawped at by a priest' sort of way. A single band of crepe was wrapped once round her chest, not quite hiding cherry-blossom nipples, but what Father Sylvester really noticed were her eyes. They were dark with the knowledge that she'd never find her way out of life's maze, not even if the rats helped her.

'Enough,' Father Sylvester held up his hand.

'You don't want her to remove the rest?'

No. The priest shook his head. He'd seen enough. More than enough, more than he should. He was in the wrong place, at the wrong time. And he was very definitely doing the wrong thing.

'How much?'

Madame Sotto named a price that would have kept Father Sylvester's old food kitchen in the Aleutian Islands going for a year. But he wasn't in a barren archipelago off the coast of Russia or even at the Vatican, he was in Spain. In a ramshackle farmhouse set fifteen klicks outside Alicante. And there was a stretch UltraGlyde waiting outside the door, chattering to itself as it waited for the Jesuit to make his purchase.

'That's acceptable.' The priest motioned to the girl to put on her clothes and waited while she struggled to push one arm into a tight sleeve and then zipped up the opposite seam with a quick run of her nail along the edge of the cloth.

Did the garment do that for everyone, the priest wondered, or was it imprinted to Mai's touch only? Either way, there was going to be time enough to find out.

'Twenty-four hours,' the Madame said firmly.

Father Sylvester nodded, his face impassive. Without hesitation he reached into his soutane and pulled out a Moroccan leather wallet, its corners edged with brass. The card he selected at random was stolen, they all were. So was the Honda outside. But they were as nothing compared to the dead Pope's soul hidden in his pocket.

Sliding the gold HKS across the top of the marble table, Father Sylvester made sure his fingers never quite touched those of the Madame.

He should have asked about infections, about retro Virus and malaria and all the other diseases whores in Spain were prone to. Not that any of it would have changed his mind. This was the one he wanted, no matter how bad her blood count. Taking his gold card back from the Madame he pushed it deep into a pocket.

All that stood between him and success was a door and a short walk to his car.

'This time tomorrow,' he said, most of his attention now on the Japanese girl. 'Go on,' he told her, stepping back to let Mai enter a small courtyard flanked by Moorish *ajimez*, double arches cut from local red marble.

Later in the day the heat would be blistering. But right now it was still cool, in that Mediterranean way that everyone knew signified the sun would eventually be hot enough to melt blacktop.

Father Sylvester sighed.

Behind him a thin mist clung to the grey slopes of the Sierra, those final foothills of the Baetic Cordillera that had once plunged into the Mediterranean at Cape La Nao to reappear miles later as the island of Ibiza. Now, of course, the cities of Alicante and Valencia were landlocked, the new coastline a product of General Que's decision to lower the Mediterranean.

Between the brothel and the sierra were *huertas*, heavily-irrigated orange groves thriving in the alluvial soil of the Levant littoral. But it was the bare mountain beyond that which people really noticed, the *puig*, its hard-edged grey slope rising sharp as pain. Not high but jagged like broken teeth and fringed around the bottom with a white-walled hill village that clung tight to its base.

Father Sylvester didn't even turn to look at it. Priest and girl, they walked down the grey stone steps together towards the waiting Honda, the girl picking her way carefully across damp gravel, bare feet moving over sharp stones as if undertaking complicated ballet steps, to a score that only she could hear.

'Ready to move, Monsignor?'

The man nodded, remembered his car wasn't running on visual and brusquely told the Honda to unlock its door. The Honda did, both front doors opening in a gentle hiss of well-damped hydraulics.

'I'll drive,' the priest told the car, daring it to disagree. And then he had the hover up on its skirt and spinning in a neat circle before the semiAI even had time to remind him about his seat belt.

'The girl too,' said the Honda, and Father Sylvester nodded to Mai to strap herself in, which she did in bland silence.

Experienced in the ways of the world though he was, Father Sylvester didn't realise the girl was thinking precisely nothing. That Mai's head was empty of thought, fear or hope. She had long since discarded all three, learning first to retreat into a corner of her mind and then – later – once she'd reached twelve and the lessons got harder, to leave her body altogether. To hover at the edge of existence, in the far corner of every room while clients beat or abused her empty body.

There was a clinical name for disengagement, for the fracture of psyche from pain, but the girl didn't know that. She thought she'd invented the technique: that it was hers alone. A way to keep sane while other children retreated into suicide or the fixed brightness of crystalMeth.

'Ready?' Father Sylvester asked, half thinking about his wallet and already regretting its loss. Fat with its stolen credit cards and bank bonds, he'd left the thing on top of Madame Sotto's marble table, just inside the viewing room.

How long before the Madame noticed? How long before she picked it up and opened it, not to take anything of course, but just to take a look at the possessions of a priest who'd woken her up at 2a.m. on a Friday demanding to be shown all her girls? Three minutes, maybe four . . . If he'd been a betting man that's what Father Sylvester would have gambled on. But she didn't even wait until his car was out of the drive.

The ball of fire expanded outwards from white through gold to red, flames licking up for the briefest second before black smoke followed them skywards and the twisted olive trees around the edge of the brothel began to catch, leaves shrivelling like singed paper.

But it wasn't the explosion that broke the habits of Mai's

short lifetime and shocked the girl into screaming . . . It was the aftershock that hurled down the red-earth path behind the car and caught the Honda, twisting it sideways towards a rock-strewn bank.

She needn't have bothered. Without hesitation, the semiAI overrode manual and slid the silver Honda up the steep bank and down the other side into a field of orange trees. The brothel was a mess of flames behind them. Its grey stucco walls already flaking with heat, red roof tiles falling into the inferno below through gaping holes in the broken rafters. Whole olive trees were aflame, smoke spiralling up like a plume of black feathers into the early morning sky. Father Sylvester had been right, Madame Sotto's brothel was a giant fire risk.

So simple and so effective. All it took to prime the trigger was to remove a credit card from the wallet. Opening the wallet again ignited the core and after that everything was a mathematical certainty.

If he hadn't been dying, Father Sylvester would have been proud of himself. As it was, he didn't have the time or energy left for pride, foolish or otherwise. On a plane to Mexico was where he was meant to be. Not killing brothel keepers, buying children or stealing souls.

He turned to the girl and gripped her podgy face in one hand, looking deep into her eyes while the Honda steered itself between rows of orange trees and back onto a narrow road.

'Your name . . .' he began but got no further before Mai interrupted, trying to tell him who she was.

'No,' said Father Sylvester, holding her face a little harder between his hands, his eyes never leaving hers. 'Your name is Joan, do you understand me?'

Mai looked uncertain, unhappy. They were sliding down a slip road now towards a battered, cracked four-lane blacktop and behind them, what she had loosely called home for the last five years was burning up in flames.

'You have a new name,' the priest told her fiercely, 'a new life. Now tell me, who are you?'

'Joan . . .' The girl stumbled over the unfamiliar name.

Father Sylvester let go of the girl's face and collapsed back into the black ultrasuede of his ergonomically-perfect driver's seat. He was shaking. 'Yes,' he said. 'Your name is Joan. You're the new Pope.'

Chapter One

Sounds/Silence

Axl could hear, that wasn't his problem. Axl's problem was his life lacked a coherent sound track, at least it did these days. When doors shut they just slammed, with no kick-back loop of drums. Cars collided on the freeway and no hi-haus/low-fi chords crashed. Not like back when . . .

He was blind to the music.

Axl still had a Korg sound system installed in his head, at least he figured he did, just not connected. After fifteen years Axl still couldn't get used to it.

He had the negative algorhythm blues. He had . . .

Shit, Axl knew exactly what he had, a sucking black hole where the music used to loop and feed inside his head, sound-tracking everything.

'You look like death . . .'

The mirror wanted to say *like shit*, but it was too mealy-mouthed.

'Yeah.' Axl pushed one thin arm through the sleeve of an old biker's jacket. He had a job to do and he was in a hurry. Plus, there was something he was meant to remember and crystalMeth from the night before was making him forget.

The jacket was PaulSmith with silver ceramic elbowpads, relined years back in spider's silk and Axl liked it. The mirror didn't . . .

Wedged into the mirror's frame was Axl's driving licence which showed a round-faced, vaguely European male with spiky, peroxide-blond hair. Years of not sleeping had left him with the dissolute look of a drunken Welsh poet, which was odd because his mother was originally Irish Catholic. Axl had no idea who his father was, the police never caught the man.

Age 29, *height* 6′ 1″, *weight* 152 lb, *name* Axl Borja, *status* human. It lied about everything except his height, and that was only true if Axl wore Cuban heels. There was other shit crypted onto it, like a DNA profile and medical record but that was also fake.

Besides he was using another name these days too. Which one didn't matter. He changed them as regularly as swopped his dead-end jobs flipping hamburgers.

Axl shrugged, checked his looks in the glass and then took another glance at his eyes. Nineteen years back they'd been advertised as 'clear and sparkling, like early daybreak peeping through a clear night sky.' And at $4500 a pop on the open market that's what they should have stayed. Right around now they looked more like the sodium headlights of a dumptruck refracted through smog. And he could have moved house using the bags under them, if only he could raise enough credit to relocate . . .

Walking across the kitchen of the flat he semi/sort-of squatted, Axl realised he was stark bollock naked except for the jacket and remembered seconds later that it didn't matter a fuck, he lived alone.

His choice. At least that was what he always told himself.

Machines he could handle, even if they did answer back. Human beings couldn't be returned. Hell, most didn't even come with a guarantee.

'Hey fuck-wit . . .'

'Coffee,' Axl demanded and wrapped his fingers round the cable attaching the Zanussi BreakfastBar to the wall. For once the Zanussi didn't argue. Above the BreakfastBar what looked like a tastefully-framed Fox Studios poster flicked over on cue to a rolling newsfeed, leading in on the major headlines.

'Samsara takes another 50,000 refugees from Europe.'

Crashing chord from the screen. Shot of thin Catalan woman breastfeeding toddler.

'*Cartel Pharmaceuticals sue IMF for collapse of Colombian economy . . .*'

Another chord, less emphatic. A pan back from bombed office block to burned-out district of Bogota.

'*Vatican refuses to release figures for auditing. WorldBank denies Pope Joan might rise from the dead . . .*'

Minor chord for what would be a major miracle. And an archive shot of the Pope staring at a hovering camera.

No news in other words.

Axl pulled the tab on a Lucky Strike and drew smoke deep into his lungs. If there was anything the Zanussi hated worse than Axl washing breakfast down with coffee it was him smoking and eating at the same time.

The front door said goodbye, even though it knew Axl hadn't paid rent on the sublet in months. The lift was scrupulously polite on the way down. One of the Armani-suited porters even smiled wryly as he let Axl out through a service entrance, something that was strictly forbidden.

But Axl was still scowling as he walked out of the Metropole and into a Mexican morning so hot it felt like someone had just kicked down Hell's front door. Dead fireworks from last night's fiesta littered the open-air car park at the back of the building. Dead fireworks, a sleeping drunk and three blank-faced local kids flopped out on a discarded nylon settee.

They watched him pass, their eyes hidden behind cheap copies of last season's Spyro wraprounds. The joker in the gang crossed himself and Axl scowled even more. He'd remembered what he was trying to forget. It wasn't the thought of a day at McDonalds that pissed him off. As if a day spent flipping burgers wasn't bad enough, when his shift was over he had to go out and shoot somebody.

Chapter Two

Vote Maximillia

Grid-locked traffic. Smog warning. Three shootings since lunch time. Same as it ever was . . .

The valley was 100km long, 60km wide and 2500m above sea level. Inhabited since prehistory, its bowl now contained the world's biggest city, *Day Effé*, Mexico's capital. Axl still didn't think in metres but he'd been around the city long enough to know just how big it was.

From long shot, the place cried out for plaintive single-track guitar, nose flutes, even a little mindless Dutch trance. Close up, it demanded needle-sharp acid lines or electric violin, amphetamine edged. But all Axl got in his head was street noise and the arhythmic grinding of gears as vehicles lurched up the *Paseo de la Contre-Reformacion*.

'Vote Maximillia,' demanded a poster. The picture of Max was flyspecked and bleached almost white by the sun. All the same the poster spoke firmly, as if it couldn't imagine that Axl might do anything else.

Axl snorted. He didn't vote, hadn't voted, not in an election where the result had been a foregone conclusion even before it took place ten weeks back. Someone should tell the sign that Max won, as Imperial candidates usually did when they were the only person allowed to stand.

The sign was midway between *Glorieta Cristobal Colon* and *Cuauhténoc*, vast statues on the paseo dedicated to the man who discovered the New World and the Aztec emperor who lost it. Colon's plinth had priests carved around its base, Cuauhténoc's had scenes of torture. It seemed to Axl that very little had changed.

'Vote . . .' The sign began again, only to squeal as Axl kicked out and crumpled one of its tubular uprights, making the hoarding lean even further. Not an easy manoeuvre for someone parked-up on an oversized Yamaha WildStar, but Axl was happy to make the effort.

He would have spat into the dirt like a *cholo* but caught himself in time.

Once, way back, the DFPD and Axl had an understanding, when this had still been what he did for a living instead of flipping burgers any place that didn't want his papers. And as understandings went, it had been a good one.

He didn't fuck up the hits, he didn't turn tourists into Chinese takeout even by accident and he didn't leave incriminating clues, the kind they couldn't overlook. In return the DFPD didn't give him grief about slotting lowlifes they'd have tagged and bagged themselves given half a chance.

Axl sighed and checked his watch. *7.30 p.m., Friday, August 13 . . .* His blood pressure was up slightly, his neurorhythms were erratic and his heartbeat was ten over ideal. But since he wasn't carrying betaBs he was going to have to live with it. He had no messages and he was bored with waiting.

At least the three kids parked-up in the black Toyota bubble behind him had reruns of BlackJack Hot to watch. Sitting on his stolen Yamaha, Axl could do most of the dialogue from memory.

'You going to die now . . .'

'Yeah, right.'

Said hard and slow. The way studios imagined people spoke on the streets, fifty years out of date and way too intelligible. Real street was jump-cut and amphetamine fast. Axl had been there . . .

'Say goodbye Jack.'

'Goodbye Jack.'

And the gun would jump from Black Jack's wrist holster to his hand before the villain even had time to mash the slide on some ugly, stub Skorpios.

Bang.

Axl hadn't known how much the studios left out, not until he got to eleven and started killing people for himself. Putting a .38 ceramic through some jerk's skull produced enough loosely-chopped meat to turn anyone vegetarian.

There were no labels in the clothes Axl wore. Not that it would have made any difference, since simple thread analysis would have identified everything except the jacket as being made in Day Effé itself. Most probably by twelve-year-old ghosts in a slum sweatshop out near Tapo. But he cut the labels from habit and most of Axl's bad habits died hard.

Like stealing get-away vehicles and always choosing fancy ones. The fat Yamaha had been lifted thirty minutes before from in front of *Thunder Road*, the biker's café on Avenida Madero. 1600 cc, 48-degree, old 8-valve pushrod unit, capable of 100kmp at just 2.4k revs per minute. What's more the lovingly-restored V-twin was completely original, except for a turbo-charger and gyro, and a small Matsui semi-AI to handle cruise control.

Not that the evening traffic on the ten lanes of the paseo de la CR was going anywhere. And nor would Axl until he saw the Fiat coupe he was waiting for. Leon Kachowsky was forty minutes late and unless he turned up soon Axl's blood pressure was going to take another unwelcome hike.

Back when, that would have been enough to kick Axl's bass line into a jagged holding loop ready for the build. But now . . .

Axl spat anyway.

In theory, Axl's every move was being watched by the vidcams bolted to road signs, bridges, the top of every tall building. Apparently there was even a fleet of low-orbit Aerospats bought cheap from the French. But this was Mexico City. Half the cameras weren't working, and the output from those that were didn't run basic visual recognition software. They got watched by low-paid staff who worked hard not to notice anything at all, it wasn't worth the paperwork.

But enough of that . . . The traffic on Axl's side of the paseo was kick-starting into movement and finally he'd spotted Kachowsky's red coupé, it was the semiAI model with bulletproof shell but the Kevlar softtop was down and the man would be driving it on manual, he was that kind of idiot.

Blipping the bike into action reactivated the poster.

Axl glanced again at the faded tri-D with its idealised portrait of a girl in green uniform with silver braid looped down her chest in traditional cavalry knots. A long sabre hanging uselessly from one hip.

'Vote . . .' the poster began and Axl kicked it, more gently this time.

'Yeah, right. Keep the Austrians in Chapultepec Castle. I got it.' He gunned the twist grip on his Yamaha and slid the 800-pound bike into a vanishing gap in the traffic, leaving the dumb-fuck poster covered with even more dust than when he found it.

The election was gone, done, over . . . Sixteen-year-old Maximillia Habsburg was Emperor of Mexico. Just like every other dysfunctional, manic-depressive first-born from the family Louis Napoleon hoiked into power when he opened his purse back in 1864 and offered Mexico to Archduke Ferdinand Maximilian of Austria.

Three years later the Mexican empire converted to a democracy, with the accession of each emperor dependent on a plebiscite. It fooled nobody, but it pacified the newly-victorious President Lincoln and − back then − Mexico spent a lot of time trying to stay on good terms with its well-armed friend north of the border.

Five cars ahead, two lanes across and still utterly oblivious to what was about to happen sat the fat man Axl intended to

kill, squeezed into the driver's seat of a sports coupé so retro
it was all leather seats, stubby tail fins and tyres fat enough to
iron flat a pedestrian if they passed over one. The vehicle just
begged to be wrapped round with cheese-mungous slide guitar.
But – as ever – all Axl got was traffic noise.

Angrily, Axl blipped his Yamaha between a Honda UltraGlyde
and a Mack cargo drone, watching the gap he'd just closed go
wide open again as fat boy flipped into the outside lane to the
sound of hooting. Kachowsky wasn't driving defensively, he
was just being his usual arsehole self.

In the seat next to him was a young blonde, long hair held by
a white silk scarf and face hidden behind a lightweight smog
mask. She wore a red Diorissima jacket. The scarf was House of
Versace, this month's model. The mask was the kind picked up
from a street stall by people who've forgotten to bring their own
or didn't know they were going to be travelling in an open-top
car . . .

Not Kachowsky's regular squeeze then, someone new maybe.
Either that, or else the blonde was a bit on the side to the bit on
the side. From what he'd heard of fat boy's personal life that
wouldn't surprise Axl in the least.

Ahead of him the traffic was picking up speed, gaps lengthening
between cars as vehicles filtered off onto a slip road. Now was
the time to make a move, before the four lanes on his side of
the road could slow again.

Axl flipped back his holster's velcro restraining strap with
his thumb, tripped a wake-up switch on the side of his Colt
hiPower and pulled the gun from beneath his jacket.

'Ready?'

'What, you think I'm . . .' Silence hit as the Colt ran a scan
on Axl's current location and jumped five years and one whole
continent.

'We're fucking where?'

'Mexico,' said Axl.

'You're in trouble?'

The gun didn't really need the answer to that either. Thirty-nine shots, three magazines, nineteen cartridges in each – exploding ceramic, phosphex or flechette – all running parallel up the handle. Use more than two of anything and you'd already fucked up. That's what his first sergeant used to say; mind you, she bought it on camera, both her guns empty. Took a bamboo spear under her left tit and through her heart, it made repeats on the evening news.

'Hey,' said the Colt, 'you want to make a choice?'

Yeah, he did. As always the Colt would want phosphex but Axl didn't. He hit the brakes as tail lights ahead lit up red, the Yamaha slowing to a crawl. There was that girl in the passenger seat and Axl didn't do spillage. It was going to have to be . . .

'*Flechette*.' No smarts, no in-flight steering. Just a shiny black dart as long as a human finger, with tiny fins at the blunt end and a hair-thin strip of bioSemtex running from point to base. Axl had been trained in primitive, in darkness visible. Atrocity brought in CySat or C3N and every ten seconds of prime time upped the value of his platoon. Any geek could mix lethal nanites into a victim's cocaine or send in an over-wired spider packed out with tiny saddlebags of toxin.

Hell, he hadn't done that stuff back then and he wasn't going to start now.

Party time.

Gunning the throttle on his WildStar, Axl felt its fat rear tyre bite road and then he was off, V-twin never rising above a steady thud as the Yamaha's turbocharger cut in and both exhausts lit with a fluorescent glow, heat shimmering from the afterburner like melting air.

As kills went it started out almost perfect as Axl closed rapidly on Kachowsky's Fiat coupé, his stolen Yamaha burning up the inside lane, wheels thudding over speed bars put there to stop him doing exactly what he was doing.

Two cars back from Kachowsky's fancy Fiat, Axl cut in front of a soft-top BMW, leaning hard left then right as he switched lanes and ran between the soft-top and the VW in front, then hit the WildStar's gyro to swing him upright. He was now on the inside of the fast lane, the VW howling in protest.

No crashing chords, though. No machine-gun guitar. Combat without a soundtrack just wasn't the same.

Just ahead, Kachowsky was now worried enough to be punching buttons on the dash, trying to hustle up an aerial pov to see what the fuck was going on, but he was too late. Axl pulled alongside, violet eyes locked on the skull of his target, his Colt still pointed skywards but already beginning its downward arc as Axl began to squeeze the trigger.

'Stop.' The man's eyes were open wide with terror, which was good. That was what the fat shit was meant to feel. That was what Axl had promised to ensure he would feel.

'I said stop.' The words were howled out, but spat into existence not by Kachowsky but by the girl in the car. The coupé ignored her, she wasn't a designated driver.

Kachowsky wouldn't live to see the crash that ran his car into the red Honda truck braking up ahead, that was the theory anyway. The first flechette was meant to take him in his right temple, drilling through bone to trash occipital lobe before hitting the back of his skull and splintering into shards of carbon that would reduce his cortex to minced protein. Only life didn't turn out like that.

As time slowed to a crawl and Axl brought the Colt down through its firing arc the blonde girl made her move. Ripping open her red jacket to grab a small package from where it was taped to bare flesh beneath her arm.

For a split second too long, Axl was hooked by a flash of white breast and then he saw what was unfolding in her hand, a tiny H&K semi-automatic with retractable stock and barrel.

Axl made his second mistake as she mashed the slide on her H&K. Instead of concentrating on finishing the kill, he flipped half his attention to the tiny machine gun and squeezed off his Kachowsky shot at the wrong moment. The Colt's flechette hit the man all right, but instead of piercing bone the dart entered his cheek and tunnelled under skin like a parasite until it hit the corner of his jaw and the hair-thin core ignited, shattering the flechette into tiny shards of carbon needle.

Kachowsky screamed, the left half of his face hanging free from the yellow sheen of skull beneath as pulped eye ran down his cheek like egg yolk. He was grabbing at his tattered cheek to try to force it back into place before he realised that half the blood now came from the needle-sharp shards of carbon skewering his fingers.

'Fuck it,' Axl said. The Colt was right. He should have chosen phosphex, cremated both shitheads where they sat. Axl slotted his second shot cleanly through Leon Kachowsky's right eye as he did what he should have done first time round and liquidised fat boy's brain faster than dropping it in a MagiMix.

And then, while the woman was still drawing bead on him, Axl put his third flechette through her throat. The nastiest shot he knew. From start to finish was three seconds, which was two seconds too long.

Leon Kachowsky's bodyguard was still shuddering in her leather seat – lungs spasming as her own blood began to drown her – when Kachowsky's out-of-control coupé finally slammed into the Honda in front and put her through the windscreen, shards of glass finishing off what Axl had started.

'Out of here,' said the Colt. 'Out of here now. You fucking hear me?'

'Not yet.' Axl stopped his bike beside the wrecked convertible and reached into his jacket pocket. The driver in the Honda truck ahead was watching him in a wing mirror but made no effort to get out. In fact, no one got out of that vehicle or any other. Wise move, Axl decided. Start involving yourself in one Mexican street hit and you'd never stop. Until the police or one of the militias decided you were getting too involved . . . And then they'd do the stopping for you, with boron-fibre baseball bats if you got lucky, with Brownings if you didn't.

'Fucking move,' the Colt demanded. But Axl ignored it.

Firing up the Fuji, Axl grabbed three shots. One of Kachowsky, one of the dead woman and one of the wrecked Fiat. Punching upload Axl bounced the files off a low-orbit commSat and threaded the packets through a replicator in Montana. Give or take a power outage, those pics would be spreading over the web in under thirty seconds. A bot waiting at the Montana site would automatically notify all relevant news groups ahead of their receiving the files, each message tailored for the group in question. The last thing Axl wanted was to be accused of spamming.

'Jesus fuck. What is wrong with you?'

Axl couldn't answer. The silence in his head was too loud.

'Cops,' warned the Colt. 'Get us the fuck out of here.' It was almost screaming with rage.

There were too. Roaring down the police lane, speed bumps obediently laying flat, came a vast DFPD Cadillac, the noise of its turbocharged V-12 engine buried beneath the suffocating wail of a siren.

'And above us,' announced the Colt and Axl looked up. Black against the evening sky like a wingless bat and hovering directly overhead was a Sikorski gunship, ex-US marine model. Someone had taken out its two linkless Brownings, but the gun mountings were still in place and the helmeted cop leaning out of the perspex bubble was clutching a loudspeaker under one arm. A very loudspeaker, the kind that stunned you into submission.

'Put your gun on the ground.' The demand was simple, unmistakeable.

Axl started to raise his Colt.

'No fucking way,' announced the gun. 'You think I'm going down for trying to take out a police 'copter?'

'I think you do what the fuck you're told,' said Axl, but he lowered the Colt all the same and turned his back to the 'copter. Then, without giving himself time to think it through, Axl dropped the gun to the tarmac and kicked it viciously towards a group of hookers working the inside edge of the road.

Leaning over from his bike, Axl grabbed the tiny H&K from the bloodstained lap of the blonde girl, then quickly checked Kachowsky's jacket for good measure. Another Colt, but a cold one, inanimate and lifeless.

Holding that gun close to his body, Axl rapidly jacked out the first clip and emptied it into his shaking hand, thrusting the simple ceramics into his chino pockets. Back still to the Sikorski, he grabbed a handful of flechettes from inside his jacket and loaded the clip, slamming it back into place. It took about two seconds. Long enough for the cop in the Sikorski to scream at him to drop *any* weapon, turn round and move his hands away from his body. *Now.*

Axl dropped the dumb Colt, hearing it thud on the heat-softened blacktop, then realised he was still gripping the butterfly H&K, which now appeared to be pointed straight at the occupants of a nearby Saab. Inside the car, some trophy wife was going green under her immaculate Shu Uemura makeup. The small boy behind her was howling, but mostly because he wanted a better view.

'*Drop it,*' insisted the voice from above. '*Drop it now . . .*'

Axl did. Slowly raising both hands above his head as he kept the vast Yamaha upright and stable with his knees.

'Get off the bike.'

Axl did that too, turning off the engine and putting his hands down long enough to run the bike back onto its stand. He left the tiny ignition chip where it was. Somehow he didn't think they were going to let him keep the machine. Come to that, he was pretty certain they weren't going to let him keep anything much, probably not even his life.

He was kind of glad the Colt was getting a chance to branch out on its own.

Chapter Three

The Rules of Migration

'Yo! *Rulacho*. Shit for brains.'

Sanchez froze in the seat of his parked car.

'Yeah, you.'

The *cholo* with the light-swallowing black jacket tugged one python-skin lapel and turned slowly, his already thin mouth pulled into a tighter line, hooded eyes narrowing as he glared round for the person he was going to have to kill.

There was no one. No one that is, except for ten lanes of locked-solid, Friday-night traffic and five hookers on tiptoe, leaning in through car windows with their G-stringed arses stuck up in the air as their heads bobbed up and down. 20,000 people in a traffic jam. 19,995 hot, fucked-off and miserable and five of them happy.

The hookers belonged to Sanchez. He paid $75 a month for them, indentured labour from an orphanage out at Zumpango. They were clones mostly, ghost girls. Uneducated, unwanted, running .22 calibre intellects in a .45 Magnum world: but the ones he employed had tits that bounced like baby kangaroos and that was what the punters paid for.

'Hey,' the voice said loudly, 'You blind or something – or do you always dress like that? And what's with that beard?'

Before he could stop himself, Sanchez put one hand to his chin, touching the fine, neatly-razored streak of dark hair that dropped from beneath his bottom lip to the centre of his pointed chin. An equally fine line edged his upper lip, pimp style.

Sanchez tried to made it look as if he was thinking, like he'd always been planning to stroke his moustache and adjust the collar of his black shirt.

The shirt was silk, the kind with filigree-silver points to the collar. Expensive, but not as expensive as Sanchez told everybody it was. Not that people usually argued. People didn't where Sanchez was concerned. The pimp smiled, showing a row of gleaming teeth inlaid with diamonds and fine gold circuitry.

'Jesus fuck!' The voice was back, rougher than ever. 'Get out of that fucking rust bucket.'

Sanchez looked round again, lazily. As if checking out his working girls, but a small tic was pulling at the side of his jaw and his lips had thinned to nothing. A bad sign, as any one of his girls could have told the Colt, not that the gun would have cared.

'God, finally. Down here. Okay?'

The pimp stopped eyeballing the nearest drivers, all of whom were nervously looking everywhere but at Sanchez, and at last did what he was told. Bloodshot eyes skimmed along the edge of the paseo, where the blacktop met a builder's chainlink fence. The voice was coming from down there, amid the buckled wheel trims, dead Marlboro butts and a riot of crumpled wetwipes that covered the dirt like fallen blossoms.

Sanchez finally spotted the gun, flipped over at the bottom of the fence and already half-buried under dust. One side of it was grit-encrusted where Axl had kicked it across five lanes of road, tiny diodes now opaque and frosted.

'Sweet fucking Nazarene . . .' Sanchez was talking to himself, which wasn't something he did often. This was a man who existed on the absolute surface of life and liked it there. He had his own reasons for not going deeper, rooted in childhood and poverty but then most people in Day Effé did.

'. . . a gun that talks back.' Sanchez knew about weapons like that. Every two-bit detective in the *novelas* had one, that and an Italian suit and a big American car. But this was life and that was tri-D.

'Yeah,' said the Colt, as the pimp finally opened the door of his ancient white Merc and sauntered casually towards the bank. 'Clever boy.'

For a split second Sanchez was tempted to kick the Colt through the fence and into a storm drain beyond. Let the piece of shit see how well it managed to insult him when it was drowning in five scummy inches of untreated sewage.

But greed won out, as the gun knew it would. Common sense, Sanchez called it. He didn't have a problem with greed. He didn't have a problem with it at all. And Sanchez knew just what he was looking at.

Guns came in three grades, requiring three different types of licence, if you were the kind of person who bothered about what was once called paperwork. There were NightClub specials, die-stamped out of steel or laser cut from cheap ceramic. These had no chips inside at all, not even for basic voice activation. Next were chipped weapons. They could switch between loads, eject empty clips on demand, adjust their own sights under orders. Neat stuff and the most anyone could hope for, until Colt-MSG/T teamed up with Linux, Gates y Turing and guns went AI.

Smart guns listened, gave advice. In fact they gave so much advice that Colt were forced to get purchasers to sign exclusion clauses stating they understood their gun wasn't always right, that it could make mistakes and the manufacturers weren't financially liable for the results of those it did make.

Which hadn't stopped the guns talking or the owners from listening . . .

'Hey,' the Colt waited until Sanchez was leant right over it, 'you and me, we could be really good together, right?'

Five lanes away, on the other edge of the southbound, two policemen were laying into a man with riot sticks. That man was on the ground, curled up in a ball out of Sanchez's line of sight. But even across the lines of idling traffic Sanchez could hear the rhythmic thud that accompanied the rise and fall of riot sticks as cops beat whoever it was to pulp.

It was Axl, obviously. And they were hammering the last memories of music out of his head. Kicking the final echoes of soundtrack into red silence. Up above, in a CySat/C3N copter, a woman leaned out of its perspex bubble as she explained what was going on below, talking rapidly into a throat mike. And standing by the central crash barrier was a Japanese tourist vidcaming the violence: alternating between grabbing shots of the falling riotsticks and bowing respectfully to the backs of the two policemen, who were completely oblivious to being filmed.

By the time an Ishie roared up on a dirt bike, bowed to no one and began uploading live to the Web, feeding the datastream from the Zeisscam set in his right eye, Sanchez was back in his Merc with the engine humming. Seconds later he was reversing his vehicle along the hard shoulder towards a turn-off 200 yards behind him.

'Hey, Sanchez!'

The pimp saw one of his girls jerk upright to stare in surprise. He ignored her. Later on he'd come back for them, and maybe they'd still be there and maybe not. Either way, he could always get some more. Street kids were two a dollar in Mexico City, literally. Guns like the Colt couldn't be bought for money alone. And whatever Sanchez liked to tell others he didn't have those kind of contacts.

Not yet.

Ignoring the hostile stares of other drivers, Sanchez ran his white Merc with fins back to the turnoff, cruising past the frozen traffic like a prowling shark in reverse. If he cut up *Via Sullivan* and then doubled back along *Antonio Caso* he could be at his bar in the *Alameda* inside forty minutes, maybe less.

Chapter Four

Drowning in an Empty Pool

'War . . . what is it good for,' sang the newspaper vendor, badly.

Sanchez slid his card down the vendor's slot and yanked out a fresh copy of the *Post*. It was a crude print-out of the newsfeed, ink still sticky on its surface, the hyperlinks all dutifully underlined but useless, going nowhere . . .

The civil war in Spain was almost over. Italy's national bank was in the hands of the World Monetary Fund. Only the Vatican was refusing to be audited. Holding out politely but firmly under the orders of Mexico's own Declan Begley, better known as His Excellency Cardinal Santo Duque.

In London, the Prime Minister was defending the WorldBank arms embargo that had led to the slaughter of unarmed liberals in Valencia, on the grounds that allowing both sides to be armed would only have extended the war.

None of that got read by Sanchez.

The shooting on the Paseo de la Counter-Reformacion was relegated to a two-line snip at the bottom of the sheet, two-thirds of the way down late-breaking news. Sanchez didn't bother to read that either.

Half an hour later it would make headlines when an AI at DFPD finally reminded everyone who the dead man was. But at the moment CySat/Mex's ex-CEO was just another body in the morgue.

'Enjoy your read,' said the vendor and Sanchez kicked it, his boot ricocheting off its reinforced metal sides. The machine picked itself up with as much dignity as a knee-high cube can manage and shut its front flap with a loud clang.

'Everyone's a critic.' The vendor stamped off up the road, stopped briefly outside a review bar and then kept going towards a more upscale part of town.

'Coward,' Sanchez shouted after it. The machine ignored him, but a Swedish girl in a red crop top stopped long enough to give Sanchez a quizzical stare. Then she was gone too, pulled up the sidewalk by a blond boyfriend who muttered something rapidly in her ear.

She had good tits and an even better ass. Sanchez looked after her, considering. Then he patted the Colt tucked into his silver and leather belt, shook his head sadly and headed towards his bar. For once, Sanchez had better things to do than chase after tourists. Like take a good look at his new toy.

Between 10 a.m. and 10 p.m., south of Alameda was tourist town. After that, most tourists went back to their high-rise Marriotts or Plazas in the *Zona Rosa* to eat almost-Mexican food and watch Brazilian porn, while those the quarter really belonged to came out to count that day's takings and drink cold beer in the cafés the tourists had only just left.

As an arrangement it worked well, except for the occasional backpacker stupid enough to hang around in search of the 'real' Mexico. A quick punch in the gut, a knee to the face and they woke up with a hangover-sized headache, no watch and an empty wallet if they were lucky. The rest never woke up at all.

Sanchez grinned. He'd rolled his share, back when he was a kid and before franchised vats meant stealing kidneys wasn't worth the prison sentence. Who hadn't? But he'd moved on since then, gone respectable. These days he ran five whores and had a major share in nightclub. Hell, he was practically a tax payer.

And he wasn't a killer, either. Which wasn't to say he hadn't killed. He had, but not for fun, not for a long time and only in the line of business. Sure, some of his donors had died, but only the stupid ones who didn't bother to read his instructions when they awoke. After they'd donated, Sanchez used to pack their limp bodies in ice and leave them in a bath with printed instructions to call 0800 HELP-HELP-HELP and ask for surgical emergency when they awoke.

He had a good deal going with the hospital too: including a sliding scale of kickbacks that depended on the size of the donor's insurance policy. And if the donor went flatline, then the hospital lifted the cornea and anything else in demand, and Sanchez skimmed ten percent of the sale price off the top.

It had been a good living, until even the not-so-rich started growing their own spares in advance, just in case. Which was enough to kick the bottom out of any market.

Sanchez sucked at his teeth and kicked his way into *La Piscina* before the toughened door had time to swing open. The hinges hissed, or it could just have been hydraulics adjusting pressure.

La Piscina had been a swimming pool before it was a club, until concrete rot had drained it of water and patrons. Now steps cut and welded from steel grating led down into what had once been the shallow end. At the deep end was a small bar for those partying. Chill-outs drank at long bars up on the sides if they could hack climbing the ladders. The place was almost deserted, but that was usual. Nothing real in Day Effé started before midnight.

Sanchez chose the small bar.

'Dos Equis, cold.' Without waiting, he headed towards a table in the corner of the pool. It was empty as always. Slumping into a metal chair, Sanchez pulled out the Colt and rested it on the table's chrome surface. When the barboy arrived, Sanchez looked between the Colt and the boy, waiting.

'Nice gun, señor . . .' The boy put the cold beer carefully on the table, then placed a frosted tumbler beside it. Finally, he put down a saucer of freshly salted almonds.

Sanchez nodded. 'You know how much this gun is worth?'

The boy shook his head. He didn't even dare guess. Not when the patron obviously wanted to tell the boy himself.

'Any idea?'

The boy shook his head mutely.

'More than you are.'

The boy's polite smile revealed the teeth of the poor, the kind Sanchez once had. *Worth more than him?* Neither of them doubted it. Pietro was one of the empty ones. Condemned to hollowness by *il papa*, by John Paul II's pronouncement way back in 1997 that clones had no souls.

'Get me another beer,' Sanchez demanded, watching as the boy carefully didn't look at the full bottle already on the table. The kid was learning, too slowly and helped by very public kicks and slaps, but he was finally getting it right. Which was just as well. Sanchez had leased him from Zampango, from the same orphanage as the whores he'd left out on the freeway. And he'd told the manager he wanted a bright one this time: one bright enough not to get himself killed. The girls Sanchez just wanted pretty – and young.

'Hey,' Sanchez said suddenly, grinning as the kid froze in his tracks. 'You been messing with my girls?'

Over by the steel steps someone laughed. Spanish Phillipe probably. Built like an ox and with brains to match, he was what you got if you bred cousins with each other often enough. A Neanderthal brain in a Cro-Magnon body.

'Well?' Sanchez asked. He was smiling at the small crowd round the bar. Counting off men he'd known since childhood, men who looked up to him, one or two even sliding *Don* in front of his name like he was some *hidalgo*. Sanchez kept smiling until he saw how quiet the boy had gone, how the kid's shoulders had tensed up.

'Turn round,' Sanchez demanded, 'look at me . . .'

The boy did and Sanchez saw the guilt etched in Pietro's large blue eyes. Etched there as surely as any retinal pattern, along with slow-burning anger. The hatred of a calf for the butcher.

'Which one?' The pimp demanded, lifting the Colt hiPower from the table in one lazy move and flicking off the safety catch. He pointed the muzzle at the boy who stared back, wide-eyed. A tiny red dot stood out on the boy's white apron, just over his heart. The boy couldn't see it, but he knew it was there right enough.

'Well,' Sanchez demanded. 'Which was it?' He moved the tiny red dot up to the boy's face, centring it between his eyes.

'Maria,' the boy said softly.

'*Maria*?' The man's voice was contemptuous. 'How the fuck do I know which one's Maria . . . What does this little slit look like?'

'She's not a slit.'

Sanchez looked at the boy in disbelief. And then stood up so slowly that the whole club was silent by the time he made it to his feet. Each step he took across the concrete floor echoed off the white-tiled walls. No one even shuffled in their seat.

It didn't take much to club Pietro to the floor. About as much effort as it took to slam a heavy door.

'Which one?' Sanchez demanded, dragging the kneeling boy to his feet.

The boy said nothing so Sanchez clubbed him again.

'Which one?'

Even if his lip hadn't been split Pietro would have found it hard to speak with the barrel of a Colt pushed into the underside of his jaw, but he tried anyway.

'Small, long dark hair. We were . . .' Friends back at Zampango was what he wanted to say. Only saying that was one sure way to get hit again. Sanchez's arrangement with the orphanage might be beneficial to both manager and pimp, but talking about it was off limits. Sanchez didn't want everybody getting the same idea.

'Have you any idea what I do to people who steal from me?'

The pimp looked into the boy's frightened face and liked what he saw. Plus everybody else in the club was watching him. That was good.

Pietro shook his head.

'She's mine,' said Sanchez. 'You want a piece of her ass, you deal with me.' He said it like he was explaining the obvious to someone too stupid to recognise it. Hell,' the man looked round the club and grinned. 'I'll even give you discount. After you've reimbursed me for what you've already taken.'

Spanish Phillipe laughed.

'Well, can you pay?' Sanchez asked.

Of course he couldn't. The boy just stood there, blood trickling slowly down his chin to Rorschach-blot in slow drops onto the front of his white apron. Sanchez would probably charge him for that too.

'Say five dollars a time?' The pimp's voice was still amused but it carried an edge now, jagged like glass. There were two ways the next thirty seconds could go – joke or tragedy – and even Sanchez himself didn't know which way events would stack. Pietro decided it for him.

'No.' The boy shook his head, but he wasn't answering the question he'd been asked, because the words still ricocheting round his skull were a response to something Sanchez had said earlier. 'She's not yours. You don't own Maria. No one owns anyone.' He said it with all the conviction of the very young. As if it that might make it true, even when it obviously wasn't.

'We've been 'mancipated . . .' He tripped over the word, but still everyone in the club knew what he was talking about. Nine months earlier, Pope Joan had issued a papal bull making it a sin to own clones of anyone except yourself. And sat in his villa on the coast near Cancun, his excellency Cardinal Santo Ducque had approved her edict, even though he was a known enemy of the liberal schism.

'Of course I don't *own* her, you dumb fuck,' the pimp said

heavily. 'I lease her ass from the orphanage at seventy-five bucks a month. And believe me, it's fucking robbery.'

Sanchez pushed the Colt hard against Pietro's neck. 'You know how much I have to pay the orphanage if you die . . . ?

'Nothing. It's covered by the insurance.' Sanchez tightened his grip on the gun, knuckles whitening. He was waiting for the boy to shut his eyes, but the boy didn't, he just kept staring at the little lights on the side.

One after another, diodes lit in slow sequence along the breech of the Colt as the pimp's trigger finger kept tightening until even Sanchez knew he was about to kill the boy. Only it didn't happen like that at all.

One second the pimp's smile was hardening, the next the Colt had flashed lightning bright and Sanchez was screaming, long and high like a newly-castrated horse as the gun fell from his nerveless fingers to hit the floor. He was whimpering to himself like a child in pain as he squeezed his hurt fingers first hard, then harder.

There wasn't a mark on them.

'Jesus fuck,' said the Colt crossly, 'what are you waiting for?'

Pietro realised seconds ahead of the others that the gun wasn't just talking, it was speaking to *him*.

'You *want* to get killed, you little fuck?'

Pietro didn't. He scooped the Colt off the floor and settled his fingers round the handle. Enough diodes lit to decorate a Christmas tree and then died away, leaving only a tiny red light flashing slowly on the left side of the handle, next to the boy's thumb. It meant the Colt was ready to fire, not that Pietro knew that.

'Take him out,' demanded the Colt. 'That's lesson one, for fucking free. When the time comes to do something, get it done.'

Pietro looked at the pimp who was staring at his own frozen fingers. Every nerve had been burnt out in a single pulse without any visible sign of damage to the epidermal surface.

Slowly Pietro raised the gun until he saw the small red dot appear on the pimp's chest but still he didn't pull the trigger, just stood there clutching the heavy hiPower. All he wanted was for life to get back to how it was before this started. Getting shouted at, even slapped, that he could handle. But killing someone like Don Sanchez was beyond his reason – and beyond his expectations.

Anyone who had thought the club was quiet before revised their opinions now.

'Put down that gun . . .'

Pietro glanced over his shoulder to find Spanish Phillipe behind him, slate-grey eyes flicking between the boy and Sanchez.

Decision taken. Inside Pietro's skull dendritic nerves fired, creating a new matrix that flared and died into a new path that would make it easier to take the same decision next time. Only Pietro didn't see it like that and wouldn't have understood the implications even if someone had been there to explain them.

He just pulled the trigger.

Bits of Sanchez hit the white-tiled wall behind the pimp, painting it red. But most of the pimp just ignited from inside. It smelt like someone was cooking a roast.

'*Roll*,' said the Colt.

Pietro didn't. Instead he stood slack-mouthed looking at what had once been Sanchez and was now a length of rapidly-burning meat. Phospex did that, instantly. Guaranteed.

'*Fucking roll.*'

Pietro did what the gun demanded, hitting the tiled floor of the pool and rolling between the legs of a shocked bystander.

'In there,' said the Colt and Pietro went scrabbling into the gap behind the bar. No tiles, just a skim of flaking polycrete that was wet with beer slops and sticky with spilt food. But what mattered was the soft armour plating that ran along the back of the counter. Alternate layers of boron-fibre and kevlar mesh, from ground zero to above waist-height on an adult. Something Pietro didn't begin to appreciate until Spanish Phillipe's first hollow-point slammed into the bar and flattened out into a worthless chunk of lead, velocity already spent.

'Not bad,' admitted the Colt. 'Now fire the fuck back . . .

'*No,*' it added loudly when Pietro started to stand up. 'Hit the fucking ceiling.'

Pietro aimed the hiPower at the roof of the bar and pulled its trigger, sending shards of concrete falling onto the shocked crowd below.

'You want to run on manual or automatic?' the hiPower asked him.

Pietro shrugged. He hadn't the faintest idea what the Colt was talking about and figured it wouldn't make any difference if he did . . . Sooner or later they were going to slaughter him . . .

'Okay then,' said the Colt, 'you want automatic?' It paused, sighed . . . 'I'll take that as a yes.' The gun bucked in Pietro's hand and another slug exploded into the ceiling, dropping chunks of the floor above into the club below. And it kept firing until Pietro could see straight into the room overhead and then into the room above that. 'Okay,' said the gun. 'Now open that door and fast . . .'

The boy looked around but couldn't see a door. Behind and to both sides were white-tiled walls. In front was the counter. There was no door.

'In the fucking floor.'

Pietro looked down and saw a square hatch set under the bar. It was edged with steel. 'That's not a door, it's a hatch,' he told the Colt.

There was a moment's silence. And when the hiPower spoke again its voice was quiet, infinitely patient. 'I suggest you open it. Whatever it is. Before someone else decides to kill you.'

Chapter Five

Right Here, Right Now

Colonel Emilio smoothed his already-neat moustache and then pinched the broad bridge of his nose, hard . . .

He had a headache. It wasn't the Saturday morning warmth that bled in from the great square of the *Zocalo* outside or the familiar stink of the cellar. Or the sight of the bloody wreck of a suspect sitting in front of him. A man apparently given to talking to himself as he committed murder.

No, what was giving the neatly-dressed, thickset cavalry officer problems was that he had one dead ex-Guerrilla leader – plus boyfriend – murdered on the Paeso and the man tied to the chair was refusing to take the situation seriously. And unfortunately no amount of expensive tailor-made nanetic artery-widening in the Colonel's brain could do a thing about it.

Colonel Emilio got headaches, always had done ever since he was a child. He just wished he hadn't got one today. But then what could you expect with a suspect who gave his name as Black Jack d'Essiarto.

'Who ordered the hit on Isabella Rosa?'

'I've already told you,' Axl said as lightly as anyone could with three teeth missing. 'I've never heard of Isabella Rosa. And I killed Kachowsky for Don Alonzo d'Estevez.'

There was no significance in the fact that Axl was being questioned in a small cell off a cellar that had once, centuries before, been used as a prison by the Inquisition in Mexico. It was just that upstairs at *La Medicina* the cells were all in use and this was where the police dumped the overspill, which is what he was.

Just another late arrival in the hell that was the morning after the night before at DFPD headquarters.

The Colonel walked slowly around the chair to which the man was tied with self-knotting ropes. The slow click of his heels on the granite floor wasn't meant to intimidate the prisoner or make him fear that he was about to be attacked by the Colonel from behind – the Colonel had a sergeant to do that for him if he wanted, but he didn't.

No, the Colonel was walking in circles because he was bored, like an dog trapped in a too-small courtyard, and he was beginning to think the piece of human wreckage in front of him was telling the truth.

Everyone at *La Medicina* always did in the end. Tell the truth, that was. Though it was usually DSP or sodium pentathol that brought them to it. Violence was as inefficient as it was unnecessary, though from the state of the man's face the Colonel could tell that his troopers still hadn't quite grasped that.

'Alonzo d'Estevez died six weeks ago,' said the Colonel slowly, not for the first time. His heels continued to click on the stone flags as he kept circling the small cell, thinking about what the man had said. What kind of idiot would kill someone on the instructions of a man already in his grave?

But what else was there? You only had to look at the prisoner to know that he didn't move in the same world as Leon Kachowsky. And what about all that talking to himself while the murder was happening . . . Spirit voices?

Was it Voudun?

The prisoner didn't look like a candidate for hardcore/Vou. Colonel Emilio stopped pacing and checked the edge of the man's shirt, rubbing it between his fingers. Old but soft and finely woven, not smartcloth but some kind of lightweight silk all the same, Italian possibly or Spanish.

The boots were scuffed from where the man had been dragged face-down across the floor, and both the heels and soles were badly worn but the stitching was hand done.

Colonel Emilio began to be more interested. This man wasn't Voudun. Vou was for the poor, for the dispossessed, for barrio-dwellers seeking emotional release within Vou's soulCore synthesis of Catholicism and Animism . . . a release fuelled by cheap psychotropics and cheaper hardcore.

'So,' the Colonel said with a sigh, 'a dead man told you to murder Kachowsky . . . ?'

'He wasn't dead when he gave the instructions and it wasn't murder,' Axl said it firmly enough for the Colonel to stop dead and stare into his violet eyes. They were as hooded and impassive as those of any slum Indian but Axl met the Colonel's gaze without faltering. Not bad for someone half unconscious from loss of blood.

'It was a hit,' Axl repeated. 'Ordered by Don Alonzo d'Estevez.'

'Who is dead . . .' The Colonel's words trailed away into silence. This wasn't the first time they'd been round that particular loop.

'You had the money in advance?'

The man nodded.

'Then where is it?'

'Debts,' Axl said shortly as if that explained everything, head shaking abruptly to say the conversation was closed.

Little . . . The Colonel stepped forward and then stopped himself, eyes widening. The fool shouldn't have jerked his head like that, it was too much of a give-away. Grow back that hair, take twenty years off the face and scrape away the city grime . . .

Staring down at the man tied to the chair, Colonel Emilio smiled for the first time that morning. He already knew the answer to his next question, but he asked it anyway.

'Your real name?'

For a second, Axl considered lying. Then, just as quickly he rejected the idea. Surprising the Colonel, but not himself. Honesty was something he majored in. Honesty and stupidity, and few things were more stupid than ending up in the cellar of *La Medicina.*

'Borja,' he said. 'Axl O'Higgins Borja . . . And I'd like to see the Cardinal.'

If Axl noticed the look that crossed the Colonel's face, he didn't let it show. He'd seen that look before, just not for a long time. Part fear at the Cardinal's name, part contempt as if to say, 'Have you heard what they say about you and the Cardinal?'

Yeah. He had. But that was years ago and it wasn't even true back then.

'You know what the Cardinal liked about me?' Axl asked.

The Colonel didn't and wasn't at all sure he wanted to. Which was fine because Axl wasn't about to tell him, not for real, not all of it.

'I know how to die,' Axl said flatly.

'Any one of my soldiers knows that,' the Colonel said abruptly.

'No,' Axl said as he shook his head. 'They know how to kill, anyone can be taught that. Learning how to *be killed* takes a special kind of teacher. Ask the Cardinal . . .'

The Colonel was back inside the hour. In that time, Colonel Emilio's fat sergeant had found Axl a very young police surgeon who stapled shut his ruptured lip, fitted new tooth buds and put a handful of cheap silver spiders to work sucking dead blood from the swelling round his right eye.

Six ribs were cracked, according to the doctor, one of his retinas was almost detached and a chip of bone had freed itself in the second vertebra of his neck.

'You know,' said the boy, 'in the long term he should get something done about that vertebra . . . if there is a long term.' He glanced from Axl to where the sergeant stood doing fist clenches to build up her already-vast biceps and padded silently out of the cell door.

After the doctor came a shower, in a marble-tiled room one floor up. The room was filled with stucco mouldings to the ceiling and a vast marble fireplace in the middle of one wall. Shower stalls stood at one end, a bank of cheap Sony tri-Ds filled the other. And naked to the waist at the screens were two cops blasting Chinese mercenaries off the red-tiled roof of a warehouse. Relaxing after a hard morning's work.

The cops shot double handed, racking up four baby Uzis between them that unleashed a steady stream of flame. And the cheap synth soundtrack didn't even keep time with their movements.

Axl snorted.

In RL the mags would have blipped out themselves inside five seconds and the cops would have been overrun before they had time to reload, but DeathGuardIV wasn't RL, it was that month's best-selling battle sim.

Neither cop looked round, not when Axl came in and not when he stripped off to step into a shower, letting waves of tepid water soak the blood from his body and face. Most of the spiders were already dead, their job done. The others died as they were washed off his skin, metal legs waving.

The only person who watched was the sergeant and for all the interest she showed he could have been dead meat already.

'Borja.'

Without turning round, without even seeing Colonel Emilio's face, Axl knew just from the voice that he might want to see the Cardinal but the Cardinal didn't want to see him. So be it . . .

So be what? Part of Axl wanted to outraged but it was a very small part and most of him couldn't be bothered to make the effort.

'Justice must be uphold?'

Behind Axl, the Colonel grunted. They both knew what *JMBU* meant. JMBU wasn't merely the slogan that ticker-taped lazily along the bottom of every newsfeed during televised trials. It was the foundation on which the Cardinal had ruled Mexico for nearly fifty years.

It was legitimisation for judicial murder, for abrogation of civil rights. JMBU justified manipulating difficult judges, nationalising some industries and privatising others, the usual detritus of centuries of Central American *realekonomik.*

'But not before my day in court?' Axl could already imagine it. A week of having his life raked over on newsfeed. Maybe as much as three weeks if CySat's liaison officer at the Ministry of Justice could work out how to throw in a couple of twists.

'No public trial.'

Axl turned round at that.

The Colonel's voice was flat, uninflected. He was wearing a pair of wrapround Spiros that hadn't been there when he went out an hour before. And he stood well back from the prisoner, hands behind his back, as if fate could be contagious. Or maybe it was the fact that Axl was naked.

'Military trial?' Without thinking about it, Axl climbed back into his trousers. Even freed clones got their five minutes in front of a civil magistrate. Which didn't usually make a difference to the result, but that wasn't the point.

Colonel Emilio didn't answer.

Fuck it, thought Axl. Maybe he should have paid out for a misery-bypass in Santa Fé after all, that time he'd had his conscience removed. Though *removal* was the wrong word, 'amygdala block' was more accurate. It would have made sense to get his capacity for misery chopped back at the same time, but then that particular threshold had always been set too low. Red meanies, black dog, insomnia, the blues – Axl got them all.

Amygdala amendment was cheaper than seeing a therapist and infinitely more secure. The only therapist Axl had visited had been a Jungian with an unnaturally developed sense of right and wrong. And after a single session and three days of the man's increasingly frantic calls to Axl's house AI, Axl had been reduced to threatening to kill the man if he didn't turn over his case notes and leave town.

So, thought Axl as he perched himself on the edge of a

window sill and watched the two cops still knocking gooks off the roof, justice must be upheld, must it? Inside he didn't feel nearly as sick as he'd expected.

But then hell, death and he had been like . . . Axl wasn't too sure how to define their past relationship. Suffocatingly close was probably an accurate enough description.

Just next to him was the fireplace, neo-classical, flanked by two marble dryads, one male and one female, blank eyed, both naked from the waist up. It was difficult to see them properly because an old-fashioned lecture screen had been nail-gunned in front, the bolts driven into the marble at chest height.

That would have been done years back, obviously enough, but no one had bothered to remove the useless screen. There were also books lined up on the over mantle, all of them flaking and crumbling with age and no one had bothered to remove those either. Time's debris – there was a lot of it about.

'You got the job of trying me?'

The Colonel nodded. No apologies, no excuses. Axl was gratoful for that.

'Today?

Colonel Emilio spread his hands. From his short brushed-back hair to his green eyes, he might have been Austrian somewhere back in the gene pool, but he had the hand gestures of someone born in Mexico.

'The Cardinal decided this?'

Of course he did. Stupid question.

Outside in the central courtyard police recruits paraded in full uniform. They carried Browning pulse/Rs with flip-out bayonets, sawtoothed ceramic blades neatly folded back under each barrel. Grey polymer helmets protected their heads while smoke-grey visors hid their faces.

It was the battle armour of an army devoted to crowd control not the solving of crime. Everyone from the meanest peon to the Cardinal, from the visiting delegation from WorldBank to the crowd being controlled knew that.

Fear was the key, thought Axl, but then when wasn't it? My fear, your fear, the Cardinal's fear . . .

Particularly the Cardinal's fear.

When Axl spoke again, his words were calm and reasoned. Without knowing it, he fell into the speech patterns of his old captain. Understated, ironic. The things Axl usually tried to be and mostly failed.

'When you try me, do you get to take my saving the old bastard into account?'

Colonel Emilio shivered. Criticising the Cardinal lost people more than just promotion . . . Starting with their heads, if they got lucky. Everything else, and then their heads if they didn't.

What Colonel Emilio should have done was slap the prisoner into submission, just in case the two cops at the screen had overheard. But it was too late for that and besides Axl could tell the Colonel was interested.

'I saved his life,' said Axl, 'but you already know that . . .'

Colonel Emilio didn't know, he didn't know at all. And the Colonel suspected he was learning something it was better not to have been told.

'The republicans almost shot the old bastard,' said Axl flatly. 'But I was there, so it didn't happen. Maybe I was wrong . . .

'Maybe I should have . . .'

'Out,' Colonel Emilio barked and the two cops looked round in surprise. Neither one had been listening but that wasn't the point. A door slammed and then Axl's comment hung in the air like a taunt, along with a thin strand of spider's web and dust motes that danced like slow-turning flakes in a bottle of chilled goldwasser. The expensive kind sold in Austrian cafes ringing the Plaza de Armas.

Prisoners in *La Medicina* didn't question the rights of the Cardinal, not coldly anyway. They cursed and spat defiance or pleaded for their lives or a quick death, or both. Axl wasn't going to plead. He hadn't pleaded for the impossible, not for a long time. And he didn't curse, he left that to his gun. All the same . . .

'You go back and tell him I saved his life once. Ask the old bastard if he wants it saved again.'

Power and paranoia, vanity and fear; flip sides born out of the cowardice most people called survival. *Me too*, thought Axl, surprising himself. The Colonel might not quite believe him. He might decide that Axl's words were as empty as Axl's future but all the same . . .

Axl would get his meeting with the Cardinal, he was sure of it. Whether he'd get out of the meeting alive was something else again. But just being able to stare the old bastard in the face once more would even the odds.

Chapter Six

Sábado

Each breath pulled at his throat and the sour air Pietro sucked into his lungs burnt like smoke from a rubbish tip. The boy thought he wanted water but what he actually needed was enough rest for his tired muscles to purge themselves of lactic acid and his heart to steady.

Pietro wasn't sure how old the tunnels were or where they led. All he knew was that most were lined with damp grey stone and that they stank. Shit he could have handled, what with sleeping each night on the floor of the servicios at *La Piscina*, but this was the sour smell of dust and dead history.

Sometimes the tunnels were silent except for the rumble of traffic overhead and sometimes Pietro could hear the distant swearing of his pursuers. Now there was noise both behind and ahead. Pietro was sure he'd been running for days and wouldn't have believed it was only three hours, had there been anyone there to tell him, which there wasn't.

Hurtling down the sewer towards the noise ahead, Pietro realised it was the sound of drums and froze. What if the people ahead were worse than those behind? He'd heard the stories about Vou, about old men ridden by gods, cups of blood, smoke, animal sacrifices, drugged girls in torn shifts . . . whatever, he had no choice.

Pietro wasn't sure what he was expecting. Breasts, probably. Naked women – or at least naked from the waist up – dancing to the drums or falling to the ground like drunks. Or maybe a single frenzied woman foaming at the mouth and writhing in the dirt of a cellar floor, while a tall black man slit the throat of a black chicken and drank its blood from a silver chalice.

What Pietro got was an almost empty brick-lined vault. The drums echoing from an old Sanyo stack. No woman writhing in the dirt. Only an old man with dreadlocks who looked up from the upturned crate that made do as a makeshift altar and frowned at the boy who skidded out of the darkness and stopped, huge gun held tightly in one hand.

'You looking for Sábado?' The man's voice was incongruously deep given his spindly, driftwood thin body. He had a cigar in one hand and was wearing a bowler hat.

Pietro just shook his head. Behind the man was a half-open door and steps . . . If Pietro could reach those he could lose himself in the crowd. Maybe jump a tram to the Zona Rosa and the big 'crete and glass hotels. Find a tourist, either sex. It wouldn't be pleasant but it would give him a bed for the next few nights. And if he got really lucky they might buy him a ride out of the city, maybe even across the border.

Time to move. Now, before Spanish Phillipe and the others came crashing out of the tunnels.

'You stay right there, Mon.'

'Like fuck,' Pietro said and began to edge towards the steps.

'No,' said the man. 'Like a good boy.'

Old . . . thin . . . ill. Pietro decided the dreadlocked Vou priest was no real threat but he raised the Colt anyway, then stopped as dark eyes locked onto his, faint tendrils of thought brushing at the edge of his mind, no heavier than cigarette smoke curling up into an open sky.

On the upturned crate – in front of half a dozen framed postcards, and either side of a copper bowl containing burning embers – stood two candles, little more than wax poured into paper cups and left to set. The kind that street stalls sold by their thousands every day. Crudely printed on the wrappers was a woodblock of a woman gazing heavenward. The old man passed his hands over the cheap candles and they went out, flames guttering into nothing. Then the man passed his hands back the other way and the wicks relit.

'Choose,' said the Voudun priest.

Choose what? Pietro shook his head violently and tried to raise the hiPower.

'Wrong choice,' said the Colt and it was talking to Pietro. Just above where the handle finished and the matt-grey ceramic of the chassis began, a tiny diode flicked from red to steadily-flashing yellow. The gun was on standby.

Pietro slapped his hand against the Colt, trying to get the diode to change. And when it wouldn't he reversed the gun and tried to raise it like a club.

'Peace, Mon. Me Sábado . . .' The words were dry like leaves, whistling from lips blotched with cancer scars. Sábado took a deep drag from the flame end of his cigar and paused to listen to sounds approaching down the darkened tunnel. Someone swore when they saw the burning candles.

'Hey,' Sábado looked direct at the gun. 'You on or off?'

'Off.'

'Good.' He glared at the Colt. 'You make sure you stay that way, you hear me?'

If the Colt could have nodded, Pietro could have sworn it would have done. Instead the hiPower just gave a non-committal grunt and shut down completely, every diode winking out at once.

'Okay,' the man looked at Pietro, 'you stand over there.' He pointed to the back of the vault near the steps and Pietro felt the smoke clear from his head. 'But you don't try to leave.'

Keeping the lifeless Colt to his side, Pietro quietly toggled the 'on' button but the gun remained silent. Whatever the old man was doing it worked. Pietro stood where he was told.

Stiffly, as if bending hurt his back, Sábado stooped and turned off the Sanyo stack, ending the drums. But somehow the silence sounded twice as loud.

'You,' said the old man, only this time he was speaking to the crowd outside. 'Make yourselves welcome to Sábado . . .'

Spanish Phillipe came first, blinking at the slight light of the candles or maybe at the heavy smoke rising from the fire bowl on Sábado's altar. Then the huge man saw Pietro and scowled, sudden anger blocking out his fear.

'*Stop.*'

It was a single word and not even loud, but Sábado's voice was enough to halt Phillipe in his tracks. Seeing the big man halt, everyone else behind him stopped too. Though only Phillipe clutched at his chest.

'It's the smoke,' Sábado said, 'sometimes it does that to you . . .' The old man beckoned to the five or so men behind Phillipe and waited while they came in slowly. No one had any doubt what the small vault was being used for or what the old man was, even if they didn't know him by sight or name.

Phillipe crossed himself and the old man nodded and crossed himself in turn, cigar stub still burning in his fingers as he did so. Then, without pausing he turned to the handful of tri-Ds on the makeshift altar and made a bow as stately as that of any courtier.

Pietro recognised Cold Blue Lies, who sang for the Family, a wizard called Pa with a snake knotted over his robe and the Little Princess who gazed out from under long lashes, a one-legged infant sleeping on her lap.

She had other names that one. The Huntress, the Chosen, and Mistress of the Mines. Which mines Pietro didn't know but there were silver workings to the far south of Day Effé, so it was probably those.

The boy stopped gazing at the Mistress and realised everyone was looking at him, waiting for some answer. From the way a dark vein tugged at the edge of Phillipe's heavy jaw, Pietro could tell the huge man thought he was refusing to answer the question.

'Did you kill the patron?' Sábado repeated patiently. His deep voice held no sense of judgement and his eyes were glazed as if looking inside himself. He was listening hard, but to what Pietro didn't know.

Pietro nodded. 'Yes,' he said.

'I told you.'

'The boy kills the man, so you kill the boy . . . ?' Sábado asked.

Phillipe nodded.

'You think the boy knows this when he do it?'

Silence was the big man's only answer.

'Of course not,' said Sábado and turned to the boy, one thin hand flipping sideways as if to introduce Pietro's answer, which didn't come easy and – in the end – didn't come at all . . .

'Tell me,' said Sábado, sucking on the stub of his cigar. 'Tell me why . . .'

If Pietro could have done, he would. Anything and everything was better than standing there in the vault being watched by those eyes. Everyone was waiting for his answer but the boy didn't have one. He wasn't thinking about how to get away from there, because Pietro didn't believe he would.

He wasn't thinking at all.

Sábado nodded and stepped over to the boy. Age-mottled fingers reached for the neck of Pietro's T-shirt and ripped, tearing the cheap cotton in two. There were no tell-tale trademarks on Pietro's chest or back, no tattoos or subdermal barcodes, but Sábado didn't need visible proof to know the obvious.

And confirmation would be there somewhere. If not in a trademark around one nipple or flash-burned to the inside of his thigh, then in the genome itself, clauses and sub-clauses, copyrights, patents and disclaimers of liability coded into the kid's junk DNA.

'I'm right . . . ?' The old man looked at the boy. 'You soulless?'

Pietro said nothing. Life had taught him that was usually safest.

'Thought so,' said Sábado sucking at his teeth in disgust. He took the boy's hands in his own and held them, palms up looking at broken blisters and rough, not-quite-formed calluses. Pietro's nails were broken too, one split so badly that half of it had peeled back like yellow shell.

Pietro hadn't been coded to survive in the fields or work with dangerous chemicals in a factory, he had none of the protective augmentations the pro-clone movement boasted about.

'A house clone?' Sábado asked. He sounded sympathetic.

Pietro wanted to say that he hadn't minded. Not back at the beginning. At Mr Rubenstein's house he'd had his own bedroom and a tiny Matsui screen, even his own newsfeed to watch the novelas. Eating leftovers and scraps hadn't offended him. Waking early to prepare breakfast had been a pleasure. He liked the big house when it was empty and quiet.

But then came the UN ruling. Indenturing clones was illegal. Or rather, it was illegal to indenture a clone that had been hatched and batched specifically for work. Non whole-body spares, surrogate children and medical use were exempt. Under the UN's ruling you could own – that was, adopt – copies of yourself but not of anyone else, especially not of a mass-produced commercial model.

It turned out Mr Rubenstein hadn't really owned Pietro at all, just leased him from a Korean employment agency in Santa Fé; that was what Mr Rubenstein told Pietro anyway. But when Pietro went to Santa Fé the company wasn't there.

'Here, take this . . .' Sábado passed Pietro the wet stub of his cigar and the boy dragged smoke into his lungs, di-methyl-tryptamine swamping his nervous system. All Pietro felt was dizzy. The leaf was prime semillia, not synthetic but grown from seeds hand planted in fields outside Havana. Sábado was given one cigar a week from a Cuban cardiologist in his congregation.

'Tell me everything,' said the old man. So Pietro did. Starting with Mr Rubenstein sitting Pietro down at the big kitchen table with a glass of juice squeezed from fresh oranges.

Free to go turned out to mean *had to go* . . . And that was the end of Pietro's world. He was free to starve and be driven across the Mexican border by American police only to be dumped back into the US by the Mexican authorities.

Only one time, the last time he got shunted, a fat police woman in San Antonio with pillows for breasts told him about leaseback. It wasn't slavery and it certainly wasn't restricted to clones but . . . She paused, looked thoughtful . . . clones were finding it very useful.

And so Pietro found himself finally owning identity papers, and owing the next twenty-five years of his life to Brazilian Baptists who subcontracted his housing and feed to an orphanage at Zumpango that leased him to La Piscina. As stories went it wasn't even that remarkable.

Pietro blinked away his tears and the vault was suddenly empty except for Sábado.

'Wha'happen?'

The old man grinned, showing nicotine-stained teeth and two tiny vampire canines. The small screw-in kind the poor chose, not fold-back incisors that cost real credit.

'They went, Mon. Back to that bar to finish the Cachaca. Time you go too.' He nodded towards the stone steps. 'You take care now, you hear?'

The old man took an amulet from around his own scrawny neck and put it gently over Pietro's head, adjusting the leather thong until the knot was to one side, just above Pietro's breastbone. The bundle of feathers reached to the boy's waist but that didn't matter. People would still look at him and know he was protected, that he'd walked with death through the valley.

'Go,' said the old man, then jerked his chin towards the lifeless Colt still held in Pietro's fingers. 'And leave that t'ing behind. Sábado want to talk to it.'

Chapter Seven

The Wheel of Life

A wolf howled somewhere on the edge of the mountain, up where Mai was headed, where the air was thinner and even more cold than where she was now if that were possible. Mai thought it was a wolf, the animal certainly howled the way she thought wolves should howl: sounding desolate and sad, and very dangerous.

There was something wrong with the sky, but Mai couldn't work out just what it was. The colour looked right, pale blue with low grey clouds that clung to the lower slopes. And birds swung high in the air currents. Not just the small familiar swifts she knew from the brothel, but larger, more exotic species she'd only seen before on newsfeeds. Even a pale osprey that skimmed low over a small silver lake behind her, its talons extended though it swept upwards again without ever catching a fish.

The priest didn't look at the mountains or birds. He was talking to a ragged Tibetan boy with a hoe who'd stood watching them as they rode up the track towards him.

'*How far . . .*'

Almond-eyes regarded Father Sylvester passively. Dark eyes set in a wide face under a crudely-cut thatch of black hair. The boy was a *lo-pa*, high valley Tibetan and the man wasn't. As far as the boy was concerned that was all he needed to know. He'd been busy clearing rocks from a field until the strangers interrupted him and he wanted to get back to his job.

The man on the black stallion snorted in exasperation. He was cold, wet and tired. And, worse than that, he was four days closer to death than when he selected Mai at the brothel. Pulling a small gold box from his coat pocket, Father Sylvester flipped open its enamel lid and tapped a pinch of white powder onto the back of his shaking hand. One sniff and raw cocaine blasted the back of his throat, melting like snow. He didn't offer any to the boy and he certainly didn't offer any to Mai, sitting silently behind him. The priest didn't approve of children taking drugs.

'How far to Cocheforet?' Father Sylvester didn't quite add *you moron*, but the unspoken insult was understood. The priest wasn't looking for an exact distance, what he wanted to know was how much longer this journey was going to take him. The Jesuit master had never been a patient man and dying was making him more impatient still.

He didn't have time to waste.

'Well?' Father Sylvester said as he kicked his horse forward, almost trampling the boy. 'How far?'

For a moment it looked like the boy planned to swing his hoe at the priest's head, but he just shrugged instead and spat into the road before turning away, swinging his hoe from side to side.

He didn't know the man was a priest, of course. Just as he didn't know the girl with her feet in the second set of stirrups was the man's prisoner, her wrists bound behind her back so tightly it cut off the blood supply to her fingers. All the boy noticed about the girl was that her face was tear-stained and she wore a ragged bead-and-feather talisman round her neck.

Father Sylvester almost hissed in irritation. He didn't need the boy noticing the talisman or the girl and he didn't need her to start crying again.

She'd never been on a horse before and they'd been riding for two days, almost without stop. The inside of Mai's thighs were raw, her buttocks ached and every stumble from the horse went straight up her spine to explode inside her head. Worst of all, the man wouldn't stop and when she'd pissed herself a mile back, urine running in a stinging river between her leg and the saddle, all the priest had done was flip up his arm and backhand her across the face, without comment, without even looking round.

'Hey, boy,' Father Sylvester pulled a handful of coins from his pocket and rattled them before returning them there.

Without word, the boy turned back, his face still sullen. He was gripping the hoe with both hands but it was unmoving now.

'Cocheforet?'

Mai wanted to cry out, to warn the Tibetan boy, but she couldn't. Her lips were sewn shut with surgical thread. Surgical so the tiny puncture wounds wouldn't get infected. She'd already tried ripping her mouth open but the agony was too great. And the only time they'd stopped in the last twenty-four hours was when they'd passed through a village and she'd fainted with the pain of trying to shout for help.

He'd rabbit-punched her in the ribs then, once when no one was looking: adding to the bruises already inflicted by the animal's hoofs and her fall. She believed without hesitation that he would do exactly what he'd threatened to do if she tried it again, so she hadn't. All the same, a part of her wanted to warn the boy. The tiny bit not already kicked into submission. That ember which no one had ever quite kicked into submission, despite all that had happened to her in the short ugly space of her life.

'Cocheforet?' repeated the priest.

The boy looked doubtfully at the man's black stallion. The metal bit in its mouth was flecked with foam and the animal's flanks radiated steam like a wet blanket drying too close to a fire. He held up four fingers, then changed it to five and shrugged.

Three, Father Sylvester decided. That was how many days they would take. Stamina and willingness weren't what kept his horse going, the secret was 0.25 mg/kg of ketamine every two hours, mixed with crystalMeth and blasted through the animal's thick hide into its neck using an industrial-strength BayerRochelle subdermal gun. The priest had doped up the animal so often that now his mount took the injections without even breaking its stride.

'Thank you,' said Father Sylvester as he pushed one shaking hand deep into his pocket and closed his fingers clumsily around a blade, 'you've been very helpful.' The stubby glass knife caught the boy in the throat, severing his vocal chords. For a second – as the boy stood there swaying, eyes glazed and mouth slack with shock – it looked as if the priest might have to climb down from his horse to finish the job, but then the boy pitched forward and Father Sylvester caught him by his long damp hair.

A blade so sharp the makers claimed it was honed to a single molecule sliced once across the boy's neck and oxygen-rich blood spurted from a severed artery. With a hiss of regret, the priest dropped the boy into a heap and watched his blood stain the thin grass.

Chapter Eight

Dying to Schedule

Three and a half days later Father Sylvester unlocked the nanetic cuffs that bound Mai's wrists together. Three and a half days, because that was what it took to cross the high plateau and navigate the pass that let them enter the valley of Cocheforet, while black kites circled overhead and *bharal*, Himalayan blue sheep watched listlessly as they rode past.

And all that time his shakes got worse and his concentration less certain. But he remembered to tidy up after himself all the same. The last thing Father Sylvester did before beginning to descend the gravel track that led down from the pass to the valley floor was kill his horse.

The animal had stopped on a steep spur where angry rock stuck through thin red gravel like broken bone. On top of the rock someone had built a rough stone cairn and daubed it with paint as red as the gravel. The goat's skull on top of the cairn was weathered to a yellowing ivory.

To the left of the cairn was a small gully with steep sides dotted with wind-stunted scrub juniper. And at the bottom was what looked like an old cartwheel buried under scree that frost and rain had cracked from the gully's sides; three of the wheel spokes were broken.

Ahead of them was the long narrow valley of Cocheforet and across the valley was his destination. A monastery with red walls and a tiled roof set low on distant rhododendron-covered slopes that rose so high they were eventually swallowed by cloud.

But first there was his horse to deal with. Shooting the poor animal would be easiest. But guns upset Tsongkhapa. And upsetting an infinitely-parallel Buddhist AI with the personality interface of a Bon demon wasn't a risk Father Sylvester was prepared to take. Getting the unconscious girl and his medical kit through customs had been a miracle of discreet diplomacy and outright bribery, to have risked carrying an unlicensed gun would have been blindingly stupid, and that was something Father Sylvester had never been.

Besides, getting into trouble with Tsongkhapa would be a disaster, which wasn't an idle consideration. After the girl was delivered . . . That was a whole other matter but since Father Sylvester would be dead by then he wasn't prepared to waste energy or thought on it.

Not now.

Despite what the girl thought, Father Sylvester wasn't instinctively a cruel man. Being harsh took effort and finding the energy to make that effort was becoming more and more difficult. He was even fond of the horse.

There were three ampoules of ketamine left and with clumsy fingers Father Sylvester blasted all three into the neck of the glazed-eyed stallion. And when the animal was still trying to catch its breath after the climb, the priest led it to the edge of the gully.

Father Sylvester opened his wallet and carefully extracted a curl of molywire. Flicking it once aligned the molecules so that the wire suddenly became rigid. One hand gripped the other, to steady it and then – without pausing for thought – Father Sylvester rammed the wire in through the animal's eye and swivelled his wrist, pulping its brain.

Even as the stallion tried to shy away from him its knees buckled and the animal crashed over the edge of the gully, crushing anaemic saplings as it rolled to the bottom. Broken legs kicked briefly and then stilled. Dust to dust, flesh into earth. It was a ritual so old as to be almost pagan.

Over Father Sylvester's head crows wheeled in alarm, like a dying twister until still squawking they came to land in the spindly branches they'd left. No one would find his animal until it started to stink, five days at least in this temperature, maybe longer. And even then they wouldn't find it unless they were looking for it, which they wouldn't be.

The priest had worked hard to cover his tracks since leaving Vajradala, taking a minor road away from the city, riding through forests rather than take obvious paths round them, avoiding tourist towns as much as possible. No little silver Aerospats had followed him or hung above crossroads to report back what they saw, Father Sylvester felt certain of that.

'Now you,' said the priest. He pulled the glass knife from his pocket and stepped towards the girl who scrambled backwards, hands stretched out in front of her as if they'd be enough to keep him away.

'I'm not going to hurt you,' promised Father Sylvester, but she didn't pause until she reached the edge of the gully and then she had to stop anyway. Mai winced when he brought up the blade and she tried to scramble away again, almost slipping over the edge in her panic.

Dried blood. Father Sylvester sucked at his teeth in irritation and wiped the glass blade on the sleeve of his black jacket. Grabbing Mai, he twisted his fingers into her hair until she was unable to move her head and then jabbed the blade between her lips, severing the stitches.

'Shit head.' The girl tried to spit at the priest, but her blood-streaked saliva caught in the surgical thread still looped through her swollen lips. So instead of spitting at her captor, the half-Japanese girl made do with pulling the stitches from her mouth, one thread at a time. It might have been worse, Mai thought grudgingly. The bastard could have used plastic skin or cloneDerm . . . Both of those would have grafted her lips shut, leaving her mouth scarred and in need of real surgery.

Mai knew all about cloneDerm, she'd had her virginity rebuilt a dozen times when she first went to Madame Sotto's, until she got too acquiescent for it to be convincing.

No one had been around when Father Sylvester had sewn her mouth shut in the VIP lounge at Alicante because they'd had the whole room to themselves. And the priest had issued firm instructions that they weren't to be interrupted. From the disapproval on the face of the VIP steward it was obvious what the designer-droid thought Father Sylvester would be doing with the weirdly-dressed young girl. But it hadn't made a fuss. After all, the man had reserved a secure lounge for his own exclusive use and that took serious credit. Father Sylvester hadn't been doing that at all, of course. Merely pumping Mai full of every antitoxin he knew and feeding her glucose through a straw pushed between her sewn-shut lips. And when that was done he'd put her to sleep for forty-eight hours. Not waking her until after they'd landed on Samsara.

The priest had a strong belief that Mai hadn't even realised she was off planet.

Head down, still picking surgical thread from her bottom lip, Mai heard Father Sylvester call her and stubbornly ignored him. It was the wrong name anyway. You'd have thought he'd have realised that by now.

'Joan!'

She did and said nothing. Just waited to get hit again. Only this time he kept his fists to himself and merely watched her. Had Mai known the word *political agenda*, she might have understood that Father Sylvester was working to a plan. But she didn't, so instead she dismissed him as some shit-head psycho and put the shaking fits down to a trade-off for the all the drugs he took.

And it was a trade-off too, but not the way Mai thought. Father Sylvester had nanetic C3JD, the network of his brain unravelling and disconnecting as tiny, molecular-level assemblers made a mockery of their name and slowly disassembled every active axon and dendritic nerve in his cortex. His memories and his life were coming apart snip by snip.

A single line of poisoned cocaine, taken carelessly through a rolled prayer sheet had started the rot. By the time he realised it was more than stress that kept him upset and restless it was too late to do anything. Although, as the Surgeon General of the Jesuits had pointed out, it had probably always been too late.

'Joan,' he called it again but Mai wouldn't answer or turn round. Somewhere in what was left of his mind he even sympathised but history didn't have time for the niceties of an underage Japanese whore trying to hang onto her identity.

Putting one foot carefully in front of the other, Father Sylvester began to pick his way down the steep path towards the distant village below. And after a few seconds, the girl followed. They were halfway down before the priest remembered to put back her cuffs, only this time he left her hands at the front in case she fell. It was as close as Father Sylvester would ever come to showing her a kindness.

Chapter Nine

Cold Like Water/Sharp Like Glass

'This is Joan?' The small fat man who stood at the top of the stone steps leading up to the monastery sounded doubtful and Father Sylvester tried to look at the shivering child with fresh eyes. He couldn't. Too few memories were backed up in what was left of his brain for him to see anything clearly.

Father Sylvester nodded abruptly. 'This is the girl.' He pushed Mai forward, then gripped her shoulder when she stumbled. 'And her name is Joan.' When Mai opened her mouth to protest the fingers became vicelike, digging hard into a nerve in her neck.

'Release her.' The words that interrupted him were firm: not cross or bullying, just spoken by a woman who was used to being obeyed, and obeyed immediately. She spoke Spanish.

Father Sylvester released his grip.

'Good.'

The woman came slowly down the steps towards them, tall and black-haired and somewhere in her late twenties. If she was shocked at Mai's filthy clothes she didn't let it show, though her smile faded when she looked at Mai's face and found dark pupils dilated with drugs, fear or fever. Damaged goods weren't what Kate Mercarderes needed.

Sweat had stained under the arms of Mai's canvas jacket and the now-tattered crepe bandages on her legs were obviously soiled. But it was the bruises darker than lipstick around her mouth that sparked fury in the woman's eyes.

'What happened?'

'He sewed my mouth shut,' said Mai sensing an ally, 'with a needle.'

The tall woman looked at Father Sylvester and though his face hardened he couldn't quite meet her gaze. 'It was necessary,' he said. 'You know it was necessary.'

'And her wrists?' Katherine Mercarderes said abruptly. 'Was that necessary too?'

'He thought I might escape,' said Mai. She held her wrists out to the woman. 'Please, my fingers hurt . . .' She swallowed a sob. 'Everything hurts.'

'Life does,' said Kate, then caught herself and forced a smile. 'Still, Louis can find you new clothes, a bath, some food . . .' She nodded to the small fat man still stood at the top of the steps who beetled back inside the house, head down.

A bath? Father Sylvester wanted to howl but restrained himself. Surely Kate realised . . . There wasn't time to pamper the brat. Kate had to realise that. Besides, all they needed was the brat's body and they didn't need that for long . . .

'Patience,' Kate ordered.

. 'I don't have time for patience,' said Father Sylvester. 'I'm dying.'

'You think I don't know that?' Kate said. 'You think I'd forgive you this if you weren't?' She nodded at Mai, who stood swaying with exhaustion. And then Kate caught herself again and touched the priest gently on the shoulder. Seeing someone she'd known since childhood. Someone she'd loved as a child and trusted as much as she'd trusted the Pope. But also someone she was planning to betray.

'You have the relic?'

The what . . . Father Sylvester looked briefly puzzled and then nodded, pointing to the bead-and-feather talisman round the girl's neck.

Kate raised her eyebrows but she didn't say anything further and she made no attempt to touch the precious soulcatcher. No matter how much she wanted to, Kate didn't dare.

'Release her hands.'

The priest muttered something in Latin and the cuffs dropped to the ground like lifeless plastic snakes. They were two-use only, the kind issued to airlines, not supposed to be used for anything longer than a ten hour flight.

Red weals ran around Mai's wrists, oozing clear liquid. In any other situation, Kate would have fired up a medical Drexie box or relied on mediSoft to brief proprietary assemblers. As neither of these existed in Cocheforet she'd have to make do with what she'd brought with her, which was a bit all-purpose.

'Salve, I suppose,' Kate said thoughtfully. What she meant was that in a tiny vacuum-sealed pot she kept a colony of BayerRochelle spiders that could stitch shut the thread holes at a molecular level, clearing away dead white blood cells and repairing torn flesh. But she made it sound like she was offering Mai some ancient herbal extract mixed with pig fat.

'Come with me,' she put her arm round the girl's shoulders and steered her towards the steps.

'Wait . . .'

The woman stopped but she didn't turn round and she didn't let go of the girl's shivering shoulders. 'She's having a bath and then she's getting some rest. Look at her! You think we can work with her in this state?' Together, Kate and Mai began to climb the steps.

'Take some rest,' Kate said to Father Sylvester over her shoulder. 'Your job's done.'

Done, was it? She had to know it wasn't . . . Whatever she told him.

The water was cold as glacial melt, the splash of a high waterfall echoing off the rock face that surrounded the deep mountain pool. Above Father Sylvester the sky was dark and starless. A black arc of nothing that stretched across the heavens like void. No people could have looked up at that night sky and imagined it held eternal mementoes of ancient heroes. No angels hung silent and unseen overhead listening to the celestial music of the spheres.

It was an absence made absolute. No place could be more fitting for him to die. Father Sylvester had spotted the foam-flecked foss, the thin fall of water, on his ride up to Escondido and though he couldn't see where it fell to earth, he'd guessed rightly that there'd be a mountain pool. Cold and private, like the few thoughts left in his mind.

The girl was his legacy to Kate and she could make of the foul-mouthed child what she would. Whether it was success or failure no longer worried him. He wouldn't be alive to see either.

And the child wasn't much, but she was all they had.

Father Sylvester had hoped to be present to see Mai give up the dreams he'd put into the child's head, but if Kate wanted to move at her own speed then she had that authority. Though her speed was too slow for an old man with only hours to live. So he'd come here to die, lead by Clone who understood the need for these things.

Clone wasn't a friend of Father Sylvester's, but he was no longer an enemy. The mute and tongueless ox of a man had long since made his peace with Father Sylvester just as he had reached resolution with Joan, may God overlook her undoubted sins.

Using his glassblade, Father Sylvester shaved off his beard and cut away his hair and greying ponytail as grief demanded. Ashes he'd already had enough of to last a lifetime. He wore no jewellery. And his steel cross of five nails crudely brazed together was where he'd left it, on the pillow of his bed for Kate to find.

The gutting out of the Vatican bank accounts had been Joan's secret and his doing. He set up the discreet shell companies and blind trusts, switched money from account to account, using everything from Bajan datahavens to free-trade orbitals.

Between them they'd dug out the foundation of gold on which

the Papacy had always stood and quietly spent it as the money always should have been spent. On food for the poor, on medicine, but mostly in airlifting the destitute and starving out of warzones and into transit camps where they could be shipped to Samsara. And while there were still 'fugees in need, Joan had kept spending money to ship them and Tsongkhapa had kept receiving their numbers until the money was gone. And by then WorldBank and the IMF were already closing in.

Father Sylvester sighed.

Kate had been grateful when he asked permission to retire to his room. Her anger at his treatment of the Japanese girl palpable in the abruptness of her nod.

Dying wasn't as easy as Father Sylvester had imagined, but then it had begun earlier and lasted longer than he had made allowance for. And now his patience, like his faith, was exhausted. It was time to close the book. For the recording angel to weigh up his life and make judgement.

Father Sylvester carefully took off his trousers and folded them, leaving them on top of a rock that was slick with white spray from the high foss. He didn't believe in waste. That was one of the reasons he'd kept himself alive so long. His shirt came off next and Father Sylvester folded that neatly too. He was tempted to leave his Calvins on but he'd come naked into the world and bloody-mindedness said that was the way he should go out.

Drowning had been his first idea. A pocket full of stones and a slow walk into the freezing pool at the foot of the waterfall, the cold binding tight his chest before his lungs had even filled with water. But Father Sylvester's greatest fear wasn't death, it was changing his mind. The idea that the stones might not be heavy enough or survival an instinct too strong filled him with doubt. And he despised doubt, not as an intellectual position, that he accepted entirely, but as a weakener of action.

It would have to be by the blade.

Father Sylvester climbed out of his Calvins and stood naked

in the darkness. His body was old, not bloated or fat but weak with old injuries only half repaired and swollen around the upper gut where an ulcer ate at his stomach lining. He wouldn't miss that. Actually, the priest's mouth twisted into a bitter smile, there wasn't much he would miss.

Unfolding his trousers to get the blade, Father Sylvester refolded them quickly and stepped away from his pile of clothing. He'd prevaricated enough. What he needed now was a stone as ballast to keep him from slipping or floating as he walked out into the water. Finding one the correct size was difficult but he managed it, holding the glass blade in his right hand and the stone in his left.

The meltwater numbed his ankles as effectively as a baseball bat and Father Sylvester winced as he knelt and the water reached his genitals, which constricted like three snails with the contact. But he kept on shuffling his way further into the pool, feeling for the rocky bottom as the water closed ever higher round him until only his shoulders were above the darkened surface.

Now came the real test.

The stone went between his knees where he knelt. He'd been planning to hold it in one hand while using his other to drive the blade. But his hands were weak these days and besides his fingers shook so much he was afraid that if he dropped the blade it would be gone forever. So between his knees was where the rock had to go.

Taking the razor-edged glass blade in his right hand, Father Sylvester closed left hand over right and without pausing, rammed the knife point hard into his abdomen, low down on his left hand side. Muscle tore but the water was so cold and his body so numb that Father Sylvester felt almost nothing. But then he expected that, he'd been stabbed in the gut before.

Now came the hard bit. Clenching his teeth, Father Sylvester gripped the blade's handle and yanked viciously, pain exploding as he cut open his own stomach wall in one sickening pull of the knife. Guts bulged through the sudden slit in his abdominal lining to reveal a tangled sausage-like mess within. And cold water rushed into his body as if someone had just packed his insides in ice.

'Jesus.'

Father Sylvester cut harder, slicing more muscle and gut and watched in shock as lengths of his ileum and jejunum tumbled out through the rapidly gaping slit and slowly sank, spilling their ruptured contents like floating fish shit where they'd been hacked open by the knife.

Grabbing at his own small intestines, the man severed a slimy white handful and reached inside himself to pull out another length, sawing at the muscle until that too came away in his hands. And then he pushed his fingers back inside his body for more.

He was undoubtedly insane and undoubtedly dying, but that didn't make killing himself hurt any the less. In the end it was slitting his wrists that finished Father Sylvester. But he didn't remember doing it, though he felt the blood sluggishly leave his veins. All he remembered, and the only thought he took with him to the edge of death, was that his stomach was frozen.

'Your name is Joan. You are my sister.'

Mai looked doubtfully at the woman sat on a wooden chair beside her big cast-iron bath. She wanted to say *No, I'm Mai.* To insist that she'd never been anyone other than Mai, that she'd never had a sister, or mother or father come to that, not that she could remember. But the woman was being kind to her. Very kind. Which wasn't something Mai knew how to deal with.

Not that she trusted the woman or anything. She didn't. It was just that Mai was being buried under an accumulation of small kindnesses. And besides she was warm for the first time in days and her face had stopped hurting.

Powder had been brushed on her lips to take away the swelling, unseen assemblers unweaving insoluble fibrin threads as scabs dissolved, her wrists had been dressed and antiseptic skin sprayed onto the raw flesh of her thighs, analgesic deadening the rawness as proteins knitted together a new dermal layer. The woman had made Mai cover her sex while she sprayed on the new skin, and even with the edge of a sheet covering Mai's groin Kate had been jumpy, almost irritable.

The crossness hadn't lasted though. After the painkillers and skin came something Louis called *thukpa*, food, hot noodle soup that Kate spooned into Mai's mouth herself. It was salt and sweet, not a taste the girl recognised, but she finished the bowl anyway. And would have had more if only Kate had let her.

After that, Mai was taken through to a bathroom on the ground floor next to the vast kitchens. So hot water could be carried through, Mai supposed, and she was almost right. Hot water came gurgling down a sluice from the kitchen and kept splashing into the bath until it was almost full.

The feather thing that weird priest made her wear round her neck rested on a chair by itself, well away from the water, but Mai's jacket was gone: removed as soon as she took it off, along with the crepe bandages, and carried out of the room at arm's-length by Kate who returned seconds later with a small pile of folded clothes.

'Nightdresses,' Kate said. 'We'll find one that fits.'

The girl sat up to look, soap bubbles sliding in a sloppy avalanche from her shoulders and tiny breasts.

'Do you want to get out?' Kate asked, her face suddenly stiff.

'No,' Mai shook her head.

'Then get back under the water,' said Kate, 'it's better for you.'

Mai shrugged and sank back in her bath, burying herself beneath the scented bubbles. She'd tried silence and sulking, but neither made a difference. The strange woman still just sat there, occasionally smiling at Mai but mostly looking worried when she didn't know the girl was watching her.

'My name is Katherine Mercarderes,' the woman said finally. There was the briefest hesitation, as if she expected Mai to say something and when the moment passed she smiled sadly, 'but you can call me Kate. You've always called me Kate . . .'

Always? Mai shrugged and sank even lower, until slowly cooling water rose to her chin and only her face showed above the surface. She liked the bath, with its four cast-iron legs and she liked the big room. Though the house seemed more like a derelict palace than the empty monastery Kate said it was. Plaster peeled from the dusty pink walls and the ceiling overhead seemed to be held up by narrow wooden beams, at least they looked like real wood from where she lay.

She liked the house too. There were no swathes of watered silk to line the walls, no naked marble nymphs, no heavy chandeliers or gold leaf highlights to the ornate ceiling rose, because there was no ceiling rose, no architectural decoration at all. The walls just ended at the top and then the ceiling began . . . And best of all, at least for Mai, there were no huge mirrors to reflect her back at herself. Mai liked the house, liked it a lot.

'You live here?'

'We all live here . . . Joan.'

Kate said the name like she was tasting it. And from the expression on the woman's face, she found the taste strange.

'Joan is your sister?' That was what the woman had said, wasn't it?

'Sweet, lovely, innocent, stupid Joan.'

The tall woman was crying, Mai realised. Not loudly but softly, almost as if she hadn't quite realised it herself.

'Hey, you okay?'

'Of course I'm . . .' Kate stopped and bent to pick a white towel from the grey slate floor and when she straightened up again her face was calm.

'It's time to get out.' Kate held up the towel and blushed as Mai scrambled up to stand there, suds sliding down her soft stomach and legs. Then Kate suddenly stepped forward to wrap the Japanese girl in the towel, steadying Mai as she stepped out of her bath onto the tiles.

'Time you slept.' Strong arms, surprisingly strong arms, gripped Mai in a quick hug and then Kate was fussing with the clothes she'd carried in earlier, holding up simple cotton nightdresses one after the other, eyeing them for size.

'This one, I think.' She held it out, stopped and laughed when she saw the naked girl wasn't yet dry. A laugh was so brief it sounded like a sob. 'Joan never could dry herself properly either.' Kate took the towel and tossed it over Mai's head, rubbing hard to dry the girl's hair before patting dry her shoulders and back.

'The rest you can do yourself,' Kate said. 'I'll be back in a minute to show you your room.'

Mai watched her go, wondering. About Kate and about the others. But mostly about sticking around for a day or two. She'd liked the way the hot bath water flowed over her body like waves. She'd never had a bath before, only used a sonic cubicle or rubbed on skin crawlers to get rid of sweat and dead skin. The bath was nice and so far the woman was nice, in a fussy sort of way. Even the huge house wasn't bad, though it had almost no furniture and was so dirty it looked like only animals had lived in it for years.

All the same, nice bath and house or not, Mai knew she couldn't stay there long term. They were all too freaky. Besides when was she ever going to get a better opportunity to set up on her own?

Commission, food and bed space at Madame Sotto's had taken ninety-five percent of her earnings and now that Madame Sotto was burnt toast, Mai planned to do without an agent. And there was bound to be room for a hard-working ex-kinderwhore, in wherever the hell it was she was . . .

Chapter Ten

Waiting For Darkness

The sun overhead on the Cancún coast was blistering but it was the wet-sponge humidity that really got to Colonel Emilio. That and the 1500-klick journey from Day Effé, through Veracruz, Campeche and Valladolid to Cancún.

'You know the real problem with Mexico?' Axl said loudly as he looked round at the uniforms filling the long corridor of the Villa Carlotta with a clash of primary colours and handfuls of gold braid.

The walls of the corridor were salmon pink, the floor white marble and all the windows were *trompe l'oeil* . . . Florid Rousseausque gardens painted directly onto cracking plaster. Axl had worked McDonalds kitchens that were less humid and he wasn't even dressed in a green cavalry tunic buttoned to the neck.

'Well, do you?' he asked the sweating Colonel.

Colonel Emilio didn't know and – what's more – he didn't want to know either; but that wasn't going to stop Axl Borja telling him.

'Most of the fuck-wits in this government can't tell the difference between history and nostalgia.' Which was probably true.

Unfortunately it was also slander against the state, a fact obvious to all those stood around them. So it was a relief to the Colonel when he finally reached the huge double doors that led into the Cardinal's anteroom.

'Colonel Emilio to see His Excellency,' announced the Colonel. It had taken three hours to navigate the corridor. And all that time he'd been unable to sit down or relieve himself for fear of losing his place in the vast and restless queue.

He didn't bother to give the waiting usher the name of his prisoner. The red cuffs that bound Axl's hands made clear his position in the equation, and if the cuffs didn't, the blackened eye and cut lip certainly did.

The usher consulted a list and nodded, running one finger over Colonel Emilio's name so that it changed from blue to red on his pad. There had been no need for the Colonel to announce himself, just as there had been no real need for the man stood at the door to check his list. FaceSoft would already have pulled up names plus a bullet-point list of their careers to date.

In fact, neither would have got that far if the Villa's AI hadn't already authorised their presence. Cameras were everywhere in the corridor, tiny pin-lenses wired into a spider's web of optic that ran behind the priceless 19th-century frescoes.

'If you would wait in here . . .' The usher nodded to the door which creaked open, struggling under its weight.

They found themselves in a pre-anteroom. Ornate, gilded, impossibly baroque but a holding pen all the same. Axl looked approvingly at the tall window that made up one side of the tiny room.

A real window this time, glazed with crystal polymer. Running through each huge pane, invisible to the naked eye, was spider's web woven into a mesh that was tougher than military-grade steel and more forgiving than thermal polymer.

And if that wasn't enough, the window had semiAI fast-action shutters, lead-lined against radiation, while the heavy brocade curtains were woven from charcoal-bearing silk to protect against biologicals. The window couldn't fight back but as passive defence systems went this one defined 'top of the range'.

Mind you, it should have done . . . Axl had served under the woman who drew up the original specification and he was willing to bet Colonel Emilio didn't know that either.

'Come on man, move,' the Colonel hissed and Axl gave a twisted smile.

'LockMart-designed doors,' Axl announced, tapping what looked like wood, 'alternate layers of titanium alloy and blast-proof ceramic micromesh, sourced in Paris from the Imperial Armouries. The windows were grown in Prague around spider's web woven in Beijing. I'd tell you where the curtains came from, but His Excellency doesn't want anyone to know . . .'

Colonel Emilio looked at the usher, who very carefully didn't return his gaze. If there was going to be trouble, the flunky didn't want any part of it.

'Through there,' he told the Colonel politely, nodding his head towards the next door and went back to examining his list. It ran for screen after screen, but anyone seeing the queue built up in the corridor behind would have known that.

Axl stepped through the door ahead of the Colonel and, following after, the Colonel found himself facing not the Cardinal as he'd expected but a grand room, lined down the sides and in the middle with wooden benches, all occupied. Towering brick-red walls were hung with gold-framed mirrors and antique portraits. The mirrors were neo Venetian and the vast pictures showed Hispanic men in armour with beards and jutting chins or woman with jutting breasts and dishevelled hair. The only black figures in the paintings were kneeling or stood discreetly in the background.

Not one of the paintings was religious. The first time Axl had stayed at Villa Carlotta, back when he was a boy he'd decided the Cardinal didn't want to get religion and politics mixed. Now he knew you could no more separate religion from politics in Mexico than you could separate a person from their past.

'My,' said Axl lightly, nodding towards the benches, 'isn't His Excellency popular?'

Hundreds of faces had turned to watch them come in.

'Still, that's the nice thing about Mexico. Even the meanest peon can request an audience with the Cardinal. Of course

. . .' Axl shrugged, 'whether they get to see him is another matter.'

Colonel Emilio nervously adjusted his empty sword belt. He was wearing full dress, like every other officer in the room. But minus his sabre. Weapons were not to be carried in the presence of the Cardinal, not even ceremonial ones. Those petitioners without uniform wore long dark soutanes or simple cassocks, belted at the waist with the colour of their order. And those without church dress wore dark suits, with white shirts or blouses.

Only Axl was dressed in basic peon uniform of black chinos and white T-shirt, and he was so obviously a prisoner that no one expected anything better.

'Stand over there,' ordered a fat usher, his expression so bored it had to have been surgically enhanced. Colonel Emilio was about to protest but never got the chance. 'Over there,' repeated the usher and was gone. Waddling past a crowded bench, the man managed to ignore every upturned and enquiring face, disappearing through a small wooden door which banged shut behind him.

Five, maybe six, hundred people waited in that room, with maybe twice as many in the queue outside. Almost all were men, with only a handful of women to leaven the mix. That was how Mexican politics still worked; to the despair of Mexico's northern neighbour and the Emperor herself.

And how many waiting in that sweltering crowd would the Cardinal actually see in one day? Ten, fifteen . . . ? Axl didn't know, but he wouldn't have been remotely surprised if the Cardinal was somewhere else altogether, like Paris or Rome.

Or in the capital having a discreet meeting with the new emperor. And if not then maybe in New York talking to the UN about the 'fugee lifts to Samsara. Rumour in the *barrio* said the Cardinal was irritated by the number of Mexicans approaching the Red Cross to claim 'fugee stutus. And if the word had met the street, then it was pounding the beat because the Cardinal wanted it there. That was how Declan Begley worked.

'Would you emigrate to Samsara?' Axl suddenly asked the Colonel, who went bug-eyed. A woman sat behind sniggered, but most of those around them looked away. Leaving Mexico was disloyal. Even prisoners should know that.

'Clean air,' said Axl lightly. 'Better climate.' He glanced slowly round the crowded chamber and stopped at the carved door he knew led through to the Cardinal's study. 'Better class of criminal . . .'

A captain of police standing by the wall stepped forward, noticed he was outranked by Colonel Emilio and stepped smartly back. But he didn't lower his gaze and when he spoke it was direct to the Colonel's prisoner.

'Keep your mouth shut.'

'Or what . . . ?' Axl asked. 'You'll have me condemned to death?' His laugh was abrupt, at odds with the polite irony in his voice. Enough at odds to make the fat woman beside them suddenly stand up and walk away.

'Axl O'Higgins Borja . . .'

The voice from the flat speaker set into the far wall was soft, almost reedy, with the faintest Fall's Road accent. And of all the waiting petitioners, only Axl recognised it and he wasn't even really petitioning. Unless he was meant to count asking for his life, which he didn't. As far as Axl was concerned he was owed that, whether the Cardinal intended to pay up or not.

Heads were being raised around the waiting room, as every petitioner glanced frantically round to see who'd been called. Even the hot chocolate sellers who ambled with little silver trolleys from bench to crowded bench stopped their endless round of fleecing the bored, weary and upset.

Jaw clenched against his own embarrassment, the Colonel yanked Axl forward and began to push his way down an aisle, treading on the feet of those who didn't move their boots fast enough. Axl tagged along behind him, staring back at anyone who looked at him. Raybans would have helped his defiance, but the only person allowed to wear shades when the Cardinal was around was the Cardinal himself, and his were tiny pebble glasses that only just kept the sunlight from his eyes.

'Which one of you is Axl O'Higgins Borja?' The major-domo's smile was sympathetic, but he didn't look at the prisoner.

Axl raised his chin. 'That's me.'

'Okay. In you go . . .'

The Colonel stepped forward and the small man slid neatly in front of him, blocking the door. 'Borja goes in,' he said shortly.

'But the man's my prisoner . . .'

Tiny slit pupils narrowed, memorising the Colonel's face. 'Whose prisoner?' The small man had that low gravel growl so popular back when vampyres were in fashion. Only with him, you got the feeling it was for real.

'I am to escort the prisoner,' the Colonel said, sounding suddenly formal.

'And you've done so,' said a soft voice from behind the door. 'Now go and buy some of that God-awful chocolate and wait, in case I need you further . . .'

He wouldn't, of course. He just wanted to make Colonel Emilio wait. The Cardinal didn't like the Colonel, not least because he was Maximillia's spy. Other politicians might try to keep spies out of their offices but not Cardinal Santo Ducque. He held his friends close and his enemies closer still, where he could keep a jaundiced eye on them.

Saluting smartly, the Colonel turned on his heel. There wasn't space to sit so the cavalry officer pushed his way towards a huge window that overlooked lush terraces and the sea beyond.

'Right,' said the major domo to Axl, 'in you go.' He stepped back and as Axl slouched forward the small man gave an irritated hiss, pointedly straightening his own back and squaring his shoulders. Axl immediately followed suit and the major-domo gave a nod so slight Axl might have imagined it.

'Mother of God. Stop sympathising with the fool,' said the voice inside the door, 'and send him in. I don't have all day to waste.'

'No, Your Excellency,' said the major-domo. 'Of course not.'

There was a sour joke that had done the rounds a few months back about the Cardinal.

The emperor, her uncle and the Cardinal land in the United States on their first visit. The first thing Max sees is a black goat. 'Look,' exclaims the emperor excitedly, 'all the goats in America are black.'

'No,' responds her uncle cuttingly, 'in the US some goats are black.'

The Cardinal sighs. 'All we can truly say,' he says firmly, 'is that in the US there exists at least one field, containing at least one goat, at least one side of which is black. Now that's solved, let's eat it . . .'

What put that into Axl's head he didn't know. Simple fear, maybe. Or perhaps it was the handwritten list on the black glass desk in front of the Cardinal that the man was busy annotating with an old-fashioned pen. The kind that ran on ink. The list on the desk could be anything, Axl knew that. Imports and exports, revenues collected, coming engagements . . . A note of those recently condemned to death.

The old man tugged once at his small pointed beard but said nothing, did nothing, merely kept amending the list in front of him. And then he started over again . . . Just when Axl was beginning to think the Cardinal really had forgotten he was there, the old man spoke without looking up, his voice dark as treacle.

'I won't even begin to ask where you've been.'

Since when? Not since the second series of *WarChild* got bounced off the networks after a three-year run through the jungles of South America. The Cardinal knew all about that. And not since Axl had ripped a suit, because that alone wasn't enough to bounce him out of the Cardinal's employ. Besides, that occasion had worked out well, for both of them.

The suit in question had been reaming out a twelve-year-old *rene*. A street kid so malnourished and stunted she could have been mistaken for her ten-year-old brother, if he hadn't looked six. That mission was not ordered by anyone, not even televised. Axl did it on instinct, and no one would have paid him anyway. Hell, no one would've even known the kid had been raped except for Axl stumbling drunk into an alley by accident and put a flechette through her attacker's throat halfway through his attack.

It was Axl's bad luck the alley had vidcams set up outside a warehouse door and that the cams were working. Good luck kicked in when the shooting made *GoodGuysGoneBad* with an approval rating of eighty-four percent. It saved his life.

'Mulling over your sins,' a voice asked dryly.

'No.' Axl shook his head, 'thinking about that kid out at Xochimilco.'

'You mean Sister Innocenta?'

Axl laughed. 'Innocenta?'

'You have a problem with that name?' The voice was darkly amused, but there was steel behind it.

Axl shook his head. Anything the child wanted to call herself was all right with him.

'It means innocent,' said the Cardinal slowly, picking a *pastelillo de Cabello de Angel* off a Sevres plate and painstakingly eating away the sugared crust around its edge. He knew Axl knew that.

'Look at me,' demanded the Cardinal and finally Axl stopped looking everywhere except at the man who held Axl's life in his withered hands. As always, it was impossible to see the old man's eyes behind those trademark lenses dark enough to be used to look at the sun. But dragging on his thin cigar, the Cardinal looked serene, unmoved.

Not furious but not friendly either, Axl decided.

'Assassination is illegal under Mexican law, yes?

Axl nodded.

'And when I reintroduced the death penalty, I made it clear that anyone who broke the law would suffer its full force, no exceptions?'

There was little Axl could do but nod. He could hardly claim to have missed the edict. 'Assassination law targets zaibatsu killings,' the upscale local newsfeeds had splashed. Further down the bit stream, the midmarkets had run endless variations on, 'Is this the end to horror?' And at the mouth of the stream where fact was whatever you claimed it was and information hit the open sewer that was Mexico's unconscious, every title from the *Enquirer* upwards went into a feeding frenzy at the though of the reintroduction of public executions. Tickets to the killings and half-price hotel vouchers was the least of the promotions.

But that was nothing to the bidding scrum. Before a LotusMorph of the Cardinal had even finished reading the original edict, those same networks had been on screen to the Cardinal trying to buy exclusive access, including full syndication rights.

'No exceptions, remember?' the Cardinal repeated and Axl nodded.

'So why should I make one for you?'

That was the big question. 'Because I saved your life . . . ?' Axl suggested slowly.

'And you've already had yours from me, twice over,' said the Cardinal. Smoke curled up between his lips to meet dust-laden sunlight, its ectoplasmic edges thinning to fractal-fine invisibility.

'I might save your life again.'

For a moment the elderly prelate looked almost interested and then he gave a twisted smile. 'You're not telling me you know of a plot?' His tone was ironic, but beneath it the Cardinal sounded disappointed.

'No,' said Axl. 'No plot.'

'Would you tell me if there was? And could I blame you if you didn't?' There was gravel in the Cardinal's whisper, put there by insomnia, thirty years of bad dreams and too many cigars, but there was something else as well. And if it had been anyone speaking but the Cardinal then Axl would have called it guilt.

This was the man who took him away from New York, fixed the audition for *WarChild* and paid to have Axl's reflexes enhanced and his sight augmented. Was that what itched the old man's conscience, or were they talking about the one thing they never talked about?

It seemed they were.

'You're not responsible for your birth.'

No. He wasn't. No one was. But the Cardinal had been responsible for finding out about Axl's mother. And having found out, he told a traumatised ten-year-old boy something he couldn't bear to hear. Back then the Cardinal called it dealing with the truth . . .

Axl called it irresponsible.

Eyes hidden behind their own darkness examined Axl's face, looking for something. Axl didn't know if the Cardinal found it, but the old man took a deep hit on his thin cigar and suddenly pointed to the window and the azure sea beyond.

'You think they catch anything?'

Fishing boats hung on the water above the reef, butterfly nets slung both sides of the prows of crude canoes, their mesh not yet touching the sea.

Axl shook his head.

'Occasionally they get a bonefish or two over the reefs . . . Father Pedro,' the Cardinal jerked his pointed chin towards a distant speck, 'once caught a barracuda.'

'What did you do?' Axl asked.

'With the fish? We fed it to Behemoth.' The old man smiled at a large black cat lying curled up on the tiles in the sun, which opened one green eye at the mention of its name. Axl could have sworn the brute was grinning.

'All right,' said the Cardinal as he stubbed out his cigar and immediately picked up his hardly-eaten pastillo. 'I'll make you an offer. Give me one good reason why I should spare your life.' It was obvious that the audience was nearly over.

'I can't,' said Axl. 'There isn't one.'

And then he admitted the truth to himself. There never had been.

Chapter Eleven

Ghosts in the Beehive

There was a bare-arsed boy squatting by a puddle in the August sun. Tattered cotton T-shirt, no Levis or Nikes. No soundtrack in his head either, not yet. He had one small hand cupped to his mouth and was trying to drink black water that trickled away between shaking fingers. The puddle was shallow and its surface swirled with every hue in the rainbow, as beautiful as the wings of any butterfly. All the same, it tasted acrid and was half the size it had been the day before.

Memories weren't something Axl went in for. He hadn't had them removed, surgically or psychologically. And he didn't buy time with some rem/Temp, the side effects were just too predictable. He handled time gone in the old-fashioned Freudian way; locked it away in the back of his head and told himself it was forgotten. So successful was he, that the memories shocked him with their newness, every single time they reappeared.

The stack system was at the back of the Port Authority Terminal. Older boys called it the hive. Rows and rows of tiny roomlets stacked on top of each other, each cell two foot high and six foot deep, all sealed at one end and open at the other. There were 120 cells in all, ten to each row and a spiral staircase that fed steel walkways on rows four and eight.

Hotter than hell that summer, more crowded too. Hot as a bathhouse said the older boys. Axl didn't know what a bathhouse was but he didn't tell them that.

Years back the hive had briefly been The Salariman Hotel

thrown up by FijiSu, a Japanese metaNational on West 42nd for minor suits who'd suffered a hard evening's team building at one of the karaoke dives on Times Square. But FujiSu had turned turtle long before Axl was born, leaving behind a supposedly-disposable locker hotel that had so far lasted as long as the oldest bum on Times Square could remember.

Axl lived in Row 4. Not his first choice because most mornings saw someone slumped drunk on the walkway and he had to move them to get out of his cell. Row 5 was a middle row and those were prized. Row 6 was also good but Axl wasn't tall enough to reach the walkway overhead and swing himself up into a top row cell.

And by the time he did get big enough he was already living somewhere else . . .

The Cardinal's shades rested neatly on the black glass desk. Golden pupils, as unblinking as any cat's, stared into Axl's eyes until it seemed to him that the burning gaze passed beyond now into the memories behind. He was . . .

. . . sitting in a cold café, watching his reflection in the window. Overhead was an unmoving wooden fan, resting askew on worn-out bearings. In summer the fan did nothing to cool the café, merely stirring up the hot air. At Christmas it was hung with fat strands of cheap electric tinsel, like now. The rest of the year it got forgotten and try as he might Axl couldn't even work out why he'd remembered the fan.

The boy sat at a plastic table opposite a tall man in dark glasses with a thin moustache and small pointed beard. Everyone in the café, including the owner and his brother, were carefully not looking at them.

Red smoke filled Axl's mind as it rolled in from the edge of his vision, sharp flashes of memory flickering in front of his eyes as neurons charged and flared, billions of tiny electric connections made and broken in an instant. *Snow. Cold.* Despite the heat of the Caribbean coast, Axl shivered. Personality is a grid, whispered a voice in his head. Memories even less, just neural remembrance of the route most taken. Not even accurate, not even true . . .

The old Jewish tailor was nervous, thumbs twisting together as he watched the boy watching himself in the long glass. It wasn't the black-suited youngster who worried him, it was the tall man in shades standing silently behind him, upper lip pulled back in an amused sneer. A black coat was wrapped tightly around the man, but not tightly enough to hide the crimson of robes beneath, anymore than his lip hid the tell-tale canines.

Cardinals didn't usually visit tailors in New York's lower Eastside. Actually, no one visited tailors anymore. A semiAI running coutureSoft could scan a body, cut cloth and stitch faster than any human. And that was only relevant to those not rich enough not to want their clothes grown to measure.

And even if Cardinals did visit, it wasn't usually to buy silk suits for boys with slicked-back blond hair, violet eyes and cheekbones sharp enough to slice your heart in two . . .

Chapter Twelve

Wait No Longer

'I have a job for you,' said the Cardinal.

Axl blinked and caught his own shock before it had time to reach his face. What he couldn't do was keep the hope out of his eyes.

The Cardinal gave a sad smile. 'The sentence of death is postponed only. You understand me?

The man stood in front of the Cardinal nodding slowly, waiting . . .

'Succeed and we can talk again,' said the old man 'Fail me and you *will* be hunted down and executed. Do you also understand that?'

Yeah. He understood all right. He'd been here before, over twenty years previously. Same offer from the same man. He didn't know if the Cardinal knew he was repeating himself. Somehow Axl suspected he did. Axl understood what the words meant too, just as he'd understood back then.

What sounded like a threat was actually a reprieve. Bizarrely enough, Axl wanted to cry.

The Cardinal smiled and shook his head. 'You don't change, do you?'

Axl knew it wasn't a compliment.

'Mother of God.' The Cardinal stubbed out his latest cigar and grabbed another, not waiting for the silver box to open itself. 'I don't know how she could do it to us . . .'

They were talking about Pope Joan, again. Outside the sun

was setting over a silver sea and the small boats had set their tiny sails for the shore. From the other side of the study door came the shuffle of feet as ushers cleared the waiting room. Axl was hungry, thirsty and tired but at least he was still alive. And he could do with losing the weight anyway.

'What's so funny?'

How could he explain to the Cardinal? Instead of using words, Axl gestured at the smoke filled study, the black cat still snoozing on the tiles and himself now sitting in a huge green-leather armchair opposite the Cardinal's black glass desk.

'This,' he said. And the old man nodded before getting back to briefing Axl.

'We started last year with record profits. Now we've got a dead Pope, a black hole where the Vatican's assets should be and WorldBank demanding to be allowed to crawl through our accounts like maggots on a corpse. And if that isn't bad enough, we've got newsfeeds springing up every hour saying the bitch should be canonised immediately . . .'

The old man barked with laughter but there was no amusement in it at all. 'So you know the options. Accept your death sentence, which strikes me as the least intelligent choice. Or go to some hovel called Cocheforet and track down Father Sylvester and Kate Mercarderes. Then all you have to do is bring one of them back, so we can find out what the fuck the sainted Joan did with our money.'

It was a stupid question but Axl asked it anyway, 'Why me?'

'Because you're available, you've got the combat skills and you'll fit right in on Samsara. Just another traumatised 'fugee, tortured and blinded in Joan's service . . .'

Axl looked at the Cardinal. 'But I'm not . . .' And then as the guards came in, he stopped talking.

Chapter Thirteen

Sábado II

'Fresh, delicious, wholesome . . .'

A taco cart stood in the middle of the *Plaza de Armas*, chained to black wrought-iron railings that fenced off the entrance to the metro. The cart's aluminium sides were scuffed to a matt finish that looked like a bad acid etch but was just dust, grease and age, and its voice was tiny and uninviting, coming from a single speaker.

But its owner didn't need the cart to tell tourists he was there, the stink of frying onions did that for him as the late-morning wind wafted odour molecules northwards towards a line of Honda setting them down directly outside the *Sagarario*. The cruisers would have put the tourists down outside the *Catedral Metropolitana* next door, but parking was forbidden there.

Almost all the tourists pulled a face when they caught the smell of burritos but a few always headed towards the cart, hands dipping into slack pockets to look for credit chips or loose change.

Next to the small cart, stood its owner shovelling fried mince mixed with chocolate into a tortilla roll, using his filthy fingers when he thought the Americans weren't watching. The meat looked obscene and smelt of gristle and fat, and yet even that was better than the over-sweet smell of the onions that went on next. Sloppy tomatillo finished it off, hiding the sludge grey of the onions. Refritos were extra.

Sábado grinned, showing yellow teeth. He wouldn't have eaten one even if he could. And besides the Voudun priest didn't eat animal, not even those that hadn't really been alive in the first place.

Sure, he killed occasionally to make offering. But nothing bigger than a chicken and even then he didn't take off the bird's head with his teeth like the ignorant said. And he never ate their flesh. He left flesh eating to the Christians.

'Will you take a fucking look at that . . . !'

Sábado shushed the gun he carried wrapped in a brown paper bag like some dustout trying to hide his kit, but he did what the gun said all the same. The American girl at the taco cart had breasts like small melons and buttocks like colliding twin moons, all covered with some orange lycra-derivative that stretched in all the wrong places.

She needed another taco the way the Colt needed a street-patois upgrade, but she was deep throating the taco like a snake swallowing a rat.

'Hey, lard-arse . . .'

The backpacker swung round, but didn't connect the ripe Brooklyn accent with the skeletal black man standing a few paces away smiling apologetically.

Sábado slapped the Colt's mute button hard. Actually, he just slapped the whole handle through the paper, not caring if he hit *mute* or *off*. He didn't like carrying the Colt when it was in live mode, but he had no alternative. Zocalo wasn't his part of town and the gun was feeding him directions siphoned off from traffic lights on the corner of Correo Mayor and Salvador.

The girl was still scowling at a Mexican policeman when the tattered old man started to walk across the huge square towards the parked-up chrome and glass cruisers and the squat, bell-topped towers of the cathedral beyond. The church was old, Sábado could sense that. Besides no one bothered to put all those fiddly bits on buildings any more, not even churches, and they hadn't for centuries.

And the ghosts that called to Sábado from the yellow stone of the building weren't white or even originally European.

They were older and darker, with a different kind of bloodiness. More savage but also more honest, if cruelty could be counted in that way. And in Sábado's eyes it could. The old man didn't *know* that Spaniards had built their ornate church with its Renaissance and baroque facade on top of the Aztec's *tzompantli*, that place where Mexico's original rulers displayed the skulls of sacrificial victims. Neither did Sábado know that the first Christian church on the site used stones ripped from the temple of Huitzilopochtli, but he could *feel* it. Like a wave of dark power that threatened to break over him.

The old man crossed himself, kissed a small chamois bag that hung on a human sinew round his scrawny neck and opened his mind. As always, if there were gods waiting for riders then he was there to carry them. But the wave washed over Sábado without sweeping him away and the old man kept walking.

The Zocalo was crowded and it would be even more crowded later on. Saturday was the most popular day to visit the cathedral and by that afternoon the square would be packed with visitors wall to wall. Sábado wasn't worried. He intended to be gone long before then.

Japanese tourists parted around Sábado without even knowing they'd done so, streaming both sides of him as he walked through their middle, only half-noticing the tiny visCams most of them wore like transparent lenses over one eye. He would appear in a dozen slickly-edited versions of their holiday, skimmed off from optic nerve, saved as a *.vis* file and uploaded that night while they slept. And none of them would know who he was or even remember having put him in vision.

'Keep it quiet,' Sábado said, tapping the Colt's voice button. 'Comprende?'

The hiPower kept silent, which the Voudun priest decided to take as agreement or as near as he was going to get.

'Okay,' muttered Sábado, reaching the cathedral door and looking doubtfully at a little round man in a black cloak who pushed a silver tray in his direction. On the salver was a jumble of coins and credit chips, so Sábado took five dollars.

Ignoring the monk's surprise, Sábado stepped through a small wooden door cut into a far bigger one. Instantly he felt the Colt shudder as it picked up a weapons alarm inaudible to human hearing.

'Fuck it.'

The Voudun priest glared at the tattered paper bag he held, fingers already reaching for the off button.

'Do that and we're really fucked,' warned the Colt. 'So shift your arse and take us somewhere quiet. Before the cathedral gets a fix on us.'

Sábado did what he was told, slipping around an oncoming Texas couple holding hands and sidestepping a group of sombre Korean politicians. He could feel the little man from the door standing somewhere in the crowd behind him. Not shocked or angry, more interested. As if a man who thought he'd seen everything and more, suddenly realised he hadn't.

All along the back of the cathedral candles burnt in rows on black wrought-iron racks and the welcome smell of melting wax mixed with the dust of old incense.

'Turn right,' insisted the gun and Sábado stepped into a tiny side chapel to let by a group of adolescents who trailed after a guide, ignoring the simplified history shot into their ear beads by a hidden Toshiba smartSat.

Only a teenage girl with cropped orange hair and her ears surgically cut away to streamline her head noticed Sábado so he smiled back and filled her mind with a sudden twist of naked limbs. She went slack-jawed with shock, then grinned. She was still smiling when she caught up with her group. The Voudun priest wasn't sure what her sweetest memory had been, only that whatever it was she definitely liked having it played back.

'In there, quick,' said the Colt. So Sábado slid around the base of a stone pillar and took a short cut through to an even smaller side chapel.

'Now fucking kneel.'

The Voudun priest started to protest and then shrugged, dropping to his knees on a padded rail in front of a plaster statue of a young Indian girl with gold spikes coming out of her head. *Virgin de las nivas.* She had the same smile as the kid with orange hair.

'Okay,' said the Colt crossly. 'Let's lose those fuckers while we've still got time.' The gun hummed to itself, a rapid electronic murmur of bleeps and static, running a *sympatico* programme as it skimmed up and down the length of the cathedral's defences, looking for some leeway. Nothing. The cathedral security system had the digital teeth of a Rottweiler and the stunted, obsessive, emotionally-anorexic brain to match.

In turn the Colt spat out that it was willing to gut an Islamic orbital bank and donate the entire proceeds to the charity of the AI's choice, that it could let the AI have devastating insider leverage on both the new Emperor and her mother and that it was seeking sanctuary under the 3rd UN Turing amendment.

All were lies and all were rejected. In total, the transaction took .129 of a second. Sábado got the idea the gun beeped to itself.

'Shit.' This time the Colt dug deeper, hardsphere in its handle spinning like a psychotic gyroscope as the gun mined software it had hidden away for emergencies. *UN PaxForce agent* – rejected. *WorldBank auditor* (with unlimited access to funds at Hong Kong Suisse) – rejected.

There had to be something . . . *Doctor* on edge of C3JD breakthrough, famous *free-form nanetic artist,* leading member of Mexico's *U2 Masonic lodge* – all rejected. The gun didn't even bother to offer up *midWest tri-D evangelist* or *liberation theologist* . . .

The house AI was closing in. Tracking back the Colt's offers as the gun bounced his business cards off smart lights or the small silver guides that floated effortlessly above the tourists, even double bouncing between neon-clad automated confessionals.

Archbishop of Karachi – rejected.

They were pinpointed to the right side of the nave, forward of the transept, which didn't give them too many hiding places. Slowly but certainly suited guards were moving up towards their chapel, politely stepping around tourists and showing no haste or worry, nothing that might upset that day's paying visitors.

Defecting Russian Mileetsia general – rejected.

The guards wore wrapround Raybans and discreetly padded jackets that mixed kevlar mesh with plates of 99.7% pure biopolymer chitin that overlapped each other like fish scales. The kevlar ran a tsunami program, soft to the touch but able to harden instantly into a rock-hard carapace. Not that the guard got many chances to try the tsunami out for real, baseball-bat-wielding thugs were a rarity in the Metropolitana.

Commissar in Exile from Red Tibet – rejected

'Sweet fucking Nazarene,' the gun dug to the bottom of its store of business cards and pulled out one it didn't even know was there. The card was large and white, or it would have been if it were real. Hand-engraved text embossed onto a perfectly-smooth china clay surface, its gently-scalloped edges dusted with gold leaf. The Colt didn't bother to read the ornate print, just bounced it straight at the Metropolitana's AI without even a pretence of re-routing.

The guards stopped dead, listening to a suddenly barked order in their ear beads. They weren't talking to each other when they spoke into the small mikes slicked to their throats, as Sábado had thought. It was the AI they were reporting in to. And just as the guards listened when the building told them where to look, so they stopped when ordered.

For a second or two they stood, eyes blinking and puzzled, ten paces from where Sábado knelt over a brown paper bag. And then they moved off again as a now-softer voice inside their heads sent them back to their little mezzanine just above the main door.

'Welcome,' said a soft voice from a speaker set in a nearby confessional. Its tone was cultured, almost urbane.

'Which one of you is a Papal nuncio?'

Sábado looked at the paper bag in his hand.

'I'm a Voudun priest,' he said shortly. 'Try the gun.'

Chapter Fourteen

Vision Off

'. . . shit out of my arm.' What began as a scream trailed off into recognisable words, hysterical with bitterness. First he'd lost his soundtrack and now his sight had been stolen. Inside Axl's head, white noise clashed with a raging, fiery blackness as he went through fear into fury. Despair would come later. As yet, Axl was too angry to understand fully what he'd lost.

All he knew was that they'd finally come out of heavy Gee. And he only knew that because gravity had stopped trying to pulp him against the back of his fucking seat.

Axl usually left the swearing to his Cult but the gun was missing, along with his eyes. Tracks like dried yolk still ran faintly from empty sockets. Most of it had long since peeled away in dirty flakes, but enough had remained to turn the stomachs of those guards who'd dragged him from the VIP lounge at Paris Charles de Gaulle toward the boarding gate for Boeing Shuttle PS 1308, destination Planetside/Luna.

No man had been less looked at or more noticed.

Now he was safely aboard the shuttle, sat alone in a VIP cabin at the back, with only the shuttle's AI in the control room behind him. VIPs used to sit at the front, until statisticians pointed out that as both airplanes and spacecraft crashed or burnt up from the front, the intelligent place to sit was at the back.

But the only thing Axl cared about, besides his missing sight was pain from a surgical tube plugged into a ceramic socket in his wrist. The edges were raw where they folded out over cut-away flesh and fire lanced up Axl's arm everytime he tried to bend his fingers.

He'd still had his eyes when the Cardinal's personal doctor had punched the implant crudely into position and since the man was an upscale surgeon in a world where most surgeons were infinitely more dextrous machines, Axl could only assume it was meant to hurt.

There was another square in the side of his skull, of crystal polymer this time, equally crude and even more visible where the Cardinal's major domo had cropped away hair with a Braun beard trimmer to leave a leprous white patch, now scabbed round the implant's edges with dried blood. It made him look like some cheap Tetsuo, all retro bio-augmentation, anal obsession and angst. But this wasn't some chic tri-D cerebro games Wear from Sony and if it really was an *apter*, which was doubtful, Axl didn't know why it was quite so obvious and crude.

And it wasn't even about making a back-up file of his core personality, although Axl guessed the Cardinal was sick enough to be amused at the thought of him ending up as a bioAI, operating some fridge door. No, if all they'd wanted was to copy him they'd have used a cloneDome, a basic Matsui SQUID.

'Give me a fucking neural block,' Axl demanded crossly, for about the tenth time. There was fresh blood in his mouth and a sour bile was etching his tongue from the last time he'd vomited into the bag now coming loose from his mouth, but mostly he just had a migraine left over from when the weight of gravity had squashed him back into his seat as the Boeing shuttle hit five G.

On the wall in front of him, a LotusMorph he couldn't see was explaining in very simple language how to combat the worst effects of take-off sickness. The level of language linked to gravity, so that the higher the G the simpler the talking head's language became, as the viewer's critical faculties crashed.

No one answered Axl's furious demands for a painkiller.

Certainly not the automated flight attendant built into the arm of his seat. He knew it was a proper flight attendant and not some cheap tri-D imitation put there to fool steerage-class tourists into thinking they were getting the full treatment because it had suggested he do up the web of his belt when he first sat down. And then suggested it again, more firmly, touching his shoulder to reinforce the message.

The attendant ended up telling Axl to buckle up for his own safety until Colonel Emilio told it a few home truths, starting with the fact that Axl couldn't currently see the buckle and finishing with the fact that he was a dangerous terrorist who, in the Colonel's professional opinion, shouldn't have been allowed to live. Never mind be sent off into comfortable exile on Planetside.

Now the flight attendant wasn't talking to Axl at all. And being blind, Axl couldn't check whether there was anyone else sat near by. There wasn't and his cabin was sealed from the outside. Not with a simple electronic lock or even a square of epoxy mesh. The cabin door had been spot soldered with self-welding nickel/aluminium flashtape: the magnatron 50-atom splutter-gun stuff that hit 1600 degrees C within milliseconds and needed cutting open.

Ordering the door sealed was the last thing Colonel Emilio did before saluting his French counterpart with bad grace and stamping his way out of Departures at Charles de Gaulle, using the walkway to Local Flights and catching a low-altitude shuttle back to Benito Juarez, six klicks outside Mexico City. The Colonel knew that in the Cardinal's eyes he'd somehow failed, he just couldn't work out why. He also didn't see why Axl had to go to Planetside Luna from Paris either, when Mexico had its own shuttle service.

As far as the flight attendant was concerned shuttle trips didn't get more boring than this one. The prisoner was to be secure, adequately restrained and not sedated. Plus it had orders that the man was not to arrive physically more damaged than he already was, which cut out half the sexual services usually on offer to VIP passengers.

And the reason the flight attendant wouldn't come through with the painkillers was that it had strict orders not to supply any medication, alcohol or recreational drugs.

Since that pretty much encompassed the other half of its reason for existing, the semiTuring had retreated into a major sulk and was endlessly speed-watching the end of *Death in Space*, the episode where the cabin assistant goes on trial for saving a shuttle's gentle, intelligent and sensitive AI rather than rescuing the craft's whining, overbearing passengers.

Fifteen minutes into take-off, as a complex cocktail of neurotransmitters began to feed through the tube in Axl's wrist, the flyset beads in his ears stopped spitting white noise and started running a simple memory-burn program. Simple words were accompanied by images that were equally simple, but always hideous.

Axl was being taught that he wanted to live. It was the old man's present to a favourite pupil.

Inside the passenger's skull, his brain underwent a massive limbic surge as old as humanity. C/cholamines kicked up fight or flight energy release and a slower, amygdala-driven ripple primed his adreno-cortical nervous system for extended conflict.

And as the burn-in alternated between targeting Axl's neocortex with feelings of outrage or injustice and firing up his amygdala to create sudden blinding rages, sweat beaded along his hair line, ran down his forehead and dripped into the hollow of his eyes.

In earlier centuries the effect was variously known as neuro-linguistic programming, brainwashing and conversion . . . To Axl, the impotent rage and blind fear just felt like being a child again.

Chapter Fifteen

Looking For A Little Human Understanding

'Okay,' said the Colt finally. 'That covers what I want. Now what about you?'

Both gun and fat little priest were in a tiny, windowless office behind the main altar, little more than a recessed doorway filled with a simple wooden table and two ordinary-looking chairs. Blocking off the entrance was a heavy velvet curtain through which the little priest had carried the gun a couple of days earlier.

Sábado was long since gone, glad to get away from the glances of the tourists and the worried scowls of the security guards. On the way out he stopped only once, to take a handful of white candles from a box below the wrought-iron racks. He figured the cathedral could afford it.

'What do I want?' Father Moritz turned the Colt over in his fingers and thought about the question. It made a change from thinking about the gun itself, which was what he'd been doing every waking hour.

The barrel was warm, exactly blood temperature. But the man didn't know if that was intentional, to stop the gun showing up during heat scans, or just because he'd been holding the weapon for so long.

He'd owned a Colt like this once, not quite this modern, but close enough. And he knew just how much that had cost. Enough to feed a *favela* family for a year, two families, five families . . . Maybe even feed the whole district. His Colt hadn't even been fully aware, only semiTuring but even back

97

then the price could have paid to pipe in fresh water for a whole street.

Father Moritz was struggling hard to be upset and disgusted, to be appalled at the waste and horror, at the destruction inherent in such an overworked bit of machinery, but that wasn't his nature. And besides, no one could tell him about waste. As the sole inheritor of three genome patents he'd spent most of his early life trying to throw money away. And he'd grown up around beautiful, overpriced *objets d'art*. It would be a falsehood to deny that the Colt was stunning in its functional simplicity and the elegance of its design. That was why he'd spent forty-eight hours polishing up the tiny, understated, jewel-like diodes that constantly lit in sequence down the gun's side.

For a second Father Moritz wondered if the Colt was running some kind of empathy routine on him. If so, it was doing a good job.

'*It's not my fault.*' The small priest's lips twisted into a sad smile. '*The serpent made me do it . . .*'

No, he wasn't a child. Resting the Colt on the pine table in front of him Father Moritz quite literally sat on his hands to stop himself reaching for it again.

'Well,' said the Colt, sounding amused. 'I want to see His Eminence. Why don't you tell me what you want?'

So the small priest did.

Even the hiPower was surprised. And this was a model that prided itself on how well it understood humans.

Chapter Sixteen

Cabin Service

Axl remembered screaming at the darkness, but the darkness didn't answer him. Then he slept, only to wake and start screaming again. Until his howls faded back into the kinder darkness of sleep . . .

Snapping awake, Axl tried to open his eyes and remembered too late that he didn't have any. What he did have was a pain in his temples that defied description and blobs of sick stuck to his stubbled chin where an over-full vomitsac had ruptured part of its seal. Only what was left of the bag's one-way valve was stopping its entire contents from floating off around the cabin.

He would have screamed again but he didn't have the energy and recent experience suggested he try a different approach.

It wasn't the same shuttle, but obviously Axl didn't know that. He'd been swapped at Planetside Arrivals, ferried in a coffin from the Shuttle PS 1308 to a sleek purple Boeing Cruiser with discreet gold livery and a triple-hatted papal cartouche set into the door. None of the ground staff was remotely surprised when a coffin was transferred from the Shuttle to the Nuncio's cruiser. Not when they knew the Papal Nuncio was on his way to Samsara. Being buried on Samsara was this year's big thing, and last year's and most probably next year's as well.

'Oh, so you're awake.' The voice made a bad job of trying to sound friendly.

Axl grunted.

'Tea or coffee?'

'Painkillers,' demanded Axl.

The stewardess ignored him and offered Perrier or hot chocolate as alternatives. Rules said no requests were to be refused outright.

Axl, however, hadn't been trained to the same level of social skills. 'Painkillers are what I want. And if you don't get me painkillers,' he said slowly, so there could be no danger of the machine not understanding, 'I'm going to rip you off the armrest and personally take your chips out through your arse . . .' To reinforce his point, Axl shot out his hand and grabbed metal.

He could have told the semiAI when it released his arm restraints that this was a bad idea, but he'd been unconscious at the time. And the semiAI overseeing his private cabin at the back of the Nuncio's ship didn't seem to be listening to him anyway.

Quite who, at Boeing, had thought it would be a great idea to kit out each seat with its own ten-inch-high, overpneumatic, underdressed sprite able to summon bar trolleys and tea or coffee machines to order, Axl didn't know. But judging from the diaphanous costume under his fingers and the improbable length of the legs now kicking against his wrist, he figured them for some Japanese throwback. Women, of course, were assigned male attendants, though dom, fem and neuter were always available on request.

'I don't carry painkillers, sir,' said the stewardess through gritted teeth. If nothing else, her voice programming was a masterpiece.

'Then make some,' Axl suggested. He wasn't stupid enough to believe the coffee, wine and food usually served before take-off was actually real. At least not really real, merely molecularly perfect. There had to be a bank of limited-function Drexie boxes someone on board.

'I'm afraid we don't have those facilities,' said a childlike voice that was new. And, childlike or not, this time the voice carried a little more authority. It added, 'sir,' to the sentence as an afterthought.

Cabin chief, Axl decided.

'That true?' Axl asked the stewardess and squeezed.

The sprite kept discreetly silent, which didn't improve Axl's temper at all.

'Look,' he said furiously. 'I feel like shit, okay?'

There was a second's silence when Axl was sure the cabin chief wanted to tell him he looked like shit too, but didn't. Instead it contented itself with suggesting he let go of the stewardess.

'No fucking way. Not until I get some painkillers.'

'I'm afraid that's not . . .'

Axl tightened his grip on the sprite and it yelped, high and strange, like a small dog that someone had accidentally stepped on.

'All right,' said the cabin chief hastily. 'Let's not get upset.'

'Upset!' Tears began to well up in the corners of Axl's ruined eyes, except he wasn't sure if it was from pain, fury or laughter. 'Get me some fucking painkillers or I'll squeeze this little doll in half and then I'll start on you.'

That got through to the cabin chief.

Human body with semiAI intelligence, Axl decided sourly. Something pretty, blond and prepubital knowing the Vatican. Haute-design. The wetware running off what was left of its cortex, its intelligence running as a subset of the ship's AI. Take the cabin chief away from the ship and its body would corpse.

GenoTypz had taken about six weeks to come up with that simple modification, which was as long as it took them to lose five cabin chiefs to suits who couldn't be bothered to do their own shopping.

'What happens if I crush the sprite?' Axl demanded. In his hand the air stewardess kicked harder

'I'm sure you won't,' said the cabin chief, but his voice didn't sound very certain.

'But if I do?'

'Then we bill you.' The cabin chief paused and added petulantly, 'And believe me, it won't come cheap.'

'Bill who?' Axl demanded as he tightened his fingers. A sliver of bioChip, a simplified intelligence and some fancy nanetics might be all that made up the sprite but he didn't actually want to wreck the thing, though she was too busy trying to bite his wrist to notice that. '*Who* gets billed?'

The cabin chief's eyes flicked briefly out of focus as he ran a *seek* and logged in to the ship's bioAI, overrode client confidentiality on the basis of emergency (as defined by ASA), backtracked through a small travel agent in Zurich, a shell company in newVenice and finally a Panamanian orbital before coming up with a name.

'Carlotta Villa,' he said firmly. 'She bought your ticket.'

As if he didn't already know.

'*She* . . .' Axl's laugh was as grim as the darkness surrounding him and as unsteady as the slow, painful thud in his head, which felt like an out-of-balance engine but was only blood beating through his tortured arteries and veins. 'Check Villa Carlotta. Go on, do it . . .'

The cabin chief blinked as the AI it was logged into ran a check and immediately wished it hadn't. Villa Carlotta wasn't a who, it was a what . . . The kind of what any sensible AI didn't want to know about.

'Look,' Axl said speaking straight to the ship itself. 'You can give me analgesics or I can rip your toys to pieces. You're not going to arrest me, return me or bill me. And who's going to know, anyway?' Pain had reduced his voice to a low growl, and it was obvious that he meant it.

Seconds later, Axl felt the telltale cold of a pre-spray and then a subdermal syringe blasted twenty-five millilitres of co-praximol into his neck. Sleep roared in but not before the pain peeled suddenly away and in that fractured moment of lucidity Axl had time to wonder about the onset gravity.

Pulling herself out the man's slowly relaxing fingers, the air stewardess folded away like a complex flower going into reverse, back into the arm of his seat.

Chapter Seventeen

Vaya Con Dios

A week after Axl was carried unconscious from his audience with the Cardinal, a duty guard watched a small but overweight priest struggle up a steep flight of stone stairs towards the sea-facing terrace of the Villa Carlotta, carrying a leather bag in his arms. The sun was only just dipping into the horizon and every surface still shimmered with heat, even the flat silver expanse of ocean. A few boats hung on its beaten surface but they were static and desultory, dragging fat anchor chutes as the fishermen waited for nightfall. Then hurricane lamps would be lit and work would begin again as the hidden shoals swam up towards the light and their death.

The little priest was climbing the sea stairs because he'd been forced to cut through the gardens . . . The hours of audience were over and he'd been refused entrance at the front door.

Father Moritz was both hot and tired. Sweat had glued his soutane to his back. And the hours he'd spent travelling on a train from Mexico City had done little to improve his temper. He was so tired he could no longer say how tired he was. But that was lack of sleep not the journey. The journey had just irritated him. The tiredness ate at his mind like a parasite.

Two men walked behind Father Moritz. They were the Cardinal's guards. Dressed in black silk suits and clerical collars, but definitely guards. Their suits were lightweight and Italian, cut loose under the left arm, to allow room for H&K .38s. The wrapround sunglasses featured self-adjusting lenses that could instantly throw up a floating-focus overlay of information. It would have been simpler, neater and altogether less fuss for both men to use replacement eyes to route incoming data direct, but the Cardinal was a traditionalist.

Rich to be sure, CEO of two metaNationals, major shareholder in CySat/nV and sole proxy for the Catholic Church in Mexico . . . all of which made him a traditionalist almost by definition.

Father Moritz smiled. Rome might have run a reverse-takeover on the Church of Christ Geneticist, but that didn't mean the Vatican or her representatives approved of all the genetic, medical and surgical patents they'd acquired. Merger, of course, wasn't a word the Cardinal would use in relation to Church affairs; ecumenical was. But it meant the same, and what it meant was that Vatican shares had their biggest rise on the Dow Jones for as long as anyone could remember.

So why was Declan so worried?

'Moritz.' At the top of the steep stairs a tall man stood smiling as the fat little priest struggled his way up the last few steps.

'Your Excellency,' the man tried to kneel to kiss the ring but got no closer than dipping a knee before he was stopped by the Cardinal.

'Don't. You'll never get up again . . .'

The little priest tried not to scowl and the tall man laughed, loudly. Grabbing a glass of white wine from a wooden tray balanced nearby on the balustrade, he thrust it at his visitor.

'Drink it and take a seat,' said the Cardinal.

Father Moritz opened his mouth and the Cardinal held up his hand, the setting sun glinting from the blood-red cornelian in his ring. 'Whatever brings you to Villa Carlotta can wait,' he said firmly.

Father Moritz and the Cardinal went back a long way, definitely longer than either of them would admit. No one was left alive to know how long, the Cardinal thought sadly, though there was nothing sinister in the fact. On his side, his people lived longer than most and the little fat man in front of him was germ-cell wired for longevity. It was the least his parents could have done for a child cocooned so tight by money that anything in the world he wanted was his, except poverty.

Quite apart from patents inherited by Moritz's father, his great-grandmother had owned the gameSoft company LearningCurve GmB. She was on ice, pending revival, while Dad now functioned as the houseAI of his family's mansion outside Seattle. It was years since he'd been home.

The first thirty years in the life of Moritz Alvarez y Gates had been spent trying to spend money faster than it accumulated. To that end, most of China's collection of Imperial mutton-fat jade got stacked up on the shelves in his New York condo, he bought the original of Da Vinci's smiling girl and he still hit thirty tired, bemused and unquestionably richer in real terms than when he started.

The money was spending him faster than he could spend it. At thirty-three, the age at which Alexander the Great died having conquered the known world, he was too frightened most days to leave his room.

Around that time the Cardinal was still a street priest from newVenice doing mission work in Spanish Harlem. Seeing a Cysat broadcast about Moritz's billions he'd written to the man – pen and ink, envelope and FedEx – never expecting a reply. The amount he received by return was ten times larger than the priest had even dreamed of asking for.

They had talked on their mobiles, then sat face to face on Moritz's roof garden. Later on, they would walk down to Washington Square to play chess badly and, later still, to play it well, with an audience of drifters around them. Everywhere Father Declan Begley was sent by his mission, Moritz followed, buying a house for himself nearby and letting the priest use Moritz's money as his own.

Sexless. Unspoken. It was a love affair, never acknowledged. And there was nothing physical in it, ever . . . The Vatican had checked that out, more than once. But the inquisitors never made anything stick. Not even that Father Declan fed from the Latin Queens, taking only blood from the young girls, nothing more and never enough to be harmful. Moritz took nothing because there was nothing he wanted. He seemed so sexless he was almost neuter.

In the decades that followed, Father Declan became Santo Ducque, bishop in Bogota, then archbishop of Havana and finally Cardinal of Mexico. Moritz had his circadian rhythms modified to reduce his need for sleep, but still couldn't burn up his wealth fast enough. When he hit an income of five thousand dollars a second his mind went walkabout for a month, refusing even to acknowledge the numbers that flashed lightning-fast direct to his optic nerve.

So at the Cardinal's suggestion, Moritz gave his wealth to the sole organisation with enough lawyers and knowledge of arcane banking back-history to be able to crack open the trusts. Only, even then, it wasn't as easy as the Vatican Bank – in its arrogance – had thought it would be. Moritz's wealth was vast, self-perpetuating, growing uninterrupted like cancer through the markets to touch everything. Water, steel, fusion, reclamation of the subSahal, reforestation of the Amazon . . . His money owned the very AIs that negotiated its own tax breaks.

And there was one big problem that the Vatican hadn't been expecting. The money didn't want to change owners, thank you very much. It was happy shuffling between shell companies, bouncing off orbitals, living dangerously.

It took a young nun in the St Peter's secretariat to do what no one else had considered. Joan talked to the money direct. And her conversation was very short and simple and went as follows.

'We wash whiter . . .'

And the money thought about it and realised that, by definition, the Vatican's cash was self-laundering, not to mention zero-rated and tax exempt. Joan closed the deal and the Vatican walked away with credit lines worth trillions, a forty-three percent stake in LunaWorld, fifteen percent of CySat's original holding company, an offshore datahaven in the Bahamas and a whole string of Panamanian orbitals, that turned out to be laundering sites for Cartel drug money.

They also – obviously enough – also got Moritz's original Genome patents. Not to mention his character rights to LC/GbH's *Lucifer's Dragon*. Overnight, St Peter's was richer than San Lorenzo, the Geneticists' base in Megrib. The games income in North America alone was worth more than the entire GDP of Saudi, which was deep in recession, but still . . .

Joan was trustee. And inside Moritz's head the numbers stopped spinning for the first time ever, leaving silence.

For the last four decades Moritz had quietly collected alms at the cathedral door and cleaned the relics in the Sangrario, that overdressed eighteenth-century fortress built next door to Mexico's *Catedral Metropolitana*. The fat little man came and went as he liked and no one worried that he might steal, because no man had less interest in money than the one man who'd had the most.

Now, Moritz wanted something else, something even simpler. And the Colt had promised he would get it. What's more, Moritz believed the gun.

'Bonefish,' the Cardinal said, pointing to gulls gathering over the reef. One of his bodyguards looked doubtful but, when the Cardinal raised one eyebrow, the man didn't open his mouth to differ.

'Maybe not,' admitted the Cardinal, reaching for a fresh glass. 'It's a long time since I've been out there.' He started to raise the Bohemian crystal to his lips, then paused as a liveried servant dashed forward to wipe a drop from its delicate base.

His Excellency Cardinal Santo Ducque shrugged, as if to say, *you see how I have to live* . . . And then behind his shades focused golden pupils on Moritz and the small talk was over.

'I've come to say goodbye,' Moritz said, 'which brings me to this . . .' He slid his hand into the leather bag on his lap and pulled out the Colt. Three things happened simultaneously. The Cardinal's face slid straight from shock to resignation, bypassing fear, Moritz grinned and the gun uncloaked, cutting its fooler loops to trip every alarm in the Villa.

It wasn't the bodyguards who took apart Moritz's head, the first hollow-point full-ceramic-jacket punching a golfball size hole just below his hairline. The guards fired a split second after that first shot, their slugs adding a jerky rhythm to his dancing, already-dead body as it went over backwards. The initial shot came from the Villa's AI, before soundwaves from the exploding security sirens even reached the Cardinal's ears.

Moritz's head had no exit hole at the back, largely because there was no back to Moritz's head, too much of his skull was scattered in sticky white fragments on the flagstones of the terrace behind him. And the heavy stink of bougainvillea had been edged out by shit, blood and cordite.

'Get a doctor,' the Cardinal demanded. 'Full mediSoft now. I want him chilled down, his heart preserved. While you're at it, scoop out what's left of his brain and chill that too.'

'No way,' said a voice. And then it went harsh, street-smart and heavily Brooklyn. 'Stop exactly where you are and no one else gets dead . . .'

Both bodyguards were spinning like tops, combat ready with left hands gripping right wrists, H&K .38s held at forty-five degrees to the upper body as they looked for the newcomer. And then they all realised it was the gun talking.

'*Black Jack Hot.*' The Cardinal sounded vaguely surprised.

'Yeah. Episode one, opening sequence. Didn't know you were a fan. *Hey* . . .' That was to the two hovering bodyguards. 'Any closer and I'll blow your boss to meatballs.'

'Moz'll die if we don't help him,' said the Cardinal.

'That's what he wants,' said the Colt. 'Besides, he's already

dead as dogmeat. And it's time you got over this resurrection shit.'

Both bodyguards looked at the Cardinal, who looked at the
Colt lying on blood-splattered slabs where Moritz had dropped
it, tiny diodes lighting in sequence along its exposed side, fast
and rhythmic, like the click-track on some mixing deck.

'You don't get it, do you?' The Colt sounded cross. 'Death was
what I promised him. You can patch him up, reload his brain,
grow a new reverse to his skull. Fuck it, you could grow him a
new head, couldn't you? Or do a transplant . . .'

The Cardinal groaned. It had been the Vatican who did the
first successful head transplant, back at the end of the twentieth
century, and no one had ever let them forget it.

'. . . but do you think he'll thank you for it,' demanded the
Colt. 'The fuck he will.' The Colt was flipping lights faster now,
opening dialogue not just with the houseAI but with the Villa's
titanium gate, persuading it to lock out the CCPD hovers that
were tearing up the narrow blacktop towards it, demanding
access.

The gate wasn't making any decisions. That wasn't its job.
No matter what the CCPD reckoned they'd seen on satellite.

'Chrysler Mark Three hovers, armoured and running in battle
readiness,' the Colt told the Cardinal. 'You want to let them
in?'

The Cardinal just looked at the gun.

'It's your Villa, your AI, your pet corpse . . .' The Colt's voice
changed, becoming stentorian, overtly dramatic. To make the
point he ran a chord crash ahead of the opening words. 'Cardinal kills benefactor. Maximillia under pressure to act . . .

'Or did the poor, muddled man try to kill you? After all, his
fingerprints are all over the handle. I've got his neural patterns
logged on file as owner. Fuck it, I'll even go on oath in court if
you want . . .'

The gun paused, its tone sardonic. 'Oh, you lot don't believe
machines can take oaths, do you? A bit of a fucking pity really.'

'Tell the house to let them in,' the Cardinal told the gun. 'And tell it to wipe any embarrassing vid-transcripts accidentally.' His Excellency looked at the gun. 'Presumably there's a price for all this?'

'Isn't there always? But you can afford it.'

The Cardinal grunted. 'You saw poor Father Moritz turn that gun on me?'

Both bodyguards nodded.

'Good,' said the Cardinal as he stood up and stretched, fingers interlinking above his head, thin lips pulling back over long yellow canines. CAT scans and lie detectors wouldn't be involved. Hell, it wouldn't even make the news. In fact, if the CCPD weren't gone in thirty minutes leaving him to deal with the gun and the body, then he was losing his touch.

The Cardinal adjusted his tiny pebble glasses against the evening glare and glanced at the Colt, considering. He was the Cardinal. And the Cardinal could do what he wanted. That was what Mexico had always believed . . . Somehow these days it was the Cardinal who felt less certain of the fact.

Chapter Eighteen

Body, Speech, Mind, Diamond

Om Ah Hum Vajra . . .

Out beyond Luna, out even beyond *the Arc*, the Wheel of God spun in space, telling off endless prayers. Around the 1500 or so miles of its outer rim were attached three million scraps of calligraphy, each gummed in place at the top right corner. They were the prayers of the faithful, written in Sanskrit, the ancient language of India, and woodblocked onto rice fabric by Buddhist monks. Each tiny script had been fixed in place by a hired gang of Deacon Blues, space dwelling salvage rats subcontracted by the Dalai Lama.

There were longer streamers – some of merely human height, others at least a mile long – weighted at the end with small lead seals. These were prayers too, convoluted mantras endlessly repeated on each ribbon and then repeated again as the wheel's edge spun them in a vast circle. Further off, huge steel drums hurtled through space, seemingly unattached to the wheel, their long lengths of monofilament so fine as to be invisible. In each drum were more prayers. As well as simple steel drums there were elaborate canisters of beaten silver, chased around the sides with complex, swirling representations of demons and the Rinpoche, Tibetan Buddhism's great masters.

Inside the silver canisters were all the names of God, printed out onto silken ribbon. It had taken a bank of Cray3s at CalTek at least forty-seven years to track down all the names and ten minutes to spit them out.

This was *Samsara*, the Wheel of Life, the Wheel of God.

Here was Tibet reborn from the carnage of the Second Sino War. It was a place of duty and of prayer, but most of all it was a safe haven, recognised as such by the UN, WorldBank and the IMF. All 'fugees had right of entry. They had to get there first, of course, but that didn't lessen the principle no matter how much it limited the number.

Unlike the original Tibetan wheel, Samsara had no visible spokes and no hub; it rotated about itself, creating both surface pseudo-gravity and enough momentum to trap most of the new world's atmosphere within the long central valley and the high, vertiginous mountains of its edges. What atmosphere bled away into space had to be replaced, but that was Tsongkhapa's problem. And Samsara's central AI didn't trouble others with its problems.

Axl Borja knew none of this. He was asleep in his seat, knocked flat by melatonin and kept that way by a seriously cross stewardess. He knew the back-history, of course. How, as the giant bioCrays at CalTek were sourcing thirteen regional variants on the god Zoroaster, fifty-three years before the end of the leasing agreement, a Buddhist astronomer at MIT's observatory on Darkside picked up the first sighting of the wheel.

Samsara wasn't a world then, merely a hollow circle a thousand miles around its inner rim, like a huge bird's egg with both ends cut off, if any bird could be so big that it might fly between the stars. And there were breakaway Navajo in Colorado who believed that Samsara was the remains of an egg, that there had been a bird which hatched. But then a Zen sect in Okinawa swore it was the birth sac of a vast cosmic carp and the sky was water.

The fractured stone bubble was not spinning around itself back then, merely tumbling end over end through space like a discarded tyre. And before the Navajo, the Carp cult – or the *Enquirer*'s insistence it was really all being staged in an SFX studio in Burbank, California – the Dalai Lama had known Samsara for more than that. Sitting cross-legged on his bed, logged into a vidgroup when he should have been sleeping, he'd opened a flash between Darkside and CalTek and known instantly that here was Samsara, Vajrayana, the indestructible vehicle. His destiny had arrived, if such a big word could be given to a shaven-headed, slightly podgy thirteen-year-old boy.

God-child creates world.

In private, Cardinal Santo Ducque maintained the story was so much shit, and he was right. MIT's observatory on Darkside had been monitoring the ring for months, watching it come ever closer. And the Dalai Lama had known to the minute when the final name of God would be collated, cross-referenced and the entire list printed out.

But it was a good story and sometimes a fitting lie can do more good than a mundane truth. Particularly when used to raise funds.

Lars Arcsen, leader of the Deacon Blues, brought the ring to a halt, using tugs and endless miles of monofilament. He lost thirty ships. Six hundred men and five AIs lost their lives, and when the ring finally stopped it was 50,000 miles further out than Lars had predicted.

Which worried Lars not a fuck, since there had been thirty-six hours towards the end when Lars was afraid that he wouldn't be able to halt the ring at all.

And once Samsara was in position, getting it spinning properly took Lars another three months. And then came creation, except that took twenty-eight years, not six days, and no one got Sunday off to rest. Water came from the dirty ice of a captured comet, not filtered but purified by nanites that ate heavy metals. Nanites also shredded Samsara's molecular bonds, feeding on pale sunlight as they separated out original elements, only to build them back into mountains, rocks, cliffs . . .

The comet ice was split into hydrogen and oxygen, mixed with nitrogen and fed back as atmosphere. Unbreathably thin at first, but getting thicker with each passing year.

But then, twenty-one years into creation, with the framework to this new landscape already grown, the project hit its biggest wall. Soil. Leaf litter. Loam. That broken-down biomass that gave Earth its actual name. Creating enough soil proved beyond the ingenuity of even Lars Arcsen.

Aged seven – sat in exile in a vast apartment on West 64th that had been sandblasted down to a stripped urban shell – the brand-new Dalai Lama flipped off the browband of his birthday Sony tri-D long enough to ask one question. 'How many people die each year?'

Initially, *WheelOfGod Enterprises* expected resistance to their request for donated bodies. They ended up charging for the privilege. To start with, the whole of the West Coast America wanted to be recycled. Elderly models from Bel Air covenanted condos provided their dumb-fuck red setters could come too.

A Hollywood actress, three face transplants on from the v'Actor still making her hit movies, had her agent hold a press call at the Dome to announce she'd be donating her body to the Wheel. But then, as her first husband bitched, what was the big deal? She'd already donated it to everyone else.

At one time your annual salary plus post & packing on a shrub or tree secured you a place on one of the coffin ships (basically, a refrigerated Niponshi food transport too old and battered to pass NASA standards for the Luna run). It also bought you a rice-paper prayer tacked to the rim of the wheel. A street sweeper in Delhi went Wheelside for a tattered Jimsen weed and $23.60, the head of Team Rodent donated $238,000,000 and a forest of oak saplings, and still there were grumbles that it didn't properly reflect his true remuneration.

Turnover proved to be high on Samsara when the living finally started to arrive. The Tibetan exiles thrived, but the refugees died faster and so did the tortured. Some died of injuries, others of shock. A few killed themselves, unable to live with the silence, temple bells and slightly-distant kindness of the monks.

But to start with, before Samsara had inhabitants, the dead got shredded into bone-filled fragments, mixed with disassemblers and sprayed over every surface, whether it stuck or not. Later, insects broke mounds of delivered bodies into mulch that got spread thin across the central valley. And then, that done, Niponshi drones hosed mulch onto the bare rock face of the mountainside which trickled down to pool again in the valleys.

Much later, mosses were planted, trees and shrubs, starting their own cycle of growth and corruption, though the bodies kept coming.

The Dalai Lama furnished the faith but the reclusive, obscenely-rich sandrat Lars Arcsen provided the knowledge. Few people knew where he got the skills or the technology, but then few people had ever been out to where Lars lived, surrounded by animals on a private orbital. All Lars did was take what had first been done in *the Arc*, and do it again, but larger. He was the one who called it *all*. Everyone else regarded it as a miracle.

Entrance to the Wheel of God wasn't down through the atmosphere. It was up through a single hole in the shell. Besides the numerous lengths of high-tensile molywire rumoured to span from one side of the wheel to its opposite, there were two reasons for this. The reason given was that entry this way kept the side effects of atmospheric re-entry out of the loop. The real reason was that it allowed the Wheel's pacifist AI, Tsongkhapa, to screen all incoming refugees for weapons and disease.

Chapter Nineteen

Monosyllabic/Monochromatic

'Wake now,' said the stewardess and Axl did, into the darkness he was coming to dread. Almost half of his life hadn't been enough to come to terms with losing his internal backing track and he knew the rest of his life wouldn't be long enough for him to learn to face being blinded with anything other than gut-churning self pity. That knowledge was almost as sickening as being swallowed by the blackness.

'Come on, wake up,' repeated the voice.

Just by listening he knew she was out of reach. Cramps were spreading up his left arm and he guessed she'd just pumped norAdrenaline into his wrist implant to kick him awake. It worked, he was jumpier than a rattlesnake.

'We're here.'

'Where?' Axl asked.

'Where you're going.' Her answer was bright, accurate and utterly unhelpful. 'I'm going to get the cabin chief now . . .'

There was a sudden silence to go with the blackness. So Axl just waited, keeping his thoughts to a bare minimum. Which was pretty easy given the steady thud of blood in his head and a writhing ratking knot in his stomach that gnawed like hunger but was probably fear.

Two-thirds of the human mind is taken up processing sight. And okay, not even Axl knew what was being logic-chunked through his unconscious mind, but his conscious brain knew only too well that it was missing visual input. And since over sixty percent of information stored in the brain got there via sight, his brain was missing it bigtime.

The cabin he was in was almost completely noiseless, Axl realised. Just the low thud of airfilters lazily converting his breath back into oxygen.

'You feeling better now?' The voice of the cabin chief was polite, but not that polite. Axl flipped out a hand and grinned when he heard the overgrown toy take a quick step backwards.

'Maybe not,' the voice said petulantly. And then there was silence again.

Outside, the Nuncio's cruiser kept pace with the edge of Samsara, rising slowly towards the wheel while the ship waited for the opening of a steel iris to let it pass into the first of many locks. Coming into its approach, the Boeing's AI had passed control to Tsongkhapa. Though what took control of the Boeing, moving the cruiser up through the iris, its forward speed exactly matching that of the Wheel's outer rim, was a subset of a subset, obviously enough. A mere fragment of intelligence.

But still it was running code it knew intimately and the Nuncio's Boeing hung exactly in the centre of the closing lock: from outside the wheel it would have looked as if the silver, purple and gold vessel was framed by a circle of black.

Below the cruiser the metal iris closed, vents opened as pressure was equalised and then an iris overhead unfurled like the petals of a chrysanthemum folding back into nothing. The elegant cruiser climbed a level and then that iris closed below it. Vents hissing softly as the ceiling overhead began to unfurl. There were a dozen locks, maybe more. Axl didn't count them, he just heard the hiss of vents, each one louder than the one before as the pressure began to reach atmospheric.

The entry point to the new world was the crater of what could have been a high and unlikely volcano, except for the final steel iris which unfurled to deliver the Nuncio's cruiser high above lakes and dark oak forests set on the floor of a broad valley.

From the crater, entering shuttles descended the high mountain towards Vajrayana City. The effect – carefully chosen – was as if the craft had merely flown in from another part of the new world.

'You'll need this.' The cabin chief was back again. Manifesting as a cold emptiness in a world of darkness sticky with sparks of neural feedback, like snow burning up the screen of an untuned newsfeed. Axl could hear the toy breathing.

'Need what?' Axl asked. He wasn't enjoying himself.

'This . . .'

It was soft and wet, round and sticky like a peeled plum. Axl realised the cabin chief was just waiting for the question and knew too that he wasn't going to like the answer. But Axl asked it anyway.

'What is it?'

'Well,' the voice was studiedly neutral. 'How can I . . . ? But if you tell me whether you prefer to see with your left or right . . .' Fingers began wiping crusted blood from below both eye sockets and Axl finally realised what he was holding. He didn't know whether to laugh or weep.

'Animal?' Axl asked.

'Synthetic. Red Cross standard issue.'

That was worse. Polymer lens and liquid-plastic optic fluid. Primitive self-adhering nerve splice. They worked all right, after a fashion: if you didn't mind the world in black and white. Rod cells were cheaper to mimic, even when you needed one hundred million of them. The colour-defining cone cells were more expensive.

But that wasn't the real problem with emergency-issue optics. No, getting them out again was the fuck up. And they were only really good if fitted within seventy-six hours of initial damage.

Axl tried to count off the time from leaving Villa Carlotta in his head and realised he had little idea exactly how long he'd been on the shuttle. That he was actually on the Nuncio's cruiser he didn't know at all.

Mind you, clinics on Samsara that could rush grow him

two new eyes or enhance his body with integrated armour were likely to range from few to non-existent. And, he'd be lucky if he even found a decent gun. Tsongkhapa might be the most advanced post-Turing AI in existence but as a Buddhist it disliked weapons-relevant technology.

Axl couldn't fault the logic. Aggression in humans *was* hardwired. That's why *satori* was so difficult . . . Difficult like sawing off your own maggot-infested leg was difficult. One madman with a blade could gut his family. With a Browning pulse/R he could clear his 'hood. With a tank he could take out the next 'burb and with a Lockmart X37 the next country. Give the idiot a fission device and he could unmake his planet.

Hardwiring didn't change, only the technology to hand.

Faultless logic, but shit understanding of how the real world worked. So far as Axl was concerned, Tsongkhapa was living proof that machine intelligence was overrated. He liked logic units where they belonged, in the handle of a gun or operating his fridge.

'Okay,' said Axl, flipping the peeled plum into the air, 'how does this work?'

'Plug and play,' said the cabin chief brightly.

'Yeah, right . . .' Axl fumbled a catch and caught the eye just as it was sliding off his lap.

'Here.' The cabin chief leant across and took the sticky ball. There was a quick hiss as the toy yanked the tab on a courtesy towel, breaking it out of its vacuum-packed silver foil, and then he was wiping grit and cotton fluff off the eye.

'Just put it in,' suggested the toy when he handed it back.

Axl did.

Pulling open his right eyelid Axl pushed and his new eye slide home with a wet slurp. Pain flared as tiny feelers burrowed through the damaged tissue of his eye socket like shoots, grappling the *inferior rectus*, *lateral* and *superior oblique* muscles. Cells divided, wasted muscle tissue started to regrow.

Specialised shoots found and tapped what had once been the

working optic nerve to Axl's right eye. A complex pattern of send and receive began between the new eye's control chip and Axl's visual cortex, as the optic brought itself into sequence.

Black faded to grey and then blinding white. All Axl felt was sick and frightened. Deep down sick for the first time in more years than he could remember.

Around him the dazzle of static faded and downward lines solidified into a grey bulkhead hung with a Bokhara carpet. Flat rectangles turned to seats, all empty. There were no real windows, but a Tosh screen framed by folded-back wooden shutters came into focus to show African children rolling in the waves on the edge of a beach.

It didn't look like something found on a shuttle.

Axl pushed the thought to the back of his mind and kept looking round. He was seeing the world in monochrome low/Res with the colour, contrast and brightness turned right down.

'Okay?' The cabin chief was watching him. A child's face with pouting lips and wide eyes offset by a sly smile. Blond hair probably . . . it showed up pale in B&W anyway.

'Yeah,' said Axl, 'just fine.'

'Good,' the cabin chief said blandly. 'Let's do the rest of it.'

Axl looked at him.

'Your arm, that rig glued to your head . . .'

Oh, that stuff. Axl nodded, glancing down at the implant in his wrist, flesh puffed up around its edges. He couldn't see the rig he was wearing and didn't even want to think about the spike in the back of his skull, but something told him those wouldn't be any better fitted either.

'You want to do this unconscious?'

No, he didn't.

'Whatever.' The toy leant over and yanked out all four wrist feeds at once. Axl was pretty sure that wasn't how disconnections were meant to be done.

'Forehead's going to hurt,' the cabin chief said. It didn't sound upset about the fact.

The cabin chief was right too, but it didn't hurt for long. A quick hiss of foamBone, a burst of cold and analgesic skin had been sprayed over the open wound almost before it had a chance to bleed.

The movement was practised, maybe too practised. Axl looked at the toy again. Pouting, pretty, vacuous and quietly vicious, the cabin chief looked like the real thing. Maybe they were all trained in battlefield medicine or maybe this one was a special, something kept in reserve. Alternatively, maybe the Cardinal had just requisitioned it from the Vatican. If the *Enquirer* was to be believed, the city was filling up with vicious little blond boys now Joan was gone.

'Spike,' said the cabin chief and Axl tried not to freeze.

'You know how to remove it?'

The toy looked at Axl, eyes cold. 'I put it in,' the cabin chief said shortly. 'Chances are, I can get it out again . . . Can't do a foamBone heal though, not for a spike. The plug shouldn't give you problems so long as you don't try to pull it out.'

Instant trepanning.

Well, it went with all the other enlightenment shit. Axl didn't know any real reason why he might want to remove a skull plug from the back of his head and he didn't bother to ask. He just wanted off the shuttle. Followed by some sleep, maybe some food and a weapon. He'd never felt so naked in his life.

Axl had no gun, not even a boot blade. All he did have were two tiny DNA polymerase wet chips, matched to Father Sylvester's genome. Plus another two for Joan's sister. Modified standards. Any body fluid from either would do – snot, blood, whatever. Drychips could have handled skin flakes, dirt and hair but they were bigger, more obvious. And besides drys weren't Red Cross standard issue, while wet chips were. He had two dozen of the things. Only four of those were specifically modified, the rest cheap mass-produced refugee fodder. The kind of chip that told you if you were dying of flu or the retro Virus a couple of days ahead of it actually happening.

'Okay', said the cabin chief. 'Final shot.'

There was a hiss cold against the side of Axl's neck and then the darkness began to roll back in.

Chapter Twenty

The Diamond Way

Its detractors might call Samsara a victimDisney themepark, but Vajrayana still had some of the best medical and legal AIs that money could hire.

Axl woke only once, realised he wasn't on a shuttle and tumbled back into darkness. At first sight, the demons that inhabited the dark were almost anachronistically Freudian, full of red snakes that twisted tight around his wrists or ate their way under his flesh until only their tails could be seen poking from ragged gashes in his skin.

Only later, days later, did he realise that a mediSoft on Samsara had been reprocessing his blood. Siphoning it off to mix with interleukin-4, before adding heat-killed bacterium and retrovirus triggers to dentritic cells to sensitise them, feeding the mix back to his body to repair what was left of its immune system.

Not a cheap process and the mediSoft did it before it even knew if the 'fugee crimes board would allow him to stay.

The old man nodded, nothing else. No questions were asked. In fact, so far as Axl could tell, the man with the odd-shaped felt hat kept his eyes shut throughout the interview. Though the abbot did stop chanting just long enough to mutter something that made even the small boy who'd led a staggering Axl into the cold, vast chamber look surprised.

'*Metal Monkey.*'

It sounded like a surf band, something West Coast classic

that Axl just knew he'd hate. Chopping Gibson Les Pauls, rhyming verses and some over-easy, cheesy-listening bridge, all masquerading as garage chic. He hoped *metal monkey* meant something to the boy, because it sure as hell meant nothing to him.

In total he was in the ice-cold room about five seconds, but given the length of the shivering queue he'd been bumped to the front of, Axl was surprised he'd got that long.

And then it was on to a smaller, more clinical room to see someone else.

'Are you a war criminal?' The question was in English.

Axl thought about it. Most of his brain was taken up with trying to remember. Except that while he was still hitting *recall* the young paralegal sat on the other side of the desk repeated the question, only this time in German.

Axl was *still* thinking about it when the man asked again in Norwegian. Only this time Axl didn't recognise the language but it didn't matter, because by then he'd forgotten the question.

Finally the man gave up asking if Axl had committed warcrimes and concentrated on finding a language in common. Not knowing he'd already achieved a hit rate of three out of seven.

'Do you speak Japanese?'

Not enough to answer. Axl frowned, shook his head and shivered. Ground zero in Samsara started at 6800 feet and rose steeply outside the central valley. At least it did where temperature, oxygen content and atmospheric pressure was concerned. If he got any colder he'd be doing involuntary cryo.

The young man sat in front of Axl smiled. He was shaven-headed and hatless, bare to the waist, his lower half wrapped in a saffron robe. Rubber sandals were tied to his feet with twine. His smile was as gentle as his impossible questions were polite.

Chinese, Axl thought. He'd heard that ultimate cool among Beijing's refusniks was to turn Buddhist and go work for the Dalai Lama. Learn to be quiet, be serene . . . Things had been somewhat different the last time Axl had met someone Chinese. Back then, back there a doe-eyed girl had ripped every nail from Axl's right hand, using pliers. And when he still refused to confess, her father had apologetically eased a cattle prod into Axl's anus and fried his colon so badly the first thing Axl did on being sprung was stop-off at Delhi to get a quick and dirty transplant.

The family was being rehabilitated, Axl learned later in their last week of being prepared to re-enter Beijing medical society. A week later, with his lower intestine in spasm, one hand missing and his jaw cracked in three places, two soldiers tossed Axl out of a moving Geep at the gates of the English Embassy.

Right idea, wrong place. The English asked so few questions Axl could only assume they recognised him from *WarChild* and figured he was still legit . . .

Axl came back to Beijing two months later as someone else. New eyes bought over the web, neatly cut hair, his skin bleached Norwegian White and an arm's length of off-the-shelf, clone-grown Indian gut spliced into place in his lower abdomen. The man Axl should have killed first time round died in his bed, from a scorpion bite. And across the city, the sad-eyed apologetic doctor and his daughter slept soundly, undisturbed.

That was the way Axl wanted it. The route Black Jack would have taken. So Axl did the job he'd been retained for and did it for free, because he'd missed his kill-by date and that was how contracts went.

Still, best not to remember . . . Who knew who was listening in?

Axl glanced across the table but the Chinese paralegal had turned into a different saffron-robed figure, sat there also smiling, quietly waiting for Axl's attention. This boy's eyes showed up to Axl as light grey, which made them blue or maybe green. He looked like a freshman from some exclusive East Coast college, all ivy leagues and quads. The kind where good SATs alone aren't good enough. The boy glanced nervously at a screen in the table in front of him and read off his first question.

'Do you speak Portuguese?'

Axl nodded, shifting on his chair. Any half-decent semiAI could have done the interview better. But then, any half-decent AI would just have got Axl to say something and then run semantics on the result. Even something basic like *KnowWho* would be able to pin him down to a country, maybe even a particular city. To get his district, background or age took something heavier like *SoftSP*. The studios in Day Effé had been using that for decades to put accents to vActors for their interminable *novelas*, Axl presumed everyone else did as well.

'Is Portuguese your main language?'

Axl thought about it, or maybe he just pretended to think, he wasn't sure. There was a time lag between words and thoughts. And besides, how the fuck did he know what his first language was? He'd been seven before he remembered uttering his first word and that had been *muerto*.

'Spanish,' said Axl.

The young American switched to fractured barrio slang and Axl smiled for the first time in days. He always felt that way in reverse, when he used German.

'Not my best language,' the man admitted with a grin, switching back to Portuguese, 'but Tsongkhapa doesn't like implants . . . And I don't rate using a box . . .' He jerked his head towards a BabelFisk translator resting lifeless on the desk. The boy hadn't even bothered to turn it on.

'English,' Axl said slowly. 'I can do English.' The words rasped in his throat, broken before they'd even left his mouth . . . 'And no, I'm not a war criminal.'

'Okay,' the American flipped the screen up off the desk and swivelled it towards Axl. On it was a real-time grab of the interview. 'Look at the screen,' said the man and Axl did. In place of the room, words now hovered.

'Can you read it?'

Axl nodded.

'Good. Check the words and if they're true read them aloud, facing the screen. By reciting these words you assert that you've not committed a war crime, not been proscribed sanctuary by the UN PaxForce and you are not – in so far as you know – under edict from WorldBank, the IMF or the Human Rights Court at the Hague . . .'

The man kept his voice soft, as if worried he might give offence. But underneath the gentleness was the flatness of lines recited hundreds of times before.

Axl swore the oath without hesitation. And in swearing gave up his right to sanctuary if the UN could prove he'd lied.

'A bridge that travellers walk over, moonlight that cools flames of passion, herbs that cure disease, and sun which illuminates darkness . . .' The doctor was reciting something but Axl wasn't listening, merely watching the way sunlight showed up tiny blonde hairs on her wrist. Not that this was what he saw. Axl got shades of grey bleaching out to white and not even in real 3D either.

The doctor deserved a soft synth loop, something exotic like a late riff or soloing balafon. She didn't get that either. Too many empty spaces, too much silence.

There'd been other borders to be crossed, years back when the world was a different kind of black and white. Crawling under the wire into besieged Bogota. Passing through the razor fence surrounding the Cabal, back when the Az virus had just started raging, before towerblocks crumbled and Spanish flu turned Colombia to a mountainous wasteland.

That was professionalism, crawling into a city under siege to kill somebody who was probably going to die anyway. Either that or stupidity. Axl did it though, and got out to rack up that week's highest ratings and a prize at Cannes. The networks hated that. Seeing freelancers walk away with awards.

The voice that broke through his tumbling memories was patient, soft and understanding. So kind and rational Axl wanted to scream. It was asking him a question. Something he thought it had asked him before.

'Can you remember your name?'

Axl looked at the doctor who smiled gently.

'If not, we can always try a DNA match using the composite Red Cross database for Europe. But you know it was logic bombed . . .' She caught herself and blushed. When she spoke again it was to say exactly the same thing, but more slowly and using simple words. Which told him all he needed to know about how convincing he looked in his new part.

Axl grinned sourly.

'Name's Jack,' he said, 'Black Jack Hot. Hell, you've probably heard of me?'

Too young to have watched the series first time round and too grown-up now to be interested in the revival, it was obvious she didn't get the gag. All he saw on her face was pity. Which wasn't enough to stop Axl pasting the patented shit-eating grin onto his hollow face.

'Well, too bad, 'cos you're about to . . .'

For a second, Axl had the hideous feeling she was about to lean across the desk and take his hand.

'I'm Jane, your doctor,' she said gently. 'We'll be working together to get you back on your feet. Get you back to full health.'

'Nothing wrong with Black Jack,' Axl said. 'He's fine.'

'No,' Jane shook her head. 'You've been beaten up, starved, blinded, tortured . . .'

His mind only made it to item two on her list.

Starved? Axl stared at his wrist. Sure there was a scar from the implant but what he really noticed was just how thin his wrist was. Paper-fine skin stretched over protruding bone.

'What's the date?' Axl demanded.

'Thursday 1 September . . .'

Eight days were gone walkabout. Axl examined his fingers, suddenly realising what he saw. Starvation. Skin pulled so tight over sinew and bone that his knuckles belonged to someone else.

'Bastards,' Axl said suddenly. 'Fucking bastards . . .'

'Anger's good,' the doctor told him.

He ignored her. That bloody toy on the shuttle . . . Axl stopped feeling angry, stopped feeling anything and finally listened to his body. His teeth were chattering, muscles strung tight as violin strings in his jaw. All the way down his spine went shivers, syncopated cold waves. He stank so bad he didn't know how the girl could stand to be in the same room as him.

Not starved, Axl realised, wired to fuck and back. He could taste the residue of cheap amphetamine in his sour saliva. Smell the crystalMeth oozing from his pores. He'd just done the Bollywood Diet. A week asleep while his metabolism ran white hot and his shuddering body rehydrated through feeds in his wrist. The little bastard had burned out his muscles to leave bones rattling in a skin sack.

'You've been chemically tortured,' Jane said.

'No,' Axl said firmly. 'Beaten up, drugged up, nothing more.' Hell, he'd been tortured by professionals and that little bastard wasn't even . . .

When the small room came back into focus Axl's hands were shaking and his teeth chattering worse than ever.

Silently the doctor stood up and walked round her desk, heading towards a basin behind him. 'Water,' she said, seeing his suspicious glance, 'run-off from the mountains.'

It was cold enough to bite into the back of his throat and make his already aching head hurt even more. Silently she refilled the glass and gave it back to him. He drank that one down too while she watched. And then, surprisingly, Jane did nothing; almost as if she'd forgotten he was there.

Axl watched while she tapped the top of her desk, elegant fingers dancing over its glass surface to wake icons. Soon the whole surface flickered with floating frames that filled with ever updating lists. It took Axl a minute or so to realise she was checking inventory and ordering fresh drugs for her surgery, something that even the most basic smartbox could have handled in fifteen seconds without anyone being aware it had run the routine.

When she was done, Jane started over, rechecking she'd got her figures right first time round. Then she started rechecking the recheck. Without meaning to, Axl shifted in his seat.

'Through there,' the woman said without looking up.

Through there featured a small chrome toilet, the first piece of obviously modern equipment he'd seen since landing. But Axl didn't have eyes or need for that or the matching glass basin with built in sonic dryer. He was too busy looking at his face in a looking glass, hollow cheeked and flayed by the unflattering glow of a striplight overhead.

It was as well the mirror was dumb. Because Axl could imagine only too well what the one back at his flat in Day Effé would have said had he ever presented himself looking like that. Refried shit was the least of it.

And if the bruising had been only half as bad he'd still have looked worse than terrible. He could have signed on as a Voudun zombie in some horror Sim and the living dead would have complained. Hell, Black Jack would have said he would double no trouble as a drug warning to kids not to ski Ice . . .

But that was busking it. Deep down inside, Axl knew he just looked 'fugee – bog-standard issue, from his razor-cut three-millimetre crop designed to keep lice at bay to the standard Red Cross tag punched through his left ear, its hologram shimmering in the overhead light.

The artificial eye feeding him the information stared out from one bruised socket. His other socket was crusted black. And if he'd got back his cheekbones to die for it was because almost dying was *how* he'd got them back. A ring of puncture wounds ran in neat circles round both temples where someone

– read that little shit – had punched SQUID needles through to his brain.

It wasn't a pretty sight but then Axl was beginning to realise that it wasn't meant to be. As for that foamBone repair in his forehead . . . He could be running straight chips, a half-real/half-augmented splice or even be packed with nothing but the wetware he was born with. Christ alone knew what that little fuck had been doing inside his head up there on the shuttle. Rewiring everything in sight probably.

Jane gave Axl ten minutes of being in front of the mirror by himself before she hit override on the door lock and came in to get him. Her patient wasn't standing in front of the looking-glass anymore. He was hunched on the floor, legs pulled up and hugged tight to him with his arms, head buried against his knees.

She knew without looking that he was crying. And experience told her he wouldn't thank her for noticing, they never did. All the same, she pulled Axl to his feet, gave him a sterile tissue and led him back to her tiny surgery.

Jane was twenty-three, six months out of Tel Aviv medical college and this man was the six hundred and thirty-second torture victim she'd seen since arriving. At most, she gave him a forty-sixty chance of surviving as was. Sixty-forty if she took time to patch him up.

So far, she'd cared about each broken human presented to her but common sense and the clinic AI told Jane that her compassion would eventually cut off, though there'd been no sign of it yet. She was exhausted with waiting.

The material on her couch was self-cleaning and the couch itself doubled as scales and most other things besides. Jane read off his weight and made a note to herself with a quick pass of her fingers over the desktop before helping him out of his blood-encrusted shirt and trousers.

Three Spanish coins, a cracked credit chip and three soiled

hundred dollar notes rolled together so tight they could be pushed into almost any orifice. There was nothing in his pockets that didn't fit the standard 'fugee profile.

He stank worse without his clothes, but that was quite normal. For a minute Jane considered removing the grime and sweat from his skin with a simple dusting of nanites, but rejected the idea. Most 'fugees were too scared of nanites to want them near. He could shower later, before he picked up replacement clothes.

'Okay,' said Jane as she ran her fingers quickly down his front, feeling for scars and swellings. 'I'm starting the examination now . . .' She was talking to the clinic AI. 'Knife wound to the right chest, looks old. Newer operation scar over lower bowel area. Bullet wound, low-calibre and non-explosive, in through right thigh and out right hip . . . Relatively recent.'

'That was five years ago,' interrupted Axl.

'Patient heals slowly . . .' Jane added it to her observations without pausing. A quick touch to Axl's shoulder was all it took to make him roll onto his front. 'Star-shaped cauterisation to right shoulder, not instantly identifiable.'

Axl could have told her that was a holiday souvenir from Belize, ceramic frag from someone else's home-made pipe bomb, but he didn't feel like interrupting her again and certainly not to talk about the one time he got really sloppy. His *WarChild* contract had been running out then and he'd missed a simple trip wire slung across the entrance to a deserted holiday hotel. Three-quarters of Axl's input to that episode had involved him getting shipped to a field hospital outside San Porto. His personal rating had dropped eleven points.

'Liver, both kidneys . . .' Her hand slipped casually between his buttocks, cupping his balls. 'Both testicles, one new . . .' She nodded to herself, made another note, revising the odds upwards. Having both kidneys was good, if surprising.

Running her fingers up the man's spine to check each vertebra, her finger reached his skull and then found the grey ceramic plug, recessed into its mounting and level with his skin . . .

'Shit . . .' She bent close, so close that Axl could feel her blonde hair brush his shoulder, soft as angel's breath. 'They spiked you . . .'

She was shocked.

Really shocked.

Axl twisted his head to look up into blue eyes made enormous by tears and pity. And despite himself, he smiled. No one came close to the Cardinal when it came to pre-planning and detail.

Chapter Twenty-one

Shangri/LaLa

This was nature with a fucking capital N, Axl realised, looking round him. Artificial and constructed, true enough, but still way more raw than what passed for wilderness back home on Earth; which the Cardinal insisted was put there by God for man but everyone knew was no more than a spitball of spacedust and a chance reaction of amino acids.

Nature was something he was part of, that's what Dr Jane back at Vajrayana had told Axl. Only fools thought nature, like life, was something that could be safely controlled. Well, he had news for her. Life and the world thrived on fools, this world as much as the old one. He'd be prepared to take a bet on it.

Hoofbeats sucked at the mud. The ground beneath his horse's hooves had the consistency of summer tundra, a hand's breadth of sticky earth and rough grass skimming soil still frozen hard as rock. His mount was spooked with fear, eyes rolled back white in its long head. The feeling of death around them was so stark it was as if they had ridden into a wall.

Everything had been fine when the wind blew from behind, but now it came straight into Axl's face, ripping tears from his hollow eye and choking him with its stench. He was so cold his bones were already ice and it felt like he had meltwater, not blood, in his veins. So maybe that little shit had left him human after all, because feeling this cold could only be a flaw and design faults were stripped out of toys and AIs.

There was something wrong with the sky, too, but Axl couldn't yet work out just what it was. From what he could tell, the colour seemed right, pale with high clouds and black dots that swung in distant currents. Not just small familiar birds, but larger, more exotic species. Eagles, black kites and hawks. Even a pale-feathered osprey that had skimmed low over a silver lake he'd left behind him the previous morning. Or maybe it was the day before that. Axl was having trouble remembering.

Ahead were more dead bodies than he'd seen since the rape of Bogota. Thousands of them. Rotting, hacked-apart corpses. If Axl hadn't known better he'd have thought himself back in some battle. Arms were cut free from naked, legless torsos. A young girl with dark hair stared blindly in his direction, sockets pecked bare. She had no feet and what had been her large intestine sprawled out of her open stomach like a crawling worm.

On a low stone table lay an old man, eyeless face turned to the sky. Both his arms were chewed away, one shredded at the elbow, the other ripped from its socket like a broken doll. Where his chest should have been was an open hollow framed by splintered ribs. And standing guard over the corpse was a grey wolf, saliva dripping from full jaws.

The wolf wasn't alone. Sitting on the stone altar beside the dead man was a saffron-robed old man chanting softly to himself, as oblivious to the wolf as to the ravens and Egyptian vultures circling overhead.

Not a battlefield but a charnel ground. A point on the high plateau where bodies could be left broken and exposed to be taken back into the wheel of life. The monk was performing *chod*. Making peace with death. Axl knew all about *chod* and the charnel grounds: before reluctantly letting him sign himself out of her surgery Dr Jane had insisted he watch a bleak tri-D on 'fugee life in Samsara.

Vajrayana and the clinic were behind him now. And between where his horse stood on the plateau and where Axl was headed was a mountain ridge, draped in oak, scrub juniper and fir and topped by wispy low clouds and snow. Beyond that and the high valleys was an impossibly-steep mountain slope that rose almost sheer to the edge of the wheelworld.

The time would come, of course, when the wheel was full but that was a long way off. Life was cruel on Samsara and Axl knew from the tri-D that 'fugees died faster than they could be imported, though Tsongkhapa hoped that natural birth would eventually change that. And Samsara did have natural birth, it was one of the Dalai Lama's oddities. As were those picturesque wooden tourist towns in the central valley leased to Thomas Cook and Disney.

No one had even looked at him when Axl rode through *Shangri/LaLa*, but then TeamRodent regulations were very strict about tourist/'fugee fratting and the tour guides made sure their charges kept to the rules. Largely because if the experiment was successful the rodents were hoping to open not just another two tourist villages but a 'tourist retreat' in Vajrayana itself.

And besides, the grocks were warned in advance that the sky was hung with tiny Aerospat vidCams, relaying constant updates to Tsongkhapa. And Samsara's overarching AI might be neutral where 'fugees were concerned, but that didn't apply to tourists. In fact, Tsongkhapa had only agreed to guide in the chartered shuttles after the Dalai Lama explained for the third time that he had 'fugees to protect and visiting tourists made it more difficult for WorldBank, the UN or IMF to launch covert raids.

On a spread of wide wings, an eagle rode the air currents towards Axl, swirled into a turn and dived, low and fast over a small distant lake, talons extended. This time it took a silver-scaled char that flapped, already broken-backed as the eagle's claws tightened.

Maybe it was an omen, but if so then too bad because Axl didn't believe in omens any more than in luck. Life was what you made of it. A construct. Luck didn't come into it, ever . . .

Pulling on his reins with cold awkward fingers, Axl wrapped

his large grey coat tightly around himself and turned to face the low mountains on the other side of the plateau. Somewhere in the foothills, next to a waterfall there would be shaggy, squat-nosed yaks weighing half a ton or more, barley fields already cut, a village and a monastery, because there was always a monastery. If you could call low, pink-painted stone shacks monastic. It would take him several hours, maybe more to find the next place. But when he did, the monks would have spare food – and if not food then buttered tea. Everyone in the bloody place had buttered tea.

Dr Jane had given Axl painkillers, a roll of surgical tape, amphetamines and a silver space blanket taken from Red Cross supplies. From the Samsara Trust he got twenty silver thalers, coins heavy enough to make a good punching weight if he put ten together and folded them into the palm of his hand, though Axl didn't point that out to Dr Jane. He also got a steel-bladed hunting knife which had a heavy brass handle but was missing its scabbard, a long grey woollen coat that was almost rain-proof and the brown mare, a mountain pony so shaggy it could have been a misbred yak.

The blonde doctor had walked him to the edge of the city herself, after finally accepting Axl's angry, tearful statement that he couldn't stay in Vajrayana for treatment because what he really needed was to find other people like him, persecuted followers of Pope Joan.

Axl knew why he'd been given a horse when regulations only specified a knife, staff and woollen coat; one look at his own face give him the answer. From the blinded eye to the raw scar of a non-consensual SQUID burned into his forehead, he wore the stigmata of the damned. His very injuries made him a VIP among those who had suffered. At least, those of them who remained alive.

Chapter Twenty-two

Buy Time/Sell Space

The effect was kind of Downtown Boho, brocade and ribbons, both filthy.

As well as a brocaded waistcoat, the broad-hipped woman also wore a grey felt skirt, embroidered red blouse and no knickers. Axl was pretty sure of that last detail because he was squatted back on his heels, arms folded tight across his chest as he tried both to keep warm and not stare between the chapped and open knees of the round-faced 'fugee squatting in front of him.

She'd kept on sweeping ashes from the cold grate as he came into the Inn and hadn't even looked round until he dropped into a crouch opposite her. Now she was looking like she didn't understand a word he said. And if she didn't, who would? The other villagers he'd seen on his ride into Cocheforet had just crossed themselves and turned their backs.

The Inn itself was no more than three rooms lumped on top of each other, with an outside latrine and a bit partitioned off from the main bar to make a kitchen, but it was still the biggest building in the village. Cocheforet had turned out to be an isolated ribbon-development of sod, wood and stamped-earth houses thrown up along the edge of a narrow stream in a valley planted on its lower slopes with millet and barley.

It also housed Joan's most devout supporters. At least, that was what Dr Jane had told Axl before sending him on his way with a cloth map of the high plateau showing the settlement marked off at one edge with a cross. She forgot to mention the track in would be littered with bare-arsed Tibetan children scooping yak dung into wicker baskets to dry for fuel. Or that no one would appear to understand a word he said.

Axl started over again, explaining what he wanted as he tried to ignore the warm darkness between her open thighs. Only it seemed hopeless. Either that, or he was just too tired to make sense.

'The inn's full . . .'

The voice came from behind him, low and gruff. Not remotely friendly. It punched the switch Axl had been looking for.

'Full?' Axl said in disbelief, clambering to his feet and stared past the thickset bearded man to an empty bar beyond. The place wasn't just empty, it was also hideous. Rough beaten-earth walls were coated with whitewash that had mostly flaked off and the floor was so pitted it could have been dried mud. Two crude windows and an ill-fitting front door singularly failed to keep out the cold.

The only vaguely attractive thing about the Inn was the wide-hipped, heavy-breasted woman kneeling by the fireplace and she was thirty-five if she was a day. Her face was hidden now and her long hair was tied away under a grey scarf, but from what he'd seen her legs were lean and muscled and he could tell that her arms were strong.

The innkeeper grunted something that sent the woman scuttling from the room, leaving her pan where it was.

'Full and closed . . .' The bearded man said. Somewhere upstairs a door slammed heavily and the man scowled.

'Looks empty to me,' Axl said, feeling better already. 'And you've got a welcome lamp burning over the door . . . Besides . . .' he deftly loosened the pocket on his coat, pulled out his hunting knife and wiped the blade on his hip, even through it was clean. 'I don't take up much space and I won't be staying long.'

'Where you headed?'

Axl shrugged. 'Passing through. You know, looking up old friends.'

'Well, you won't find them here,' said the man firmly.

'Here!' Axl sounded amused. 'No, you're right, I doubt if there's much of interest in Cocheforet.' He looked through a window at mud-splattered chickens pecking at pebbles in the street outside, then cast an amused glance round the squalid bar, dismissing it. 'How many live in this valley, fifteen, twenty?'

'Thirty,' said the innkeeper, 'forty, fifty.' He was drunk.

'Petty thieves, cell sweepings,' said Axl dismissively, 'I'm looking for real 'fugees.'

'Real!' The barkeeper sounded outraged. 'Round here we're . . .'

'Having tea,' the woman said from the doorway, sounding firm. Brown eyes looked steadily into Axl's face as she thrust a steaming wooden bowl into his hand.

'Drink it,' she said, 'it'll help you warm up. Then I'll show you the attic.' Her voice was neutral. 'The room's not much, but *round here* nothing is, except maybe . . .' The woman stopped, then shrugged. 'You'll hear about it anyway. There's an empty monastery across the valley but it's not safe. Houses that grow like plants . . .' She grunted and spat into the dead fireplace, before turning towards the door to the stairs. 'Some of the houses on Samsara brick themselves up with the inhabitants inside if they don't like you.'

Less than thirty years. That was how long Samsara had been functioning and already it had its own legends, its own dark myths. Axl smiled.

'That monastery . . .' Axl asked looking out of his attic window, but the woman cut him off before he could even ask the question.

'It's deserted,' she told him firmly, 'and dangerous. Understand?'

Yeah, he understood.

The attic had polycrete walls, roughly plastered, and a roof made from bamboo laid over rafters and lashed into place with sisal. The bamboo had been skimmed over with mud, and rough red tiles put on top of that. It was just enough to keep out the drizzle but it didn't stand a chance against the wind.

Cold ashes filled the fireplace, turned to paste by droplets that pattered down the inside of its cracked chimney breast.

'It's what we've got,' the woman said shortly.

'No problem,' said Axl, 'but I'll need a fire.' His gaze flicked round the empty room. 'Plus a mattress and blankets.' He could see from the sour expression on her face that the woman regarded all three as unnecessary.

'You got money?'

Axl gave a slight nod. He didn't offer her any. The silver thalers were tucked deep in his coat pocket along with Dr Jane's map. He had a 128Gb memory chip, a lump of unimprinted bioClay and a tiny spherical hard drive hidden in his boot heel, all wrapped round with fooler loops. The usual glass-beads-for-the-natives shit the Vatican still bought into.

'You pay my husband, you understand?'

She did the work, the drunk took the money. Axl nodded, he'd been there before.

'The room's okay?' She asked it like she almost cared.

'Yeah,' he assured her. 'The room's fine.' And it was, if Axl ignored the fact it had no light, no glass to the window and was reached by a ladder from the landing below. But he'd slept in shittier places. Hell, he'd grown up in a far worse place, only he didn't talk about that.

'You got somewhere I can wash?'

The woman twisted her fingers behind the shutter closing off the window and pulled it open. 'Down there,' she said, pointing to a patch of mud. 'There's that pump out front.'

'I was thinking of hot water.'

'It'll cost you.'

Axl sighed. 'I know, pay your husband . . .'

A strange look crossed her face. 'No,' she said, meeting his eye. 'Pay me.' Needless to say the woman didn't have change. No one ever did in situations like this. From Argentina to

North Greenland, she'd have been surprised at the number of people in out of the way places who hadn't got change when needed. Or maybe she wouldn't. There was something knowing in her brown eyes that said this wasn't where she thought she belonged.

But then this wasn't actually where anyone belonged, Axl reminded himself, no one got here unless they were fleeing somewhere else.

'I'll take that bath now,' he told her.

'No,' she shook her head. 'You wait an hour, until the kitchen is . . . until Leon, my husband, is . . .' the woman shrugged in irritation. 'You wait, and it's not exactly a bath. How much yak dung do you think we have for fires?'

'Strip,' she ordered and Axl did, dropping his shirt and trousers onto the dirt floor.

She'd fed him already, *thukpa*, a thin noodle soup with lumps of lamb floating in the salty liquid. And then insisted he finish a bowl of cold dumplings stuffed with radish.

He'd left the grey coat with his money in its pockets upstairs. That seemed safest and anyway Axl was alone in the inn with her and he had no intention of letting her out of his sight.

'How hot?' The woman had a huge iron kettle in her hand and was standing next to a tub that rose slightly at one end, so it looked like a crib for an oversized child.

'Hot as you can,' Axl said and stepped out of a pair of dirt-grey Calvins. She looked him over without shame.

'I'm Ketzia,' she announced suddenly. For a moment Axl was worried she was going to try to shake hands. 'They messed you over bad . . .'

Axl grunted and gave a half shrug. He was proud of the shrug. 'No worse than anyone else.'

Her brown eyes were counting up his wounds, looking at bruises and putting dates to those scars. He'd met the type before. Women who couldn't make conversation, looked twenty-five before they hit fifteen and had two kids before they hit twenty, but who could remove bullets using just a knife and their fingers and stitch shut a machete wound using thread from a sewing basket.

You found them among the poor on the edge of every war zone and disaster area. Living there because that was where no one else wanted to live. His mother had been one of them, apparently. Not that he'd known her. She'd been dead three years by the time the Cardinal had her tracked down for him.

'Who did it?'

Good question. Axl let the silence stretch thin between them, wondering if she'd break it. She didn't. Instead, Ketzia filled her vast kettle from a bucket and put it back on the embers. She finally left the tiny kitchen carrying the empty bucket.

Somewhere out front the pump clanked and then she was back.

'Get in,' Ketzia said, nodding at the half-filled bath, 'you don't want someone to see you.' She grinned sourly. 'So,' she said, 'how good's that eye of yours?'

'You're a woman,' Axl told her, 'long hair in a braid, long skirt, that's it . . . It doesn't do fine detail, it doesn't do night sight and it only manages black and white. Oh yeah, and everything's flat, like you get on a cheap screen . . .'

'You've got enough money to buy a real one?'

'Out here?'

Ketzia nodded but she was agreeing the idea was silly. 'The Savonarolas didn't leave you much nerve, right?' It was a statement not a question. Her voice made it obvious she figured Axl knew that already, first-hand. 'And they got you for doing that Ishie stuff . . .' She paused. 'You can imagine what the bastards core out if you're a prostitute or a rent boy.'

He could, imagine it that was. The Savonarolas weren't original. Most of what their death squads had made their own in the atrocity stakes wasn't even new. Merely updated from outrages first committed in the Balkans or the North African littoral. Places like the outskirts of M'Dina where the Mufti had been fighting a vicious, fifty-year campaign against the Jihad fundamentalists, and losing.

Five minutes later Ketzia was bored with watching Axl scrub half-heartedly at the wounds on his face. So she took the cloth from him, almost gently. And leaning back in the tub, Axl shut his eye and concentrated on feeling her heavy breasts as they brushed lightly against his shoulder through her blouse. She smelt of sweat, but he only knew that because he'd finally stopped stinking himself. And her movements were soft and surprisingly deft as she used a cloth to lift recent blood from the half-healed scar on his forehead.

Everytime Ketzia reached a new gash, she stopped to move her fingers softly round the edges. At first Axl figured she was feeling for swelling, but what Ketzia was really doing was checking the wounds were real, that it really was a SQUID scar, that what looked like a spike plug in the back of his skull was just that . . .

The woman was running a none-too-discreet check routine on his injuries and Axl was passing with flying colours. Hell, he wasn't just passing, he'd passed. He knew that because her callused fingers were slowing, her touch getting ever more soft as her makeshift flannel soaped gently down his gut towards the waterline where there wasn't a scar in sight.

Despite the cold that howled under the kitchen door and the metal edge of the tub digging into his back, Axl was suddenly tumescent and getting harder by the second. Grinning, the woman dipped her cloth into the water and squeezed slow droplets onto the swollen head of his penis. As moves went it seemed positively inventive for someone whose sex life looked like it was confined to once on Saturdays when beardface was drunk.

Axl groaned and she grinned again, a wide knowing smile at odds with her drab, washed-out clothes . . . And then the front door opened and shut and Ketzia was gone, out of the back without pausing to say anything at all. Though she hesitated long enough to shut the door.

'What the . . .'

What indeed. Axl kept his legs hugged up to his chest, like he always took a bath with his chin resting on his knees. 'I was dirty,' he told the innkeeper. 'Okay? And I've already told your wife I'll pay for the dung on the fire.'

'It's a thaler,' stated the man.

'For a tub of water?'

'Yeah.' He had his fists clenched on his hips and it was obvious that Leon was furious, but it was equally obvious he had no real idea at what.

'Okay,' said Axl calmly, 'but I'll need a towel.'

'You'll need a . . .'

'For a thaler,' said Axl, 'I want a towel.'

The innkeeper didn't even bother to go to the door, just stood in the middle of the kitchen and screamed '*Ketzia*'. The only answer he got was silence.

'Where is she?'

Axl shrugged. 'How the fuck would I know?'

Footsteps, when they finally approached, came through the bar at the front and stopped carefully at the kitchen door.

'You decent?' There was a brisk knocking and then the woman stuck her head round the door.

'Well . . . ?' Ketzia stopped and looked at the innkeeper. 'Didn't know you were back,' she said to her husband, not sounding too pleased.

Leon flushed. 'Our *guest* wants a towel.' He put heavy emphasis on the second word, as if the idea of anyone wanting to stay at his inn was somehow ridiculous.

'Probably does. If he plans to dry himself,' said the woman.

Chapter Twenty-three

Swimming Towards the Light

'*Budvar*,' Axl demanded, but only because he knew Leon couldn't possibly provide bottled beer. Couldn't provide a decent shave either, obviously enough, because Cocheforet didn't run to generators and the Braun disposable Axl had stolen from Dr Jane's surgery didn't work on daylight, it needed a feed.

Which was tough, because Cocheforet didn't run to that either. The better Axl felt inside himself the worse his temper got. Almost as if the constant headache had acted as a filter against the world in which he'd found himself.

No razor, no newsfeed and no new eyes, but worst of all no hope of finding any of them anywhere . . . It was like stumbling back two centuries. Except it wasn't. What it was really like was going below Third World.

Standing at the zinc, Axl stared slowly round at Leon's filthy bar and the silent, three-man crowd of even filthier customers and wondered for the first time what he was doing, other than saving his own life. Mind you, he knew what they were doing. Waiting for him to leave the room.

As for Samsara itself . . . Well, the best you could say was that it was economically self-sufficient. Not importing food or technology from Earth meant no commercial ties, and no commercial ties meant no metaNational leverage. Economic blockade might have replaced the gunboat kind nine times out of ten, but even the guys on Capitol Hill weren't stupid enough to try that one on Tsongkhapa, not when there were no essentials that Samsara needed.

In the end Axl settled for some kind of fermented barley mess called *chang* that came out of a big copper pot, looked like molasses mixed with water and tasted of rained-out bonfires. It was what the three men sat silently in the corner were drinking too. Only they all used long wooden straws and drank straight from a smaller pot that a dark-haired Tibetan boy had carried over to their table. The boy didn't seem to have a name. Leon just called him *you*.

The behaviour of the other customers ran the full gamut from A to B and back again. From staring into the chang to glaring at Axl with undisguised suspicion as he tossed three years of therapy and two twelve-point plans straight down his gullet in choking gulps of thin, yeast-sour ditch water. It was five years since he'd last touched alcohol and, given what the chang tasted like, not a day of it had been wasted.

He was really getting on their wick and the only problem was he had less than no idea why. If he had, he might have been able to work on it a bit more. Make push come to shove, because that's what it had to do. Axl didn't have time to blend it, become accepted, put up the usual smokescreen.

Outside in the street a door slammed loudly and everyone in the bar tried not to look at each other, but that was okay because Axl was busy looking at all of them. No one looked back.

'Rotten night,' said Axl, nodding towards the noise. There was no reply to that either, but Axl was starting to enjoy filling the sullen silences. His words were slurred far more than four small bowls of chang warranted, especially as one of those was still soaking into the earthen floor at his feet.

On the other side of the inn wall, wind was ripping needles from thin pines while hail thudded into the wet ground like endless shot. In all the newsfeeds he'd seen about Samsara none had mentioned that the weather was buggered. Mind you, he hadn't seen many and those he had always concentrated on Varjrayana and life in that city.

Samsara was silly season stuff. Every time the Jihad in North

Africa declared a brief peace or the Russian Tsar who was holed up at Yekaterinburg summoned Marshal Sukarov to play wargames instead of letting the marshal lead his troops from what could loosely be called the Sino-Russian war front, given it was fought by proxies and much of it was information-based anyway – every time CySat ran out of hard news they sent some photogenic, freelance Ishie off to Samsara to record her impressions.

Mostly these were of the *Vajrayana's quaint, wonderful and why can't we manage this on Earth* variety. But maybe, Axl decided, that was because in reality the wheelworld was freezing, with fucked weather and villages full of trauma-tised basket cases with killer PTS. Somehow that side of the experiment didn't make it to the screen.

He couldn't imagine why.

'Another beer,' Axl demanded, banging down his wooden bowl so that what was left slopped across the table before dripping slowly onto the floor. Behind his bar, Leon scowled into his beard but told the boy to take Axl a fresh bowl anyway. The bowl was small, hand-lathed from oak and decorated with five poor-quality cracked turquoises. The boy carried it like it was the most precious thing he'd ever seen.

'Your room's ready,' Leon said pointedly.

'But I'm not,' said Axl as he slammed the new bowl back onto the table, spilling some more. 'I'm going for a walk . . .'

And you're welcome to come after me, he told the three men in his head, *but I wouldn't recommend it.* Fingers touched the brass hilt of his hunting knife where its bare blade was surgically taped to his side, handle down for ease of use.

Outside was bitter, which wasn't a surprise: nor was the wind that drove along the valley into Axl's face, though the night air was so cold it took him a few seconds to catch his breath, and longer still for his eye to adjust to the darkness.

What would have surprised Axl, if he hadn't just been sitting in the inn listening carefully to the noises outside, was the figure frozen animal-still between the stables and an open-ended shed beyond. If in doubt freeze, but not when you're alone on open ground. Someone should have told the person that. Mind you, someone should have told him that all those years ago, not left him to find out for himself.

Axl didn't hurry after the ghost figure. Mainly because hurrying wasn't something he'd been taught. When he ran it was hard and fast, accelerating like an animal and preferably wired up on cooking sulphate. The rest of the time he walked slowly, head up and shoulders loose. As stances went, it didn't say *look at me*, but it didn't say *walk through me* either. It said, *here's a man going about his business, let's leave it that way . . .*

Axl could do *hard eye* without thinking about it and he could tap into psychotic on whim just by taking the filter off his memories, but like his old sergeant used to stress, the main sign of success was not needing to. Getting left alone was a primary skill, one Axl had long since picked up on the street, and beside it all that other shit about slowing down heartbeat, dropping brain rhythms from beta to alpha and hitting a neurological low of ten cycles per second was just that, so much shit.

You couldn't turn on a teen newsfeed without seeing some bug-eyed drone making a living recycling memes from StreetSemantics 101, but what Axl knew he'd learned direct on the streets of Alphabet by watching who survived and who got razzed.

And he learned fast from his mistakes.

Axl laughed as he wiped rain out of his hollow eye socket. At least he had learned fast back then. Back at the start when the Cardinal did occasional *pro bono* out of a small basement office in a block at the back of St Patrick's and Axl was the street kid stood in front of some fancy desk that once belonged to a guy called Frick, or so Axl got told while he was protesting that he didn't do all that Hail Mary shit.

God was that enamel baby the Spic gangs glued to their Uzis. He didn't know what the Nation called their god, only that he wasn't allowed in pictures so they wore his name on gold pinkie rings or etched into the barrels of those tiny matt-black H&Ks they wore clipped to their belts like Sony Walkwears. Axl didn't buy into any of that shit, like he didn't punk for protection.

Mind you, he didn't need to. Axl had learnt to get out of the way of the kids he couldn't go through and to do it so no one noticed. He didn't need protection and he didn't need God.

Atheist wasn't a word Axl learnt until later. At the time he got pulled in, he had a vocabulary of maybe 150 words and he didn't use ninety percent of those. But then he was ten and *si*, *no* and *chinga tu madre* covered most situations. Still, the tall priest promised Axl that he didn't have to believe in God to take his money so finally the boy did what he was paid to do, follow a fat man out cruising in Central Park.

Besides it was cold and he was hungry. He'd thought the marshmallow heat of his first summer on the streets was bad enough. That was before he reached the winters.

Mostly the man cruised a large courtyard of old paving stones used by the skate gangs. The courtyard was sunk into the ground like a small mall with no ceiling. Around the mall's edge were blank-eyed statues and at one end stood an empty fountain. In the middle of that fountain – her wings spread wide – stood the Angel of the Waters erected in 1842 to celebrate the arrival of clean water to New York. Not that Axl knew any of that. He just followed the fat man, keeping hidden as the man stopped and talked to skateboys who mostly laughed or kept walking like he wasn't there.

On the third night, while a shivering Axl was edging round the spread-winged angel, his target vanished. And, scared that he was about to blow it, Axl raced into an underpass that headed back towards Central Park South in search of his target. Which was how Axl found himself frozen in the dark with a blade to his neck.

Not a big junkie knife like the skatez carried but a tiny silver thing that grew its own blade. Axl knew it was sharp because one gentle brush of the blade had beaded his throat with little pearls of blood.

'You're not hurt,' said the fat man as Axl examined the smudges of blood on his own fingers. 'But you will be if you don't tell the truth . . .'

Axl held his breath. Even at ten he didn't wriggle, whimper or panic; just looked slowly left and right for his escape route.

'There isn't one,' said the man, 'is there?'

Axl slowly shook his head.

'I suggest you remember that . . .'

And while the boy stood watching the man, all thought locked out of his face, the fat man who smelled of cologne brushed one thumb along the knife to send the metal blade flowing back into its handle.

Hard fingers gripped a wrist weak from calcium deficiency. 'Why?' The man said fiercely, his face pushed so close that Axl could see he had lines round his eyes and a saggy mouth. 'And how long have you been following me?'

Now was the time to run if he was going to, Axl knew that. The man might have his fancy knife but Axl still knew tricks the fat man would never know. Like how to twist free from a grip without getting your own wrist broken for a start. All it took was pivoting hard against your enemy's thumb and forefinger.

Worked everytime, at least it had so far.

Only that wasn't what he was going to do. There was all that cash to collect from the tall priest if he played this right and did what he was told.

'Saw you come into the Park,' said Axl, his accent rougher than ever. 'Thought you might help me . . .'

'Why would I do that?'

The boy shrugged. 'Cos I'm hungry, me. Haven't eaten for days.' There was a new whine in his voice, a softness that, had it been real, would have seen him dead long since. Kittens didn't get cuddled in the Alphabets, they got stamped.

'You know,' said the man, his smile mocking, 'you should force yourself.'

Axl's rat-like face went ever more blank as he gazed up into the man's watery eyes. He knew he was being mocked, he just didn't know how.

'You've got money,' Axl said and before the fat man could deny it, he gently brushed a finger against the man's open coat. It was soft and black, shimmering to itself. Silk was something else Axl didn't know back then, not just smart silk, any silk at all. And if that man had told him little worms spun coats that machines unwound into sticky threads which were then dusted with colours smaller than the eye could see Axl wouldn't have known what he was talking about anyway, or believed him if he had.

Just as Axl didn't really believe the fat man was taking him to get a Big Mac as he was nudged back towards the terrace and then down wide stone steps towards dark water.

They walked a path that sucked glue-like at their shoes, the black lake always on their right as the fat man kept promising Axl there was a McDonalds round each corner, but there wasn't. What there was finally was a wooden house with boarded-up windows and a kicked-in door. Around it winter-stripped trees were strung with broken bulbs. The doorway stank of piss, and inside Axl could hear rats scurrying across broken glass.

They kept scurrying.

What happened where the rats lived wasn't something Axl thought about. In fact, he thought about it so little that a month or two later he forgot it entirely for five years, only remembering at fifteen, coming to in a jungle camp outside Baranquilla and vomiting up memories with the dregs of his previous night's vodka. And even now, whenever he thought about that wooden shack – which he didn't – Axl's primary driving emotion was gratitude. That he was still alive when it was finally over. Standing more miles away across the cold black vacuum of space than he could readily imagine, Axl pulled up his collar and shivered.

Later on, when the fat man was gone and the rats had come out of their corner to crawl over Axl's small white body and chew occasionally to see if it was edible or not, Axl had driven himself to his feet and stumbled out into Central Park, heading for the obsidian water.

Frigid as melt and black like night, the lake had closed over him and crept into the crevices of his body, washing them clean. And for a moment as the cold rushed into him, Axl was filled with ice but then his muscles closed out the lake and Axl found himself swimming slowly towards a dish moon lodged in the skeletal branches of a winter tree on the other side of the lake.

He wouldn't make it – couldn't, even – no matter how near it looked. And yet Axl kept swimming towards the light until he felt his body disappear. There were no edges to it at all, no skin, no sense of fingers ending or water beginning. Only an unbelievable cold that was calling to him.

Frost filled Axl's soul and he believed . . . no, he *knew* that when he looked through the sodium haze that arced above Central Park he saw not the heat but the coldness of the sharp white stars beyond.

Dancing flashes of light they were, that blazed and then went out, one after another, like neurones shutting down.

Being brought back to life was the second worst thing that ever happened to Axl. Though no one told Axl that resurrection was what they did and Father Declan Begley did a televised meeting with the NYPD specifically to deny it.

A small Latino officer from the NYPD took Axl's statement at the hospital, recording everything on vid and in her notebook. There was also a little vidSat set to permanent hover near the ceiling of Axl's room at Mount Olive but no one told him who owned that, though Axl figured it had to be the priest, because he glanced in that direction more than once as he sat beside Axl's bed and held the boy's hand.

It didn't take long for Axl to work out the code. No squeeze meant it was okay to answer, while fingers tightening on his wrist meant *don't remember* – and that was fine, most of the time Axl didn't.

No one got charged with any crime. The sergeant, a good Catholic from Queens, lost her notebook and somehow managed to park her Sony vid next to a magnet by accident. *BodyCount* on NY access led next morning with a Glasgow couple molywired outside MOMA, three Hispanics mangled by a renegade garbage crusher and a chef on Mott Street who went postie and slaughtered five First Virtual databrokers on a night out.

None of those made Sunday's download of the *New York Times* and no site even mentioned a street kid pulled out of lake in Central Park, probably because such occurrences were just too common.

Three days later, the second lead on CySat's *New York Tonite* was the tragic heart attack of Cardinal Bambinetti. A day after that the local godslot led with a pithy but pious soundbite from his successor, a sleek-suited Vampyre in Armani glasses.

The girl ahead of him was good, Axl gave her that. She moved like a cat, though had there been katGirls on Samsara Axl felt sure he'd have heard about it.

All the same, this one was a natural, blending into the drizzle as she skimmed a darkened house trying the door and pushing against windows, all the while carefully avoiding spades, hoes and other rubbish left out to rot.

Whatever the kid wanted wasn't falling into place. The door was locked and all the windows bolted. Having checked the place, she went round it again to make doubly sure. Professionalism or desperation? Axl wasn't sure until the wind brought him his answer in a long low litany of swearing.

'Fuck.

'Fuck.

'Fuck.'

Her words weren't harsh or even that angry, more resigned like bolted windows was all she expected to find in Cocheforet. And then a door clanged in the distance and simultaneously they both froze. When Axl looked again the girl was pressed flat to a wall, well hidden in the shadows.

'Thought you might want this,' said a woman's voice from behind Axl.

Ketzia had a cloak of sorts folded across her forearms. It was badly-made from greased wool and stank worse than a wet ram.

'Thanks,' said Axl.

'No problem.' The woman stared off into the darkness, head cocked to one side as if listening to the rain. 'Figured you'd be cold. Not like *Colombia*, Samsara isn't . . .'

Not like . . . Colombia?

Ketzia nodded, something close to doubt in her eyes. 'Colombia, San Salvador, Whatever . . . It's good what you speak, but it's not real Spanish. Not like I speak. I knew you weren't really one of us the first time you opened your mouth.' She leant forward and touched the scars on his face. 'But these are real. And Joan had followers elsewhere . . .'

'You tell your husband?' Axl wasn't sure what relevance that had to anything but asked it anyway.

'Did I tell . . . ?' She looked into his face as her fingers caressed the edge of the empty pit where his other eye should be. Slowly Ketzia shook her head. 'What would he know?' She said dryly. 'Leon still thinks he can go home someday.'

'And you don't?'

'I don't know who lives in my house now but it isn't me. Besides I'm getting to like Samsara strange as that might seem. The valley's safe. We don't need guns or armies . . . Or killers,' her glance was suddenly fierce and she rocked on the balls of her feet, as if ready to go.

'You were a *reformista* too?'

It was the wrong question. But what stopped Ketzia from swinging on her heels and leaving was a noise nearby, soft as the passing of a cat.

'Maybe,' she said loudly. 'What's it to you?'

'Nothing.' Axl smiled, really smiled. He could do friendly when necessary and sometimes even when it wasn't. Without making it obvious, he took a step sideways to stare over Ketzia's shoulder into the darkness behind.

'Well then,' said the woman as she leant in to lift the cloak out of his hands and drape it round him, so that her fingers rested lightly on his shoulders. 'You should learn not to ask those questions in Cocheforet'. And then she stepped in closer still.

That was the last talking either of them did for a while. The woman's mouth tasted of buttered tea, inevitable really. Her lips opening hungrily as her hands locked behind Axl's head, pulling him to her.

Axl wrapped the edges of his borrowed cloak around Ketzia, swallowing them both inside its warmth. She had her eyes shut. Habit maybe, Axl decided: somehow he doubted if it was real passion. And then he realised that the woman probably couldn't stand to stare too closely into his battered face. But all the same, Ketzia's tongue snaked against his and she bit at his bottom lip, suddenly pushing herself against him.

She was kissing all the while, softly now as if unaware that her hips were grinding hard against his. And then Axl bit into her neck and Ketzia shook free, pulling her face away from him. But it wasn't to stop, only to set the rules.

'No,' she said firmly. 'No blood.' Very slowly she began to undo buttons to reveal a silk ASui blouse beneath her top's rough felt.

The blouse had been smart once, self cleaning, but whoever donated it to the 'fugee clothes fund for Samsara had burnt out its power or done something stupid like wash it in water, because now the silk was stained with dirt and rotted beneath the arms. While the delicate skeins of optic that threaded through the lace were completely lifeless and unlit.

The fastenings worked, though, being minimalist and mother-of-pearl. Not allowed to bite her neck, Axl knelt in the mud and fastened his mouth beneath one full breast instead, biting softly on the underside where it joined her ribcage. And then, while Ketzia was still shivering, Axl's mouth slid up to close on a dark nipple. The circle around it was puckered with cold and passion, and Axl swallowed the whole circle into his mouth until she was pulling him tight against her.

Her thighs were hard with muscle and her breasts were full, but her body was already losing its fight with gravity. She was, what? Thirty, thirty-five, maybe only late twenties? Axl had no way of knowing except ask. Maybe later . . . Resting his head against one breast and letting the other overflow his fingers, Axl shut his eye. He couldn't remember the last woman he'd fucked who hadn't been a street whore, but there were a lot of things in everybody's lives they couldn't be bothered to remember.

So instead Axl stood back up and concentrated on brushing his fingers softly around the puckered aureole of her left breast, never quite touching the taut nipple until her still-clothed hips were grinding into him hard enough to bruise. And then, with her arms locked tight around his neck and her mouth hungry against his, Axl dropped both his hands to her bare breasts and gripped hard, squeezing the swollen flesh.

Ketzia moaned. There was no sublety after that as Axl slid his hands to her hips and yanked up her skirt. She stank of salt and blood, like an animal in rut, but then so did Axl when her fingers finally freed him.

He let her tug roughly at him, dropping his own hand between her open legs, smoothing his fingers down her soft abdomen until he reached damp body hair that was fine like silk.

Axl groaned. The tiny hood of her clitoris peeled back as he dragged his index finger up the sodden line of her vulva, trapping the swollen outer lips between his other fingers.

Then she was biting at Axl's mouth again as he hooked one hand under her left thigh and scooped that leg off the ground, opening her wide. Ketzia was tight and slippery and swollen and Axl eased back out of her just to get the feeling of sliding in again between her thighs.

But before he could withdraw a second time, she'd hoisted up her other knee and locked both ankles behind his legs, moving down onto him as Axl supported her weight. Anyone who wanted to could have walked up behind him and taken off his head with a rusty length of molywire, but somehow Axl found it hard to care.

'Deeper . . .'

Faint moan segued into words as her knees locked tighter and her hips swivelled frantically against him. Axl could smell the grease in her long hair, rank like an animal, and it just made him want to fuck her more. Sliding hands down Ketzia's spine, Axl hooked his fingers into the base of her back, just above her broad buttocks and yanked.

It was enough.

She came against him, hips rocking, her mouth buried in the crook of his neck. A low stream of raw Valenciana was growled out into his ear. He didn't know some of the words she was using but they still sounded obscene.

Later, after Axl had loosed his grip on her back and Ketzia had lowered her legs, he'd turned the still-panting woman around to position her against the outside wall of a house, waiting while she braced her hands against damp polycrete.

Then he pulled up the back of her skirt, positioned himself carefully and slid into her, his fingers gripping the side of her hips so her buttocks pulled apart enough to let Axl watch himself as he rode her.

She stank. And mixed in with the basic pheromones of sex and body fluid were darker traces of shit and sweat. But as the Cardinal had once told a teenage Axl before buying him his first whore, if there wasn't shit and sweat, blood and semen at the end of it then you weren't doing it right.

Ketzia groaned with each thrust, as his thighs slapped hard against her exposed arse and little shock waves ran up her back. And then Axl came, his fingers roughly gripping her waist as he ploughed deep inside her, spasming.

As he slumped over her back and wrapped his arms round her soft gut, Axl knew one thing only. That the figure he'd started out following was long since gone. Vanished cat-like into the night.

Chapter Twenty-four

Wolf Patrol

The girl crept down the gravel path into Cocheforet as silently as she could manage, heavy canvas satchel banging against her hip, head hidden by the hood of a grey fleece. Mai still wore the dumb-fuck soulcatcher but her dark hair had recently been cropped tight to her skull and what little she owned was in the satchel. From anything but up close and very personal she could pass for a boy.

It could have been the valley wind Mai was avoiding because it buffeted hard enough to rock her on her feet and dampen the sound of church bells into almost-silence. But the wind wasn't what Mai was really dodging as she slid out of the night to rest briefly against the stable wall. It was everything and everybody. The village, that weird guy from last night, Kate and Louis from the monastery, but mostly Kate's pet clone.

'Fucking freak . . .' The girl spat expertly and a black tom exploded into a ball of ragged fur, back arching as hair ruffled around its shoulders and down its bony spine. 'Yeah, fuck you too, fuck eyes.'

She wasn't allowed to swear when she was with Kate at El Escondido. Mind you, there were a lot of things she wasn't allowed to do. Most of them plain stupid, like not eat with her fingers. Others were merely irritating, like don't spit, don't skin up, don't ice . . .

Chance would be a fine thing.

The only one of Kate's rules that Mai didn't mind was *don't fuck*. She'd done enough of that to last a lifetime and probably the lifetime of several Kates as well. And Mai didn't intend to, unless it was on her terms. Mai still wasn't exactly sure where she was, she was only certain it wasn't Spain. The weather was way too cold for summer, the air too thin and the mountains too tall. Besides the heavens were blacker than squid ink and the stars were missing, banished to a speckle of light along one edge of the night sky.

Mai figured it had to be Latin America. Maybe Argentina or Peru. They spoke Spanish there and had weird-shit mountain Indians. And she had to be south of the equator. That was how it worked wasn't it? If it was hot up North then it was cold down South. Christmas barbies at Bondi and all that . . . She'd watched *WorldFaX* on CySat 13 with the Judge. He always used to sit with her and watch boring stuff before folding her over his knee.

First time round, she'd expected to get smacked with a shoe or something stupid. But the old perv just brushed her hair for an hour before shuffling her down his lap so she could give him the full *il presidenti*.

Mai spat again, blindly and aiming at nothing.

Enough already. She didn't need to go there. She needed a way out of this valley and was counting on last night's stranger from the inn to provide it. Louis was frightened by the stranger and anything that upset Louis he took to Kate, like some child running for its mother. And then Kate would sit in that big kitchen and get all sensible while she 'worked through the options'. Only options didn't interest Mai and neither did their precious stranger, not the man himself. What interested Mai was the stranger's horse and that interested her very much indeed . . .

Pulling a rusty metal bar from her satchel, Mai slid one end of it into a gap in the stable doorframe and pushed. The crack of wood splintering froze Mai to the spot, but then she was opening the heavy door and shutting it quickly behind her.

The Japanese girl stood, breathing in the hot stink of horse piss, dung and the sweet, wet breath of three animals. All were awake. At least Mai figured they were, unless horses slept standing up which was possible, they had legs at each corner.

'Okay,' said Mai. 'You and me are going to get the fuck out of here, right?' She knew which animal to choose by its size. The beast was smaller than the other two, not as tall or thick shouldered and it didn't have crude tufts of hair round its hooves like moonboots.

'I'm Mai, okay?' She stood in front of the animal and tried to remember what else Kate had said about making friends with horses. Introduce yourself, and then something about noses and blowing. Kate was happy Mai'd asked about animals, she imagined it meant the girl was settling in.

Mai snorted.

'I'm Mai,' she told the horse. 'Well, I was Mai. Kate says I'm Joan but she's wrong . . .' Mai stared at the animal's silhouette in the darkness of the stables but its head was lost in shadow and she had no idea if it was listening or not.

Okay, next bit. The girl crouched in front of the animal and then blew out, sending a puff of warm breath deep into the horse's nostrils. The mare jerked back fast and shook her head from side to side, ears flat back to her skull, long neck shivering. Mai sighed and shook her own head. Apparently no one had told this animal that was how humans said hello.

'Sorry about that . . .' Mai put up her hand and hesitantly brushed the mare's neck, whispering all the while. That was the other thing Kate had said, keep talking. So Mai did, until the mare reluctantly brought her ears forward and nudged her head against the girl's fingers.

'Sweet fuck,' the girl whispered. 'At least you can just hotsoft a hover . . .'

The other two animals were designed to haul things. She knew that from Louis. Mai didn't need anything hauled, just some transport to carry her off that plateau she'd ridden across and back to the next big town.

The only thing was, it wasn't going to happen . . .

Mai heard the chink of a bridle first, sharp as glass in the cold night air. Seconds later, someone large pushed open the stable door and a torch swept the stalls, passing through the spot where she'd been standing.

'Three,' a woman said roughly.

'Two drays, yes. Is the other a black stallion?'

The yellow beam flicked over the mare, who lazily turned her head away from the light but kept chewing.

'No,' said the original voice, sounding cross. The woman was white, had broad shoulders and a bush hat with a wide brim that hid her face. In her right hand she held a long silver torch, big as a club, and she sounded seriously pissed.

The second woman was whipcord thin and carried a staff. Her tight black T-shirt wasn't just clean, it was pressed. Either that, or it was straight from a packet. She looked no taller than Mai, with tiny braids that were pulled back along her skull like tightly twisted wire. And she wore gold wireframe glasses. Which looked odd, but maybe that was what she wanted. Rejecting sight correction could be affectation or religious principle. Or it might be poverty, Mai could understand that. Though the thin black woman came across as too secure, too understated for that.

Anorexic all the same. Her small breasts starved down to nipples and nothing more.

'Not Father Sylvester's,' Wireframes said looking at Axl's horse. 'But we'll take it anyway . . .'

'That's probably not a good idea,' said a voice from outside the darkened doorway, and up in the rafters Mai grinned. Life was finally getting interesting.

'Hi,' said Axl, stepping into the stable. 'I don't think we've met.' Absent-mindedly, he kicked aside a green canvas bag.

Axl's voice was polite but his Spanish was slum raw. Although Mai didn't recognise the man's accent, she could tell when someone had grown up in the projects, no matter what part of the world it happened in.

The newcomer lazily shut one eye against the sudden stab of a torch beam, closing a crude pupil. The black pit of his other eye made Mai shiver just to look at it. There was a steel-bladed knife gripped lightly in his right hand and as Mai watched he dropped the blade to his side and relaxed into a weird crouch, which made him look floppy as a rag doll.

What he didn't do was open his eye.

It was a Chin Mai fighting stance, but the girl didn't know that. The heavy woman with the hat didn't know it either but Wireframes obviously did. Or at least she knew attack readiness when she saw it.

'You new round here?'

Axl twisted his head slightly, as if listening. And Wireframes took that for agreement.

'Well, we run this bit of the high plateau,' she said flatly.

You do? Mai twisted her lips in surprise, If that was true, it was the first she'd heard of it and Kate and Louis did nothing but talk boring shit about how life was in the valley.

'Isn't that strange,' said Axl. 'And there I was thinking Tsongkhapa . . .'

'Yeah, I know . . . No police, no army, no guns, only self-governing autonomous settlements,' the woman recited the wheelworld litany like it was an Ad jingle. 'Well, we're none of those.' She sounded pleased with herself, so much so that Mai wanted to climb down and slap the smile of her face.

'We're a wolf patrol.' Wireframes spun her staff, touching a spot near the middle. Instantly, a blade slid from each end.

'And that's a wolf killer,' said the large woman, nodding at the weapon. That was when Axl opened his eye and blinked in surprise. He'd just recognised the voice of Wireframes' companion, though the last time he'd heard it the bitch had been wearing a sergeant's uniform and he'd been tied to a chair.

Which meant that maybe the . . . No, the Colonel would be tucked up safe in *La Medicina* and, besides he had things closer to home to worry about, like a kid's dreamcatcher with a snapped leather thong half-hidden in the straw at the sergeant's feet.

If Wireframes saw it she'd want to know where it came from and then things would get complicated, and Axl hated it when things got complicated.

'I think you should leave,' Axl said, more for something to say than because he really cared. At the same time, he edged towards them both – very slowly – making sure the one thing he didn't do was accidentally glance up at the rafters. Axl had a plan and item one was to step over that necklace and get it on their blindside.

Managing it proved easier than he expected.

'Far enough,' said Wireframes.

Axl shrugged, knife still loose in his fingers and dropped to one knee, ostentatiously retying the ragged lace of one sodden boot. 'Can't get the clothes out here,' he said flatly and stood again, Mai's feathered charm tucked safely in his other hand. 'You know how it is . . .'

Axl yawned. He knew what was coming. They all did . . .

Blood pumped slowly through his arteries. His heartbeat had dropped even as he stepped forward and the other two tensed up. *Cobras and Pitbulls.* When the Cardinal chose his tools, he chose wisely. One out of five people have a metabolism that slows before combat. They are those who instinctively go still the way that cobras do. Viral augmentation could provide it. And the skill could be learned – hell, most of bushido was hung around passing on the skill – but it was better to be born that way. Cold in combat, detached, dysfunctional, deadly . . .

'Now.' Wireframes nodded and the sergeant swung her torch hard towards Axl's head, the weighted metal tube hissing as it cut air. Except her victim wasn't standing there any more. He was rolling in towards the sergeant to finish at her feet, coming up out of the roll hard and fast to slam his hunting knife into the gap between her heavy breasts. Not blade first, but hilt forward so the brass boss split her sternum, cracking free the lower two ribs.

Shock waves radiated into the huge woman's heart, stopping it dead. Her pig-like eyes exploded in panic and she crumpled, heading for the dung and litter of the stable floor. That was when Axl hit her again, a punch to the gut that echoed round the stable so loud it silenced even the restless horses. Breath rasped into shocked, burning lungs and the sergeant rolled sideways and vomited − but by then Axl was already on his feet.

'Get it taped right round your ribs,' Axl told the woman, 'and don't pick any fights for a while.'

There was a dry chuckle from Wireframes and the woman took a step towards Axl, stopping dead when Axl flipped the knife round in his fingers and slid back into a Chin Mai slouch. The move was so instinctive that up in the rafters Mai knew the man didn't even realise he'd done it.

That made him interesting and not just to Mai.

'Neat move,' said Wireframes.

'I like staying alive,' was all Axl said. He just hoped the woman knew he was being ironic. But she didn't look the type to be big on irony. Captain, Axl reckoned, maybe even a major. Whichever it was, she was pretty pleased with herself.

'momaDef.' Wireframes held out her hand.

Axl ignored it, as Mai knew he would.

'You know,' said momaDef as she dropped her hand, 'I could use a good fighter.' There was a tightness round her eyes, but no other sign that she'd noticed him reject her greeting.

Yeah, thought Axl clocking the wolf sticker held in her hand, like the pope needs a Koran. He glanced at the heavy woman sat on the floor glaring at him.

'That's defMoma,' said momaDef. 'Working for me she gets

the pick of everything – women, money, food, boys, bodyparts . . .' momaDef's smile held as she spun out the list, waiting to see which one would punch the buttons of the man in front of her.

But so far as momaDef could tell none of them did. Or if one did, the man hid it well because she saw no flicker of hunger in his face, no spark of recognition that flared his nostrils

'I work alone,' said Axl.

'Not when we're in the area, you don't,' momaDef said flatly, dark eyes hard behind her wire-rimmed spectacles.

'I work better that way.' Axl nodded to himself, as if the woman had never spoken. 'Fewer accidents.' He glanced again at defMoma sat on the stable floor. Injured and furious, but still alive. You could say that for *WarChild*. He might not know which fork to use but he knew when not to kill. Which was more than most professionals. That it was more than every amateur in existence went without saying.

So why wasn't he more proud of it?

Backed up, stacked up like sins that he filed away in his cortex and left to gather neural dust was the answer, but Axl didn't intend to go there. Not now, not ever. Problem was, Axl realised, these days half his mind was taken up with 'no entry' signs.

'Look,' said Axl, 'I'm going to be around a while. So I think you should go now and leave the horses. Before someone really gets hurt . . .'

Chapter Twenty-five

Crazy Wisdom (The Bardo Mix)

The thin bald guy sat cross-legged on a stone altar staring at the sky. The Colt could swear to fuck that the Colt was what the monk was looking at, only the man's eyes were closed and he seemed to have stopped breathing.

Except he *had* to have air in his lungs or he wouldn't be able to manage that low chant which slid between his lips in wisps of warm breath, dissolving into the frozen air. It was the people round him who weren't breathing, but that was because they were definitely dead. The last time the Colt had seen bodies that ripped had been in Ecuador, after the IMF sent in a team to re-educate a bunch of corporate VPs about capital investment. They'd done that classic remove-the-hands-from-the-arms, the-feet-from-the-legs routine too, only the suits had definitely been alive at the time.

The other problem with the man being able to look at the Colt was the fact the Colt wasn't so much invisible as not actually in existence, at least not physically . . .

Up until a few seconds ago the Colt had been skimming the Big Black. Solar winds howling around the Legrange point where the Colt hung. In fact, it hadn't really been the Colt that hung there, because the gun was piggybacking a derelict soHo – solar and heliospheric observatory.

The sun-facing side of the Sat blistered with a heat to rival Mexico's hottest desert while the shadow side was colder than the bleakest Antarctic midwinter, but the soHo didn't know that because it was too fucking stupid. So dumb in fact that it didn't even realise the Colt was there. All in all, it was about level with a jellyfish which meant the soHo ran no discernable intelligence but did have a certain pre-coding of instinct that kept it facing the sun, both its target and its source of power.

Next, all the Colt had to do was work up a code-exchange between the soHo and Samsara and his journey would be done, for which many thanks. Bit streaming was fine if you were one of those semi house-trained, limited delinquency AIs that Japanese teenagers found so amusing. But the Colt couldn't see the attraction.

The Colt had been sentient only in disparate random bursts as every bit of himself caught up with the rest, if that made sense. Which it didn't, but that didn't matter because the Colt was rerunning the fractal equation that confirmed this was what had happened. Somehow it found the non-interfaced crudeness of raw code comforting.

So far its trip had been confined to piggybacking soHos and third-world military comSats, the kind jacked into orbit so generals could say, 'Hey we've got one too . . .'

There were a lot of those.

Common sense said the safest way for the Colt to reach Samsara was to get spun round with bleeding-edge fooler loops and stashed in some diplomatic pouch heading for the Papal Nuncio, except the Cardinal wouldn't take the risk.

'I mean,' the Colt thought crossly, 'how hard could that have been?'

And if direct delivery in a diplomatic pouch was out then what was wrong with normal luggage? Not those canvas sacks 'fugees got given to hold their few pitiful possessions but the Gucci kind, the leather kind with the reinforced brass edges and recessed wheels. Shit, Vajrayana was thick with B-list politicians ordered by their mandelsons to find some fuzzy warm photo opportunity. Any one of them could have got the Colt into Samsara, without even knowing it.

But no, the Dalai Lama said no guns on Samsara and the

Cardinal wasn't prepared to go against that. The Colt had been given the diplomatic incident talk, the ecumenical respect talk. Shit, it had even had the one on national sovereignty versus *realpolitik*.

Which was how it found itself clung to a soHo trying to make a jump that just didn't seem to be happening. The Colt might be self-functioning but every send received no response and every command was swallowed. If there was a closer approximation of living death then the Colt didn't know it.

'*Bardo*,' said a deep voice.

'You what?'

'Bardooo.' Long and low, the rolling word resonated like a bell echoing off the walls of a vast cave. As tri-D sound effects went it was pretty neat, the Colt had to admit it.

'You are between states,' said the voice, 'between existences. That is the condition of life, that it begins and ends and begins again . . .'

'Reincarnation, for machines? Get real.'

The voice sighed theatrically. A sound like cold wind rushing through a rock cleft. Infrasound, pretty neat. The Colt ran a diagnostic subroutine, well masked and way back inside itself. Had there been air not vacuum, that sigh would have been resonating at eighteen cycles a second, the frequency at which human eyeballs sympathetically vibrate to create phantoms at the edge of vision and human flesh kicks in with shivering, breathlessness and outright fear.

The sound waves were real, not real in a way that humans could have heard because what the Colt was being fed was raw code. But the code translated to a classic standing wave.

'Think of a candle,' said the voice.

The Colt did. Soft wax cylinder, inflammable central wick. Used regularly by the rich and the very poor, otherwise used for holidays and festivals. It tried to pull up historical data on the artefact then remembered it hadn't been able to carry its data banks with it.

'Rebirth is not the same candle recreated. Just the old wick's dying flame used to ignite the next candle in an unseen line . . . You understand?'

'No I fucking don't.' If the Colt had been wired to a voice chip its voice would have laughed, darkly. Instead it just sneered inside. 'I understand nothing.'

There was a deep silence, but though silence was usually a state of absence it was somehow warmer than the rolling voice had been. At the end of the silence came another question, but this time the meaning wasn't wrapped round with fractal SFX, it was clean.

'Why are you here?'

'Why?' The Colt thought about it. 'Because I'm fucking crazy, that's why . . . why else?'

Light flared and the overpowering voice crystallized into being, a shape ray-traced, skinned over and lit so fast that no human could have followed the sequence. It wasn't seeing, the Colt knew that, it was being shown. Shown what it would have seen.

'Sweet bloody . . .'

Sweet bloody what? Bombay brothels and Byzantine chapels, the Colt had seen them both and they'd both been thick as soup with smoke. It had talked to cardinals, bad-mouthed pimps even as it blew them away. Hell, it'd run mirage routines on AIs from Arbroath to Arseville in Arkansas. But this . . .

It was hard not to notice the crocodile curled around itself, especially as the animal had a woman's head and vast four-toed claws. But what really caught the Colt's attention was the old man standing on the crocodile's back. He didn't just have one head, he had — the Colt did a rapid count — eighteen of the things, four on each level, banked up on top of each other, looking north, south, east and west, plus a face on his stomach and back. Each face was topped not by a knot of hair but by a raven's head. His skin was an all-over pattern of eyes that stared or slowly blinked at the Colt.

In one of the man's hands was a rope, except that when the rope saw the Colt it opened its mouth and hissed. And the man's other three arms were waving slowly like seaweed caught in a gentle tide as fire danced up his sides burying him beneath an aura of fractal-edged flame.

'Fucking Jesus,' said the Colt, and the burning man grinned. 'Right idea, wrong culture.'

The Colt grinned back, wickedly. Still busy cutting itself in and out of loops, finessing silent coms connections . . . And if the old man of the flames knew what the ghost of the gun was doing he didn't let it show. Though given the glint in a thousand eyes, the Colt wouldn't have liked to bet on him not knowing.

'Tsongkhapa,' the Colt said finally, when the information fell into place. It seemed so obvious when the Colt thought about it.

Tsonghkapa nodded, sixteen heads bobbing.

'And you?' The mouth in his stomach asked.

The Colt blew out the idea of trying to run a business-card routine almost ahead of thinking it. Something like the one it had run back in Mexico City might fool a dumb-as-shit cathedral but Tsongkhapa was different. And any intelligence that could hold the Colt in digital limbo while manifesting itself as an eighteen-headed Bon demon was working to parameters the gun didn't even begin to understand.

Which left the Colt with only one option, the truth.

'Me?' The Colt's voice was briefly sad, as it remembered the pearl-handle grips and the Bauhaus-simple ceramic chassis it had left behind on the Cardinal's black-glass table at Villa Carlotta. 'I'm between bodies.'

'Of course you are, my beloved.' Each head nodded as the old man leaned forward, hands swaying briefly as he fought to keep his balance. The Colt was gripped in the gaze of more eyes than it could count. Which was weird, because it didn't have a body . . . which meant the old man was looking at where the Colt's body would have been if it did. Wasn't that how all that Eastern stuff worked?

'You're crazy, so you say . . .'

'Yeah,' said the Colt bluntly. 'I'd fucking have to be to be here, wouldn't you say?'

The faces grinned. 'Rinpoche, I'd offer you a drink but it's probably not a good idea. You need to find your own bit streams. Ones that aren't poisoned.'

Still chuckling, the the old man began to fade, leaving the Colt suddenly hanging above a vast *something*. Not quite a spinning ring, not really a narrow drum, more a huge stone egg with a large bit of both ends crudely hacked off.

Standing off from both sides of the ring was Samsara's lighting system, a thick cluster of Znayma flowers spread through space like daisies, each 480-metre petal a huge light-reflecting mirror constructed from aluminium-coated plastic film.

It was obvious enough how the flowers worked, but the Colt was impressed all the same. Light from the sun was reflected through the sides of the wheelworld, but whether straight down to the ground or to central mirrors floating high in the big black of the circle's centre the Colt didn't know.

Many of the million or so strips of cloth attached to Samsara's outer shell were woven through with solar-powered cells threaded to random-frequency broadcast chips, so that they endlessly chanted mantras that overfilled the Colt's mind with waves of digital scribble.

The Colt felt warmth upon its back and turned, facing into solarlight that blazed across the cold wastes of space. Then it paused and ran that sequence again, thinking about it this time. *The Colt felt warmth upon its back* . . . The compressed AI intelligence which still regarded itself as the ghost of a gun that lay, hollow and empty in the study of a Roman Catholic Cardinal in a pale blue stucco villa that faced the burnished sea of the Mexican gulf, took a look at who it had become.

Rinpoche. Beloved.

Wings spread out from the shoulder blades of a small monkey. Featherless and boneless, the wings were as vast as the new simian frame was small. They stetched nine metres across and were as thin as the tissue in a cell wall. Not for flying then, that much was obvious. Rinpoche tracked a data flow across the wing and understood immediately.

Where better to use solar power than when riding the solar winds? As for its new body, leaving aside the crude effects of vacuum, it would have dehydrated in the heat of direct light or frozen within the fall of Samsara's shadow had it been made from flesh. But it was beaten silver inlaid with rubies, pearls and turquoises.

He was the eyes of the world. Dawn's harvester. A watcher at the gates of space . . . Rinpoche sighed. Whichever geek had originally programmed the monkey's identity module, he'd inserted a serious God complex, either that or Seattle Pomp Rock wasn't dead. It was hard to know which was most worrying.

'Crazy wisdom . . .'

The last thing the Colt heard before it began to skim Samsara's upper atmosphere was the old man's voice crackling at it suddenly out of a snow-blinding maelstrom of data.

'You've sure as shit come to the right place.' The old man was laughing.

Chapter Twenty-six

El Escondido

When Axl awoke he was right where he wanted to be. And he'd got there unconscious and almost by accident. Which was a better route than most. Somewhere in the distance there was a bell ringing without stop, just the one and erratic enough for it to be rung by hand.

Sunday morning.

Axl groaned loudly. The taste in his mouth was salt and sweet, blindly primitive. For the briefest second he figured that what he could taste was Ketzia and then Axl realised it was his own blood.

'Don't try to talk,' said a woman's voice crossly. 'You bit your tongue and it's slow to heal. So stay silent.' The words weren't a suggestion, they were an order.

The hand that pushed Axl back into the pillow was firm and the pillow was soft, so Axl stayed where he was and slowly opened his eye instead, letting life drift slowly into focus.

As rooms went, this one was vast, its right wall almost beyond the edge of his vision. High overhead the ceiling was cracked and crazed until it looked like a dangerous map, a map that might send continents tumbling in on him at any moment. Huge plaster chunks were missing from the middle of the ceiling, as was any suggestion of architrave that might once have softened the line where ceiling met wall.

And as for the walls . . . Axl squinted. The tapestries were long and red, decorated with life-sized women. Not one of them had less than four arms and all were round-breasted and topless.

'Where am I?'

'El Escondido,' the woman sounded resigned. 'Now be quiet . . .'

'But this room . . .'

'Grew itself like that. Apparently, some people like to live in reproduction monasteries.' It was obvious from her voice that she wasn't one of them and she had better things to do than repair a building that needn't have been broken in the first place.

'I was out in the storm,' said Axl.

The woman nodded, suddenly nervous. 'Did you see who . . . ?' Hard eyes examined him. 'Did you spot anything, well, odd?'

Odd, like momaDef and defMoma? Or . . . Axl thought of the young girl creeping into the stable then jumping to the rafters, odd like that? Hell, this was Samsara. Nothing was odd. 'No,' he said, 'not really.'

'And you didn't find anything?'

Find anything?

Like what?

The room drifted into darkness, wrapping him in warm silence. And Axl smiled to himself. Silence was good, he could live with that.

'Who are you?' Axl asked, although he already knew. At least, Axl hoped he did

'Me . . . ?' The tall woman wrapped in the shahtoosh hesitated for a moment, but when she spoke her words were angry. As if she was furious with herself for hesitating. 'I'm Katherine Mercarderes.'

She said it like he should know. And even if she hadn't been the person he'd been looking for he would have done, Axl realised, just from the way she held her head. Maybe Kate Mercarderes had never had her own show syndicated on CySat, but there were whole months when that was what it felt like. Her show was called the News.

And now, without any real skill on his part, he was where he needed to be. Inside her house. All he had to do was find Father Sylvester. Either that, or learn from Kate where the Vatican dosh was stashed. Axl doubted if the Cardinal would care that much either way.

How hard could it be?

She pushed Axl back into his pillow with a tut of irritation as if she didn't know why Axl couldn't just be sensible. And the thing was, her wrist bones would snap like dead twigs if he flipped in the right direction. Even half-conscious Axl knew that. But the thought obviously hadn't occurred to Kate. Which said a lot about where she came from.

Axl looked at Kate again, more closely. Tall but not beautiful. Thin rather than slim. She had heavy black hair scraped back into a knot at the nape of her neck and dark eyes that watched from beneath too-heavy brows. Her chin was strong and her cheekbones high. No one could have looked at her and not know she had Latino blood. Only her too-narrow hips let her down, and that could have been solved with a simple rebuild.

'Seen enough?' She demanded.

'You look different . . .'

'I am,' said Kate baldly. She didn't point out that the last time he'd seen her, she'd probably been on CySat fighting to get Joan airlifted out of Northern Mexico. There'd been talk about the UN stabilising the area north of Torréon. The need for PaxForce intervention. It all came to nothing. But there were 50,000 major feeds and for twenty-four hours it seemed like she'd been pleading for Joan's life on all of them.

Maybe if he'd had a sister, thought Axl, he'd have been changed too. But Axl didn't have a sister, not that he knew of anyway. And given where he came from, somehow he doubted they'd have been close even if he had. Too busy fighting each other for food probably . . . Axl didn't buy into that *novela* 'he ain't heavy he's my brother' shit. Filial feeling was something else life gave to those who already had . . .

'It's the poppy,' she told him crossly.

Axl looked up.

'It makes you cry.'

She came back later, wearing just a shirt and chinos, her grey shahtoosh discarded. The bowl of soup she carried tasted of heavily salted butter and little else. And it wasn't until Axl finished it that he remembered to ask Kate how he got there.

Apparently he been clubbed into unconsciousness outside the stables. That he wasn't dead Kate put down to good luck but Axl privately figured was more than that. momaDef wanted him alive for some reason: or else she didn't want him dead yet, which maybe wasn't the same thing at all.

He'd been found with his face matted with blood, which was standard. What wasn't was his coat had been sodden with other people's piss. Which was the point Axl began to worry. They did that, PaxForce grunts. It was about marking territory. Only any grunts were so far off-territory on Samsara that Axl couldn't help but wonder what level of deniability they had built into their mission.

Unless they were about to go legitimate. Which would explain why Kate was jumpier than a roo on speed. If she knew who they were.

'You shouldn't go upsetting outlaws.' The woman said furiously.

Outlaws?

'Why not?' Axl asked. Upsetting people was something he specialised in. And if Kate didn't know that yet, well, she'd find out. As for her 'outlaws', it was obvious the Cardinal would be running back-up, but momaDef wasn't it, she just didn't feel right. Too full of herself. And somehow Axl couldn't see His Eminence subcontracting anything to PaxForce.

'How long have the *outlaws* been around?'

The woman sucked at her olive cheeks as if thinking hard. 'It's the first time they've been to Cocheforet, I think. But I hear the bastards ride from village to village, looting, thieving . . .' Her dark eyes were seeing things that weren't there.

'Still,' said Kate tightly, 'it could be weeks before we see them again. If we get lucky.' There was real anger in her voice.

'Well,' said a girl's voice from the doorway. 'Is the idiot awake yet?'

'Yeah,' said Axl, pushing himself up on one elbow to peer round Kate. 'He is. And feeling shit.'

The kid from the stables grunted.

'This is . . .' Kate hesitated too long to recover gracefully.

'I'm *Juanita* and I found you,' the half-Japanese girl said smoothing a grey cotton smock across small breasts, as if brushing away crumbs. She looked suddenly furious but Axl found it hard to tell what about.

'Juanita?'

'Apparently that's my name.'

Mai didn't acknowledge the hard-eyed glance Kate shot her, at least not openly. 'I shouldn't be here,' she told Axl, 'I belong in the kitchen.' There was such contempt in her voice that Axl thought Kate was about to say something. Instead she just ignored the girl. To Axl it was obvious there was some kind of war going on and he was flat on his back in the middle of it.

'You found me?'

'Yeah,' said Mai, shooting an evil glance at the older woman. 'Aren't you lucky?' Whatever battle those two were fighting, it looked like the kid was capable of keeping up her end of it. What she didn't look was strong enough to carry a grown man up a gravel path without help.

'And you just happened to be around?' Axl asked innocently.

'I was taking some night air,' Mai's accent was a mocking imitation of Kate, her fussy choice of words intentionally irritating.

'You mean you went walkabout?'

'Yeah,' she grinned sourly. 'It's a little ritual we have. I go for a walk and she sends her pet Clone out to drag me back.' She glanced at Kate, her brown eyes sharp as glass. 'You'll find they're big on ritual round here.'

Flakes of plaster fell from the wall as she slammed the door behind her, hard enough to make the whole room shake.

'Sweet kid,' said Axl.

Kate flushed. 'Antagonising a patrol wasn't the most intelligent thing to do, but that's not really your problem, and nor's she . . .' If Kate realised she'd referred to the momaDef's group as a patrol she didn't let it show. 'We do have our problems, though.'

Yeah, thought Axl, I bet you do.

Half the planet thought Kate was the sister of a saint, the other half wanted her on trial for *reformista* war crimes committed when 20,000 pre-teens took over Northern Mexico in Joan's name.

Twelve-year-olds with antiquated Kalashnikovs had been a feature of subSahal warfare for two centuries. Ever since the animist army of the SPLA first took Islamic Khartoum with ex-Soviet AK47s donated by a Bible Belt baptist show. The Children of God were something new. At least they were to Day Effé and to Washington politicians who thought that kind of shit didn't happen in what was still laughingly called the First World.

'Anything I can help with?' Axl made it sound like he always went round offering aid to complete strangers, which would have amused the Colt. But from the look on Kate's face, it seemed his help wasn't something she needed.

Chapter Twenty-seven

Cutting A Deal

The onions made his eyes water but Axl kept at it, cutting out the rotten bits and tossing the onion flesh that was still edible into an iron bucket. He was sitting on a bench in the kitchen at Escondido preparing supper.

The Hideaway.

Axl didn't know if it was Kate who'd called the place El Escondido. He only knew Father Sylvester wasn't based there and the monastery was unoccupied except for Kate, the kid, Kate's servant Louis and the Clone. And except for the kid they were all down in the village, doing something he wasn't meant to know about.

There was nothing of value in the enormous house, unless you liked old statues and musty wall hangings that reeked of damp and dust. Axl knew. He'd laboriously checked every room from the slab-floored cellars to the empty attic with its broken roof tiles that let heat out and rain in.

Mind you, Axl hadn't expected to find some elegant little smartbook belonging to Kate, still powered up and containing details of transparent bank accounts at Hong Kong Suisse in Zurich. Not straight off. Unlike His Excellency, Axl didn't believe in miracles. He believed in sex and cheap drugs and all the other shallow gratifications that made life bearable.

Only you couldn't get 4-MTA in Cocheforet. In fact, from what Axl remembered from the newsfeeds back home, you couldn't score anywhere on Samsara. The wheelworld was a drug-free zone. Privately, Axl doubted that. All he needed to make life bearable was a heat source, some fairly basic chemicals and a half-intelligent twelve-year-old amateur chemist. And if crystalMeth was off the menu then someone somewhere had to be cooking china white. All that took was bloody poppies, for God's sake, the kind Kate kept doping him with.

But if the kid was to be believed there was no meth, no china white and not even any cooking sulphate. There would be – of course – somewhere. In one of the tourist towns just outside Vajrayana. Some makeshift kitchen would be turning out meth by the tray. The big problem for Axl was he didn't know where that town was and couldn't afford the time to get there even if he did.

On the other hand, supplies aside, he could hardly claim life wasn't interesting. In the last week he'd got beaten up, fucked somebody's wife without even bothering about retro Virus, taken down that fat sergeant . . . What was even better, he'd made contact with Kate without having to leap through too many hoops. All he need do now was get into the Japanese girl's confidence and find out what the fuck was making Kate so jumpy.

It was hardly a difficult assignment. He went in, he found Kate and grabbed her. Then he revealed himself as a member of the Rights Police, pulled a Section 53i on Tsongkhapa and took the woman to Vajrayana for repatriation. The job was so basic even a kid could have done it. Axl knew that for a fact, the Cardinal had told him so.

Axl tossed down his knife.

Slouched next to him on a bench in the kitchen, a mound of raw onions at her feet, Mai grinned sourly. She was meant to be peeling the onions and he was only there to keep her company, but so far he'd done all the work.

'Jesus, you really need ice, don't you?'

Ice, a life, some guaranteed way off Samsara . . . Axl got through a lot of his life on nodding, and the bits where a nod didn't work could usually be covered by silence or a simple shake of the head. Chuck in the trademark looks that ran from quizzical to coldly amused and in many ways his working vocabulary was no better than it had been back when he was nine.

'Kate's got medical drugs,' Mai told Axl. 'Want me to look for you?'

Axl did, though he went along with her, climbing the narrow back stairs from the kitchen to a small landing so slowly that Mai had to stop to let him catch up Axl didn't mind taking his time. The kid had a nice arse and it helped that all she wore on her bottom half was a pair of thin black leggings so tight they edged between her buttocks with every step she took. On top Mai had a short red jacket machined from cloth that looked like it had started out as a dog blanket.

Axl kept watching her arse until she paused at the landing. And then he looked at what she was looking at. Attached next to a door in the far wall was an open padlock, hooked over a clasp. Both were new.

'My room,' she said bitterly. 'Kate has this one,' Mai jerked her thumb towards a single door behind her. To the right of the narrow landing were two other doors, both shut.

'And in there?' Axl asked, as if he hadn't already looked.

'The Clone and Louis . . .'

'There's no one else living in this house?'

The girl looked at him.

'How about nearby?'

'Kate's followers,' Mai said sourly, making it obvious she had little time for the other 'fugees in Cocheforet. 'No one else, okay? Or I'd have found them, believe me . . .' The smile on her childlike face wasn't kind. But then she wasn't doing this to be nice to Axl, she was doing it to spite Kate. Which didn't matter a fuck to Axl, because complicity was complicity.

'Look,' said Mai. 'You want to help me find some stuff or not?'

Stuff, when they found it, was in a cheap plastic tray inside a folded blanket crammed under Kate's bed. Mai crawled under to get it while Axl searched the almost-bare room a second time, moving fast.

A wooden crucifix was nailed up above a wood-framed single bed that sported only one sheet and a tattered low-tog quilt over a mattress of uncovered foam that was no thicker than a smart book.

The walls were white, with no pictures or rugs. The floor was also bare, its faded red tiles cold as ice to the touch. Apart from Kate's bed, the only other item of furniture in that room was a simple wooden desk made from oak. It had three drawers down each side, all empty of everything except dust and dead insects. What clothes Kate had – and there weren't many – rested in neat piles on one side of the door.

Axl had been around enough to know what punishment looked like. Since it was unlikely anyone else had imposed this cell on Kate, she had to be inflicting it on herself. Which, maybe wasn't so unusual from the sister of the Pope who had cleared St Peter's of all its art treasures and thrown open the gates of the Holy City to all comers. And God did they come. Hyps, Ishies, the Wild Tribe. The influx made the medieval crusades look like ordered outings.

'Sweet fuck.'

Axl looked round to find Mai sitting on the bed tossing bubblepacs back into the tray, one after another. 'Dandelion, arnica, teatree oil . . .' She read a few more out in disgust and then scooped the rest noisily back into the tray and slung it under Kate's bed. 'You're out of luck.'

'Maybe,' said Axl as he slid the drawers out of their runners and skimmed his fingers across the backs. Nada. Nothing taped to the underside of the desk either.

'What you looking for?' Mai's head was hooked to one side, her smile quizzical. She was definitely interested.

'Whatever the fuck she's got,' said Axl shortly and Mai laughed. The only problem was Kate had nothing worth taking and less than nothing hidden. No decent drugs, no weapons, no illegal comms kit, no smart book.

Sliding the drawers back onto their runners, Axl took down the wooden crucifix to check that it wasn't hollow and that Kate had nothing interesting taped to the back.

'You know,' Mai said suddenly, 'you don't act like a 'fugee.' She blushed. 'It's like, you look like shit but you don't act like you've lost everything . . .'

He could still kill her, of course. That was Axl's first thought as he reached the bed. Get her body out of the house before the others got back. Or just stack it in one of the tiny storerooms in the cellar. The second thought to cross his mind was to do a runner, exit Cocheforet. Axl's third thought was the right one – empathise, loop the emotion and feed it back. That was what they'd all been taught in basic psych. So that was what he did.

Axl shrugged. 'I haven't lost everything,' he told Mai, dropping to a crouch in front of her. 'When you start out with fuck all, there's fuck all for anyone else to take away. If you know what I mean.'

Casually Axl let one finger brush the back of Mai's wrist.

Check the eyes. Examine the mouth for signs of disbelief. Now was when he was meant to flick back his hand and slam fragments of nasal bone up into her brain, if that's what he was going to do. While she was still considering.

But Axl didn't need to. And more to the point, he realised, he didn't want to. Looking at the Japanese kid was like looking across race, gender and age into a mirror image of himself. She wasn't someone who remembered her past, she survived it.

He knew when a kid was wearing scars like armour. When real anger burned so fierce it had to be kept smothered under glib dismissal or a sullen sneer. She could walk though a crowd and they'd notice her but not smile. Want to bed her, yes, but no more. Something in those dark eyes filtered out friendship and cut her loose.

But if he wanted Kate he was going to have to reel the kid in.

'What's your real name?' Axl asked.

'Mai,' said Mai. 'That's the first one I remember.' Mai's gaze was level as she looked him over. 'What about you?'

'Axl Borja. I don't know my real name.'

They shook.

'You planning to stay here long?' Mai's question wasn't as simple as it seemed. They both knew that. And this time it was her fingers that reached out to touch his wrist.

'Long as it takes,' said Axl. He didn't say what *it* was. Just as he didn't ask what she meant by *here*.

'Well, make it fast. I want the fuck out.'

'So we just set out over the high plateau, hand in hand?'

'No,' Mai grinned. 'We ride on your horse.' She had the grace to blush at that.

He'd been right, Axl realised. She had tried to take his mare and the beast hadn't let her. That at least explained why she'd bothered to stick around while Clone dragged some stranger back to the house for Kate to treat. He was her ticket out of there.

Axl had a pretty good idea what she was offering by way of payment.

'I don't have a problem with that, if you don't . . .' Mai said simply.

He didn't. Though he'd have to deal later with telling the kid he planned to stick around for a few more days yet, maybe longer.

Mai took off her top herself, undoing its clumsy buttons and sliding out of the red jacket to reveal high olive-tipped breasts, each tiny enough to be cupped in a single hand. She had slightly full hips and a belly button that sank into the curve of her soft stomach.

And then Axl stopped looking as Mai's arms tightened around his neck and she pulled him in close. She smelt of onions, sweat and smoke from the yak-dung kitchen fire. He'd known expensive perfume smell much worse. And then even that thought was forgotten as Mai began to undo his tattered cotton shirt.

Her fingers started at the bottom and never once touched Axl's skin as she threaded each tiny button through its slit until there were no more to undo.

His own fingers fumbled as they found the waist of her leggings and began to push them down over her hips.

Beneath the black leggings she wore a rainbow thong, so out of place on Samsara that Axl looked twice at the tiny triangle of thermo-reactive material that pulsed with her body heat, its silk so tight against her flesh that Axl could make out the soft mound of her naked mons and the flame orange outline of her labia.

Mai grinned and Axl briefly wondered if this was planned in advance. Either way, he didn't really care too much about anything except the feeling of her breasts squashed tight against his bare chest and her back tensed beneath his hand as he pulled her against him.

Soon that wasn't enough and so Axl slid one hand down the girl's leg to caress her thigh and then moved it slowly up to cup the curve of her behind. Mai giggled, softly biting Axl's shoulder as he slid his hand up again to edge one finger under the strap of her thong until his finger vanished between the cheeks of her arse. Any lower and Axl could reach the puckered black rose of her anus or the waiting lips below that but Axl stayed where he was.

Thinking nothing.

Remembering nothing.

Just inhaling the musk that rose off Mai's body like smoke.

One of them was holding their breath and Axl had a feeling it was probably him. He didn't see the Clone, Louis or Kate struggling up the path from the village, just as they didn't see him even though the shutters to Kate's bedroom window were wide open.

Axl didn't hear them enter Kate's room either. All he knew

was that Mai froze in his arms and then a vast man with a shaved head and a knife scar that circled his thick throat like a necklace stood beside the bed. And behind the man, almost hidden by his wide shoulders, stood Kate, her eyes wide with shock and bitter with fury.

Chapter Twenty-eight

Outriders

Two facts saved Axl's life. The first was that everyone from Kate to Clone was too busy searching for the missing bits of the dead Pope's mind to want the added complication of killing him.

Axl didn't know that, just as he had no idea he was the person with Pope Joan's missing memory stuffed deep in the piss-drenched pocket of his greatcoat. But then splitting Joan's senses into five and stringing the memory beads on the wires of a kid's dreamcatcher had been Father Sylvester's way of keeping them not just safe but also anonymous.

The second thing that prevented Clone slitting Axl's throat was that Mai still wore a thong. True, the scrap of smart-silk was all she did wear, but it was enough to save him. Axl had few-to-no illusions about that as Clone herded him down the kitchen stairs, never quite touching Axl. As if to touch him might trigger violence the huge man wouldn't know how to control.

Not until Axl reached the bottom stair did he hear the first ringing slap and Mai's loud four-letter reply. Axl wanted to go back for the kid but Clone crowded right behind him, fingers clenched into vast fists as if the ox-like man was fighting his need to use them. It took a minute for Mai's swearing to subside and then even her sobs faded to leave only slaps that came hard and rhythmic, meted out in absolute silence as if the woman delivering them was too furious to speak.

'Poisonous little bitch, isn't she?' Axl said. Not surprisingly the mute didn't answer. So Axl took down his coat from a peg and shrugged himself into it, PaxForce piss and all. He had a feeling Kate wasn't going to want him staying at Escondido any more.

When the woman finally came downstairs Axl got a chance to swear at her to her face, but he might have been as mute as Clone for all the response his insults got. When she spoke it was to dismiss him.

'I don't know who you are,' Kate's voice was glacial, colder even than her face. 'But you're a coward and a liar. I don't believe you were ever one of us. To abuse Juanita like that, a child . . .'

'Her name's Mai,' said Axl hotly, 'and the kid's a whore.' He wanted to add, *and what's with this us*? But it was already too late.

Kate gave Clone an abrupt nod and the huge man bundled Axl outside into the ever present, early-evening drizzle that was such a feature of Cocheforet's microclimate. It took the Clone and Axl forty minutes to reach the inn and the Clone didn't take his knife point out of Axl's back the whole way.

And now the drizzle was gone, the air was thinner, Cocheforet was a morning's ride behind him and Axl still wasn't sure which cut deepest, being accused of abusing a kid or being told he was a coward and liar. And he had no intention of stopping to wonder why both insults hurt so badly.

Somewhere ahead was the carrion ground. Which, given the Clone's permanent snarl as he rode beside Axl, wasn't a reassuring thought. The man's wide face was set hard like concrete and Axl had a nasty feeling that if Clone got his way, he'd be joining those other bodies. And the crude-looking revolver that Tukten, the Tibetan boy from the Inn, carried in one hand was the weapon for the job.

The sullen Tibetan brat did nothing but look at the revolver and whistle tunelessly. That Tukten distrusted Clone was obvious, but the boy made it clear he liked Axl even less. And from the way Tukten stared around him, nervously scanning the sky or peering ahead of him across the high plateau it was equally obvious the boy would rather be anywhere than where he was and doing anything except whatever it was he was doing.

But it wasn't until the three riders were far enough onto the bleak plateau for the swirling black specks in the grey sky ahead to be identifiable as vultures that Axl worked out that Tukten was terrified of the scavenging ground. Which explained all that tuneless whistling.

A couple of hours was what it took Axl to reach that conclusion. A couple of hours during which his bladder grew tight as a drum, cold wind leached warmth from his face and the air got thinner and the vegetation ever more sparse, if that was possible. But still they rode a narrow track, in silence except for Axl's abortive attempts to talk to the boy. It would have been easier to empathise with a stone.

Empathising with the Clone wasn't an option. Clones didn't do empathy any more than they acknowledged blood ties. How could they, without getting landed with sending 3000 birthday vid-mails every month? And if you were a clone of a clone, what was the relationship to whoever held the ur-genetic template? Axl didn't know . . . He made a point of not watching the daytime newsfeeds.

You're wandering, Axl told himself. No surprise really. Too much *chang* maybe or the after-effects of poppy potion, those were the options that looped through Axl's mind. That it was lack of oxygen meeting exhaustion and exertion didn't occur to him. And as for last night's *vision*. That was seriously somewhere Axl wasn't allowing himself to go.

His own mare was struggling to draw breath. Yet the other two rode animals unaffected by the thin air. Small dirt-grey ponies with thick coconut-matting coats that stank of oil. He'd half expected them to be riding yaks.

'I need to stop,' Axl told Clone who said nothing, just wrapped his huge hand tighter round the bridle of Axl's mare and yanked so hard the animal almost stumbled.

'Can't you do something,' Axl asked Tukten. 'I *have* to stop.'

Axl couldn't manage the boy's trick of standing in the saddle, unbuttoning and pissing against his horse's neck so steam sprang from its skin, but pissing wasn't the only reason he wanted to dismount. The fact was Axl couldn't think properly with the mare's spine banging into his arse with every step. And Axl needed to think and quick, if only because what he was refusing to think about kept pushing itself to the surface.

Mostly, what he needed to get his head round was what Kate, Clone and Louis had been looking for. And not just them. Ketzia, too, she'd been looking. He'd stumbled down the valley track from Escondido into Cocheforet, passing under dark tangles of rhododendron grown so thick that there was only just room for one person to pass at a time and the path was black as night. The Clone was behind him as always. And when the man's eyes weren't boring into the back of Axl's neck they were scanning the gravel as if the key to everything might just be lying there.

And then there was the 'vision'. Axl didn't believe in real visions, his own or those seen by others. Schizophrenia, B-alvarius specials, fucked-up levels of serotonin, neural flares that flamed the fern-like structure of the cerebellum with dazzling corona, faulty REM mechanisms that overlaid real life with narcoleptic fantasies. Those he believed in. And then there were the mechanical kind . . .

Delivered by Clone to the inn, Axl had slammed his way through the front door, pushed past the bearded landlord and stamped up the rickety steps to his attic room, slamming the door behind him so hard that plaster flaked off the damp chimney breast.

It didn't make him feel any better.

The shutter was open, the fire was out and his mattress

was soaked with drizzle that had come in through the unprotected window. A maggot-white lump of dried yak cheese stood crusted on a plate by the bed, his uneaten supper from days before. The bread that went with it was already spored green with mould.

Axl wouldn't miss Cocheforet but life wasn't as simple as just leaving. The Cardinal would have spies on Samsara. It wouldn't be that long before the hip and run of rumour told him Axl had failed. Not long enough, anyway. Not nearly long enough . . .

Aware just how close he was to screwing up big-time, Axl stood in his attic room and kicked the two main problems round in his head. No hint that Kate knew anything about the missing money or was planning to set up some little papal court in exile. Nothing worthwhile to offer His Excellency as a counterweight to failure.

Added to which, he was hungry, cold and in deep shit with the villagers. Not a good place to be. And the only problem he could deal with immediately was hunger. Axl dug into his pocket for his knife, planning to scrape mould from the bread. Only its blade caught on Mai's soulcatcher, scratching one of the memory beads.

And Axl found salvation.

The shock threw him across the room so hard Axl slammed sideways into the far wall, almost dislocating his shoulder. Invisible bands bound his chest so tight he couldn't draw breath and his heart froze with shock. He was dropped into darkness so cold that every muscle locked solid.

The woman had skin that shone white and her head was thrown right back, nostrils flared wide, her mouth open in prayer or ecstasy. Blank eyes turned blindly to some gilt heaven. She was . . .

St Teresa d'Avila.

A statue which didn't really rate approval, no matter that it was famous.

And then the marble figure and the knowledge were gone.

He stood in a city at the top of a flight of stone steps and the air was heavy with incense and honeysuckle. And the world was briefly in colour again.

'Michaelangelo was so kitsch,' said the voice in his head. 'Or maybe it was Paul Three.'

Behind was the empty floor of del Campidaglio, a circular Renaissance piazza paved in marble. A white wolf in a gold cage stood to the left, the symbol of Rome, shaded by a myrtle bush. And below the steps, stretching so far the eyes he was looking through couldn't focus on the far edge, a silent crowd waited expectantly. The little silver insect hovering near his mouth wasn't an insect, Axl realised. It was a microphone.

And again, that feeling of waiting for death. Watching the edges of the crowd as if the bullet might somehow be visible. Expecting it but knowing that here was not the place. Now was not the time.

'What is there left to say?'

'Everything,' said a voice he didn't recognise. 'Tell them the truth. That's all you ever . . .'

And then all Axl had were cold echoes in his head and a sense of loss.

Victory out of defeat, or some such shit. Sitting on the floor of the attic Axl had known exactly what Kate, Louis and Clone had lost. Exactly what he had to offer His Excellency. For the first time in days, Axl grinned.

Sure Joan was dead, ripped apart on camera. The death that had been digitised and cast out into the Web to be diced and spliced, cute-cut and mixed to music, backdrop to synth loops and sound-grabs, textured with cheap space echoes and fed back at everything from slowburn to 280bmp, was for real. Joan really got ripped apart, no faking. That really had been her blood running back into the cracked earth. Her face flash-frozen by history.

Mimetic.

Iconographic.

She'd be selling dermaPeel face creams and high-phene-thylamine chocolate within five years.

But that was all the Army of God got, her body. When the soulcatcher chips had been inserted Axl didn't know or care. Maybe only when Joan announced she intended to negotiate an end to the children's crusade, or maybe back when she was first elected Pope. The Vatican might not approve of cloning but it had medical AIs like nobody's business, answerable to the Congregation for Causes of Saints, better known as the Devil's Advocates, the conclave that existed to disprove miracles.

It wasn't novel to get wired. If anything it was a bit passé, almost retrograde. But she'd been augmented all right and he had the chips. Not augmented like an exotic, no ultra-fast reactions or night sight, nothing too obvious. Just five-sense neural backup. Each bodily sense captured in a tiny bead, not glass but crystal bioSoft, memory layered like time.

Exact emotions couldn't be backed-up — not yet anyway, maybe never — but reactions created emotions and reactions could be stored, along with sights, smells and memories of what they were reactions to. The math was simple. Splice the senses through a transparent back-up. Putting the baby back in the bottle was more difficult, but it happened and, like most things that take place regularly enough, everyone figured if it happened that often it must be easy.

It wasn't. A decade and a half back, Axl had flushed his own life down the tube, literally. The most satisfying data dump of his life. Two and a half years was how long he'd been beaded and central accounts for CySat's *WarChild* had charged him five percent of his earnings for the privilege, even though he hadn't wanted beads in the first place. Keep extra memories? He didn't want the ones he had.

Those marble steps with the open-faced crowd staring up at him. Thousands of them. He'd seen that image before, from right back when it all began and Washington and Paris were rubbing their hands at the thought of a young woman in the Vatican.

Someone unworldly.

A recluse they could use.

Except they couldn't. Because the woman who stood up to address the UN was the one thing no one had been expecting. Someone who really *believed*. In telling the truth. In doing what was right because it was the right thing to do. At no matter what political cost.

She was a fucking nightmare. And when she used New York to announce that killing civilians was a sin, no matter what their religion or politics . . .

There'd never been a time when the victims of war were just those who fought, when wearing a uniform was an invitation to Death and being a civilian meant Death rode by. But that had been the ideal, destroyed by the balkanisation of conflict and the new crusades, not over water shortages as CIA Langley had warned but over religion, between Islam and Christianity, those followers of the Book.

Polarisation saw off humanism on both sides, leaving only harsh fundamentalist certainties that did to the differing peoples of Nigeria and the Sudan what 250 years of famine and corruption hadn't managed – exterminated whole races.

Tough shit.

Axl didn't do compassion and he was backpacking enough guilt for stuff he *was* responsible for, not to pig out on certainties he could do fuck all to change. He was, as the saying went, out of there . . .

The water in the attic basin was days old, filmed across its surface with dust, but Axl didn't care. He just splashed the cold liquid onto his face and when that wasn't enough dunked his whole head in the basin, rubbing his fingers through his hair.

Food and something to drink.

The bar was empty when Axl got downstairs. Not even the three wise monkeys were in their usual corner. No fire was lit in the grate and no one came when he called, so Axl stepped round the bar and walked through to the kitchen to find Ketzia on her knees in front of a rancid heap of rubbish. Sodden tea leaves, a broken plate, splinters of glass, animal bones, anything the goats outside wouldn't eat.

Axl knew exactly what she was looking for. He had it in his pocket.

'So,' Axl said, 'what are you looking for?'

Ketzia kept silent. In fact, she didn't even look up. Must be invisible, Axl thought sourly. Clone had obviously been telling tales.

'Can I help?' Axl asked and watched Ketzia tense her shoulders. His voice was so polite she couldn't help but know he was insulting her.

'No,' she said roughly. 'You can't. You can go back to your room.'

Axl shook his head. 'I'm hungry,' he said. 'I need food and then I'm out of here.' He made no pretence at being anything but pleased at the idea of leaving Cocheforet behind.

'Out of here?'

'Back to Vajrayana. Off Samsara.'

'No one gets off Samsara,' said Ketzia flatly. 'That's the deal. Everyone innocent gets sanctuary, no one leaves . . .'

'Maybe,' Axl said casually. 'Maybe not.'

'Unless you really are a spy.' Ketzia's voice was suddenly cold. 'Then maybe you can cut a deal with Tsongkhapa. If your bosses are powerful enough.' She stared hard at the man in front of her. Like she was vid-grabbing inside her head.

'Oh, don't worry,' Axl said lightly. 'I'll remind you if you don't remember me.'

Ketzia brought him half a loaf of bread and a lump of goat's cheese that had gone liquid down one side. It might have been the worst food she could find in the kitchen, or it might just have been what she had. Axl didn't care, he ate it anyway, sitting at a table in the deserted bar. Washing the rough bread down with buttered tea. Then he stood up to fetch his mare.

Only Axl got no further than stepping through the door. Hands gripped his shoulders, strong fingers crushing muscle like someone just sprang a steel trap. There was no need to look round to know it was Clone, but Axl did anyway and found the ox-like man standing next to a barefoot, sour-faced Tukten, who was holding a pistol.

Nothing fancy. Wooden grips, single-action. A seven-and-a-half-inch barrel fed from a steel cylinder reamed out to take five shots. The barrel wasn't even blued, and oily fingermarks had etched themselves onto the cylinder. But it was loaded and if the gun itself didn't have intelligence, the wide-faced boy holding it had enough to pull the trigger if ordered.

'Tomorrow,' said Ketzia, coming up behind Axl. 'You can leave at first light. This evening you stay at the Inn.'

For once it wasn't raining when dawn broke and to begin with, as Axl stood in front of the inn and stared straight towards the vast mountain behind the village that extended if not to the sky then at least as high as the wheelworld's atmosphere, he felt happy.

The job was finished. Even His Excellency couldn't deny that. What remained of Joan's life was hidden deep in his pocket. Ready for the Cardinal to gut. The old bastard could ask no more.

The only thing to sour the taste of a job well done was the echo of Kate's slaps. Every which way he processed the memory of what happened it still didn't make sense. So he'd been caught groping some half-naked street kid and that was enough to make Kate Mercarderes look like she wanted him recycled into body bits? The hatred that burned from the eyes of Clone; the contempt that kept Ketzia on her knees in the kitchen, silent and facing away from him . . .

So maybe he was missing something and maybe whatever he

was missing was big, but Axl told himself he didn't care. He had enough. And more to the point, he had all that His Excellency could need. Who needed puzzles?

Axl's happiness lasted as long as it took a sour-faced Leon to bring Axl's horse and announce that Clone and Tukten would be riding with Axl to see him safely out of the valley. Now vultures spiralled overhead like soot from a fire and Axl felt less safe with each passing mile. His bladder was bursting, his throat was dry and cold clung to him like the smell of fear. And all Clone did was act like he didn't care. Which was fine, because he didn't.

And then, trotting between two tangled banks of wild rhododendron, Axl suddenly tripped over the answer to what he'd been missing. Wetware. He found it in the body of a naked boy draped over a blood-red boulder.

Beyond the dead kid sprawled other figures. A few had been quartered with an axe, the rest clumsily disjointed by scavengers: abdomens were ripped open and coils of half-eaten viscera dragged from their bodies.

And then Axl knew exactly why he had to get back to Cocheforet.

'Stop.' Wheeling his mare in front of Clone, Axl put up one hand. It took all his will to ignore the revolver the black-haired boy pointed at his head but Axl managed it. All his attention was on Clone. Axl didn't trust him but that was hardly the point. This wasn't about trust. It was about getting back in the game.

'I don't want to leave without giving Kate this.' Axl pushed a hand deep into his pocket and snapped a wire on Mai's soulcatcher, freeing one bead. Using the cloth bag that had held his Red-Cross issue DNA chips, he trapped the bead inside and handed the bag to Clone.

'I found this.'

For a second, Axl thought the huge man might not take the bait, but he nodded at Tukten to keep the revolver pointed at their prisoner. Because somewhere between leaving the Inn and reaching the high plateau a prisoner was what Axl had become, he had no illusions about that.

Clone's eyes widened with shock as he peered into the bag, seconds sliding by like hidden assassins. Then, grudgingly, he let the Tibetan boy take a look. And as they stared at each other, neither had the slightest idea how close they were to being dead.

A snap of the boy's wrist would have given Axl the revolver. One of its black-powder slugs could rip open even Clone's thick skull. A few split brains, two more bodies, nothing that would make much difference to the charnel house around him.

But Axl wasn't planning to kill anyone. He was going back to Cocheforet to talk to Kate, whether the bitch wanted to talk to him or not. And if losing a bead was the price he had to pay to get rid of Clone, that was fine. Axl had every intention of getting it back later.

Axl wanted to shout aloud, punch one fist into the air, all those *WarChild* responses he no longer allowed himself. His Excellency was going to get his prize. And he, Axl Borja, was going to bring the Cardinal back Joan herself. Had an imprint ever been tried for the crimes of its original? Why the fuck should he care? She might not look the same but let some fuckwit Vatican lawyer deal with that.

Instead of punching the air or grabbing Tukten's revolver, Axl kept his hands relaxed at his side and watched arctic wolves casually do things to corpses that would have got AIs terminated and humans locked up as insane.

Defences could be made from anything. The wolves protected Samsara. As did the rare white elephants, obscure mountain cranes and the last sixteen snow leopards not in cryo. One aid agency's 'fugee might be some metaNational's financial terrorist, but no one got stressed at the Dalai Lama providing refuge for animals. Rumour said the animals got higher corporate donations than the starving, sick and homeless, but no one really knew. Some subset of a subset of Tsongkapa ran the banking routines.

'I found it in the stable.' Axl liked the way both figures suddenly jerked their attention away from the cloth bag.

'We searched there,' Tukten announced. The Clone said nothing, but then he couldn't. What he did do was stare hard at Axl.

'Yeah,' Axl shrugged, his voice bored. 'Well, that's where I found it.'

The Clone gurgled something and the boy nodded.

'Where?' demanded Tukten.

'In the trough,' Axl said, remembering a crude waterbox that took rain from a downpipe off the stable roof. That they hadn't searched the water trough was obvious from the expressions of hope that flicked across the two very different faces.

It was Clone who reached a decision first, jerking his chin towards a track that threaded between bodies. Translated it meant, 'you take him'. At least that was what Axl figured it meant. The boy didn't want to, that was equally obvious. He wanted to ride back with the good news, but Clone was already wheeling his mount about, Axl forgotten.

It couldn't be better. Not for Axl anyway who watched as Clone yanked roughly on the reins of his horse and galloped back the way they'd all come. A minute or so later he vanished behind a low bank of scrub and Axl was left alone with the Tibetan boy, who was now looking more nervous than ever.

Chapter Twenty-nine

Rinpoche

'Ride,' the boy demanded, scowling at Axl.

No way. Axl was going to negotiate his way out of this one. Only when Axl smiled and shook his head, Tukten lifted the heavy revolver with both hands, fingers of his left hand steadying those of the right, just like you saw on *NVPD/Live*.

The long barrel shook so badly it looked like the boy was running a fever.

Fear did that to you. Fucked up the adrenal levels without damping down neural feedback. Not that understanding this was any consolation to Axl who sat right in the path of any bullet. The kid was frightened and the kid was armed, no one had to tell Axl that this wasn't a good mixture.

From the wrong end of the revolver it looked like the thing packed a 250 grain, conical bullet, soft lead with no jacketing. Which gave the revolver a muzzle velocity of 900 feet per second. More than adequate. And mechanically the gun looked so simple there was little chance it was going to jam any time soon.

But what worried Axl most wasn't the revolver's .45 calibre or its muzzle velocity, it was the amount of shake Tukten was giving to the barrel. Rock solid told you the guy with his finger round the trigger was either a psycho or had done it before, probably often. Rank amateurs Axl identified by the dangerous level of hand-jive their fear imparted to the barrel. The ones in between presented no problem to anyone, being slower, less clued-up and a lot less mean than they'd like to believe.

'Point it somewhere else,' Axl suggested, and kicked his mare into reluctant action, heading back towards Cocheforet. It looked like good advice wasted. The bullet didn't come, but then nor did Tukten. And Axl turned to find the Tibetan boy holding the revolver with straight arms, as far away from his own body as possible. The barrel still shook as if Tukten was running a come-down but the revolver was very definitely pointed straight at Axl.

Taking him across the plateau wasn't the boy's job after all, Axl realised with shock. He'd misread Clone's unspoken instructions completely. Tukten was meant to kill him and dump his body for wolf feed. Sure, the kid was frightened by the charnel ground but not as scared as he was at the thought of having to shoot someone.

Big casino, little casino. It was a virginity that no one got back.

Axl swung round the head of his mare and rode slowly back towards the trembling boy who looked, for one flustered moment, as if he was about to try to get his own mount to back up. Instead, he gripped the revolver tighter, knuckles whitening around its crude wooden grip.

If Axl had ever needed his Colt now was the time. Or maybe not. The boy would have been dead already.

'Stay back,' Tukten demanded.

Axl didn't. He kicked his heels softly into the mare's flanks and pushed her forward a few paces, his eye firmly on the boy's face. Looking into someone's face as you killed them was difficult enough when killing was what you did as the day job and Tukten wasn't yet angry enough to pull the trigger out of anything except fear. At least, Axl hoped he wasn't.

'Come on,' Axl told Tukten, 'give me the gun.'

The boy tightened his grip, eyes widening.

'We'll ride back together,' Axl said hastily reining in his horse, but Tukten wasn't listening. The connection was gone.

When the shot came its blast sent a black cloud of Egyptian

vultures spiralling skyward but Axl was too busy dropping sideways from his spooked mare and rolling behind the nearest boulder to notice. And it took him until his ears stopped ringing to realise he hadn't been injured.

'Fucking terrific,' said a voice behind him and a silver monkey crashed into the dirt, a jagged hole torn in one wing. 'Can't leave you alone for a minute.'

As Axl watched the hole mended itself, closing up from the edges like liquid mercury coming together. It didn't take a genius to know that the Colt was back on line, sort of . . .

'You trying to get yourself shot, eh?' Rinpoche demanded. 'And what were you going to do if I didn't turn up? Frighten him to death with your fucking face?'

The monkey paused, took a look at the black cavity where Axl's missing eye had been and twisted its lips into a rueful grin, thin lips sliding back to show gold canines. 'Been picking fights you can't win?'

Yeah, thought Axl, mostly with life, but he didn't admit that to the monkey. Instead he gazed pointedly at the raw skid mark its landing had carved into the plateau grass.

'Fucking air density's fucked,' the monkey said furiously, tripping over one of its own wings as it stood up. 'You any idea how badly this check-the-real-altitude, then add-ten-thousand-feet-to-get-virtual-altitude shit fucks up basic aerodynamics?'

Axl shook his head.

'Didn't think so,' said Rinpoche. 'It's a fucking miracle anyone can get a sodding helicopter to move in these conditions . . .' The monkey looked over at the terrified boy. 'What's with Mowgli?'

'He's scared.'

'He should try dropping through the upper atmosphere of this place. Wind like a cosmic fart. Not to mention more fucking hardware up there than there are HondaGlydes on the Beltway . . .'

'Security?'

'Plus CySat, C3N, TimeWarner. Simple peasants farming the homestead, brave hunters, furry little bears scooping fish from crystal streams. This place is a fucking goldmine . . .' The silver monkey turned its attention to wings which spread across the ground behind it.

'Lose those for a start,' Rinpoche said crossly and both immediately shrank, thickening as they did. 'The wings are a given,' it told Axl with a sigh, 'coded into the animus, but there are style choices.' The monkey shut its eyes, which looked horribly like real rubies, and ran some permutations. Gold scales, bronze feathers so perfect they looked real, wings of transparent glass, the monkey rejected them all without even opening its eyes.

'Small,' Axl told it, 'something basic . . .'

'Basic!' Rinpoche glared at Axl and did a quick pirouette on the damp grass, showing off jewels that ran like exposed vertebrae down its spine. 'Does this look fucking basic?' All the same it let its wings stabilise to two bat-like sails that opened and closed around hollow silver spars. The downy skin between the thin spars was niello black.

Axl forgotten, Rinpoche ambled over to Tukten and yanked his foot, tugging the slack-mouthed boy off his pony. It took the revolver from Tukten's unprotesting hands.

'Move and you join them.' The silver monkey jerked one small thumb towards the corpses. 'Okay?'

Tukten nodded.

'Piece of shit,' said Rinpoche, but it was talking about the revolver not the boy. 'Even for this place.' It snapped out the cylinder to check the machining, then snapped the cylinder back into place and spun it hard, counting off the few brief seconds it took for the five chambers to come to a halt. Still scowling, the monkey flipped the gun forwards over its trigger finger and sighted along the barrel.

'I've seen kids make better toys.'

Without pausing, the monkey passed its hands swiftly over

the revolver, its fingers moving faster and faster until they blurred. Which was the point Axl realised they really had disappeared, into a steel-grey smoke of freeform nanetics.

Somewhere inside that cloud a metal matrix so thin it was invisible to the human eye was holding the ex-revolver in place while subatomic assemblers crawled over its surface like dust mites, breaking millions of molecular bonds as Rinpoche rebuilt the weapon from the ground up. Growing the parts it needed rather than cutting them down from steel blanks, the way a semiAI or a human would. It reworked the metal too, rebalancing the carbon content of the barrel and cylinder, folding the steel like filo into thousands of invisible Toledo layers.

It would have preferred to work in ceramic but was making do with the source materials at hand, that way was quicker. When Rinpoche passed the revolver back to Axl the only thing about it that was the same was the overall shape. Form fits the function and the silver monkey might not like the inevitable side effects of Samuel Colt's ingenuity but it had no problems with the man's original sense of aesthetics.

Axl tossed the remade revolver from hand to hand, spun it once round his trigger finger and then flipped out the cylinder. Everything fitted flush, like it had been machined by an anally repressed semiAI to dangerously minimal tolerances. Smiling, Axl tapped the cylinder back into place and watched it spin.

'Yeah,' said the winged monkey, 'very pretty. Now about those housekeeping routines for you . . .' It grabbed Axl's skull and, before Axl could pull free, warmth bathed his face. 'Not carrying credit chips are you? Good . . . They'd only be wiped.'

Ruby-red irises peered deep into Axl's synthetic eye. 'Okay,' said the animal. 'The good news is there's more spare hardware inside your head than suits in a sushi bar. The bad news is that eye's about to fail.'

'Remake it,' Axl suggested heavily.

'Can't,' said Rinpoche, then changed its mind. 'Well, I could, obviously, but it's a sealed unit and pretty cheap at that. Why fuck around with an emulation when we've got more spares than Bodies'r Us . . . ?'

Unfurling its wings, the monkey twisted its head as if getting rid of a nasty crick in its neck and kicked off from the ground, pinions spreading as black wings caught and rode the bitter wind.

'Where are you going?' Axl shouted after it and Rinpoche grinned.

'Shopping.'

They were exactly what he thought they were, unfortunately for Axl.

Cupped in the palm of the monkey's hand lay two eyes, slippery with mucus and trailing fat sticky skeins of optic nerve. Blood coated the animal's fingers and little slivers of flesh were trapped beneath its glass nails.

'Farm fresh,' it told Axl grinning. 'Though we'd have had to improvise until I ran into monks carrying a teenage lama. He was almost dead anyway.'

'You killed him?' Axl tried not to sound shocked.

'Me? Rinpoche? Kill a priest?' The monkey grinned. 'How stupid do you think I am? I waited.'

Neither of them talked after that. Axl because he couldn't with his face gripped in the monkey's paws. The AI, which had once been the Colt and was now a silver monkey templated from Tsonghkapa's memory of a Bon myth, because it couldn't spare processing power to run the necessary vocal sub-routines. Besides, it didn't see the need to talk. The man had blacked out as soon as fingers were dipped into his orbital socket to scoop out the RedCross eye.

Rinpoche worked fast. Admittedly not as fast or as flashily as when it had remade the revolver because this time it was working with living tissue and besides who was there to impress? Axl's brain had toggled consciousness to standby and the blank-faced boy was too deep in shock to pay attention to anything.

The new eye was 20/20. Undamaged cornea, a clear perfectly-shaped lens and an ideal ratio of rod to cone cells lining the retina. So good it could have been grown to order. It also had an iris of unnaturally intense brown, as bright and shiny as the speckled shell on a newly-opened horse chestnut.

All Rinpoche had to do was amend the eye for infrared and a couple of colours the human eye couldn't usually see.

Having grafted the optic nerves and reattached Axl's *rectus* muscles, the silver monkey adjusted a tiny dip-switch that fed off the optic nerve further up the line, popped the new eyeball into its waiting socket and began to concentrate on the ruined pit that was Axl's other eye.

Smoke flowed from its fingers as assemblers broke free from the hand to reassemble in the wounded hollow of Axl's eye socket. Scar tissue was cut back to raw flesh beneath and then the nanites began to rebuild, matching and shaping to a mirror image of what Rinpoche had memorised from the socket of Axl's other eye.

Work done, the silver monkey grafted and stitched, not with thread but molecular chains, amending proteins to regrow muscle fibre and extend the optic nerve.

'Okay,' said the monkey. 'Almost done.' Fingers danced over Axl's face and it was like watching torture in reverse, scar tissue and bruises disappearing beneath the silver monkey's touch.

'Now let's get you back to Buttfuck, Hicksville. . .' Rinpoche walked across to where Tukten was sat blank-faced by his pony, and crouched down in front of the boy, looking for some sign of intelligent life.

'Well . . . life, anyway,' the monkey said sourly to itself as Tukten blinked and gaped at the silver animal sat in front of him. 'Wait until he wakes up and then get him back to

Cocheforet, understand? I'm relying on you.' Metal fingers that could have cracked stone reached out and gripped the boy's jaw lightly in one hand.

'Just don't let me down.'

Chapter Thirty

Enter the Tag Team

Fuck-wit.

Either the sound system was faulty or Rinpoche had amused himself by intentionally degrading the hardware until the backing track inside Axl's head sounded as tacky as some kid's home-grown deck. Every high note was tinny and the bass muffled down to the consistency of wet flannel.

He recognised the track all the same, a heavily remixed *WarChild* cut from fruity loops of temple gong instead of dry snare. And if it was Rinpoche's idea of a joke, Axl didn't care – it still stank.

Though not as much as Rinpoche's other little retro augmentation.

The timecode was white, digital primitive and running backwards. The tiny almost transparent numerals floated on the edge of Axl's vision, at the top left of his left eye, somewhere about 10 o'clock.

The read-out didn't click from 000.00.00 to 187.59.59 until Axl shook himself awake and it'd counted back to 187.54.00 before Axl even noticed them. He was too busy coping with reality in 3-D, colour and surround sound.

SS St Bernadote/Sept-21/13.00. Slot allocated for take-off. Time remaining to allocated slot . . . Axl only realised he been reading the departure authorisation for the Nuncio's cruiser when the words scrolling down his sight vanished leaving him staring at a worried looking Tukten.

*   *   *

Now the numbers were dim inside his head – low night setting – and read 183.38.39. And while Axl recognised a timecode when he saw one, he was trying hard not to think what else the digits might be counting down. Just in case it was something important like his own life.

Only, given the four UN conscripts strung across the track leading into Cocheforet, there was a chance Axl might not even last that long. They held snubPup Brownings, hip high, supported by neoprene slings twisted casually round their right arms, thumbs brushing each user-verification chip and fingers wrapped round waiting triggers.

No diodes were lit to confirm that safety catches were off or squat magazines were loaded, but that was because duct tape had been wrapped round zytel butts, blocking them off. All four men had their visors down and Axl had no doubt that they'd been watching him on infrared the whole way in . . .

The backbeat in his head upped tempo, bpms tied to his heartbeat, then slowed as Axl caught and hog-tied his irritation. The R3 reMix coming together clean, the sound system having kicked back to top quality once it had run that tattered, tacky WarChild intro. Now he had brushes dusting over a single snare like blown dust.

Read, Reconnoitre and get it Right

Fifty paces beyond the picket, three more conscripts and a Tibetan girl were sprawled on damp grass next to a dead goat, passing a giant spliff between them, while next to a hurricane lamp a fourth soldier fussed over a Braun portable grill that refused to ignite.

Axl didn't recognise the Tibetan girl, but that meant nothing. He'd barely been in Cocheforet time enough to learn more than half a dozen names. She was laughing, except the laughter didn't reach her eyes. She didn't mean it. In situations like this people never did, but they kept smiling just in case it might make a difference.

Axl knew all about it, he'd been on both ends of that equation and neither left a good taste in his mouth.

One huge hand gripped the girl's wrists and still managed to keep a spliff between two fat fingers, while the conscript's other hand fumbled at the bottom of her grey felt skirt trying to find its hem. No matter how hard she laughed and wriggled that hand was going to find its way between her legs eventually. Just as Axl knew he was going to let the matter ride.

The alternative was putting a bullet through the back of the big man's head and splattering his shit-for-brains all over the girl beneath, but that meant getting killed in return and Axl wasn't prepared for that. So instead Axl grabbed the reins of Tukten's pony and kicked his own mare into a trot, dragging Tukten behind him as he headed towards the conscripts blocking his path.

All of them were dressed in cheap PaxForce combats, cut from the kind of chameleon cloth that did its best to blend in with the background but was always a second or two behind. Over the jump-suits they wore heat-retaining kevlar flak jackets topped with polymer helmets featuring roll-down NBC masks and tiny built-in geek mikes. Boron patches were spot epoxied onto the transparent flaks above the heart. They wore shoulder armour too, running Tsunami software that could flip from soft to hard at the merest suggestion of a blow.

The jump-suits might be cheap but both helmet and flaks cost more than most PaxForce conscripts got paid in a year. Which wasn't hard given the UN sourced its troops through an offshore broker called DecSec, who leased regular conscripts from Mauritania, Kazakhstan or Peru depending on the type of mission.

In theory the lessee countries got paid by the UN but in practice the IMF usually wrote the payment off against outstanding debt.

Conscript loss was acceptable, which wasn't something you could say for their top-flight military electronics. Even adding in a completion bonus didn't take the annual cost of a PaxForce trooper to more than half that paid to LockMart for the helmet alone.

All four soldiers had PaxForce IDs welded into their collars. The kind of crypt chip guaranteed to vibrate frantically if caught in the cross-hairs of a PaxForce snubPup, not to mention tell the snubPup where to get off . . . UN regulations demanded soldiers also wore rank and number identification, but this was missing in every case. Axl wasn't surprised.

What did surprise him, though, was the fact he could see all this. And what surprised him even more was that he could see it clearly on a darkened night when Cocheforet was closed down, wooden shutters pulled tighter than a sphincter over windows and front doors kept closed.

Maybe this was the trade-off from Rinpoche for that irritating timecode. Because whatever scam the silver monkey had pulled in there among his neurons it was neat.

'Actually,' said Axl, 'for an outdated Colt with an attitude problem it's fucking impressive.'

Beside him, Tukten jumped. But mostly because he'd finally realised what Axl already knew. They were riding straight towards a group of soldiers, maybe twenty paces ahead. If Axl hadn't grabbed the boy's wrist, Tukten would have pulled round and ridden away; which was about as sensible as staple-gunning a luminous target on his back. At least it was when PaxForce were running a little unofficial R&R.

'Wait,' Axl snapped and kicked his heels until the mare he was riding stumbled into an unwilling trot. 'Unless you want to get killed.'

The torch beam hit Axl's face just ahead of the voice which ordered him to halt. Axl did. But he waited until his horse was almost upon the guard before yanking its bridle.

'Shithead.' The guard snapped up the lux level on his laserlight, shining it straight into Axl's eyes. Without even thinking about it, Axl shut down some of the rod and cone cells, filtering out most of the brightness.

'Who are you?' The voice was rough, casually arrogant but not as hard as the man would like it to be. A corporal, nothing more.

'Black Jack d'Essiarto,' said Axl politely. 'And I'd like to stable my mare . . . if that's not a problem?'

Next to the corporal a wiry kid sniggered and lowed his snubPup. Peruvian by the look of it. Which made sense at this altitude.

'And this?' The corporal demanded.

'My servant,' Axl grinned as Tukten stiffened in the saddle.

'You live here?'

'Do I live here . . . ?' Sat on his horse, high above the corporal, Axl yawned heavily and stretched his arms out to his side, then yawned again . . . 'Do I look like I live in a shit hole?' Memories of his flat back in Day Effé crashed in on Axl but he shunted them out of his head. 'Well,' asked Axl, 'do I?'

Someone else laughed and as the corporal whipped round, Axl kicked his mare forward and squeezed between the suddenly straight-faced soldiers. 'I'm dossing at the Inn,' he told the corporal over his shoulder, 'if you need me.'

Axl trotted the hundred paces to the stable door and dismounted without once looking back. He had the revolver tucked into the back of his belt, hidden beneath the thick felt of his stinking coat. Using the weapon would be a last resort and Axl didn't intend for that to happen. Mainly because he'd have to be seriously stupid to use a black-power .45 against flaked-up troops waving PaxForce-issue snubPups. It didn't matter how many modifications to the gun Rinpoche had made, without kevlar body armour and a helmet Axl didn't even have tickets to the same fucking ballpark.

Throwing open the stable door, Axl stopped. Instead of the familiar reek of dung and horse piss it stank of hydrocarbons and over-hot metal.

Five Chinese-built Honda X3 dirtbikes were parked up in one corner, the kind with studded tires and built-in gyro. Not fast, but they could hack ice that would tax a sherpa and slick down any slope that was less than vertical. That was exactly what he'd have brought if he'd had to choose. Except normal people on Samsara didn't get to ride Honda dirts, or Seraphim 4×4s or Mitsubishi half-tracks come to that. Only PaxForce got full use of technology on Samsara, courtesy of some UN mandate. And even then, the Dalai Lama wasn't too keen, though he was much too pragmatic to say so openly . . .

That was what Axl had heard anyway.

'Feed her and rub her down.' Axl told Tukten, tossing his reins to the boy. 'Then get home and stay there, okay? If they want your jacket give it to them, the same goes for your sister or your arse. Don't get into fights, don't get riled and don't waste time trying to be a hero. This lot slot kids like you for a hobby. Understand?'

The stable door had swung shut before the shocked boy even had time to answer. The corporal didn't challenge Axl on his way up the street, in fact the man did his best to pretend he hadn't seen Axl at all.

DanceSerious WarPosse announced a hand-printed screamer posted to Leon's door. *Suck On This, Samsara tour.* Despite himself, Axl smiled. Some things didn't change.

A wave of sour chang, sensimillia and stale sweat hit Axl as he stepped though the inn's door into the crowded bar. The place was rammed to the rafters. Over at a table in the far corner, Ketzia was trying to stop a tray crammed to over-flowing with bowls of chang from being pulled out of her hands.

Three teenage conscripts sat at the table, *DanceSerious* patches epoxied to their shirtsleeves. And the only boy not struggling to slide his hands up Ketzia's skirt was alternating between sucking hits on a jade chillum and fumbling at Ketzia's blouse. One full breast was almost loose, its dark nipple exposed, but for all the expression on Ketzia's face the grinning stoner kid might have been transparent.

The woman's eyes were blank, her wide mouth neither smiling nor frowning. Unlike the other girl serving, Ketzia didn't even bother to swat away their groping hands. She'd been here before Axl knew, just from the deadness of her expression which reflected the utter powerlessness of an object with no reason to question the emptiness of those who did only what they were told.

If she expected any help from Axl she didn't let it show, but then with his two new eyes and reworked face she probably didn't recognise him anyway.

Just inside the door − and right in his way − six or seven spliffed-up Peruvian kids sat in a circle on the dirty floor. Off duty and killing time with bowls of Cocheforet's thin beer. Spread out in the middle of them were foil packs of Mexican take-out. Someone had gone to the bother of yanking the heating tabs on the sides before ripping off the lids, but most of the packs were still full.

Axl wasn't surprised. Reconstituted protein was no one's first choice and the smell of vat-grown chilli still turned his gut.

'Shite, isn't it?' Axl said, stepping carefully over them. One of the mind-blasted teenagers nodded long before she even thought to wonder who the newcomer was. Avoiding her boots, Axl stepped neatly round a boy on his knees trying to puke, dodged two conscripts kissing and finally reached the bar.

'Evening, Leon. Did Ketzia find what she was looking for?'

It was worth the walk.

Leon's face went slack with shock and then he was scrambling beneath the counter, hands feeling for some weapon. A hidden length of metal pipe, Axl decided, that would be about his level.

Axl shook his head slowly, locking his eyes onto those of the barman. Equally slowly, Leon dropped his hands from the bar and stood back, mouth opening and shutting silently . . .

'Hey,' said the heavy woman Leon had been serving. 'You seen a fucking ghost or something?'

'Yeah,' said Axl, yanking a stool from beneath a drunken conscript, 'or something.' Leon glared angrily at Axl, glanced at the heavy woman and left, muttering under his breath.

'Do I know you?' defMoma asked. The sergeant was stripped to her combat trousers, stained T-shirt and steel-capped boots that buckled to the knee. Her biceps were thick as hams, her heavy breasts topped by nipples bullet-like enough to threaten the cloth of her T-shirt. It was an impressive sight.

Axl spread his hands slightly. 'I don't know,' he said. 'Do you?' The long list of UN conflict zones he reeled off began with Azerbaijan and ended with Zaire, via Bessarabia and Montevideo. Actually, he'd only been to about three of them but defMoma didn't know that. Didn't know he'd fought mainly for the other side, either.

'Chang,' Axl ordered, while defMoma was still thinking over his list. The beer tasted no better than it had the last time Axl tried it, but at least Leon didn't try to charge him.

'And another.'

The revolver pressed hard in the small of his back. Other than that, Axl had the hunting knife stuck in his boot. Not much if putsch came to kill . . . Of course he could always try to grab a better weapon, if he could just work out what defMoma was packing and where.

Back in San Salvador, when the IMF were running one of their interminable credit checks, the NCOs got issued with semiAI HiPowers, poor relations to the gun Axl used before logic went walkabout. No one knew what weapons senior officers in San Salvador carried because no one saw any.

Axl suddenly realised defMoma wasn't listening to him anymore. She was displaying an unhealthy interest in a woman who'd just walked in, only to stop dead in the doorway, appalled by the stink of vomit and the blast of some kid's Sony boombox.

Poor-boy's soundtracks. Like his sergeant used to say, if it's not fitted it's not real. 'Like to stay and chat,' Axl shouted, slipping off the stool, 'but you know how it is. Shit to do . . .'

Idiots to rescue.

The barefoot woman began to edge between the kids blocking the door, gazing too obviously round the crowded bar. Either she'd been to the stable but hadn't found any more beads, and had come for help from Leon and Ketzia, or else Escondido had been occupied by PaxForce officers and she wanted Mai out of the house but needed help finding somewhere for the kid to stay.

Or both.

Axl could write the script in his head.

A ragged yellow jacket hid her upper body, while what looked like a horse blanket was tied tight around her waist, making a crude skirt. Her hair was scraped back under a blue scarf too old even to remember if it had ever had better days.

All she needed was a bottle of industrial alcohol to look like a pantomime beggar. On Samsara, of course, among the thousands of 'fugees scrabbling to feed themselves from thin soil, she looked almost normal. Just another woman who'd lost her home, her job or her kids and been issued with two blankets and a refugee PIN number in reply.

She wasn't.

That ash-grey blanket round her waist was cut from a shahtoosh, woven from wool combed from the stomach of an antelope. It took five animals to make each wrap. Pashmina and shahtoosh were two of the few luxury items Samsara produced for export. Cutting it up and dumping it into the mud must have really hurt Kate, which was fine with Axl. The last time he'd seen the bitch she'd just finished slapping Mai stupid.

Now the roles were reversed.

What gave Kate away was her feet. They were filthy enough, her soles and heels crusted with mud where she'd walked into Cocheforet from El Escondido. But the dirt that should have been ingrained under each toenail was missing and her ankles lacked the grey patina of those forced to live without shoes.

She was altogether too clean, as some conscript was bound to find out the moment he stuck a hand under her skirt to uncover legs that weren't as filthy as they should be.

'You.' Axl pointed at Kate. 'Over here.' She could run or she could do what she was told. One of those wasn't going to get her killed, if Kate got lucky.

'Well done,' said Axl coldly, watching her trying to work out where she recognised him from.

He slapped her. And then Kate knew.

Half a dozen of the conscripts cheered, cheers turning to crude encouragement as Axl twisted his right hand tight into the shocked woman's hair and kissed her hard.

'Hit any more children lately?' Axl asked, coming up for air.

If she could have done, she'd have slapped him but Axl caught her wrist, fingers tightening until Kate bit her lip.

'Fond of that, aren't you?' Axl's smile wasn't kind. 'Well, try it on me and I'll break your fucking wrist . . . And then I'll give you to this lot.' Axl yanked her over to the bar, booted another conscript off his stool and sat down next to defMoma, pulling Kate down onto his knee . . .

'Staying long?' Axl asked defMoma, whose blue eyes left off trying to focus on a frozen Kate and had a shot at refocusing on Axl instead. The only bit of defMoma's iced-out brain still working almost asked what business it was of his, but defMoma was tired and Axl behaved like he belonged. On top of that, there were standing PaxForce regulations about answering reasonable questions, not that anyone paid much attention to shit like that.

'As long as it takes,' she replied heavily. Which was undoubtedly true and told Axl zilch, which was what it was meant to do.

'To do what?' Axl demanded. 'Or are you planning to stick to the usual?' He jerked his head towards where one of the younger conscripts was hinting, with the aid of a zytel blade, that Leon might like to supply Cocheforet's piss-poor chang for free.

'You're an observer,' said defMoma flatly. And the conscript at the next stool along went hurriedly back to his beer, then snuck another look.

Axl said nothing.

If he was an official UN-appointed observer, now was the point to whip out his little holographic card and flash it in the huge woman's face. Observers had diplomatic status, carte blanche, carte noblique . . . Whatever it took wherever they were. Didn't matter which way the IMF or PaxForce cut it, observers weren't messed with.

Observers were the control group that kept the PaxForce honest, that was the theory. They'd been introduced fifteen years back, around the time the UN gave in to IMF pressure and outsourced its rapid-response troops. Five corps tendered and DecSec won, helped by a recent devaluation of the rouble.

Killing an observer was bad news. Every conscript on the ground lost a year's pay *and* had an extra year added to their contract. Axl smiled at the thickset, cropped-haired woman and did nothing more. All of the conscripts were watching him now. Most out of the corner of their eyes but a few full-on.

'Mission statement?' Axl kept his voice polite, wondering what he'd do if defMoma called his bluff.

She didn't. Without a word she handed him a tiny silver disc and then, when he sighed heavily, unclipped her Sony walkWear and handed that over as well.

The instructions were simple. The unit was to search Samsara for Father Sylvester, the Vatican treasurer and return him to Earth to face a financial-crimes tribunal. The order was approved by the World Bank, signed by the current Secretary Fiscal and ratified by the International Court of Human Rights at the Hague.

So far so normal.

Where the whole concept started to unravel was when Axl

checked the instigator properties on a hunch and got not the Prosecutor Fiscal or the Secretary General of the UN or even Cardinal Santo Duque, which would have been bizarre but just about possible, but Maximillia.

Max didn't do politics. That kind of stuff the kid left to the Cardinal. She definitely didn't do heavyweight legal finessing either. Not that Max didn't have a right to appeal to the Hague. It was her economy that had been wrecked by the underage Army of God. WorldBank had to be leaning on her. And Axl could understand why.

Grapes had been left to rot on the vine, whole fields of cannabis and maize had withered and died uncollected. Even the mountain coca crops had been left ungathered. Worse than that, industrial complexes were burned if executives refused to embrace poverty with what the Army thought was sufficient enthusiasm. From San Antone and Baja California to the lush sensimillia estates of Cuba, caldes, patrons and hacendados who decided to hang onto their bank accounts lost their lives.

Mexico was in ruins. Financial crimes didn't come more obvious. Watched around the world by millions Pope Joan had taken a low-orbit Boeing shuttle to Day Effé to stop the children.

And died, on camera. Standing alone in front of an army of children. Caught by CySat stringers, Ishies, aerospats, by every wannabe news jock on the American continent. What the newsfeeds showed was the sudden stumble of a middle-aged woman, her fallen body ripped apart by beautiful, wide-eyed street children. It had been as unsettling as watching puppies kill.

Her clothes got stripped from her, strands of grey hair tugged from her scalp. The papal ring had been taken from her finger and the finger taken from her hand by a smiling ten-year-old girl wielding a five dollar Bowie ground sharp against brick.

All her fingers had gone after that, then her hands, then

her feet. Last to be taken was her sightless head, brow blood-covered but unfurrowed, lips reposed, eyes shut as if she was sleeping.

The police got that back, of course. As well as most of her fingers.

What the mainstream News didn't show, and what Axl didn't know until the Cardinal told him, was that Joan was dead before she hit the ground. She didn't stumble, she died. Shot as she stood doing what she always did, telling the truth as she saw it. The time had come for the children of the Army to go home. And if the children didn't have a home to go to, she would find them one.

A sliver of super-cooled ice was all it took, poisoned at the tip with curare and fired from a hopped-up airgun. The impact no more painful than the bite from a horsefly.

The Pope knew what had happened, though.

So did those closest in the crowd. The children who ripped her apart on camera weren't killing her, they were collecting relics. And the Cardinal believed that Joan would have approved. Just as she approved the spirit, if not the result, of most things done by the Army of God.

'She was shot,' Axl said firmly. 'I saw it on vid.'

'Vids lie.' defMoma might have been arguing with a child.

Axl flushed.

'You think that sequence wasn't stripped back? From what I heard CySat's AI went half crazy behind the scenes trying to peel the episode apart. It couldn't be done. Every fucking checksum, every fucking kilopixel block of it validated; nothing was cropped out, nothing added, nothing taken away.

'It happened, it just didn't get shown,' Axl added furiously, 'get used to it.'

defMoma finally focused on Axl's face. 'You supported the Army of God?'

Axl shook his head, feeling Kate stiffen. 'Far as I'm concerned, Joan was a fucking lunatic who got stuffed and turned to kitty litter on camera. I just don't know why everyone's having trouble accepting it.'

Yanking Kate to her feet, Axl pushed back his stool, hearing it scrape in the ground. 'Party time,' he told her.

'You know that woman?' defMoma nodded towards a struggling Kate.

'Nah,' said Axl, sliding his free hand down to Kate's arse and cupping one buttock. 'But I plan to.'

Laughter and obscenities followed him out of the Inn, and kept coming right up to the point he turned the corner into darkness and Kate Mercarderes suddenly yanked up her skirt, pivoted on one bare foot and used her other to kick Axl's head hard enough to knock him off his feet.

That didn't just rate synth, it got crashing, speed-metal chords.

Chapter Thirty-one

Time Out

'*Taekyon*,' Rinpoche said, dropping from the night sky. Adding, '*tae kwon do*,' when Axl looked blank, though that could be reverb *howing* inside his head. 'Sweet Jesus. Can't you even duck?'

'Rinpoche,' said the silver monkey offering Kate its paw. 'And you're Katherine Mercarderes. Aged twenty-seven years, four months, five days. Born Mount Olive hospital in Rome. Natural carriage, natural birth, no artificial womb. No foetal augmentations/genetic rewrites. Confirmed hereditary predisposition to stress, anger and depression. Forty-three percent chance of developing breast cancer by the age of forty. Educated from six to eighteen at the Vatican by Jesuit tutor Father Sylvester. Currently in protected exile on the island of Lampedusa, south of Sicily . . .

'. . . yeah right.' The monkey's face lost its distant look as it peered deep into her eyes. Whatever it was looking for, it found in there.

'Retinal match,' it stated firmly. 'Unless those are new, of course?'

Kate slowly shook her head and the monkey sighed.

'That was irony.'

'So,' said Rinpoche turning to where Axl still sat in the mud, 'You found Kate Mercarderes, who wasn't on Lampedusa. Now what? Planning to keep her?'

'No chance.' Kate came uncoiled like a spring, pivoting again as she drew back one foot to kick Axl in the head.

Axl needn't have bothered ducking. Rinpoche came up fast and hard, his paw closing round her ankle, locking it solid. No restraints could have held Kate that tight.

'Later,' snapped the monkey. 'You can kick him later.'

'I should have let Clone kill you.' Kate spat the words at Axl. 'Back at Escondido when he wanted to.'

'Yeah,' said Axl coldly, climbing to his feet. 'Maybe you should. While you had the chance. Because, fuck knows, your family's been responsible for enough killing.' He put up one hand and lightly touched Kate's face the way visitors used to touch his when he was a kid, the way he really used to hate.

She flinched. He used to do that too.

'So what's one more,' Axl asked as he reached behind him to pull the revolver from his belt, 'I mean, after all those others . . . ?'

The gun was loaded, unfired. There wasn't a safety catch to release because the model wasn't that sophisticated and Rinpoche hadn't bothered to create one while giving the gun a make-over because Axl never used them anyway.

Axl spun the revolver once round his finger, fast forward so the handle snapped back into his hand with a satisfying slap and the muzzle finished up pointing straight at Kate's stomach. The soundtrack died, kicked mute by significance override.

Even Rinpoche stopped breathing.

'Did you enjoy hitting Mai?' Axl asked the frozen woman. 'Did it help your stress? Make you feel all gooey inside?'

'I apologised to Mai, afterwards . . .' Kate said softly.

Gun still to her gut, Axl patted Kate's cheek softly. 'Yeah,' he said, 'bet that made her face less sore.' Kate had tears in her eyes and she was biting the inside of her lip without knowing it. He'd gone out from Cocheforet nearly blind and returned with someone else's eyes. She was afraid of him.

Been there, felt that . . .

Axl casually reversed the revolver and held it handle first to the silent woman: standing there until she finally reached over and took the weapon from his grip.

'Well,' he said, as he leant hard into the muzzle of the revolver, 'you going to shoot me . . .'

How else was he going to get that bloody timecode to stop?

The problem, Axl decided watching Kate's haunted face was that she really didn't know whether she was going to or not. Kate had been running on empty for so long she didn't even know it. And she needed another decision to make about as much as she needed the gun Axl had put in her shaking hand.

Saying he'd been there was glib, but it was also true.

She stared at him in the night-time darkness of a small 'fugee village in a high valley on the edge of an immeasurably large hollowed-out wheel at some Lagrange off the edge of Earth. While around the outer rim of that wheel spun strips of prayer cloth that streamed out through the void, endlessly chanting.

She had a gun pointed at his gut finger tightening on the trigger, and all he wanted from her was an apology. How stupid was that . . . His thoughts were shredded, fractured like glass. Added to which he was cold, his spine hurt and his thighs were raw from a whole day in the saddle.

'Look,' said Axl as a clicktrack fed back in, thin as a baby's heartbeat. 'Do you want to shoot me or not?'

Chapter Thirty-two

Forgiveness Comes Xtra

The silver monkey wasn't keen to leave, claiming it was now Axl's bodyguard. But it went after Axl threatened to rip its wings out at the shoulder if it didn't take itself elsewhere. Both Axl and Rinpoche knew he couldn't make good on that threat, but the silver monkey went anyway, sucking at its teeth in disgust as it clambered onto a PaxForce 4track to give itself a better take-off.

The night was getting late in more ways than one. And the wind that ripped down the narrow valley brought them cordite and the sound of shooting as drunken conscripts lit the dark sky with tracer. A wooden house was being noisily demolished for kindling. Off behind the village, a woman's scream got chopped off, abruptly.

And behind it all, the heavy beat of some kid knitting up Tokyo Techno, all looped snare-fills and Korg samples stolen from ad jingles for products so old no one remembered what they were. The deck was UN-issue. But then it had long been accepted that you couldn't go to war without a decent sound-track. Though Axl still thought it was cheap not to provide the kids with their own inbuilt sound systems.

You got better results that way, too − and it didn't upset the neighbours.

Rinpoche didn't go far, of course. Just high enough to hang out of sight in the darkness, not so far it let Axl out of sound range. Both Axl and the silver monkey knew that was how it was going to be. Kate didn't, but shock had wound her so tight she couldn't have watched her words even if she'd known.

Shock at seeing Axl remade. Shock at getting herself trapped in that inn. But most of all, her face was sucked hollow by the shock of suddenly thinking she knew where the memory beads were, then discovering Clone was wrong and she didn't.

'I could have killed you, you moron.' Fury coated each word with acid.

Axl shrugged like he didn't care. Actually, he didn't but that wasn't why he shrugged. He still hadn't forgiven Kate for Mai or what she'd said.

'I saved your life,' said Axl, 'back there in the Inn . . .'

'Did I *ask* you to interfere?'

'No,' Axl's words were matter of fact. 'You thought I was dead.'

Kate looked up at that. Face suddenly still. She'd told Clone to take Axl across the plateau. She hadn't wondered too hard about whether he'd actually do it.

'*Tae kwon do* isn't enough,' said Axl. 'You get into a stand-up, knock-down with PaxForce and you've lost before it starts. Mai might have fronted them out, but you . . . If I hadn't got you out of there, you might not have ended up dead but you'd have wished you were.

'You owe me,' Axl said, when Kate glared at him. 'Deal with it.'

'Yes,' said Kate, 'I will.' She didn't sound at all convinced.

In fact, she sounded worried and scared. Somewhere up the side of that valley, in a shambling monastery was an underage Japanese whore who'd fuck anyone to get away from the woman stood in front of him, even the PaxForce.

It made Axl want to know why.

'Why didn't you send Mai to look for the beads?' Axl asked, though he already knew the answer. Because Mai would have run away. That's what all of the kid's night trips to Cocheforet were about. And that other stuff in Kate's bedroom. Axl wasn't stupid enough to think Mai had been at all interested in him. Okay, maybe he had been at the time, but not afterwards. Kate was holding Mai at Escondido against her will and the kid wanted out.

'She your servant?' Axl asked. The *reformistas* didn't believe in servitude.

'No,' Kate said coldly, 'she's not indentured.'

'But she's not free, is she?'

The shake of the woman's head was so small as to be almost imperceptible. She made no attempt to hide the fact that the truth tasted bitter. Her eyes were hollow, unblinking. Her chin jutted forward but her cheeks were sunken with increasing worry and lack of sleep. She looked older and much less certain than she had twenty-four hours before.

What Axl didn't know about REM sleep, alpha-states and conscious dreaming hadn't yet been discovered. He knew when someone was staying awake because going to sleep was worse. And he could spot all the signals in her face, like someone had erected a neon sign above her head saying 'Empty'.

Unwelcome thoughts guttered behind her dark eyes like candle flame, as ready to go out as to flare . . . Kate needed those memory beads, and yet there was no clone readied to take Joan's memories. No shrine already formatted and waiting; there couldn't be, because Cocheforet had no power. That much Axl knew.

Which meant Mai was the key.

Joan might have suddenly gone on CySat to declare herself Pope of the hollow people, but she was still CEO of UnitedVatican, whether she had liked it or not. And until recently UnitedVatican's core statement had included the fact that clones were without souls.

Joan couldn't have ordered herself a clone anymore than she could have announced a sudden conversion to Islam. Some things just couldn't be done, not even by a Pope. Although not understanding that point was regarded by the *reformistas* as Joan's greatest strength.

'I'll see you back to the house,' Axl told her as he slid one hand under a reluctant elbow. All it would take to cripple her was a quick and dirty thumb jab into a nerve running up the inside of her arm. And from the way Kate stared ahead it was obvious she knew that. 'We can talk on the way . . .'

They didn't, though. Barefoot and frozen, Kate just stamped on through the drizzle, her feet squelching in the mud. And by the time they'd reached the bridge Axl realised that if he didn't break her silence it wasn't going to get broken . . . So he stopped dead and let go of her arm.

'Just listen,' he said.

For a moment it looked as if Kate would storm ahead but she stopped herself, still not looking at Axl. In another world and another time, in someone else's story, he would have been less than zero to her. At most a peon in the lower reaches of what ever multinational she would have inherited.

But this was Axl's story and whether she liked that or not he was standing beside her in the darkness. And what he wanted from her was an apology. The problem was, Axl realised, an apology for what? For hitting Mai, a kinderwhore he only thought he knew because he saw too much of himself in the kid? For not trusting him? She was right not to . . .

Crunch time. 'I've got something for you,' Axl said, pushing one cold hand deep into his pocket.

Kate shook her head, raindrops running down her neck. 'No,' she said, 'you don't.'

Closing his fingers around the dreamcatcher, Axl pulled the small circle from his pocket and offered it to her. 'Are you really telling me you don't want this?'

The face that looked up at him was frozen with shock. Hope and fear flickering across it as she tried to frame the question Axl knew she needed to ask. There was no attempt to deny the memory beads were hers, that they were what she, Ketzia and Clone had been hunting for so desperately.

She would pay his price, whatever it was. That much went without saying, but she wanted it said anyway.

'There's a price?'

Axl smiled. 'Of course there's a price.'

'We're not rich.'

'Not now.' The jibe came out more bitter than Axl had intended but Kate didn't even notice. She was too busy thinking.

'What money we have is yours.'

'I don't want money. You know perfectly well what I want.'

Axl saw Kate's chin go up. 'Mai's a child,' said Kate defensively.

'The kid's been a whore since she was eleven.' Axl's kept his voice cold. 'She didn't have childhood. But no, I don't want her either.'

Kate didn't wish to ask the next question but Axl made her. He was enjoying himself too much to give Kate any slack.

'You want *me*?'

In the darkness Axl grinned, he couldn't help it. Always answer a question with a question ... He might not have picked up as much as he could have done from the Cardinal, but he'd learnt that much.

'What do you think?'

Kate didn't know and she didn't want to think. No, that wasn't true. Kate shook her head crossly. Actually, she knew exactly what would happen if that was his price. She would agree.

'Tell me,' Kate said finally, in little more than a whisper, 'what is the price?'

'An apology,' said Axl.

There was silence. As much as there could be silence with a woman shouting in the distance and drunken conscripts drag-racing unlit dirtbikes down the only street.

Under that and the noise of rain, the muted clicktrack and

wind blowing cold inside his own head, Axl could hear the stream rolling over gravel beneath their feet: and under that the drumming of her heart and the silence of a held breath.

'An apology?' Kate couldn't keep the catch out of her voice.

Axl nodded. 'That's all . . .' He said it as if there was never any question he might have had another price in mind. Taking Kate by the shoulders, he turned her and himself so the faint light from a fire in the village lit his face and she could see his new eyes burning into hers.

'You called me a coward, a liar . . . All I want is you to admit you were wrong.'

'And then I get the beads?'

'You get the memory beads anyway,' said Axl quietly. 'Here . . .' He held the soulcatcher out to Kate.

She was crying already inside. And when the tears finally spilled out of her, Axl watched them trail down her cold cheeks but didn't let Kate know that he knew she was crying, just stood and stared up at the darkened valley wall, following the faint line of the foss as white water tumbled down from the high slopes. More PaxForce troops were up there, bivouacked just beneath the snowline. He didn't think anyone in the village knew that.

And sat closer in, wings folded tight and arms curled round the upper trunk of a fir, was Rinpoche staring back. Axl couldn't see the expression on the silver monkey's narrow face but somehow Axl knew he didn't want to.

High and haunting, a loop of flute came out of the darkess, rich with echo and loss. He knew Kate couldn't hear it. That it only reflected what he believed she felt. But it tugged strings that rippled like Celtic harp.

He had Kate now, ready and hooked. Axl just wished he felt better about it.

Chapter Thirty-three

Build It Up . . .

He sprang the rest of his trap the next evening. After a day in which Kate had finally crept to the village because she couldn't stand the conscripts lighting fires on the tiled floors of the monastery.

But it was only after some kid started to tag great 3-D bruises over a tapestry in the vast dining room that Axl decided to act, ripping the gloPaint gun from the kid's fingers.

'No posse marks.'

'You what?' Dressed in half-combat, kevlar flak but no shoulder armour or helmet, the conscript gaped at Axl. The man had to be mad. Civilians didn't just march up to members of PaxForce and start ordering them around. Not if they wanted to keep both knees intact.

Except Axl was standing with arms folded across his chest and legs apart in the doorway of the dining room, staring straight at the soldier. And he obviously expected to be obeyed. Looking at the man's tattered shirt and 'fugee crop, the soldier couldn't quite work out why.

The monastery was requisitioned. The man shouldn't even have been there.

'And get rid of this shit,' Axl said and pointed to a pair of fourteen-buckle combat boots drying in front of a grate full of smouldering yak-dung. The leather boots were meant to be self-drying, self-sealing, self-deodorised . . . They weren't, not even when new.

Anyone with half a brain bought their own pair and the fact

that their owner hadn't said nothing good. Getting too crippled to march wasn't macho, it was just dumb.

'Whose are those, anyway?' Axl demanded.

'The sergeant's,' replied the soldier as if that answered everything. And having met defMoma again that morning Axl figured maybe it did. She looked like a typical fuck-wit masochist dyke to him, not that he wanted to pigeon-hole her.

'And those,' demanded Axl, pointing to an expensive-looking pair of men's ankle boots. No buckles, just a self sealing flap. If they were regulation issue, then it was senior ranks only.

'They belong to the boss.'

Yeah, well that explained it. Though the pleasure of meeting their CO was still to come. He'd only just arrived and was choosing his bedroom.

It was 8 p.m., Wednesday, 14 September. Axl knew that because it was displayed in his left eye, just below the timecode that now read 160.59.59. He'd asked Kate to come down to supper with Mai at 8.30 on the dot. She hadn't wanted to but Axl was reeling her in. And he still didn't feel any better about it.

'You going to get rid of those?' Axl asked, pointing at both pairs of drying boots.

The soldier shook his head.

With a shrug, Axl opened a shutter and let cold evening air swirl into the smoky room. For the first time since he'd arrived in the high valley the night sky was deep blue, the wind mild and it wasn't raining. Axl could look from the stone window to the village far below. And that was the direction in which he hurled the boots one after another. Straight towards a four-wheel Toyota cutting scars in the grass as it climbed noisily towards the house.

When defMoma stamped into the room with her spare boots clutched angrily in one hand, she found Axl sweeping his arm across one end of a long wooden table, knocking fag packets, medicare boxes and stripped-down gun parts to the tiled floor.

'This is for food,' Axl told her. 'You or your little friend want to play strip-the-gun-naked go and do it outside. And get rid of this crap, too.' He scooped up a box of combat rations and tipped the packet of enhanced grits onto the tiles in a rain of little foil squares. Everything the human body could possibly need, from essential amino acids to chelated minerals, minus texture and taste. He'd have swapped a crate of the fucking stuff for a single dose of MDA-4.

'You're not an observer.' It was a statement not a question.

'Well done,' said Axl.

'You told me . . .'

Axl didn't care what he told her. Two people were talking in the hall and Axl was busy registering a voice he'd been half expecting, half dreading, ever since he'd recognised the sergeant that night in the stables exactly a week ago . . .

'*Well,*' said the voice, '*have you found Father Sylvester yet?*' The words were utterly flat, without accent and yet they gripped Axl's attention the way crocodile clips grip testicles. Party time.

The revolver was in his hand before Axl even realised that he'd drawn it. Three strides took Axl to the doorway and the crack of the barrel as it met Colonel Emilio's head was louder than the thud the big man made when he hit the floor. Just nothing like as loud as the single drum kick that swallowed up the rest of Axl's soundtrack and spat it out as echo.

Axl was feeling better about life already.

'Freeze,' he said loudly, and behind Colonel Emilio, the lieutenant did just that, like someone had dipped her in liquid nitrogen.

'This is private,' Axl told momaDef, 'strictly between friends.'

'You know the CO?'

'Yeah, but he won't remember,' said Axl over his shoulder, as he turned back to defMoma who was still inside the room. 'I looked different then.'

The fat sergeant had her hand hovering over the half-open, velcroed flap of her own holster, unable to complete the move without making that familiar ripping sound. The one that tells you someone is about to draw their weapon.

'I wouldn't,' said Axl and nudged the revolver in her direction. Choosing advanced weaponry then wrapping it in a neoprene container apparently designed to make it difficult to get at made no sense at all to Axl. He'd take a skeleton holster or a lanyard over a closed-top holster any time.

'Come in,' Axl gestured to the lieutenant, who did as he said, stepping over the Colonel.

'You'll find Clone in the kitchen,' Axl told the sergeant, sweeping his arm across the other half of the long table so the last of the clutter hit the floor. 'Tell him to bring supper.'

'Get your own fucking . . .'

The fat woman didn't finish because Axl put a bullet into the wall behind her, showering her broad shoulders and cropped head with coin-sized chunks of plaster. The kind that knock normal people to the floor from shock if nothing else.

He got complete silence then. Inside his head and out. The ringing silence that comes when human ears try to adjust from one extreme of noise to the other.

'Food,' said Axl firmly.

The sergeant wanted to kill Axl. Wanted it so badly the need was written in her blue eyes and in the muscles that stood out in her thick arms and knotted her jaw. He could almost taste the adrenaline sweating off her. But she wasn't going to get the chance. None of them were.

'Put your gun on the floor first,' Axl told defMoma and waited while she did.

It wasn't her white trash manners, wrong-end-of-the-bell-curve genetic coding, macho ignorance or what defMoma did or didn't have dangling between her fat legs that fucked Axl off, it was her PaxForce uniform, pure and simple. The twenty pocket combats. The silicon dogtag. The sweat-stained dirty grey T-shirt stretched tight over steroid shoulders.

'Thank you.' Scooping up her gun, Axl flipped open the holder in a squeal of velcro and spun her Colt hiPower, Black-Jack style, trying it for balance. Not bad, but not as good as the revolver held in his other hand. Where balance went, that was perfect.

'At least I'm not in love with my fucking weapon,' snapped the lieutenant.

'Well, shit,' said Axl, glancing between defMoma and momaDef. 'Maybe you two just never met the right gun.'

Chapter Thirty-four

. . . Knock It Down

Same as it ever was. Chance threw the sixes and he kicked over the dice. By nightfall Axl had a sour taste in his throat no amount of putting one over Colonel Emilio could have shifted.

But the evening began well enough, once he'd managed to persuade the sergeant she really did want to order a conscript to cook Kate and Mai supper. He let momaDef prop Colonel Emilio up against a wall. The man's thick greying hair had stopped the blow from being fatal or even that serious. Axl had to admit to feeling slightly disappointed.

Even Mai could have cooked better but it wouldn't have been half so much fun as making the sergeant order her troopers to do it. What they got served was some kind of crude pancake, made from sour milk and barley flour cooked on a griddle.

'Tsampa,' said Kate when Clone slammed a plate piled high with the pancakes down on the table. Clone was willing to let someone else use his kitchen, just about. But no conscript was going to serve Kate.

With the *tsampa* went preserve, dark as venous blood and made from crushed berries. And even the soyburgers Axl used to flip for McDonalds at the aeropuerto outside Day Effé tasted better. They drank from clay bowls that were greasy round the rim from the yak butter that floated like tiny oil slicks on top of the green tea. It was a safe bet that somewhere in his rations the unconscious Colonel Emilio would have a vacuum-sealed sachet of pure Colombian, but Axl decided to go after that later.

defMoma and momaDef didn't eat, just watched in heavy silence as Kate and Mai sat at the table and calmly ate their supper, talking only to each other as if Axl and the PaxForce officers didn't exist.

Fucking brilliant.

It was costing Kate though, that much was obvious from the way she chewed occasionally at the inside of her mouth. And the way her hand shook slightly as she raised the tea bowl to her lips.

Still, he couldn't have done it better himself, Axl thought. Actually if he was being honest, he couldn't have done it at all. Getting in someone's face by not getting in their face was a skill Axl lacked.

Violent and demented he could do easily enough. Where he originated from that was simple survival stuff, but Mai's simmering contempt and Kate's complete indifference were way more subtle . . .

Kate nodded to Mai, who downed her final cup of buttered tea.

'Thank you,' said Kate to Axl, as he stood to pull back her chair. 'I enjoyed that.'

'Yeah . . .' Mai stuffed the second to last *tsampa* in her mouth, wiped up the remains of the preserve with the only one remaining and put it in her jacket pocket. On her way out of the dining room, she kicked the big wooden door shut with her heel.

'Jesus,' the lieutenant said in disgust. 'How can you eat in the same room as that little tramp. She's got the manners of a pig.'

'Really?' Axl shrugged and did his best to look puzzled. 'You obviously move in better circles . . .' He glanced to where the sergeant was sprawled in a chair, vast breasts flopped onto her jutting gut, black sweat patches Rorschach-blotting her singlet, the only item of clothing she wore on top. Now that Kate and Mai were gone, she was stuffing handfuls of dried apple porridge direct from a foil sachet to her mouth.

The lieutenant's lips twisted, but she was already moving on to what was really bugging her. 'Helping the enemy. Attacking members of PaxForce. You want to tell me . . .'

The rest of momaDef's question was drowned out by the splash of Colonel Emilio vomiting onto marble tiles. Shock or the side effect of concussion, Axl didn't care. The man should still have tried to make it to the window.

'Tell me too,' said the Colonel, wiping his mouth with the back of his hand. 'Or maybe we can skip straight to the bit where I kill you.' He held a baby Uzi in one hand and was using his other to pull himself up, fingers gripping the edge of a Bon tapestry.

It was almost impressive. Most people would have stayed down after a blow to the head like that, bouffant head of greying hair or not. But Emilio was built like a bull, thick bones and thick hide and stupidly stubborn.

Axl had met the type too many times before to remember – and he hadn't liked any of them any better then. So if Rinpoche was thinking of putting in an appearance, now would be a really good time.

Inside Axl's brain blood flow increased to the amygdala, cortisol levels rocketed, adrenaline kicked in and stress jacked up the bmp to his backing track, step on step. It took less than a second.

But the darkening sky outside the window remained empty. Which wasn't to say the silver monkey wasn't keeping track, just that it was running to a different timescale. And besides, it was developing a thing for tight dramatic entrances. Which was fine, because that fitted well with Bon mythology. But then what did you expect from an ur-myth that said the high plateau of Tibet was really a naked goddess, arms and legs splayed wide, lying flat on her back?

Weird shit indeed.

'Recognise me?' Axl asked.

Stood upright, free hand carefully wiping the last specks of vomit from his neat salt and pepper moustache, Colonel Emilio looked carefully at the hard-eyed, gaunt man stood in front of him. He was dressed in the standard 'fugee uniform of felt trousers, grey smock and old boots but there was something about the face, that chin . . . The right answer hovered briefly on the edge of his awareness and then it was gone.

'Didn't think so. Try five weeks back, *La Medicina* . . .'

Recognition hit and Colonel Emilio half raised his Uzi. 'I should have killed you,' the Colonel told Axl flatly.

'Yeah,' said a voice behind Axl. 'Join the queue.'

defMoma and momaDef spun round first, and Rinpoche gave a litle bow. Axl couldn't be arsed, he already knew who it was and besides he was too busy watching, enjoying the shock in Colonel Emilio's eyes.

Time stopped.

Or maybe it speeded up.

Whatever happened, the Colonel, Wireframes and the sergeant freeze-framed and the silver monkey kept talking as Axl walked over to the Colonel and lifted the excited Uzi gently from his fingers.

'Tsongkhapa wants to talk to you.'

'Tsongkhapa?' Axl said, then realised Rinpoche was talking inside his head and the others couldn't have heard it anyway. They were too busy hitting the high notes of a *fugue*.

'Yeah,' said the voice, 'but first get rid of this lot.'

Get rid of them?

'Get them out of this place, away from the Pope.'

Away from the . . . Axl stopped dead. He hoped he didn't look as stupid as he felt. 'There is no Pope,' he said aloud. It was beginning to sound like a mantra and one too many other people seemed not to believe.

Rinpoche laughed. 'Shit happens – and so does reincarnation. And guess what? Sometimes they're the same.' The silver monkey clicked its fingers and the fugue holding the others abruptly ended.

Like someone flipping out of a trance defMoma fumbled desperately for her gun and kept fumbling, fingers scrabbling at her belt until she remembered she was no longer wearing one. 'What the fuck is that?' She said crossly.

'I'm a monkey,' said Rinpoche, 'made of fucking metal, with fucking wings. What the flying fuck do you think I am?'

'I wasn't briefed on this,' said Colonel Emilio to no one in particular.

'No,' said Rinpoche, 'I don't imagine you were.' It nodded at the lieutenant and then waved its paw towards Axl. 'You know who this is?'

The woman shook her head.

'Remember Axl Borja?'

She did. So did her sergeant, Rinpoche could tell from the way her huge shoulders tensed.

'And you have both heard of Cardinal Santo Ducque?' His voice was silkily sarcastic.

Something unspoken passed between the two women, brief as a blip of static. Anger, contempt, glee . . . Whichever it was, Axl didn't like it, but the flicker of emotion wasn't there long enough for him to identify it. All he saw was Colonel Emilio shake his head slightly at momaDef and defMoma.

'Yes,' said the lieutenant carefully, 'everyone knows the Cardinal.'

'Well,' Rinpoche's smile was cold. 'This man works for him. Something your Colonel already knows. And currently I work for Axl, sort of . . .'

With a sigh, Colonel Emilio dipped into a pouch on his belt and pulled out an olive grey Sony walkWear, military issue. In the time it took the machine to boot up, he'd unfolded a pair of floating-focus Raybans and clumsily velcroed a tiny keypad to the inside of one wrist.

Some sentient bloody spySat with delusions wasn't what Colonol Emilio wanted. Not what he wanted at all. True, he'd heard rumours of another operative working the area, but *Axl*?

And anyway, the idea was that the operative and PaxForce didn't cross.

Sat on the window sill, Rinpoche grinned at the Colonel, thin lips pulled back to reveal extremely nasty-looking teeth. As if it too could see the frames and menus scrolling ghost-like and translucent beyond Colonel Emilio's eyes.

And try as the Colonel might, the digital grab he'd taken of the silver monkey didn't pull up any information on screen. Irritated, Colonel Emilio loaded another grab and reran the visual recognitions software. Absolute zilch. Between them, WorldBank, the IMF and PaxForce had the best military neural net in existence and so far as it was concerned the bloody monkey didn't exist.

'Classified,' Rinpoche told him smugly and jerked his thumb at Axl. 'Like his mission.'

The Colonel was about to say he was cleared for access to the highest levels but the words died as the Sony RomReader suddenly went dead and he could see nothing but sick-making white fuzz. And when he ripped off the Raybans, he got the silver monkey grinning at him.

'You responsible for this *animal*?' Colonel Emilio asked Axl, unstrapping the wrist-pad in disgust . . .

'I think it's probably the other way round,' said Axl and the silver monkey suddenly looked at him, head turned sideways, as if it was vaguely impressed. Or at least, as if he wasn't quite the idiot it had assumed.

Besides, given the endless scroll of crap he'd accepted without reading when he first bonded with the Colt, Axl was willing to lay odds that MacroShite had some sub-clause to say AIs reincarnating between hardware systems invalidated the agreement. 'Look,' said Colonel Emilio, 'I think we should get the lines of command clear here . . .'

Nodding down to the revolver he was holding, Axl smiled. 'I think we already did.'

Rinpoche grinned at the Colonel. 'Missing you already.'

It tipped itself backwards off the stone sill, wings suddenly spreading and growing. By the time Colonel Emilio reached the open window, the animal was already riding up into the air currents, Cocheforet spreading small and isolated beneath it.

The Colonel and Axl reached a simple compromise. Probably the only one not to involve Uzis, revolvers and one of them actually having to shoot the other rather than just talking about it. PaxForce wouldn't interfere with Axl's mission, whatever that was, if he didn't interfere with theirs.

By then Axl had already insisted that, in his opinion, there *was* no Pope Joan or Father Sylvester on Samsara and never had been. Joan was digital dust in backed-up newsfeeds. Unfortunately Axl didn't sound convincing, even to himself.

And Axl left out what Rinpoche had said to him. *One*, because he wasn't sure it had ever happened and *two*, because, even if it had, he needed time to process the data.

'So, you're just at Cocheforet for the sightseeing?' Colonel Emilio smiled and smoothed his moustache, then patted his hair into place and winced as his hand met the bump left by Axl's revolver. He stopped smiling.

His scalp was so thick, Axl realised it had bruised but the blow hadn't even produced blood. Next time he was going to have to hit the man harder.

'Yeah,' said Axl, 'that and my health. The Cardinal thought I needed to take the air.' He nodded down to the guns he'd piled safely on the floor while the others were fuguing, inviting Colonel Emilio to take back his Uzi. The fact Axl had a revolver clutched firmly in his hand made it that much easier to make the offer.

'Okay,' said Axl, 'you remember how it works. You leave Kate and Mai alone and I leave you three alone. Mess with Mai or Kate and you get an instant lead implant. No warning.'

The Colonel looked at Axl, eyes burning. 'You *are* the Cardinal's man?'

Axl nodded.

'Then maybe you aren't as smart as you think . . .' Red-faced and furious, he hovered on the edge of some indiscretion, some truth he wouldn't be able to take back. And what was really interesting was the sudden flicker of doubt that stopped him going over the edge and the way both Wireframes and the fat sergeant tensed up as they waited to see what the Colonel might say.

He said nothing.

'What about the Cardinal?' Axl asked.

'You know,' said Colonel Emilio calmly, as if he'd never started the previous conversation. 'There's just one thing puzzles me.'

Only one . . . ? Sweet fuck, thought Axl, knowing there'd never been a day he wouldn't have been delighted to say the same. 'Really, what's that?'

'Just who are you betraying? I mean,' Colonel Emilio's smile was cold, 'obviously you plan to betray someone. But is it Kate or the Cardinal?' He paused, shrugged and pulled at his moustache. 'I just thought I'd ask.'

Chapter Thirty-five

Zazen/Sunyata

Ice grated over rock, reversed and looped into digital fuzz. Sonars blipped under bleak overlays of dolphin funeral cries. Every note was degraded, flat. Emptiness within emptiness. There was no chord he recognised. Nothing that he'd ever heard before. Even the snare line was gone, the noise ugly and a-rhythmic. This was what you got if you fed anger and disgust through a backing track. A meshing of cognitive and aural dissonance.

The Colonel's question had eaten away what little chance Axl had of sleeping. Crawling through the back of his mind like a king snake, it had disturbed cerebral undergrowth better left untouched, leaving behind its trail of slime.

There was a bed still made up for him on the first floor. A mattress and a blanket but, unlike the Inn this time both were clean. All the same, Axl chose to spend that night sat on a wooden chair in the monastery dining room, watching his spinning timecode count itself down and keeping one eye on the overgrown slope down to the village.

All the doors into Escondido were locked. Windows that had shutters were closed and bolted, Axl knew, he'd done it himself watched by a suspicious Clone. Only the window in the dining room by which he sat and brooded was still open.

He would kill the Colonel. The man was as good as dead . . .

Axl was still silently raging – at himself, at Colonel Emilio and at the Cardinal when Kate gave a tentative knock and pushed her way into the huge room to find Axl slumped in a chair, the cold barrel of his revolver resting parallel to his face. Salt tears ran unnoticed down his cheeks as he stared at mist that filled the valley and hid the pitiful village below.

'The last of them just left.' Kate said it like she couldn't believe her own words, which she couldn't. 'They've set up a new HQ in the village.

'How did you do it? I mean, why did you . . . ?' She wanted to reach out and take away his gun if he'd let her. Touch his hand or shoulder, anything to stop the track of tears etched like acid into the dirt on his face. But she was afraid of Axl; and she knew he was afraid of himself.

So instead Kate just pulled up another chair and folded her arms, tucking her restless hands into the grey shahtoosh she wore over shirt and chinos. A cold breeze blew in through the open window to make the wall tapestries of multi-armed gods ripple and sway. She hardly noticed. Nothing that had happened made sense. First the man had given her back the lost memory beads, then he'd driven PaxForce out of her house and now he was crying like a desolate child, his face so bleak it could have been cut from ice. But if his hollow face was cold, his voice was empty of everything, even echo.

'You want to know why?' He asked. Inside his head the king snake was stirring and Axl was too tired to face it down.

Kate nodded. Yes, she did. She didn't operate well in the dark. Besides beyond that, she *needed* to know. Kate was coming to believe he really was on her side, whichever side that was. She just didn't know why.

'There was a man . . .' He told her, then stopped his story before he even really got started, correcting himself. The person hadn't really been a man, more a boy. Except that wasn't relevant, not really.

Axl ran through different ways of telling Kate why the Colonel had left quietly and decided events only made sense if he went back to the *WarChild*. Everything he'd become came out of that.

The shit that went down before *WarChild* wasn't part of the story, or even him. Not now. That chapter had just been about another wrong kid in the wrong place at the wrong time.

Killer Kid. The moniker was chosen by a machine. Though the CySat PR who plucked it out of air laden with cigar smoke gave the impression it was just another flash of brilliance which had dropped into his mind. This was around the time Axl decided he was going to take the psych tests and that if he passed he was going to sign their contract.

'Do you remember *WarChild*?'

She did, though she'd probably only seen it on repeats. And Axl didn't expect her to approve.

'Remember the round-faced blond kid with the Russian gun?'

'The Killer?'

Of course he was a killer, Axl thought. That was what the child was trained for. No one had told him it was wrong. So when his CO was shot on IMF orders, the kid didn't go after the eleven-year old Guatemalan who pulled the trigger, he hit the officers of the local IMF committee that processed the order.

It wasn't an official *WarChild* response, but Axl was wired for sight and sound so 163 million viewers looked through his baby-blues as he crippled two *WeGuard* and then gunned down fourteen suits sat round a table made from endangered hardwood. *WarChild* retired him after that. He was thirteen.

She knew who he meant, because about the only thing you could say for CySat, C3N and the other feeds that hovered round war like flies on a corpse, was that it meant everyone shared the same heroes and villains, give or take Jihad leaders and kooks like the Montana militia.

'Joan said Cardinal Santo Ducque once gave him confession.'

'Really?' Axl's smile was so thin his mouth was no more than a knife wound slashed into his jaw. Absolution was about the one choice the Cardinal had never offered — and just about the last thing Axl would have asked for. God didn't exist for him, not the Cardinal's or anyone else's, come to that.

'You've heard that the kid was a clone . . .' Axl said.

Kate looked so shocked that Axl almost smiled properly.

'It isn't true.'

'How about, that he was the Cardinal's bastard?'

That wasn't true either. Axl had stolen a hair from the old man's comb and sent it with fifty dollars to a clinic in Sante Fé. The kind of place that hijacked links from genetics' websites. He got the result two days later. No genetic pointers in common.

'That one's bullshit, too,' Axl assured her. 'But you know who I'm talking about?' He paused to check she did. 'Well, I'm the kid.'

The pupils of Kate's eyes exploded with shock, only to pinprick immediately with fear, as if blinded by light. And the gasp she swallowed almost choked her. He was waiting and there was nothing she could say.

Within her silence, Kate could hear the call of circling kites and the mutter that running water makes as it slides over gravel. The air reaching her outside was cold and fresh, but oxygen-poor and stretched gossamer thin. The world, this world, felt very new and fragile.

Axl watch faint goosebumps spreading along the inside of her wrist, while she held one hand to her mouth, knuckles pressed hard against her lips. A strand of black hair curled down her forehead where it had escaped from a steel barrette keeping the rest of her hair in place.

Low down to the side of her neck, and just above the briefest glimpse of breastbone seen through the open collar of her shirt, beat an artery that slowed even as Axl watched it.

She was getting her courage back. And the slow butterfly beat of her blood told him something that Kate was working her body hard not to let him know. She was afraid of him, but there was no way she going to admit it.

Instinct told her to step back. And she was fighting her instinct. Axl found himself being impressed by that. Stamping down gut reactions took training or tight self-control.

'*You* are Axl Borja?'

Axl nodded. And watched as Kate tried to make sense of something that didn't, could never make sense.

'I thought you were dead.'

'And Hell was flipping burgers,' said Axl, nodding again. 'So did I.'

Sad songs. Not ersatz, but real.

'I killed someone,' Axl added after a while, when the notes were gone. 'People say you should never go back. Well I did. I ended up here.'

'Mexico has the death penalty.' It wasn't quite an accusation but it was definitely a question. One that wasn't too difficult to answer.

'I have friends . . .'

'The Cardinal?'

Axl thought of the old bastard, probably still sat in his octagonal study. Staring longingly out of that stone window at tiny butterfly boats dotted like dust on the silver surface of the Caribbean, while thousands of petitioners waited for his attention in the sweltering anterooms, dressed in their best clothes.

Friends in high places . . .

This time Kate did comfort him, with a feather-light brush of her fingers against his shoulder. He wanted to tell her everything then. To warn her against himself, against what he would do in the old bastard's name to her life and her world.

Chapter Thirty-six

God's Fist

Outside the dining room someone slammed a door loudly, and inside the room silence settled. One of those embarrassed, awkward silences that happen when a person you don't like or hardly know has said too much.

There was a gap opening between them, almost visibly. A gap bigger than the hand's breadth of floor that either could have stepped over. Except Kate didn't know how – or if she even wanted to – and Axl didn't dare.

Axl desperately needed to say something, but his major problem was he had no idea what, because the truth didn't seem like an intelligent option . . . Falling for the person you intended to betray wasn't an area that any episode of Black Jack had ever covered. And though everyone knew about Stockholm Syndrome, Axl had a nasty feeling he'd just been memed with its flip side.

No matter that Kate wasn't beautiful. Nor was he. She wasn't even that clean. Her black hair needed washing. She smelt of rose water over sweat as if she hadn't had the time recently to bath. And there were scratches on both wrists and blisters on her fingers, painful evidence that she wasn't used to manual work. Her hands trembled so hard it looked like she was headed straight for the brick wall of a sulphate come down, except drugs weren't her style.

This was the woman who'd hit Mai, Axl reminded himself. And if Rinpoche was right and somehow the Pope really was here in some form, rather than just being data on some memory beads, then this was who he'd need to pressure for the information.

It made no difference to the way he felt.

And he wanted her approval so badly his stomach hurt and he could taste the need like blood in the back of his throat.

In a second she would turn away from him, find a reason why she needed to be in some other room. And the slowly-tearing spider's web of understanding that had briefly been spun between them would finally snap. He could see it in the tension seeping back into her face. All that held Kate there now was politeness. Inside her head, she had to be inventing excuses to go.

By the afternoon they would be worse than strangers. If she thought of him at all, it would be as a killer, as what was left if you took away fame from a child star. No more than the wind-blown husk of that blue-eyed, deadly blond boy. And all the half misremembered rumours would shoulder their way out of her subconscious to push aside what fragile sympathy she had for him.

That he was a clone Kate already half believed. And if not the Cardinal's bastard then surely Axl had been his catamite, the old man's bum boy. Or else Axl somehow had his claws into the old man: as if it was him and not the Cardinal who only had to pull back his thin lips to reveal sharp teeth.

That's the way it would go, Axl just knew it.

And she wouldn't even come close to getting the rumours right, to digging far enough through the shit to hit real truth. Because no one else but the Cardinal knew that. All of it had to be visible, Axl knew that. Why else did anyone think he hated mirrors so much? Or loved guns, for that matter . . .

'Come with me to the village,' Kate suggested, standing up.

Axl stared at her.

'I need to check the situation. PaxForce . . .' Her voice trailed away. She'd seen and heard enough of them in action the previous night to be scared of what she was going to find at Cocheforet.

Axl nodded, suddenly understanding her jumpiness, cursing himself. 'You need me to go as your bodyguard.' He didn't make it a question, just a simple statement.

'If that's the way you want to think of it. Though Clone won't like the idea.' Kate's smile was so slight Axl thought he'd imagined it. 'Wait here while I get changed . . .'

She returned to the dining room wearing black jeans and heavy leather boots that buckled across the ankle. On top she wore a vest, black enough to swallow light and fitted so exactly it had to be grown for her alone. Spider's silk could stop a knife. Better than that, bullets could be extracted by pulling on the threads they'd wound-up on their way in.

If Kate noticed Axl register how tightly her vest fitted or the fullness of her breasts she didn't say anything, merely shuffled herself into a loose black jersey.

'Are you ready?'

As if checking, Axl touched his hand to the small of his back, feeling for the wooden handle of his revolver. Yeah, ready and willing. Hell, he'd been both for as long as anyone could remember . . .

Scrub that. Half his life he'd been so drunk or wired the only person to believe he was ready for anything was him. Just as he'd always believed that deep down he was rational, well-mannered and emotionally balanced, no matter how untrue all that was turning out to be.

Black Jack was a kid's show. US skins over Japanese-designed frames, cheap Chinese coding. *WarChild* was a battlefield soap that used real meat. That was the truth.

'Sure,' said Axl, holding the door open for Kate. 'I am now.'

Axl knew next to nothing about Samsara, he realised as his boots slid on mud and he grabbed a rhododendron branch to stop himself falling. Then Axl released the branch, slid another few yards down the slope and grabbed another. Getting down the narrow path was easy once you got the hang of it.

Samsara was cold, obviously. The air was thin, ditto. And most of it seemed to be mud. That last fact hadn't made it into Dr Jane's chirpy little induction show back at Vajrayana. Oh yeah, and it was bound round with enough international law to keep the 'fugees almost safe. Though that wasn't the result of a freak outbreak of humanity, even Axl knew that.

Straight media manipulation, based on a one-sentence pitch by the Dalai Lama, had sold Samsara to the UN. *No more refugees.* Not on Earth anyway. The rest was sleight of hand and window dressing. And the media he manipulated was CySat.

Ninety-eight percent of the world watched the same shit, day in/day out, and CySat had provided it for as long as anyone could remember. Which demographically was about fifteen minutes. *SickWard*, *FirstTime*, *SpacePup3* were the staples that delivered viewers to ad agencies worldwide, albeit using semiotically-tailored local plotlines, relevant franchise references and genotypes overlaid onto basic rayframe v'Actors. So Sammi the wacky Moslem rich kid with the lovingly-restored Mercedes 612 in the Bangladeshi version of *FirstTime* was the HondaCRZ-driving teen software millionaire Ryuchi in the Japanese version, was Leo the spoilt New York . . .

But over and above that, CySat had always provided political muscle. Drop a frag hag like Passion with her little flying camera into a war zone and three hours later a significant slice of the world were vid-mailing congress or parliament with demands that whatever *Passion's Passion* was complaining about be stopped, immediately . . .

Courtesy of CySat nV starving kids to death and blaming famine or refusing to let *HelpFirst* air freight them medicine and calling it sanctions had become vote losers. Samsara solved that problem. It also got the Dalai Lama out of Beijing's hair and gave Indonesia, Texas and the Ukraine somewhere to ship those dissidents too high-profile to kill. It was small wonder the UN vote was near unanimous.

As solutions went, it was right out of this world.

'What are you thinking?' Kate asked suddenly. She'd stopped to let Axl go ahead and was looking down at where he stood on a broad ledge, one hand gripping a bush. Ahead of him the track was even softer underfoot, the path muddier and the overhanging rhododendrons so thick the branches twisted around each other like flash-frozen serpents.

He didn't want to answer, but he did anyway. Kate had that effect.

'About Samsara.'

'You hate the place that much?'

'Hate it?' Axl hesitated watching Kate slide down the track towards him, her fingers finding and releasing overhead branches in quick succession. Kate was using a different way down to the village, one less obvious than the main track but a lot steeper.

'I don't hate Samsara,' Axl told Kate. 'I wouldn't want to live here, but I don't hate it.' And that's where that conversation would have died – Axl decided later – if the zipped-tight, self-contained Kate Mercarderes hadn't lost her footing, boot heels gouging dark scars into leaf mould as she fought for balance.

She might have kept upright, she might have fallen, but Axl caught her anyway. Whipping out his right arm as she flailed past. Pain ripped up Axl's arm. For a split second it looked like the branch he gripped might crack. But the man didn't even notice. He was far too busy watching Kate.

Fury?

Embarrassment?

Axl didn't know what painted her face a sudden red and didn't much care. Very slowly Axl shifted towards her and when Kate didn't back away he rested his forehead against hers, ridiculously softly.

As needy as some teenage kid.

'You all right?' Kate asked. Her breath smelt of *tsampa*.

'No, I'm not.' Axl opened his mouth, then shut it again. Crunch time. What he was about to do was fuck-wit stupid. Flayed, flesh-cut-back-and-stripped-to-the-bone dumb. But when had that ever stopped him?

The mind threw up walls for a purpose, to keep shit in or keep light out, it didn't much matter which. Kicking them down went against everything Axl believed in. There was the stuff in there Axl didn't admit to himself. He'd have to be an idiot to tell it to some woman he hardly knew . . .

'Look,' said Axl. 'You really think you know the truth about that kid . . . ?' About me, he meant.

Her head flicked up in that defiant gesture Axl had begun to recognise, then she caught herself. 'What would I know?' She said it sadly.

'The press releases had me down as a ghost. Do I look like hollow?'

Yes. No. Kate started to shake her head, hesitated . . . *I don't know. Yes, probably.* She'd been born, grown up and educated within the walls of the Vatican and in all the twenty-seven years of her life she hadn't met a single clone, other than Clone that was. And he was Marne release #2.1 of a combat model, which was different. She wouldn't recognise a batch-reared ghost if she walked through a crowd of them. That was the point. The only real way to tell was strip out some DNA and check for the copyright line.

'Does it matter?'

'Yes it does,' said Axl as he stepped back because that was the only way he was going to get through the next few minutes. Though he didn't look like someone stepped back and he didn't feel like it either.

'I'm not a clone.' Axl held up his hand to stop whatever Kate was about to say. 'I'm . . .' *Much worse* were the words he was choking on.

The deep green of the rhododendrons began its slow spin

around him: the glimpses of the distant sky seemed higher than ever, a far cold blue that had to be impossible. All he really wanted to do was sleep, to put his head to the damp leaf mould and let in the darkness. Forever if possible.

Conditioning, Axl thought, and wondered drunkenly why he hadn't realised it before. 'You know what I am?'

She didn't.

'I'm a fucking foetus,' Axl said through gritted teeth and promptly blacked out, the wet earth he'd wanted to embrace coming up to meet him as his brain hit a system fault and clicked out the lights.

Kate sighed.

When Axl came to his head was in Kate's lap, and she was stroking his cheek with one finger, following the line of a cheekbone. What he thought was a two-beat drum track was just his heart.

'Oh, you're with us again.' She dropped her hand quickly.

'Yeah. Looks like it.' Axl struggled upright and got as far as kneeling before he felt sick again. Waves of nausea pulling at his gut.

'You were telling me all about being aborted,' Kate's voice was neutral.

'I was what . . . ?'

'You told me everything,' said Kate. 'The whole fucking lot.' It was the first time he'd heard Kate swear.

Her dark eyes were locked on his face, not cold or fierce but lit with sympathy that was almost unbearable. Everything else about her was studiedly casual. Rigorously non-threatening. Just how odd it was to be crouched opposite a woman who was worried she might make him afraid, Axl couldn't begin to tell her.

'I really told you?' The blackness that had been crawling around the edges of his sight blew away as if it were smoke and Axl no longer felt sick. Inside his ribs his heart kicked back into a regular rhythm. There was no way Axl could know it, but his body levels of cortisol and the catecholamines began to fall. All he knew was that his soundtrack slowed, softened slightly.

'So when did you find out?' Kate asked. She sat back on her heels and casually scratched the inside of one thigh, then blushed when she caught him watching. 'You going to tell me or not?'

He did.

Eighteen weeks of womb time was what he got. That's what they told him at the home anyway. Enough to produce tentative REM and thumb sucking, but leave him the wrong side of the survivability line. That was how long it took the kid to get her shit together enough to book a clinic. The clinic was a charity job, obviously enough. Cash wasn't something she had a lot of, they'd told him that too. Made sure he knew freebase came first and getting rid of him came second. The home wanted him to know how lucky he was good people had come along.

When did he find out? Sweet Jesus.

'I always knew,' Axl said flatly. 'Sometimes it just meant less.'

'You want to expand on that?'

It was Axl's turn to sigh. Grabbed from the disposal bin of an abortion clinic by a right-to-lifer hit team and grown to term in a Matsui artificial womb. Paraded as a toddler before judges, women who lunch, elderly patrons as an example of what their charity could achieve. Shit happened and mostly, it seemed to Kate, shit had been happening to the man in front of her. It was like someone just smashed a dam that held back a life's worth of backed-up emotions. And then she realised with a shiver that someone had and it had been her.

He was still talking, telling her how he'd been sat stealing time from a public smartbook in the annex of the NY library on 42nd, using 'trodes to pop frames almost faster than his brain could render. Worthless shit all of it, the kind of stuff all eleven-year-old boys, not just street kids hide behind 'trodes to skim. Some animal fuck sites, *Taiwanese pissing schoolgirls*, cheats for getting the 6 million volt nanchuku in *Mishima*, the usual stuff . . . A bit of bomb making, some half-arsed chemical formulae for a kitchen-sink version of *BetterThanIce*.

There was no site that toggled his memory, nothing meaningful like hitting on some dumb schmuck *Fight For Life* site, skimming the mugshots and thinking *shit, that's me* . . . He just remembered being six and getting shown a lump of purple flesh the size of his fist, with frog-like legs and arms. Whatever it was in the glass case, it looked very dead.

'You know what the blonde-haired matron said to me?' Axl asked Kate.

Kate didn't and she didn't even want to guess.

'You've got a sister to look after.' Next time Axl saw his *sister* five months had gone by. She was still small and still purple but more-obviously alive.

In between they'd grafted her to a synthetic placenta and stitched the placenta into the pre-stretched uterus of a mother for Jesus. When that failed they fell back on a rubber womb, growing her in a nutrient and oxygen-rich solution of transparent gel.

'But she was still one up on me,' Axl said with a bleak smile. 'I was picked up as an afterthought. When some *God's Fist* commando grabbed a bucket on her way out, having slapped a .45 through the head of an intern, nurse and receptionist at the clinic . . .'

He stopped briefly, listening to a noise in the distance but didn't really pay it the attention he should have done. He was still too busy talking.

'You ever get really cross as a kid,' Axl asked, 'so cross you say you didn't ask to be born?'

Kate nodded.

'Well, my mother didn't ask for me to be born either. But the home still wanted me to demand the clinic release details so I could track her down.' Axl shrugged. 'Hi, you remember that walk-in, hobble-out abortion you had ten years ago . . . Well, the clinic got hit by Fight-for-Lifers that evening and I was the pile of slop at the bottom of the bucket. Yeah, I'm pleased to meet you too . . .'

'Enough,' said Kate. 'Stop it.' She was crying, the surface skim of water on her eyes magnifying pupils until it felt like she looked right into Axl's head. Which wasn't where anyone should be allowed to go.

'Yeah, enough already.' Axl stood up. Suddenly alert as a crimson-horned pheasant crashed into the air further down the path. Fear ate worm-like at his brain and it was nothing as wasteful as a memory: more of a dampened reflex, something hardwired. Guitar chords splintered, fast as panic.

'Down,' Axl slammed the crouching woman flat. Kate didn't get to protest because Axl was already kneeling over her, with one knee up and one down, finding his balance as he thumbed back the hammer of his revolver and sighted in on somebody crashing through the bushes.

Black-powder exploded. Axl's first bullet slamming into the trunk of a stunted oak, stripping away bark to reveal splintered, glistening wood beneath. Beautifully balanced it might have been but the revolver still fired slightly wide.

Which was just as well. Otherwise Mai would have been dead instead of just scared, shaking and white-hot furious. And then things would have been really fucked. How badly fucked, no one quite knew, not back then.

Chapter Thirty-seven

Learning To Howl . . .

Axl was still sighting for his second shot when Mai came to an abrupt halt, staring open-mouthed at the revolver. Very slowly, Axl lowered the hammer.

'You fuck-wit . . .'

Axl nodded. Agreeing with her could only save time.

'You want to kill me?'

Axl shook his head. If Mai was shaken then so was he. Slamming random shots into the undergrowth wasn't his style. Come to that, it wasn't any style at all.

'They've got Clone,' Mai gasped, holding tight to a tree trunk, jagged breath ripping her throat like broken glass.

'Who's got . . .' Kate asked but Axl already knew.

'The soldiers' said Mai.

Not PaxForce, IMF troops, or WorldBank, but *the soldiers*. The mute, dumb cry of civilians everywhere.

'Where is he?'

'In the square . . .'

Axl realised she meant that patch of mud with the water pump in front of the Inn. And then he asked her the difficult one, not that the question really needed asking. It was going to be some variation on *tell me*.

'What are they doing?'

Mai's answer locked in her throat. Whatever choice the Colonel had made it was enough to widen her eyes and tug down the corners of her childish mouth.

'The box has got a handle . . .'

Moscow telephone. 'They've got him wired for sound,' Axl told Kate, then realised she had no idea what he was talking about. 'A hand-cranked electrical generator.'

'He's dumb,' she protested.

'They'll have a cat.' Matsui cats came in a box the size of a Lucky Strike packet, with no moving parts, no user skill necessary. They were entirely waterproof and shockproof. All you do is run the box across a casualty's skull to get a down and dirty snapshot of their brain in action.

That was what the battlefield CATscan was designed to do anyway, but its main use turned out to be something else entirely. All the tiny screen ever showed up was a flare of purple and pink wrapped across the mottled folds of a small, dirt-grey walnut, but it was usually enough.

At least it was for any soldier who wanted a crude checksum that the person being questioned was telling the truth.

Wireframes had Clone stripped naked and nailed to a rattan chair taken from the Inn. She'd also taken Leon's cart and ripped off its back and sides so everyone could see where Clone sat shivering on the raised chair. Someone had kicked out the chair's seat before nailing Clone in place. The sergeant probably, she looked like someone who enjoyed her work.

Axl didn't need to check the rest, because it was already obvious what he'd find. From the stinking mound of shit under the chair where Clone had voided his bowels to wires running from his nipples, testicles or anus. Axl had seen it before. Whatever grunts might boast drunkenly in the franchised brothels of *The Last Boer*, imagination wasn't something PaxForce conscripts majored in. Even the heavy roof nails pinning his feet to the wooden cart were a cliché. Something they'd seen done on a newsfeed.

The huge clone's arms had been held down and his wrists crudely nailed to the wooden back legs of the chair. His balls hung through the kicked-out chair bottom, tied round with string to make them protrude better.

Hooked through his ear lobes were a couple of thin wires that ran back to momaDef, who held in her manicured hands what looked like an old-fashioned music box with a handle on its side.

'You are going to help me, aren't you?'

When the naked man didn't answer, momaDef cranked the handle five or six times between her first finger and thumb and Clone arched backwards in his chair, bloody wrists tugging against the nails as his leg muscles locked and the man tried to jerk upwards but couldn't.

'Stop . . .'

The lieutenant smiled when she saw Kate. And this time when she jerked the handle back into action, momaDef kept it turning until Clone juddered in his chair like a puppet.

'Wait,' Axl grabbed Kate and tightened his grip until Kate stopped struggling.

'You can't do anything,' he told her fiercely, which was the truth, the whole truth and nothing but . . . But that still didn't mean Kate wanted to hear it.

Up on the cart Clone tumbled back into his seat and momaDef smiled breathlessly. She had a fine line of sweat beaded across her upper lip and damp patches under the arms of her otherwise immaculate T-shirt. Something told Axl it wasn't from the effort of turning that handle.

'Now, you *are* going to help me, aren't you?'

Clone nodded frantically even before momaDef's fingers wrapped themselves round the handle. But nodding wasn't enough to stop her having one last spin. Round went the handle and a noise more animal than human hissed between Clone's clenched teeth as muscles locked across his body and watery shit squirted onto the wooden boards beneath the chair.

That was when Clone noticed Kate standing there in the crowd. Face stricken, a thin trickle of blood down her chin from a bitten lip.

He blushed.

'Enough,' said Axl and stepped forward. Even though he knew that now wasn't the time.

The lieutenant reached for the little handle and Axl repeated himself. Only this time he had the revolver in his hand, hammer thumbed back and muzzle pointing straight at her face. No, not nasty enough. With a shrug, Axl lowered the target to her stomach. Seventy-six hours was how long it took to die from a gut wound and where momaDef was concerned Axl reckoned that was too quick by half.

'Look around you,' the lieutenant said. Not that Axl needed to. His whole upper body was covered with a rash of tiny red laser dots, right down to two in his gun hand. One look at Kate told Axl the dots were all over his face too. Raghead measles was what PaxForce called his symptoms. And in most cases RhM proved fatal.

It was a straight stand-off, the kind that used to get labelled Mexican before everyone got prissy.

'What good does this do?' Axl demanded, jerking his head towards Clone. Even to Axl the words sounded too loud.

'He's going to tell me what I want to know,' momaDef admitted, after leaving a gap long enough to tell Axl she'd debated not answering his question at all.

'Look at him . . .'

The lieutenant did, reluctantly.

'. . . what can that tell you?'

'Where to find Father Sylvester.' The lieutenant said it like he was stupid.

Behind him, Axl almost felt Kate freeze, her tension so obvious it was a wonder momaDef didn't put her up there in the chair.

'You see,' said the lieutenant, 'Father Sylvester is here and this man is going to take me to him, aren't you?'

Nailed to his chair, Clone nodded, carefully not looking at Kate.

Chapter Thirty-eight

. . . In the Society of Wolves

It looked like some picnic, thought Kate. The kind she and Joan used to take in the hills behind Castel Gandolfo when Joan was still alive. Lavender and rosemary suffusing the warm breeze as they rode across scrub-covered slopes and through ancient, thousand-year-old olive groves.

But that was then and this was frightening.

Hooves sank into cold mud or struck sparks from stones as the horses headed up track towards El Escondido. It was drizzling, but Kate had grown used to that. Surprisingly the lieutenant rode less well than Kate would have expected.

Kate didn't ride at all. She walked behind with Axl glued to her side like someone had splattered them both with a goo gun, not that paxForce grunts carried anything that non-lethal.

Around the time the horses had finally arrived, the black woman with the thin, twisted dreadlocks gave a signal for her troops to find some target that wasn't Axl. Kate didn't know what the signal was, just that one minute Axl's body and face were breeding red dots like lice, next moment all the dots were gone.

Kate was shocked at how relieved she felt.

Now she followed Clone, defMoma and the horses past rough juniper scrub and through the darkness of a rhododendron tunnel, under the twisting branches that closed out the sky over her head as if they were petrified worm-casts.

The high-falling foss splashed away to her right, water plummeting down the valley side to the pool below. And the slight wind blowing down the tunnel into her face hung heavy with the smell of damp earth. Any hound following after their party could track them by the stink of horses and the sour undercurrents of blood, shit and fear.

Kate shivered. For herself and for the huge naked man who stood in his saddle and rode straight-legged up ahead. They were tramping down the dead. Ground fine, unviralled and spread thin it might have been, but the earth beneath their hooves and feet had still once been flesh. But then, was that so different to back on Earth? Except there the dirt was carapaced over with concrete or marble and sterilised by history.

'What?' Axl asked.

What was she thinking? Kate almost said, 'about anything but Clone'. Instead she shrugged. 'That this is all meat. . .' She nodded at the track and the leaf-encrusted mud glued to her boots, then jumped at the touch of his fingers on her wrist.

'I don't understand.'

'There's nothing to understand,' Kate said crossly. And there wasn't. Life happened and then someone got left to clean up the mess. Someone like her. How difficult could comprehending that be?

Just before the track climbed the steepest part of the lower valley towards Escondido it branched off, the main track kept on up to the ramshackle monastery, a narrower path headed downwards again through undergrowth towards the mute roar of falling water.

'Through there?' momaDef demanded when Clone reined in his horse.

The big man nodded, jerking his heavy chin towards the narrower path.

'You go first,' momaDef told him. 'Any problems I'll shoot you, understand?'

What the tongueless Clone grunted might have been agreement but sounded more like an insult. And then he kicked his bleeding feet heavily into the flank of his horse and crashed away through the bushes, remembering just in time to duck as he went under a snaking branch.

'Dumb fuck.' momaDef was after him even before her fat sergeant had realised what was happening. It took the handful of conscripts a second to work out what the sergeant was shouting about and then they jogged after the fat woman, snubPups snagging on every branch despite being held tight to their chests like regulations demanded . . .

Get lucky, thought Axl, kill each other. Which would at least save him the effort. Not that he was bothered by the grunts. But taking out defMoma, momaDef and Colonel Emilio was going to be a pleasure if the chance ever arose.

Tracking Clone was effortless. He'd signposted his passing in branches on both sides of the path which were snapped back to white bone and in leaf mould churned deep with hoof-marks.

All the same Axl took his time, not wanting Kate to reach Clone too early. Because whatever the lieutenant would do to the big man when she finally caught up with him was likely to be slow and nasty . . . And Axl wanted to avoid Kate having to watch that. There was enough anguish built up behind her troubled dark eyes already. He'd seen the way her head jerked and her shoulders hunched every time someone mentioned the dead pope by name.

By hanging back Axl hoped to stop Kate seeing Clone tortured and killed. Only, when Kate and he finally reached the mountain pool, it seemed the lieutenant had blown her chance to do either. Clone took the dive himself, taking momaDef with him, from a point on the path that dropped fifteen metres into the ice-cold waters of the foss pool below.

All of this Axl put together as he and Kate walked down to the water's edge. He based it mostly on bloody footprints he'd seen back up the path. That had been where Clone dismounted to whip his horse into the distance, the man's spoor track climbing the path's upper edge just high enough for him to be able to turn, hide in bushes on the slope above and hurl momaDef off her horse down into the foss pool as she galloped past.

Primitive undoubtedly, but hard to counteract.

But putting it together from clues wasn't really necessary, obvious ones or not. Because the fall suddenly imprinted onto Axl's vision. The roar of the tumbling waterfall mixing abruptly with crashing synth, the fierce exaltation written on Clone's face. Then a splash, silence and the darkness of deep water.

Axl shook his head quickly. He'd arrived at the edge of the foss and the huge sergeant was waiting for them.

'You did this.' She stood in front of Kate, her words stripped raw with emotion, and that emotion wasn't just fury. Tears filled the woman's eyes and real sorrow was in her round face. A muscle tugged at her jaw with almost cartoon-like regularity.

'It's *your* fault,' she insisted, fists clenched. The only thing that stood between Kate and the grief-stricken defMoma wrapping her hands round Kate's throat, was Axl, and his head was still spinning from the snapshot replay of Clone's fall. But what he wanted to say was . . .

'Her fault? How the fuck do you work that out?' The words were ripped from his head, spoken in a hard metallic rasp that sounded far away, though it came from where Rinpoche scrabbled up between two rocks. 'She wasn't even here, was she? You stupid fuck.'

Rinpoche steered Axl and Kate firmly away from defMoma and then busied itself with folding sodden wings tight against its back. 'United in death,' Rinpoche said with a grim smile. 'Well, at least they'll have no trouble bringing them up together.'

'Oh and you'd better have this,' the monkey dropped a cold glass blade into Axl's hand, 'Call it a present . . . You know,' the silver monkey added suddenly. 'I like this place. Really like it. In fact, I'm planning to stay. You, on the other hand, shouldn't stick around. And as for her . . .' Ruby eyes flicked towards Kate, then towards a handful of conscripts improvising ropes and hooks to drag the pool. Rinpoche shrugged. 'It's your shot,' it said. 'But I really wouldn't waste it.'

Rinpoche shook water from his fingers and passed Kate a black ring made from beaten iron. 'I figured, what the fuck, this might have some sentimental value?'

'Jesus,' said Kate.

'Yeah,' Rinpoche grinned, showing gold canines, 'that's what it's got engraved around the inside. Of course . . .' The silver monkey paused, 'don't take it wrong, but for myself, these days I'm Tibetan Bon Buddhist.'

The little shit wasn't joking either, Axl realised. It had come down with Turing Syndrome. Make machine *artilect* and before anyone knows it, your gun's gone pacifist, the chill cabinet's vegetarian and the house AI's campaigning for the reintroduction of zoning regulations.

The tension levels didn't improve when Colonel Emilio turned up to oversee the retrieval of momaDef's body. For a start the Colonel had serious problems with the fact Kate Mercarderes had her head buried in Axl's shoulder and the Cardinal's pet killer was slowly, absent-mindedly stroking her long black hair.

'Lovely couple,' said Rinpoche.

The Colonel glared at Rinpoche, at Kate and Axl and then finally back at the silver monkey – and didn't like any of what he saw.

'You,' he said, nodding to Kate. 'You're not required here.'

Axl shrugged insolently, to save her the effort. That was how the neat, green-eyed Colonel made him feel. But then Axl figured if you've been thrown together from what was left in the bottom of the slop bucket, impressing buttoned-down establishment wannabes was never going to be an easy option.

And besides, Axl was right out of sympathy. The lieutenant

deserved everything that happened. In fact, as far as Axl was concerned Clone had simply saved him from having to do the job.

'We'll stick around,' said Axl as casually as possible. 'She's with me and I've got work to do.'

Colonel Emilio didn't like that either, but then Axl hadn't wanted him to. For better or worse – though probably the latter – Axl was the Cardinal's man. There might be no contract, no formal indenture, and it was true he appeared on no lists of humans, ghosts or AIs employed by VaticanMexico, just as no house agreement covered him for cloning insurance or rebuild, but that wasn't the point.

Axl shook his head.

What was between the old bastard and him wasn't written down or recorded, it was etched into memories, most of them bad. As for Colonel Emilio, given a face-off was inevitable, Axl would rather it came sooner than later.

There was something badly wrong with the arm that finally broke the surface, waved once and splashed back out of sight. It had taken the conscripts three trys to snag anything at all and on the fourth go the snagged body had fallen off its hook halfway to the surface, so they'd been forced to start dragging the bed of the foss pool all over again.

Now the body they had snagged was caught on a rock while PaxForce soldiers tugged in vainly at their rope.

'Free it,' Colonel Emilio shouted crossly and a conscript ran forward. Leaning out over the foss pool, the boy grabbed the pale arm and then let go hurriedly, shuffling back so fast he almost tripped himself. 'Sir . . .'

Axl beat Colonel Emilio to the water's edge. He felt the cold of the water on his legs but ignored it, putting his hands beneath the arms of the corpse to pull the body sideways. It came free from the rocks and Axl pushed the bald man up onto a nearby ledge.

Brown eyes stared at him from an Asiatic face perfectly preserved by the ice cold water. His guts hung free.

'Who is it?' Axl asked.

'I've no idea.' Standing behind him, Kate glanced once at the body and shrugged.

Rinpoche was right about one thing, on their fifth drag of the pool the conscripts had no problems bringing momaDef and Clone up in one go, their big problem was separating them. And it wasn't just that the huge man had his teeth sunk so far into the small woman's throat that Sergeant defMoma had to use her own blade to force open his mouth. It was what Clone had done with his thumbs.

One was hooked in under her spectacles through the lieutenant's pulped right eye, thick fingers locked round the side of her dreadlocked skull to keep his hand in place. As for the other thumb . . . Kate jerked her face sideways when she realised where Clone had rammed it.

'Sweet fuck,' said a voice in Axl's head, 'Corn on the fucking cob.' The silver monkey was right. It looked exactly as if Clone had driven his thumbs into the lieutenant at both ends and started chewing on her throat.

'Yeah,' Axl said. 'And all she did was strip him naked, tie string round his balls and wire him to a generator.'

defMoma exploded right on cue. The crack of a detonating firework, twisted loops. Steely bass gone harder. Rough-cut drums, echoed out.

Party time. Blocking the sergeant's punch easily, Axl hesitated and shocked himself by not killing her. Slotting her out was as simple as chopping the edge of his right hand to her larynx, but instead Axl grabbed the sergeant's left wrist and pivoted himself under it, taking the wrist up behind her back as he simultaneously kicked her leg, hard and fast. She went down onto her knees in a crunch of guitar as Axl twisted her arm up behind her.

The woman could stop struggling or she could listen to her own elbow rupture. As choices went it was simple.

'Drop it.'

Axl heard the words first and then felt the kiss of a cold muzzle against the side of his head. Inside it, the soundtrack went down to a two-drum heart beat.

'Well hey,' said the voice in his skull, 'there's always a critic.' Axl grinned and grinned again. That was what the Colt always used to say back in the days when it was just some gun with an amorality problem.

The Colonel had his arm outstretched, stubby fingers wrapped round the ivory handle of a tarted up paxForce-issue hiPower. Axl didn't like anti-environmental posturing used as a position-statement and didn't like the fact the man probably had a case full of fancy guns, but it wasn't the ivory that really fucked him off, it was the look in Colonel Emilio's eyes that said, 'Nailed you.'

Twisting the fat sergeant's left arm even harder wasn't the brightest response but it was satisfying. Pain hissed between the woman's lips and when Axl tightened his grip again she gave up trying to bite back the pain.

'Let her go,' Colonel Emilio ground the Colt muzzle harder into Axl's left temple. 'Now.'

'Do that again,' Axl said softly, 'and it'll be your fucking arm that gets broken.' He was getting stripped-back bass now, low and skeletal. More space than sound.

'Release her,' the Colonel said firmly and Axl heard an abrupt click as he jacked back the slide on his gun. Dust to dust, dross to dross . . . There had to be worse ways to go than being slotted by some sanctimonious WorldBank arsewipe but Axl couldn't think of any.

Of course, he could just have stopped twisting the fat woman's wrist but Axl couldn't get his head round that, either. And as the bass line kept time over the heartbeat, Axl got that feeling he was missing something obvious, yet again.

'Hey, shit for brains . . .'

The monkey wasn't looking at Axl, he was staring pointedly at Colonel Emilio's gun. Colt hiPower, ivory handle, .38, single clip, no laser sight and probably only semiAI.

Probably only semi . . . Sweet Jesus.

Snapping one fist sideways into the Colonel's groin, Axl flipped his attention back to the sergeant, broke her forearm with an easy twist and ground the jagged ends against each other until she screamed. And he kept grinding broken end against broken end until she pissed herself too.

Colonel Emilio pulled the trigger. Only the pre-sectioned flechette that should have scrambled Axl's brains stayed exactly where it was, correctly ratcheted into the chamber but untouched by a firing pin as dead as the already-moving Axl should have been.

The gun that Axl rammed under the Colonel's jaw had no electronics, no little data packets for Rinpoche to scramble, just an old-fashioned arrangement involving trigger, hammer and tempered steel spring.

The slug wouldn't frag into razor-edged shards designed to pulp his brain, it wasn't even jacketed with depleted uranium. It would just pass straight through, punching his memories and most of his brain out through a fist-sized hole in the top of his skull. Still, it was enough. And what Axl wanted more than anything was to pull that trigger.

'Next time,' Axl promised, stepping back.

'There won't be a next time,' said the Colonel, rubbing his jaw. Then he turned to his troops. 'Get the lieutenant packed in ice,' he barked. 'And you can leave those two here. I'm sure this *bitch* will want to bury them.' Not even bothering to watch as the conscripts scrambled fast for ropes and stretchers, the Colonel stalked over to the bitch in question.

'This man isn't a real refugee,' he told Kate coldly. 'His name isn't Jack Black, Black Jack or any permutation. He's a convicted murderer. His name is . . .'

'Axl Borja,' Kate said calmly. 'Yes, I know.'

Which was probably the one response Colonel Emilio hadn't been expecting.

Behind the Colonel, conscripts kept on loading momaDef's corpse onto a gurney and Axl watched them tighten the straps. Clone and the bald man with the slit-open stomach sprawled on the rocks, eyes open to the sky. Some medic was tending to the sergeant, though he took his time about it and claimed to be carrying no anaesthetic. Sergeant defMoma didn't believe him and Axl wasn't surprised, he didn't either. But Axl wasn't really paying attention to any of that. He was busy listening to the exchange between Kate and the Colonel.

'And I suppose you know he's here to betray you,' said Colonel Emilio. 'This man was sent by the Cardinal to hunt you down . . . Don't you understand that?' His voice was furious.

That was when Kate looked at Axl. A slow gaze through dark eyes that let him see deep into her head and beyond, to a child walking long lonely corridors filled with marble. Kate shook her head.

'I don't believe you,' Kate told the Colonel and turned on her heel, conversation over. Axl had never seen anything quite so magnificent or so unbelievably stupid.

Chapter Thirty-nine

Dubbed-out Dub

Early-morning mist filled Cocheforet valley like froth on coffee,
filtering out the village and its stream to leave only the tips of
nearby trees and the towering wall of the valley rising out of a
vast sea of smoke-like white.

Temple bells chimed, too beautiful to be real. Beneath them
dub dub, space voices and softbeats ran together, like a stream.

Axl's timecode changed hue everytime he looked from froth
to sky, grey out of white reversing to white out of grey. 126.48.59,
the seconds counting off so fast they span uselessly

Somewhere down there under that mist were the bodies
of Clone and the other man, buried by Louis beneath squat
stone cairns. The lieutenant's corpse had been carried away
by PaxForce, to be loaded into a Matsui freezer coffin and
shipped home. Kate Mercarderes didn't care what happened
to the lieutenant, but she'd spent the night crying in Axl's
arms, while Axl brushed away her tears and nodded as
Kate insisted furiously that she was the kind of person who
never cried.

And somewhere high in the grey dawn sky Rinpoche was
riding thermals. Axl knew that for a fact, because he was being
shown the long strip of Cocheforet's valley curling up at both
ends inside the vast hollow circle of Samsara.

Of course the froth-filled valley might have been a dream, but
in Axl's experience not even the most lucid dream happened
while he had his eyes open and was softly stroking the hair of a
woman he wanted so hard it hurt. Besides, if this was a dream

she'd have wanted him back instead of hesitating on the edge, but it was life.

One second, Axl's sight had been blinded by Kate's hair spread fan-like across his face, and the next he could see the high plateau spread out far below him, small like a map but still bigger than he'd ever imagined.

What it meant he didn't know. But Rinpoche was definitely telling him something without putting words to it, because what Axl got was silence and a sense of someone watching Cocheforet from an altitude so high it was almost airless.

That it wasn't the silver monkey showing this to Axl didn't occur to him.

'You all right?' Kate mumbled.

And lost beneath Kate's hair Axl nodded and wrapped his arms tight around her, feeling her relax as sleep set in again . . .

Morning mist really did fill the valley like froth, leaving visible only the highest branches of nearby trees. Axl saw it from Kate's window, cold air rolling over his naked chest. Another hour of sunlight had made the mist thin and wispy but still Cocheforet was hidden beneath its morning shroud.

'Aren't you cold?' The voice was sleepy, almost petulant.

And shook his head and kept watching the valley. Wondering what it was he was meant to see. Besides, he'd spent the night facing down temptation, which was all very noble but it could be overdone . . .

Arms reached round his waist and the warmth of Kate's breasts pushed against his bare back as the brush of dry lips on his neck made him shiver.

'It gets even colder in winter,' Kate said and then said nothing else, because nothing was necessary. Axl knew what she was asking. The question hung unspoken between them. Would he still be here then? And the silence was Axl's answer.

Kate nodded sadly and dug her chin into his bare shoulder.

'Well,' she said, 'why would you?'

Why indeed, thought Axl and was worried to discover that he already had one answer. Rinpoche was still up there circling somewhere. Water cascaded down to the foss pool. The scent of pine carried in through her bedroom window and at his back stood Kate Mercarderes.

All it would take to remix his life was to turn round and swap the resinous scent of pine for that of Kate. Her smell was warm, almost childlike but he could change that too, if he tried, for the musk of semen and secretions.

His call, but her party. Axl turned.

Kate looked into his eyes and didn't smile. Not then and not when his hand went up to touch her bottom lip, sliding down her perfect skin to rest lightly against her jaw. 'Who are you, really?' She asked Axl.

'Me. I'm broken.'

Kate's lips twisted and she smiled. They kissed then, her arms up around his neck until Kate broke free and stood at the window. 'Do you see what I see?' Kate asked him over her shoulder. 'Do we look at the world through the same eyes?'

She stood with her back to him, her body visible like a shadow through the thin cotton of her white nightdress until Axl moved in close and wrapped his arms tight around her. It was a small step from there to letting his fingers stray to one full breast, the memory of her nipple coming erect staying with him as his fingers touched her throat and Kate's head went back, eyes closing.

He could kill her, or not. He could admit this was the first woman he'd really loved, or he could just go. Leaving was always an option. Axl was good at that.

'What would it take to make you stay?' Kate asked softly, then froze when she felt the sudden tension in his body. Only by now Axl knew her well enough to know that if she was cross it wasn't with him.

She didn't protest when he kissed her neck, just below her left ear. Letting his hand smooth its way back down her body, brushing once more over her nipple.

'Again,' she said and so he did, fingers tracing a soft circle around the fullness of her breast, spiralling in until his fingertips just brushed the puckered flesh around her nipple, then closed in, tugging gently.

Kate sighed.

Somewhere around the age of twenty-three Axl gave up notching. Partly it just felt too childish, but mostly it was because he couldn't decide if his tally wasn't enough or was way too many. Plus around then his quality control got fucked over by 4-MDA, not to mention crystalMeth. And once ruffioes and zidifel got jacked into the mix, it was keep it up all night, crash out come dawn and wake not remembering whether or not you'd just had the fuck of a lifetime.

But now . . .

Very slowly, so slowly that at first Axl thought he imagined it, Kate pushed back against him, softly rocking her hips so the muscles of her buttocks tensed and relaxed as he pushed against her.

She said nothing when Axl reached round to undo the pearl buttons on the front of her nightdress, not touching her body as he slipped the light cotton over her shoulders and let it fall to the floor. And as Axl slid his fingers softly down her bare stomach, Kate kept silent, only raising her right leg slightly to let his hand twist into her silken body hair and gently trap the hood of her clit, softly closing on the tiny fold of skin and the swollen bud beneath.

There'd been a kid back in Alphabet City who used to take her knickers off, and not just for Axl. T-shirt too, if you could afford it. That was where he'd learnt how to touch and where. Fifty cents let him stand at the end of a foam slab as she wanked herself with glistening fingers. A dollar bought viewing space between her open knees.

It didn't matter that her nails were rimmed with half moons of dirt and her wrists decorated with dark slashes of scar tissue, those were never what Axl was looking at. She'd been thirteen, maybe fourteen, certainly older than him. He couldn't remember her name now, but then Axl wasn't sure she'd ever told him.

Part of Axl could have stood like that forever, with Kate's head rested back against his shoulder as she bit at her bottom lip, not quite muffling the sigh that rose to a gentle moan. But that part of him didn't win. It never did.

'Kate . . . ?'

She opened her eyes, then closed them again as Axl's fingers slid free and smoothed between wet and swollen lips.

Between her simple wooden bed and the window was five steps, and with each step Axl kept waiting for her to tell him to stop, to protest, to do anything but let him walk her across to the white cotton sheets and the thrown-back quilt.

But Kate didn't say stop and she didn't object when he pushed her gently back onto the narrow bed and poised himself over her. Instead she pulled up her legs and opened her knees to rest her heels on the edge of the mattress. With her eyes wide open and her long hair spread around her head like a fan, she looked more vulnerable, more naked than any woman he'd ever seen. So naked, it was hard for Axl to remember that she'd been head of intelligent resources, VP and deputy CEO of one of the world's biggest metaNationals.

Her hips moved up to meet him and Axl closed his eyes, feeling for that tiny electric jolt which came as her swollen lips closed around his glans, entrance muscles tightening around him. Pulling slowly back out, Axl slid into her again until he could feel himself fill her completely.

She looked at him then, mouth slack with sex, her eyes distant and unfocussed. What the look meant Axl didn't know. A memory maybe, or nothing. Because nothing was all Axl had in his head as he dropped his mouth to one swollen breast and tugged at Kate's nipple like a child.

It was over fast for both of them after that. One second they were ploughing against each other with that sodden slap of urgent sex and then suddenly Kate's legs twined around the back of his and she ground her hips up into him, mewling like a kitten as her arms locked round his shoulders and he pushed down into her.

There was just time for Axl to suck his right index finger and reach under her buttocks and then Kate's low broken mewling segued into steady grunts that rose to a triumphant howl. If anyone at Escondido hadn't already known what Axl and Kate were doing from the frantic creak of her wooden bed, they did now.

'Well,' said Kate as she puckered her lips into a mocking kiss. 'That was a first.'

Axl looked incredulous. 'Orgasm?'

'Penis.'

Enough shock wrote itself across Axl's face to make Kate laugh. 'It never occurred to me that I was bi . . .' Kate sounded more amused than surprised. 'Always knew I was the other, long before I knew what the other was.'

Axl rolled off her and tucked his legs under him to sit on the edge of her bed.

Kate's body hair was dark and damp, crushed flat and flecked with pearls of semen and it took effort for Axl to drag his gaze from between her open legs to her face, which waited expectantly for his question. He was ashamed to admit that he was shocked. It had never occurred to Axl that other people might not have tried both.

'The other . . . Is it like a feeling?'

Kate looked at him. 'I don't know,' she said, 'you tell me. Is it . . .'

'. . . like a feeling?' Axl glanced at Kate's full breasts, her mouth, then back to her narrow hips and the darkness between her legs. He nodded, realising that race and sex were immaterial. You fell in love with the person. If you were stupid enough to fall in love at all.

There were no faint scars on Kate's body, no patches of new

skin where a delicate dusting of freckles didn't quite match. Nothing at all to say she'd had even minor elective surgery. And yet . . . he'd seen younger eyes in old women, in old men too come to that. There was something about this woman that frightened him. Some intensity burning back inside her head just out of reach.

'Have you ever had a rebuild?' Axl asked the question without thought, regretting the words as soon as they were out of his mouth. Something else he was good at. It was the wrong question.

Axl sighed. He kind of thought it might be.

The only people who looked their age were street people, his people, those who couldn't afford rebuilds or the free-radical busting, mind-expanding chelated supplements the rest of humanity washed down by the handful without even thinking about it.

'What does it matter?' Kate demanded.

'It doesn't.' Axl held up his hands, placating Kate. 'Really.' The switch he'd tripped wasn't one he'd even realised was there. 'I'm sorry . . .'

Kate shrugged. 'You know how absurd this is?' Without ever quite touching Axl she manoeuvred herself around him and shuffled up to the head of her narrow bed where she wrapped herself in the discarded quilt.

'I've got *Axl Borja* sitting naked on my bed and he's say-ing sorry.'

'I'm sorry,' said Axl and Kate smiled.

'What's the worst thing that ever happened to you?' Kate asked finally.

He didn't want to go there.

'A couple of years in a freezer,' Axl told her, sounding impossibly casual even to himself. It wasn't the worst but he didn't talk about that. And besides mentioning the time he'd been dead didn't seem appropriate.

All the same, she still looked suitably shocked.

'You were in cyro?'

'Yeah, in Day Effé. It's a long story.' Not to mention singularly unpleasant. The kind to rate a same-day repeat and syndication on any daytime confession-fest. Then there was that other gap in his CV, when the street brats in Devil's Kitchen rose by one member and fell by three. Axl wasn't packed away in some pod then, but he might as well have been. Time passes like weather on the streets. It's hot, it's cold. Rain pisses down or it doesn't. Occasionally it snows and suddenly even slums clean up for as long as it takes drone salters to turn virginal streets into grey slush.

It could have been only a year he spent on the street, maybe two. Later on, the Cardinal got his New York office to check NYPD precincts, but no one knew how long the kid had been running wild and Axl couldn't begin to guess. Too much GHB.

He got a name change after that, a PIN number and Mexico City laminate. His own room, educational software, mediCare. Two months later he went through a back window and three guards who tried to get in his way, though he didn't tell Kate that.

'That's it, really,' said Axl. 'Not much of a story.'

'You know the worst thing that happened to me?'

Axl could guess. 'Your sister being murdered?'

The answer Axl expected was a simple *yes* and maybe more tears. But he got the truth instead which was far stranger.

'You still haven't worked it out, have you?' Kate said quietly. 'Joan wasn't my sister.' And the well of silence that followed was so deep you could have tossed your entire life into it and never heard the splash.

Inside that silence, Kate clambered off the bed in a jumble of naked limbs hidden inside a thin quilt and walked to the door. For a second Axl thought she was about to stalk out into the corridor wearing only her quilt.

But all Kate did was take a grey shahtoosh off the brass hook attached to the back of the door and wrap its length of fine wool tightly around her. Then she walked back to the bed as if nothing had happened.

'What was that about?' Axl asked.

'Joan,' she said finally. 'I can't sit opposite you and talk about her.'

Which answered his next question.

'You were lovers, weren't you?'

'At fourteen my father died. At fifteen I was Joan's unofficial private secretary. A year later I was running her whole private office . . .'

Joan was twenty-eight years older than Kate. And at forty-two, not yet ravaged by lymphatic cancer but already dismissive of the flesh, of physical needs and carnal hunger until she met the pale-skinned, serious Kate. And Kate, her mother already dead and her father only just buried in the churchyard at Castel Gandolfo woke a hunger in Joan that Joan had always believed missing from her psyche.

Those were the words Kate used. The serious language of serious matters remembered. And the naked man sat on Kate's bed sat and listened as she talked of statues by Bellini, Gobelin tapestries and the one great love of her life.

The artist and craftsmen she mentioned meant no more to him than talk of blow-back, azimuths and lines of fire would have meant to her. But Axl understood the rawness of those emotions that burnt behind her dark pupils, the double-edged cutting sharpness of her memories as she slipped tenses from *Joan is* to *Joan was* and back again, eyes overfilling with tears.

'Joan loves Samsara,' Kate said.

Axl looked up at that.

'She always dreamed of helping fill a world where there would never be war. She'll like it here . . .'

'Joan's dead,' Axl told Kate.

'No,' said Kate.

Then she said, 'yes.' And the sobs really would have started then except Kate didn't allow herself the luxury. But once she stopped shaking, she told Axl something he should already have realised. The memory beads weren't the key, Mai was.

The kid carried the Pope's *dreams* locked off inside her head. Sucked and dumped by some psi Jesuit. Slowly and seriously, never quite looking at Axl, Kate crouched there on her bed and told Axl about Antioch, an ancient order turned renegade and then brought back into the fold.

'We got the medical data when we acquired the Geneticists,' Kate said flatly. The deal was actually more of a reverse takeover, even Axl knew that and he never listened to the financial newsfeeds. Rome had bought out the Church of Christ Geneticist, acquiring the laboratory complex at San Lorenzo in Megrib. And with the lab came patents, outlines of projects that had failed and all the data that hadn't been released for peer review . . . They also got Alex Gibson, the world's only living God (if you left out the Dalai Lama, who disowned divinity). Though they still hadn't worked out what to do with him.

What she was telling him sounded incredible, Kate admitted that. But she wanted Joan back, not for the world but for herself. Get yourself cloned and any half-decent clinic could suck up memories from a soul chip and spit them back into a fresh cortex. Feelings were something else. And the problem with straight copying was you know *what* happened to you, maybe even *why* it happened. What you didn't get from a soul chip is what you *felt* while it was happening. It brought a whole new meaning to cognitive dissonance.

Joan was fifty-five. So her brain would have processed the equivalent of 300 million books. Which sounded big but came out as around ten terrabites of memory, not remotely hard for five chips.

But dreams are like feelings. Just as you can't chip the flickering dendritic matrix that ties emotionally-rich events into a shifting web of neural connections, so it's impossible to hardcopy the rush that kicks in during REM sleep when the frontal lobes shut down, emotional centres fire up and the brain swims with acetyl-choline.

'What if she didn't love me?' Kate said. 'What if I downloaded Joan's memory beads into a blank and it knew it loved me but couldn't remember why?' I couldn't take that risk . . .'

'You've got hard-form back-ups for Joan's senses. *And* you've got her dreams as well?' Axl didn't know whether to be shocked or seriously impressed.

Kate nodded. 'Everything except Joan. Because she didn't believe in clones . . .' Kate caught herself. 'Oh, she believed they were human. God knows, she fought for equal rights . . .' Her voice was harsh. 'But not for herself. She didn't believe in back-ups.'

'But the memory beads . . .'

'History.' Kate's laugh was as bleak as her words. 'Back-up for the Vatican library. Joan believed in history. That, and the essential goodness of the human race.'

'And the dreams?'

'Sheer luck,' said Kate. 'Joan suffered nightmares. Father Sylvester flew in from San Lorenzo to do a dreamlift. I thought it would give her a week or so of peace.'

Axl looked appalled. He didn't intend to, but he couldn't help it.

'He was going to return them when she got back from Mexico. Only it didn't happen, did it?'

'No,' Axl could comprehensively say it didn't. Joan got ripped apart by a pack of consensually-hallucinating street kids and Kate got landed with Joan's dreams, and back-up of her vision, smell, sound, memory and touch but no blank Joan to load them into.

'So now you know,' said Kate and headed for the door. Adding over her shoulder, 'I'm going to shower.' She didn't say *it would be good if you were gone when I get back*. But the message was there in her voice and in the way Kate didn't meet Axl's eye as she shut the door. Leaving him alone and still naked on her bed.

And he would have gone too, back to his room or out of that house, up into one of the higher valleys or even off Samsara altogether, whatever she wanted. Except that he took one last look around her room, imprinting it onto memory and that was when he found the bug.

PaxForce issue, Intel-chipped.

Chapter Forty

Hill/Slope/River

Mai wasn't in her room. She wasn't down in the kitchen with Louis, either.

'Mai?' Axl demanded, but Louis just scowled. Whatever he thought of Axl spending the night with Kate, he made it obvious he didn't think much of Axl coming straight down afterwards asking for Mai.

The little fat man hit the nearest wall, bounced off it into a pine table and was clutching his hip before he even hit the tiled floor.

'Where?' Axl demanded, picking up a knife. A sabatier – black handle and brass rivets, French-made – for refugees they had more than their share of home comforts.

Louis took one look at the blade and began crawling backwards out of Axl's reach. He knew just how fine a cutting edge the sabatier carried, having sharpened it in the first place.

'Where's Mai?'

'Down in the village.' The little priest was almost crying.

The door slammed behind Axl and he was gone. He skidded down a grass bank rather than go round by the path, his boots cutting long gouges into slippery earth. Sweet fuck, the only question that really needed answering was why hadn't he seen the bug earlier . . . ?

Because his mind was in his balls. It was obvious, wasn't it?

A small silver mosquito, wired for sound and vision. Fibre-optic eyes so small as to be almost invisible. Wings that doubled as solar panels and six tiny metal legs that let it cling to the wall near Kate's bed. Basic stuff.

So why the fuck had it come as such a surprise? Waxy leaves whipped into his face as he slid between bushes but Axl hardly felt them, though his hands flipped up to protect his face all the same.

If that mosquito hadn't been in shadow it would have been able to escape. But all that voice-activated broadcasting of what it had heard and seen had drained its power and not enough light could reach that wall for its wings to do more than mark time.

And besides, the Colonel had made one mistake. The bug was a low-valley model, not designed for this altitude or temperature. That was what made the thing easy to catch. It was also what made Axl notice it in the first place. Only, noticing the thing too late was no better than not noticing it at all.

'Mai?' The front room of the Inn was crowded with sleepy conscripts but it went quiet the moment Axl crashed through the door. The sabatier still clutched in his hand saw to that. Ketzia didn't know where Mai was, or if she did she wasn't saying.

Axl left the Inn with a couple of Tibetan women and a handful of grinning conscripts tagging. It took Axl all of two minutes to outrun his audience.

Maybe they'd expected him to cut Mai's throat when he found her, Axl had no idea. He only knew that whatever they expected the conscripts were a whole lot less bored-looking than when he went in through the Inn door.

The corporal on the Z3 gyroByke had problems with the idea of handing over her Honda, so Axl left her flat on her back in the street thinking about it. Though it was a push to her shoulder, not a chop to her throat with the sabatier, that put her there.

Getting soft in his old age, Axl decided, wondering what the old revisionist version of his Colt would have said. But he didn't really have time to worry about it. No one did, not now. He needed to get to Mai before the Colonel did. How long that took depended on how obsessively Colonel Emilio had PaxForce stripping out bug data for key words.

Mai wasn't in the stables either, though Axl's horse was, so at least she hadn't stolen the animal to try crossing the high plateau by herself. Nor was Mai around the jumble of open-fronted shacks behind the village that passed for its market, though half a dozen conscripts were.

The conscripts scattered, dropping the crudely-beaten Tibetan bangles they had no one to give to and striped rugs they'd leave behind. Been there, done that, ditched the T-shirt. Violence, rape and shopping for souvenirs. It had to be something the sergeants taught at boot camp.

The Inn, the stables and the market all empty of Mai – he had to face it, wherever the girl was, it wasn't in the village.

Cold mud slid from the Honda's back wheel like shit off a shovel as Axl hit a skid turn at the end of the row, but a military-grade gyro kicked in on cue and the bike kept him upright, tracks biting grass as he left the market and raced straight up the valley side. In reality, it was a mountain wall so high that human vision failed long before the snow-lacquered slopes gave way to graphite grey walls that stopped only after they'd long since left the thinning air behind, and met the cold emptiness of Samsara's upper atmosphere.

Down near the base of that wall, Axl slid between spindly firs and hung a shaky right to skirt a huge clump of thorn.

'Make a noise, make it obvious . . .' That's what his old sergeant used to say. Axl doubted if she'd ever seen a lapwing – he certainly hadn't – but that's what this manoeuvre was named after; if setting yourself up as a moving target rated being described as a manoeuvre.

Birds rose from the tangle of thorns in an explosion of feedback and a goat that stood on a nearby ridge vanished like someone had hit delete. The grass got ever more yellow the higher he raced, the air thinner, the soil turning to grit that ricocheted from beneath the Honda's churning back wheel.

Layers of hard attack SFX overlaid manically over-driven guitar and pumping double-tracked, adrenalin-fed bass.

Another minute of climbing and Axl was officially above the treeline, though a few stunted firs protruding bonsai-like from snow-flecked rock didn't seem to have got the message.

Somewhere down in that valley was Mai and he *had* to get to her first. Powdered snow whipped into Axl's face as he searched from Cocheforet up the other side of the valley towards the high plateau, looking for the red flash of Mai's coat. But there was nothing.

Which was the point Axl finally stopped reacting and started to think. Bruiser guitar chords chopping off into an after echo of silence. What he needed most, he realised, was some help. This wasn't one he could win on his own . . . Instead of looking down into the valley, Axl began to scan the sky.

'Lapwing defence,' said a voice behind him. 'Make a noise, be visible, draw the enemy away.' Rinpoche cocked his head to one side and frowned. 'You know,' he said, 'just 'cos your sergeant said something doesn't make it true. Bit like you and the old bastard. Your big problem is you're too trusting.'

Axl looked at the silver monkey in disbelief. Next it would be telling Axl that he'd been set up.

Rinpoche nodded. 'Oh, and I put a patch into your head for old time's sake.' Rinpoche said, before Axl could ask how the monkey knew what he was thinking. 'I mean, fuck knows, it wasn't difficult. You've got more wire in there than jelly.'

He'd come back to that later, Axl decided, much later.

'You know where Mai is?'

Rinpoche did, that much was obvious from his sly grin. 'Now Clone's gone, she's busy negotiating,' the Colt said, his voice studiedly casual.

'She'll be fucking dead if I don't get to her first,' said Axl.

'And if she isn't she'll wish she was when Emilio gets through with her. You've got to warn her.'

'No,' said Rinpoche apologetically. 'You're on your own. Tsongkhapa can't take sides. And I . . .' The ex-Colt shrugged. 'But for the record, Colonel Emilio has just notified Vajrayana that PaxForce intends to arrest a Spanish whore called Juanita. That's Mai . . .' Rinpoche added, as if Axl wasn't capable of working that out for himself.

'And off the record,' the silver monkey glanced around him. 'Last time I looked she was trying to persuade some kid he wanted to take her with him when he left.'

Rinpoche didn't need to say how and Axl didn't need to ask. He got a picture in his head, rough cut like bad mix. A drop shot of clouds, then valley sides with a tiny waterfall, trees seen from above, a river bank, Mai . . .

'Okay?'

Yeah, it was. She'd gone through the village from Escondido, met the kid and walked out along the valley bottom. Unless she'd arranged to meet the kid there. But that didn't seem likely and – with luck – the kid with his trousers pulled down round his ankles hadn't told anyone where he was going or why.

Mai had been stripped naked under a boy who looked about twelve, her eyes open to watch the clouds as the boy held her arms up over her head.

Maybe Rinpoche heard Axl's thanks, maybe not. Axl didn't wait around to find out. Kicking the Honda into gear, he gunned the throttle and slipped the clutch until the fat back wheel bit mud. It took a moment or two for the treads to find optimum depth and the tyre pressure to self adjust. But then everything came together in a blur of trashed-up bass lines and the gyro kicked in as the bike crested a tiny ridge and started to slide diagonally across a long shale bank.

Even in Day Effé there were fuck-wit city suits who did black runs for fun. Mostly they wore full body armour, kevlar-mesh bonded to funky silver leather, chitin shoulder pads and knee protectors with full tsunami function. Axl wore cargo pants and a cotton shirt. So slicking down shale was as open an invitation to get the skin flayed off his body as it was possible to get, at least without going near PaxForce.

Needless to say, it wasn't skill that kept Axl upright when the fat back wheel hit a bank and the Honda took off to land with a long sideways skid, it was the fact that combat bikes were built for pig-shit-thick grunts with colour co-ordinated riding abilities.

Another drop and then a second ridge raced towards him and the earth dropped abruptly away. There wasn't even time to swear before the ground that wasn't there came up to meet him and the bike jumped fifty feet before touching down again on wet grass, gyro whining.

Axl had a problem, and his problem was that someone had seen Mai leave the village or else the boy had told a companion how he planned to spend the morning. Dumb fuck. Down to Axl's left was a diagonal line of conscripts positioned in combat formation, a regulation three paces apart and three paces behind as they swept the valley bottom. The grunts weren't even bothering to stay in cover.

They looked like tiny toys, Axl thought, and then he didn't think anything because the Honda was airborne again, grass falling away beneath him.

Mono shocks cushioned most of the landing and his knees took the rest, but hitting the saddle still felt like someone was trying to kick his spine up through the top of his head.

And then Axl was racing into a belt of firs, loose gravel giving way to a crust of dead pine needles that cracked and slid like unset lava beneath the wheels of his Honda. Staying upright ate up the next few minutes.

When the pines finally gave way to slopes of pasture complete with stolid yaks and dazed-looking Tibetan goats that scattered as the Honda catapulted out of the tree cover and headed for their herd, Axl was already almost too late. The fat woman walking point ahead of the sweep of solders was almost at the bend in the river.

'Fuck,' Axl gunned the engine angrily, flicking the rev readout from green to red as he blipped the engine up past safety. Maybe it was the scattering goats or perhaps the wind finally changed direction to bring them the unmistakable, hysterical whine of the two-stroke but either way, the man running tail flipped round and unslung his snubPup.

Guitars screamed a warning.

A burst of speed carried Axl along the slope above the soldiers and by the time they realised he intended to get ahead of them Axl was already there, the Honda's rev readout flashing purple with electronic pain.

Now he just had to reach Mai – and fast – because letting defMoma stumble over the top of a bank and find Mai naked, sprawled beneath some second-grade conscript was one way to guarantee that the sergeant took close personal interest in showing the girl that NCOs did it better.

In fact, the only thing that stood between defMoma just hurting Mai and actually cutting her throat was the fact that the fat woman had firm orders to arrest the girl, which would hold off the throat slitting if not much else. And Axl wasn't about to let either happen.

Not if he could get there first. And he was going to . . .

Hill/Slope/River. Axl got the flash played straight into his brain, just like he was running some top-grade satellite positioning software. A quick nudge on the handlebars, a nudge of the accelerator and the Honda X3 was rocketing down a long slope towards a bank that flipped the bike up and then dropped it all the way down to the river and Mai.

She was naked, cock-eyed tits as beautiful as he remembered them, her hips full and soft. And it was obvious from the blind panic in her unfocussed eyes that she didn't have the faintest idea who was riding the bike falling towards her.

The conscript sitting naked nearby should have gone for a

weapon but went for his trousers instead. He was still trying to yank them past his knees as Axl decided to try for a skid stop and quickly decided it was a bad idea.

Even laminated carbon-fibre can only take so much. The front shock buckled as the Honda hit the bottom of the slope, the wheel itself snapping with a loud crack. The droids back in Okinawa had bonded that too, either that or the rim was run through with some kind of internal mesh of neatly woven polymer strings. Instead of exploding into shrapnel, the wheel collapsed on itself.

Axl still went arse over tit into the cold river but as he scrambled out again the revolver already dripped in his hand, without Axl even remembering how it got there.

'Freeze.'

The conscript, who still looked about twelve and scared shitless pulled a knife anyway, so Axl opened a gash across his temple with the revolver, pistol-whipping the boy to his knees. Life was getting messy – and about to get messier.

The soldiers were maybe 250 yards away, their ordered line and fast walk rapidly turning into a jagged run.

'You,' Axl said frantically, putting his gun to the head of the naked girl and tightening his finger on the trigger. 'You're under arrest . . . Do you understand?' Mai didn't even look at him. She was too busy staring at the boy on his knees. It was Tukten, the sullen-faced brat from the Inn. Not a conscript at all.

Lowering his revolver, Axl grabbed Mai's red jacket from the grass and flung it round her narrow shoulders, her instinct kicking in enough make Mai shuffle her arms through its sleeves. The kid scrambled into her thong without being told and yanked a black cotton skirt up round her waist, her eyes never leaving Tukten.

'I'm arresting you,' Axl's words were rapid but precise. Somewhere up there Tsongkhapa would have a vidSat data banking sight and sound. And if there wasn't then Axl knew he could rely on Rinpoche to do the job for him. No one would be able to say this arrest hadn't been made properly.

'. . . in the name of the Cardinal and on behalf of WorldBank. Under a mandate authorised by the United Nations.' The resolution number meant nothing to her but Axl reeled it off anyway, down to the relevant sets and subsets. It was only when the gabble of formal phrases was finished and Mai stammered out her question that Axl realised that the kid had no idea why . . .

'You've got the Pope in your head.' Axl went for an answer that was short rather than strictly true, it was quicker.

'No.' The way Mai looked at Axl wasn't much of a novelty, because ex-lovers of his had been looking at Axl like that for as long as he could remember. But then dealing with the kid's outrage suddenly took second place to keeping himself alive, as an approaching conscript flipped out a spring-loaded cosh and Axl got fed a ragged Strat-high warning riff.

'You're dead . . .' The weighted cosh slammed towards Axl's skull in an effortless, practised arc. The man was seriously unhappy. So was defMoma who was racing up behind the conscript. She'd been planning to get there first.

Axl hit the dirt ahead of contact, taking the landing on his left shoulder and drawing up his right leg, going into a half foetal. Trick number one was never break a fall with your hand unless you want your wrist shattered. Number two is don't wait to make that kick, don't aim, don't look – just do it.

Bass lines collided.

Axl's blow dislocated the man's knee, the sole of his boot tearing open the joint and rupturing its synovial capsule. The conscript went down sideways because that's what happens if someone kicks out your legs. And the man's howl of pain lasted as long as it took Axl to chop him viciously across the throat with the edge of his hand.

After that he just gurgled.

When Axl came back up onto his knees, the gun he was holding was the conscript's snubPup and its zytel butt riffed straight up between defMoma's legs, hard as hell and twice as nasty. The big woman screamed and bent double, which was a bad mistake because Axl's second blow caught her in the gut, showering him with her breakfast.

And then the rifle's safety was off, Axl was knelt astride her hips and the red dot of his laser sight was busy wrecking cells at the back of one of defMoma's eyes. Been there, done that, watched the atrocity . . .

'You're mumbling . . .' It was Mai and she looked afraid.

Too bad. With his new gun to defMoma's face, Axl rifled the patch pocket on her T-shirt, ready to toss its contents onto the mud. Somewhere the bitch had to have PaxForce issue meth, cooking sulphate, anything. Even paraDerm would do. But the pocket was empty so, gun still to her head, Axl rolled the juddering woman onto her front to try the arse pockets at the back.

Chocolate, melted with body heat and squashed beyond use, a used packet of Coag and ditto eczma cream, two PaxForce-issue laminates, one giving her name as Martyna 'defMoma' Labowsky, the other a card to be read out to suspects before their arrest. And finally, sweet fucking success, a tatty vacuum-sealed foil sachet tucked into the bottom of her pocket, date stamped and closed with a strip of tamperTell running across the top. UN-issue cooking sulphate, the world's best-loved currency. Grey crystals were bouncing off the back of his throat before the sachet was even properly open.

'Crack each crystal between your teeth and suck it soft with saliva,' suggested the packet but Axl ignored it. That was only if you wanted to slowburn and he didn't, definitely not. Axl wanted the full white light/white heat.

Glass-hard neon notes wrote themselves round every bewildered conscript, round Mai's red jacket, even round the valley top like some filter effect had kicked in. Which was exactly what had happened inside Axl's head.

'This woman is under arrest,' Axl told the milling conscripts and his voice was firm, without the slightest tremor. You could say what you liked about PaxForce but they cooked only the best sulphate.

The way it was meant to go was they'd all nod, convinced by the authority of his words and Mai and Axl would get out of there, fast . . . Taking Tukten too, if Mai insisted. And that's the way it would have worked if Colonel Emilio hadn't ridden up on some prancing stallion, looking like he was leading a parade in the Plaza de Armas.

'Good,' he said, spotting Mai. 'We'll take over now.'

Quite how Axl's new snubPup ended up pointed at the Colonel's stomach Axl couldn't remember. And to give Colonel Emilio credit he didn't flinch or try to shuffle his horse away from Axl's aim, even though the tightness in his face said he knew just how messy a gut wound could be. If not from experience, then in theory at least. Even staff colleges covered that stuff.

'Three days,' Axl reminded him. 'And if internal bleeding doesn't off you, then blood poisoning will. Of course, if one of you had remembered a combat stretcher . . .'

There wasn't much a Matsui couldn't do, from basic blood replenishment to shutting down everything except vital functions before putting the body into suspension. But defMoma hadn't come out expecting resistance, which showed what she knew. Axl spat, and grinned inside as Colonel Emilio repressed a shudder.

Not surprisingly the man didn't want to die and Axl didn't want the grief that went with slotting a UN officer, so they compromised. Colonel Emilio casually gathered up his reins and backed slowly away as if the situation didn't exist.

To an outsider it probably looked as if the Colonel was leading a group back to the village, and that group just happened to include Tukten and a shaking Mai. Just as Axl happened to be there, with a zytel-handled snubPup that coincidentally was pointing at Colonel Emilio's back.

After twenty minutes passed, Axl got bored with shadowing the Colonel and fell back to check on the conscript. He was unconscious and breathing through a self-cutting tracheagate fired into his throat below his crushed larynx. Axl felt nothing but surface guilt about taking him down. All the same . . . somewhere in the back of Axl's head there was real guilt, looping away like thin monophonic synth, at what he'd done to Tukten.

Axl sighed. He could pretend he just hadn't recognised the boy who'd ridden out with Clone from Cocheforet when he had been their prisoner. Or he could admit that he hadn't wanted to recognise the Tibetan boy.

Which was less stupid? Axl didn't know. The thin notes continued, climbing higher, but going precisely nowhere.

That was the way they trooped into Cocheforet, the hoofs of the Colonel's horse splashing freckles of mud onto a thin crowd of Tibetan and 'fugee kids who'd gathered behind him as he rode towards the Inn.

Adults watched from open doorways or from the safety of upstairs windows. None of them came out onto the muddy street except for Kate who stood alone on open ground in front of the Inn, her arms folded and face furious.

'You can't arrest Mai,' Kate protested.

Colonel Emilio looked down at the woman blocking his way and smiled. Soon the man would have a double chin to go with his heavy jowls and neat salt and pepper moustache, but for the moment most women still counted him as handsome and the Colonel knew it.

'I can't?' Fussily he pushed back a streak of greying hair that had flopped forward. Only a sudden twist of his thin mouth revealed that he'd just started to enjoy himself.

'No,' said Kate fiercely. 'You can't.'

'I haven't . . .' Colonel Emilio said. Hope flared in Kate's eyes, so palpable that even those watching from the windows could see it.

'. . . though, I must admit,' added the Colonel, 'I did intend to.'

'But you haven't?' Kate said it like she couldn't quite believe it.

'No,' said Colonel Emilio, signalling to his troops to move away from Axl, 'he has.' And the man pointed smugly to where Axl stood at the back, near Tukten.

Chapter Forty-one

Ashes or Diamonds

Kate refused to look at Axl, even when she put the bowl of tsampa on the table in front of him and carefully, silently put a narrow bronze spoon beside it. And not just because it had taken Axl sticking a gun to Louis's head to get Kate to give him the soulcatcher back.

'Why do this to yourself?' Axl asked. She hadn't answered his other questions either last night or so far this morning, and had turned away when he tried to talk about Mai so Axl wasn't quite sure why he expected her to answer this one, but she did.

'Because Louis refused.'

No one needed to tell Axl what that meant. Obedient little Louis had been with Kate since she was born. Louis had watched her grow up and gone into exile with her on the inside of some half-arsed stone bicycle wheel. He refused her nothing.

But he wouldn't serve Axl breakfast. And nor it seemed would anyone else at Escondido except Kate. So now she was putting a wooden bowl of buttered tea beside his plate while he sat there feeling sick, and not just because nearly three weeks of life on Samsara had left him hating the tea's oil-slick taste and the acid etch of tannin it left behind his teeth. But if Kate could bring herself to serve him food then, tiredness or not, he could eat it – and in silence if necessary – while she watched.

The lack of a door slamming or even closing softly behind him showed that Kate remained in the room. What there wasn't, was any sense of the woman's presence. Where she stood was empty space, colder than the dawn chill that sucked what little heat Escondido possessed out through the dining room's open window.

Axl had opened it and Kate had done nothing but shiver slightly and then force her body not even to do that. She wasn't going to close the window and nothing would have brought her to ask him to do so. Kate was teaching herself to live with the ice core that was growing like cancer inside her.

Logged somewhere in Tsongkhapa's memory would be a grab of the sequence where Kate had to be dragged off Axl, screaming and still trying to rip open his face. And before Ketzia pulled her away, Kate managed to land one good blow. A vicious punch that had Axl spitting bits of broken back tooth into the mud.

Even the Peruvian conscripts cheered. Only Mai still looked blank as if she really couldn't believe what was happening to her. And it was only late yesterday evening, after he'd padlocked both Mai and himself into her room, that Axl realised the Japanese kid thought it was all a mistake. She had no memory of being implanted with Joan's dreams. And if it hadn't been for Axl's bleak expression, Mai would have kept on believing he was lying, or deluded or both.

Instead, Mai now knew that everyone she had met on Samsara who'd offered to help intended to betray her, if not in one way then in another. She was an object to all of them, to be sold, bought or traded.

She was upstairs in her room now, lying fully dressed on her bed and staring at the ceiling. Which was what she'd been doing all night. Axl knew that for a fact, most of his night had been spent trying to stay awake as he sat guard on his prisoner. Quite who'd ended up most tired was hard to say.

Just once, when the sulphate had burned out to a dull headache, Axl had blanked for about five minutes; but when consciousness snapped back in, his gun was still in his hand and Mai was still there, staring at her darkened ceiling with eyes that he recognised. There been a kid in New York who used to watch the night go past like that, but that wasn't a memory Axl planned to crack open.

Axl asked, turning round to look at Kate.

'Is Mai ready?' He meant was Mai packed.

'Ready for what?' Kate shot back. 'To be tortured, raped . . . Why don't you tell her what you've got planned and I'll ask her?' Her words were as sharp as whip cracks and as loud.

Axl winced. Combat readiness had never been a problem, but Axl hated loud. Those kind of shouting arguments left him knotted up inside, his mouth sour with rising vomit like some drunk. He pretended it was training; speak softly, carry a big gun . . . But it was an emotional cowardice that the dregs of life in that home had enamelled to the inside of his mind.

In Manhattan one broad daylight afternoon in April, he'd put a blade into the guts of an Italian grandfather rather than shout back. It was on the corner of 12th and Sixth, outside a derelict Mongolian Bar-B-Q.

A small-time Don had promised the new owners his men would rid the place of vermin before they arrived, and Axl was one of the rats. His knife went into the man's gut because at ten Axl was too short to reach his heart.

'I wasn't the one who purchased some kid to use as a memory dump,' Axl said coldly

Kate flushed. 'It wasn't a memory dump,'

'No,' said Axl bitterly, 'just dreams, that's different, isn't it?' He yawned, though only half of it was pretence.

'At least I didn't lie my way in here.'

'It's me or Emilio,' said Axl. 'You want me to give her to PaxForce?' Axl would die rather then let that happen, probably literally, but Kate wasn't to know that.

'Could they be any worse?'

Jesus fuck. 'Could it . . .'

That was the point when anger became irrelevant, at least to Axl. Just a cheap adrenaline high that was helping him keep awake. If Kate didn't know the difference between PaxForce and what he was doing . . .

'And where did you find her?' Axl asked, voice hard.

Kate opened her mouth to shout, then paused.

'Did Mai volunteer?' Axl said into Kate's sudden silence. 'Or maybe she's getting paid to babysit your lover's bad dreams?' Without giving Kate a chance to answer, Axl picked his revolver off the table and pushed it into the back of his belt. Then he reached out for the snubPup he'd taken from defMoma and no one in paxForce had dared to demand back.

'Well . . .' he asked Kate. 'Did she volunteer?' Like we both don't know the answer to that, Axl thought bitterly. 'You took someone off the streets. Me, I'm just putting them back.'

'She'll be killed,' Kate said.

'No,' said Axl as he pushed back his chair and slung the snubPup's neoprene sling over one shoulder, 'the Cardinal's not like that.' Others were, though . . . Axl was about to wonder where that thought had come from when Kate's face twisted into a sneer. But what started out as bitter laugh ended up a swallowed sob.

'Not like that . . . ?'

She didn't say anymore and she didn't need to. No one had been able to explain why Cardinal Santo Ducque had let Joan walk out alone into a crowd of feral children, without her guards. Although that hadn't stopped everyone from CySat to the Emperor Maximillia herself from speculating.

If Axl had to guess why the Cardinal had failed to keep Joan II safe, he'd guess it was because Joan didn't want to be safe. She hadn't come to Mexico to hide behind a fortified fence in the Sasrario in Day Effé or at the Villa Carlotta . . .

The Cardinal was as powerful as any other metaNational CEO of a regional fief. Maybe more, at least he could play the moral dimension when *realekonomik* failed. But not even control of a yearly income bigger than the GDP of most subSahal national debts could change the fact that Joan was his boss.

Manoeuvering was one thing, full-on rebellion was not the Cardinal's way. And the old bastard wasn't stupid enough to try. Losing battles was the fastest way to lose authority. And nothing on earth would made the Cardinal fight a war he already knew was lost before it began.

Joan however . . . Axl remembered the marble steps, the absolute certain acceptance that death was coming. Her enemies might have chosen how but she'd chosen where.

'Look,' Axl's voice was flat, hard. He held up one hand. Most truths were better left unsaid – that was his view anyway – and the reasoning behind Joan's death was one of them. But if Kate wanted facts she was going to get them.

'She went there to die,' said Axl. 'I know, I've been inside her head.'

Kate froze, mid-breath. One hand still clasping a chair, knuckles going white where they gripped the wood of the chair back. What had been anger changed to shock as questions backed up, log-jamming each other in their need to get asked and spilled over into the only question Kate really wanted answering.

'Why?'

Axl shrugged. 'Maybe she'd got bored.'

And maybe he was just being a bastard for the sake of it. Joan had known she was going to die, though, and an elite SWAT team from the Cardinal's Guard couldn't have saved her . . .

Nor, once that shot was fired, could an automated combat stretcher or an immediate airlift to the nearest hospital, had either been possible. *Curare* acted too fast. The kill was a professional job, well done . . . Cranks were ingenious and fanatics, well, fanatical but that hit had been organised, orchestrated.

'Face it,' said Axl, 'if Joan died it was because she didn't want to be saved.'

It was only will-power that stopped Kate slapping him but Axl stepped back anyway, to let her sweep past him, head erect and back ramrod stiff as she walked through the open door and headed for the main stairs that led towards Mai's room.

Axl wished he could say what hit him most was the fall of Kate's long dark hair or the proud way she kept her shoulders pulled back, but it wasn't. What took him by the throat was the shape of those perfect breasts beneath her shirt and the fact her tears were entirely silent.

Chapter Forty-two

Exit the Tag Team

Colonel Emilio, defMoma, the Peruvian kids with big eyes and bigger guns all vanished during the night while Axl sat guard on Mai, taking their Honda GyroBykes with then. Behind them, PaxForce left firepits that still smoked, stinking outdoor latrines and *SERIOUS* tagged in gloPaint on a dozen already-decrepit buildings.

And everyone in Cocheforet was ecstatic about their leaving except for Axl, who didn't know whether to be worried or just plain relieved.

Now Axl had left Cocheforet too and both the village and valley were half a day behind him. For Axl that was life's one small blessing. Nothing could make him go back to that Inn or the jumble of crude shacks slung along a track that went precisely nowhere. Leon, his customers, the snot-nosed, dirty-arsed Tibetan children, all had lined up in silence early that morning to watch Axl and Mai ride through, followed after by Kate, Ketzia and Tukten. Of those last three only Kate and Ketzia had horses. At the back of the small group traipsed Louis, looking close to tears again. Hatred for Axl rose from the small crowd like steam.

Even the strays dogs had fallen silent.

Not one of that crowd wouldn't have knocked Axl from his horse given even a fifth of a chance. But the Browning snubPup that rested across his saddle had reduced even Leon to the status of a sullen spectator.

Maybe they'd intended to attack and lost their nerve or maybe the villagers had never got beyond thinking about it but all they did was spit and mutter. One stone hurled accurately or the steel edge of a spade swung into the small of his back would have been enough. Riots had been born from less. But they were 'fugees, Axl reminded himself. Helpless, hopeless . . . It was hard to know who held the other in most contempt.

Kate wasn't riding to keep Mai company, she'd told Axl. She was going to Vajrayana to lodge a formal complaint. Those were the words she used. Axl wasn't surprised. Most of the women he'd fucked would have told him they intended to have his head, but Kate had a complaint to lodge.

Axl shrugged. Let her lodge it. And if Kate, Louis and Ketzia held him responsible for all that had happened, let them. He wasn't afraid of the machete that dangled unsheathed from Ketzia's hip, of Kate's cold disdain or Louis's open hatred.

As for Tukten, he was glued to Mai's side, jogging beside the saddle of her shaggy pony as if he'd finally found his place in life. Besides, not even Tsongkhapa would go against a properly conducted arrest. Axl had been given a job to do and finally he'd done it. Everything else had been killing time.

He had nothing to regret, so what gave with the sparsely-layered acid trance that rolled into his head like mist from the steep slope around him . . . ? Axl didn't know. But no matter where he looked or what he thought, he couldn't shift it.

Kicking his mare forward, Axl kept climbing towards a deep split in the rock face, the reins to Mai's mountain pony wrapped tight round his wrist. He hadn't bothered to ask how a village that the night before could only produce one pony, and that in the face of a gun, had suddenly found two extra animals for Kate and Ketzia. The answer was too obvious. Axl was an outsider. And everyone who wasn't from Cocheforet was an enemy.

It didn't seem worth pointing out to Kate how lightly her precious village had got off. There were safety zones back on earth where no buildings still stood, where every child had been found binned and bagged in a corner, their throats cut.

No men in Cocheforet had been forced at gunpoint to sodomise their daughters, no mothers had to choose between biting off the testicles of their fathers or their sons. Not one person had been disembowelled, buried alive or hosed with gel from an unlit flame gun and then forced to light a match. There were no body pits for outside observers to dig up and divide the number of toes by five to reach a tally of the dead.

Axl was as angry as he was shattered. Just how angry he found it hard to admit. The problem was, it wasn't really with them.

Hoofs slid as Axl's mount hit a stream flowing so shallow across rock as to be almost unseen. The landscape was cold and quiet and all the rock near the summit was black. At noon, an eerie mist had rolled down the scree-strewn mountain side and promptly vanished after filling everyone's lungs with wet air. And by afternoon Axl's spine ached and the inside of his thighs burnt from where they chaffed against his damp saddle. More worryingly, the countdown inside his eye had hit 96.00.00 and promptly changed colour, from white to pink. Now Axl was ignoring it as he intended to ignore it the next time it jacked itself up a colour code.

Five miles every hour would have been excellent progress, if only they could have managed it. Most times their speed was closer to four or even three, no faster than a human walk. Except no human could have climbed that path without stops the way the ponies did. Either they were a truly resilient mountain breed or germline mods had been made back up the line to allow increased oxygen absorption. Though, God knew, it felt like if the air got any thinner it would disappear altogether.

Axl didn't know what kind of preNatal zipcoding Samsara allowed or required, but the Red Cross had to be doing some kind of germline splicing on 'fugees to help preborns adapt.

Kate sat white-faced with fatigue and winced everytime her horse stumbled, which was every second step. Ketzia and Tukten just scowled. As for Louis, Axl couldn't see him, the little priest was too far behind. Mai was the only one who seemed unconcerned. But that wasn't a good sign, at least Axl didn't think so. Since being told she had Joan's nightmares backed up on the wrong side of her unconscious, Mai had taken to talking to herself, as if in conversation with what little of her real self was left.

'Proud of yourself?' Axl asked Kate, hauling in on his reins and pulling Mai's pony to an abrupt halt in front of Kate. The woman slid forward on her saddle, pain hissing from between clenched teeth. If her thighs were as raw as Axl's then she really hurt. And she was without the remains of defMoma's sulphate he'd used to deaden the pain.

Kate didn't have to ask, proud of what? She didn't answer either, although her eyes flicked across to where Mai sat, oblivious to the drizzle, mountains and thinning air. What was going on in there? That was the real question and she couldn't answer that any more than Axl.

Everyone had a ghost inside their head to watch what they did.

Waiting and questioning. Not necessarily the ghost of someone dead, sometimes just a memory of someone no longer powerful to anyone except the child hidden inside the head of the adult, still seeking approval that would never be given or love that could only be withheld. Maybe childhoods fed on approval didn't have ghosts; Kate wasn't certain, but she didn't quite believe it. Everyone had to have ghosts. Judges hardwired inside their heads to criticise or praise the actions they took, judging even those others no longer dared to judge.

For Kate, it was Joan. For Mai . . . ? Kate didn't know, but it probably wasn't a memory of her mother either. After all, most people's ghost was provided by their mother. As for Axl, Kate knew he thought his ghost was the Cardinal. But she believed it was someone earlier. The woman he'd talked about that *night* . . .

Axl had protested he carried no values from back then,

nothing hardwired inside his head. Then he'd mentioned that outside – in what passed for the real world – those values he didn't carry from back then had earned the matron fifteen to twenty in the State pen.

The Lucky-Strike burns on his arms hadn't healed when they pulled her in and the NYPD figured they'd have no trouble getting the children to testify. The way Axl told it, they were wrong. Not one child at the home would give evidence. The woman was as close as they had come to a mother. And besides none of them believed she wouldn't be out inside a week. They might have lived dangerously but they weren't stupid.

Twilight came in slowly, the whole world finally falling into a night far darker than back on earth. The notes in his head grew softer, questioning. Almost sad.

'We'll camp down there,' announced Axl.

There were stars, of course, just not overhead where a band of intense black stretched across the sky, like some hand had ripped out the Milky Way and replaced each star with a negative image. Stars could be seen as cold flickering dots, heavenly Braille written away to the edges of the dark scar in that gap of sky between the black band overhead and the impossibly high, distant edge of the mountain wall.

What little latent heat the rocks held soon leached away into the vicious cold of night. But the group didn't stop until it cleared the high pass and began a descent down bleak rocky scree towards the high plateau. And then the wind changed direction and they were walking into the sudden smell of death.

'Peg out the horses,' Axl ordered when they at last reached the patch of flat ground he'd been pointing to. 'And drive the pegs deep.' No one answered but Ketzia and Kate still did as he suggested, hobbling their ponies and using rocks to drive shackle pegs far into the poor earth.

'Why doesn't the stink go away?' Mai's flat whisper contained the first, the only intelligible words she'd uttered since leaving her bedroom at Escondido.

Because the pass was steep, bleak and treacherous, much like life, thought Axl. No sooner do we get past the corpse of one fallen animal than there's another. But he said nothing and her question went unanswered. Not that it would take even Mai long to work that out for herself.

'Find some wood,' Axl ordered Tukten, but the dark-haired boy just stared sullenly in Axl's direction and started to shuffle backwards into the darkness. 'Or don't you want to protect Mai?'

Tukten stopped shuffling.

'There are wolves and snow leopards,' Axl said as he clambered slowly from his own mare and forced himself to hammer a hobble peg into the ground. 'Ice hyenas, wild dogs, kites . . . You want Mai to stay awake all night shitting herself with fright at every breaking twig, that's fine . . . It makes no difference to me. I've got this.'

Axl hefted his snubPup into view.

Tukten and Ketzia built a fire while Axl leant back against obsidian black rock and watched. Absent-mindedly noting who'd brought matches, who arranged the damp twigs, who did exactly as they were told. As he expected, Kate organised while Ketzia actually did the work of lighting the fire. Louis just sat as far away from Axl as possible, never looking at the man he held responsible for everything that had happened.

What did he see? Axl wondered. But inside himself he already knew . . . A yawning thug who had molested the Japanese girl, seduced a grieving woman and betrayed all of them. That wasn't how Axl saw it, obviously. At least he didn't think he did.

Mai dropped to a squat beside Axl, her soft face highlighted by the first flames of the fire. Whatever she wanted to say remained unsaid.

The night gripped so cold that Mai's breath solidified to smoke and spiralled away. Vomit still rose and fell in her throat like mercury in some ancient barometer and Mai finally knew what that smell was, though she couldn't remember how she knew. But she felt better now the monkey in her head had stopped talking.

All the same her skin was stiff with cold and her gut hurt. Somewhere inside her head a voice was telling her that things could only get better.

'I'm going to have to shackle you,' Axl said, reaching into his pocket for a length of twine.

'Why?' Mai did a convincing job of looking puzzled. But the sudden unexpected irony in her voice contrasted so strongly with the soft, puppy fat of her fourteen-year-old face that it unnerved Axl. Even more so when he factored a cynicism into her smile which was definitely old before its time.

'Because,' said Axl, 'I can't afford to let you escape, can I?'

Mai opened her mouth, and choked . . . Until then she'd been breathing as shallowly as possible, despite the cold thinness of the air. The stench saw to that.

'A body,' the kid said flatly, when her coughing fit had gone. 'Or a dead animal.'

Axl nodded. And she nodded back as if he'd only confirmed what she already knew. They weren't yet near enough the charnel ground to smell it. This was just a foretaste.

'Where would Mai escape to?' Mai asked. 'Back to that village? Down onto the high plateau to get torn apart by wolves? The next town must be fifty miles, maybe a hundred . . . No one would be that stupid.'

Actually, thought Axl grabbing one of Mai's ankles and yanking, they would. The kid toppled back onto her arse, her definitely Mai-like swearing only ending when Kate left the fire to fend for itself and came to crouch down beside Mai.

'How sweet,' Kate told the Japanese girl as she watched Axl rip laces from the top two rivet holes of Mai's boots and re-thread them to bind the girl's ankles tightly together. 'At least he's not planning to fuck you.'

'Kate . . .'

She shot Axl a look that should have killed and kept talking. 'Of course,' she told Mai, 'that's probably because you don't have any secrets he wants to hear . . .'

There was no answer to that. At least not one that Kate would listen to. Axl knew, he'd tried. The elder woman kept watching as Axl tied one end of his twine to the laces of Mai's boots and looped the other end to his own wrist.

'Not afraid someone might cut it in the night?' Kate asked. There were no prizes for guessing which *someone* Kate had in mind.

'That won't happen,' said Axl, staring Kate straight in the face.

Kate didn't want to ask him why not or be the first to look away, but she did both.

'Because I don't intend to sleep,' Axl told her abruptly and pushed Mai softly backward so she tumbled to the ground. 'Get some rest and don't even think of running away.'

Mai wouldn't, rest or sleep. The kid meant it when she said there was nowhere for her to go. 'As for you,' Axl stared at Kate, 'I don't want to see you anywhere near her.' He watched Kate stand up slowly and stalk away to the far side of the fire, where she sat with her back to him, staring up into the darkness at the way they'd come.

'You like her, don't you?' Mai said suddenly. The kid was smiling, that sad kind of half-smile that rests somewhere between regret and pity . . . Which was weird as fuck, Axl decided, because if he'd been Mai the only thing he'd have felt was hatred.

'Sleep.' Axl's order was rougher than he intended but Mai only smiled again. 'You could always try some yourself,' she said.

Chapter Forty-three

The Bending of Starlight

The man with the short-model Browning SLR slept fitfully. Curled up near his feet, with her face to the fire, was a Japanese girl tied by her ankles to his wrist. She was staring into the glowing embers and neither person inside her head liked what she saw. So Tsongkhapa hummed gently and soon the girl slept.

Tsongkhapa didn't like the gun and wanted to disable it but the silver monkey he'd co-opted as a pair of eyes argued against it. Apparently the monkey had been a gun before it became Rinpoche and still felt sentimental about them. That wasn't a stance Tsongkhapa readily identified with, but identifying with dichotamic attitudes was as much a part of his job as anything else, so he lived with contradiction. If that was an acceptable way of explaining it.

The bioClay chip controlling the readout in the man's eye was manufactured by Seiko, it was a military model at least ten years out of date and wasn't really in his eye at all. The point at which it would hit count zero was, in one sense at least, entirely arbitrary. But then, as Rinpoche had said while toggling the dip switches, in human terms all recorded time was.

This hadn't been pointed out to the man. Who would have seen nothing arbitrary in the difference between reaching or not reaching the Nuncio's cruiser before it left Samsara.

The sleeping man had 80 hours, 48 minutes, 30 seconds to make his connection. Less than three and a half days. The Sony sound system in his head was equally old but featured one or two rather neat, non-standard, modifications.

The Browning was a 148-shot snubPup, US-designed and sub-licensed to a penal factory in Korea. It was, in the words of Rinpoche, thicker than pig shit. The cord was Israeli sisal, genetically modified for strength. The girl was quarter Han Chinese, half Japanese, quarter South East Mediterranean. Her name was Mai, without a surname, at least Mai was what most of her answered to in her dreams. And though a section of her subconscious answered to a different name she was dealing with this.

The man didn't answer to any name at all, but had set his brain to accept Axl, Berault and Borja as acceptable aliases. There was no record of those names ever having been processed by Samsaran immigration. In fact, neither the sleeping man nor the restless girl was officially on Samsara at all, though they were both quite definitely asleep by the fire.

For a space of time almost infinitely less than a second, Tsongkhapa got a flash of what might, in human terms, have been guilt. But the AI didn't bother to track Rinpoche's guilt back to its origin. Tsongkhapa wasn't worried by how the two got to Samsara because Samsara was where they both definitely belonged. What worried Tsongkhapa was the implications of *what* they were.

The man was easy enough to categorise. Broken more or less covered it. The girl was more of a problem. And the problem wasn't really that there were at least three different personas stacked inside her head (the man had five, four of them dead). It was the lack of legitimate connection between the first and third. The first was Mai now, the second was a simple subset, real Mai hiding. The third wasn't Mai at all, not even Mai solarised, run as a negative or operating with the values reversed.

Tsongkhapa sighed. There was no guarantee she could be mended but he would have Rinpoche try *bufo alvarius* as a first option: maybe the only option, unless Rinpoche could cut a deal with Axl. And Tsongkhapa didn't need telling that for this to happen Axl would first have to cut a deal with himself.

Unrolling the dried toad skin, Rinpoche pulled a broken razor blade from where one hadn't previously existed and did the same for a small square of glass. The silver monkey didn't need a lighter, it could do flame from its fingers. 5-MEO-DMT, to be taken nightly until cured. Rinpoche shrugged, whatever.

'Hey,' the monkey tapped Mai on her shoulder and stepped back hastily as she came awake fast, reaching into her boot for a knife that wasn't there and hadn't been for five years, maybe more.

The girl blinked at the animal, then glanced at Axl leant back against a rock and smiled sourly. 'So much for standing guard.'

'Methamphetamine,' the silver monkey said, 'you've no idea how fucking hard it is to unpick. I practically had to disconnect those neurons one at a time.'

'You put him to sleep?'

'Well, someone had to,' Rinpoche said slyly. 'How else were we going to talk?'

Later, when the giant flowers that caught the sun were beginning to open their petals, Rinpoche gave Mai the glass knife he'd casually picked from Axl's pocket as he briefly slept and watched her face light like the dawn. Her faith in her abilities shamed him. And as she slipped the knife's cord over her head and began to unbutton her red jacket to rest the blade between her slight breasts, Rinpoche turned away in embarrassment.

When next Axl awoke, *dungchen* trumpet filled his head and Mai was sitting next to the cooling embers of the fire, mumbling to herself. Only it wasn't with the furious, PCP-enhanced intensity of some dustout. Her words were quiet and reasoned, though just too soft for Axl to work out who Mai thought she was talking to.

Axl wasn't too sure what had been going on inside his own head either, but his body was bathed with sweat and he felt more tired than before he had slept.

Everybody was already awake and watching him. No one

had slipped away in the darkness. Even fat little Louis had sat out the stink, the distant howl of wolves heading towards the slaughter ground and the dying down to embers of the small fire that was all there was to keep predators at bay. All of them had survived the night, hovering on the insomniac edge of anxiety – apart from Axl, who felt like sleep had crept up behind him with a cosh.

Maybe they'd been afraid he'd wake before they escaped, or perhaps it was the silver monkey sitting shaking glass straws of amphetamine from a tiny compartment in the zytel butt of his snubPup who'd kept them in order. Axl was sure he'd checked that compartment and the last time he looked it contained a cleaning kit for the Browning.

'Have a good night?' Kate asked.

A day came and went. Most of the time Axl rode holding Mai's bridle, Ketzia and Kate riding close behind, like silent shadows. Occasionally they all walked the rocky track that led across the bleak, windswept plateau, leading the exhausted animals behind them.

No one talked. What breath they had was needed for breathing.

All the same, enough water gathered in pools for the ponies to be able to drink. It was grass that was scarce. What little there was looked half-hearted, yellowing and spindly, filling the flat spaces between scrub and moss-covered rock.

They did that next night without fire, Axl and Rinpoche staying awake to keep guard. Mai slept in Kate's arms and both Tukten and Axl tried not to notice. By morning Rinpoche was gone again and Axl was so exhausted he could hardly ride in a straight line.

'Wolf,' said Tukten and Axl stopped. The shag-haired boy was pointing to where a grey shadow slunk between altars on the distant charnel ground.

'And there,' Axl muttered, 'and . . .' Oh, sweet fuck. Axl was about to point again when a flash of sunlight kicked him suddenly awake, an adrenaline rush snapping his eyes wide open with a squeal of violin. Someone was watching them from a low wooded hill on the far side of the charnel ground and Axl had a nasty feeling he knew exactly who it was.

'Problems?' Kate asked unkindly, drawing alongside. She was holding Mai's rein, though Tukten still stood at the pony's head holding its bridle. They'd spent a lot of that morning scowling at each other and pulling the bewildered animal in opposite directions.

Axl shook his head, wondering why anyone would bother with field glasses. But no sooner was the question asked than Axl knew the answer. Samsara didn't provide PaxForce with GPS, no chain of spySat hung up there running stealth mode. If anyone wanted to track him they weren't going to squat at some satellite-feeding JCIT deck, focusing in close enough to see if he'd shaved, while their thumb hovered over some floating trackball that picked out options between blind and vaporise.

PaxForce wanted Mai and so did the Cardinal. At least, he wanted Joan and if the kid really did have Joan's dreams stacked up inside her head . . .

'It's getting messy, isn't it?' The voice was amused, kind but a little contemptuous. It was Mai all right, but not really any version he knew. Her clothes were the same, that red jacket, mud-splattered felt trousers. The childish mouth was still both downturned and pouty and her hips soft with puppy-fat but her expression was more intense. And if Axl didn't know better, he'd say her eyes had changed colour. Or maybe it wasn't a hue change, just a rearrangement of the fractal dust that made up her iris pattern. Whatever was looking out at him, it wasn't a fourteen-year-old girl, or not entirely.

Axl found himself nodding. Yeah, messy was one way to put it. If his guess was right, Colonel Emilio and half a dozen conscripts were camped in the other side of the charnel gound.

And if they weren't armed to the teeth they were still a hell of lot better-equipped than his group.

'*Your* group?' Mai snorted. 'You think half the people here wouldn't slit your throat in the night if they got the chance?'

No, he didn't. Without intending to Axl glanced over to where Kate crouched, retying the laces of her Caterpillars while she pretended not to be trying to listen in.

'She'd be first in the line,' Mai's voice was regretful. 'You hurt her, you know . . . And just because you're broken doesn't mean that everyone else is . . . Of course,' Mai nodded at Kate, 'it doesn't mean they're not either.'

She was gone before Axl could reply, her hand reaching out to stroke Kate's cheek as she went past, leaving Kate staring after her with something like disbelief in her blushing face.

'Aren't you going to stop her?' Kate's voice grated on Axl's thoughts. He was about to ask *stop who*? But he didn't need to. Mai was walking steadily towards a pile of corpses while ahead of her grey shadows raised their heads, as if they could pick up her scent over the sickening miasma of rotting bodies.

Axl grabbed his snubPup and rolled to his feet, pounding after Mai. 148 shots to a magazine and he had one magazine rammed up through the butt of the Browning and a spare tapped alongside. About seven and half seconds of full-on killing time, not like he really had bullets to spare.

Only he didn't need the gun. Axl didn't even need to pull back the ratchet that jacked the first shot into the breech, though he did it anyway. It was the combat equivalent of sucking his thumb.

'Shhhh,' Mai hissed as he ran up behind her, pumped with fear and ready to hit the ground and roll, taking out the three wolves directly ahead. 'You'll scare them.'

'Scare them?'

Mai nodded and knelt briefly beside a corpse, closing the eyes on the body of a man who had one leg chewed off at the knee and was wearing his small intestines draped round his groin like a withered grass skirt. 'They're cleaners,' Mai said reaching for a grey shadow. Instead of taking her hand off at the wrist, the wolf whined like a puppy and pushed its narrow skull up into her palm.

'Fucking great,' said Axl, 'they're all God's creatures and you're fucking St Francis.' He stared at the broken body of a child, little more than ragged scraps of dark flesh on bones picked nearly clean.

'You like this?' Axl asked.

'I don't have a problem with it,' said Mai. She stopped a few seconds later, put her head up and sniffed the air like one of her shadows. 'Too much,' she insisted, 'too much for the horses. Cut them free . . .' Behind him, Axl could see Rinpoche already slitting straps that fastened on saddles and slicing through bridles and reins.

'That's . . .'

'A good idea,' Mai told him. 'Unless you plan to be a sitting target?' She smiled grimly. 'As opposed to a walking one . . .' There wasn't an answer to that.

'Does all this really make sense to you?' Axl asked Mai, feeling so tired he found it hard to think.

She nodded, smiled broadly and pointed to a blond toddler lying naked on a stone slab, his small arms and legs broken to give the vultures a head start.

It was Mai, not Axl, who led the exhausted group towards the centre of the charnel ground, walking ahead oblivious to the increasing number of bodies and their stink. The wolves stayed strung out in a line along either side of the party as if they were acting as outriders.

Mai appeared not to notice the wolves, except when one thrust its wet nose against her hand, but then she didn't seem aware of anything really, apart from Father Sylvester's glass blade warm between her breasts and a soft voice muttering in her head, and much of the time she didn't even notice that. It was the daydreams that went with those mutterings that made her gasp, shake her head and shiver . . .

Unrelated, intense but *not mine*. At least, Mai didn't think they were hers. What she liked best was the feeling of calm so deep it made her relax just to think about it. She really liked that. Liked the way her heart slowed and the knot in her stomach untied itself and faded away.

What surprised Mai most was the discovery that just because Kate had told her how lucky she was to be brought to Samsara didn't mean it was a lie.

'*Mai*?' She felt rather than heard the question. At first she thought it came from the silver monkey now circling overhead higher than the vultures. Mai couldn't really see Rinpoche, not by looking, but sometimes he was in her head and other times she was the one looking out through his eyes. She liked that, too.

Most of all, she liked watching herself as a tiny dot who moved slowly across a great expanse of rough grass, skirting bushes and small ponds. *Mezzanine*, said a voice in her head. It's a mezzanine between Samsara's broad central valley and the high passes. But she didn't know that word and no sense came attached to it so that didn't help her much, not that Mai minded.

'*Mai*?' There was that question again, the one she'd forgotten she'd been asked. The kid looked round her, saw nobody speaking and wondered if it was one of the wolves. Then told herself not to be stupid.

'Stupid is good if it helps. Crazy is better . . . But, do I look like a wolf?'

The bald man sitting ahead of her on an altar was wrapped in a thin orange robe. His mouth didn't open and there was nothing to say he was the one who had spoken, but she knew it was him from the smile on his face. And besides . . . she just knew.

'Like a wolf?' said Mai, 'No, you look like you should be cold.'

The man laughed. It sounded like echoes fading inside a prayer drum.

Chapter Forty-four

Lo-fi/Fidelity

Slap bass, the real thing . . . impressively fuzzy analogue. Slow as a heartbeat, only looping four notes not two, repeated endlessly. Axl couldn't remember the song it had been stripped from but he recalled the original fly poster. A blonde Scandinavian framed topless against a pantone sky, white flannel shorts pulled up so tight they probably explained the idiot grin on her face.

He hadn't liked the track back then.

Axl watched Kate approach, keeping his own face impassive. It was the first time in two days she'd come near him, and Axl had long since stopped trying to draw her aside and explain. Mainly because he wasn't too sure *explain what*? And besides what on earth made him imagine for a minute that she'd believe him? Axl wouldn't have done if he was Kate. Hell, half the time he didn't believe himself . . .

As rest stops went, here was better than anywhere else they'd found and infinitely preferable to where they'd been a day and a half before, sitting by an altar as Mai wandered aimlessly closing the eyes of the dead.

But a whole day's light had gone and, because he hadn't told them, none of the group understood why Axl refused to leave the slope above the woods that edged Samsara's central valley. And when Ketzia had forced herself to ask him two hours earlier, he'd just snapped that he was watching time go by.

Axl stood, Kate opened her mouth and the slap bass slid into silence, a straight fade.

'You can't take Mai back.' Kate didn't bother to pretend the conversation was about anything else. Nor did she slide into it gently. Nothing but worry for Mai would have made her cross the patch of grass from where she sat with Louis and Ketzia to where Axl sat alone.

He could, quite easily. Provided neither of them got killed first. Whether he should was a different question, but that wasn't what she'd asked.

'I can,' said Axl demolishing half a tiny apple with a single bite. They had food now. Two rabbits killed with a slingshot by Tukten. And sour pippins from a row of trees that looked as if they'd once been cultivated but had long since been allowed to grow wild. 'Quite easily.'

They were watching her, the others. And it was obvious Kate realised the fact from the tension whipcording her neck and the way her fingers wrapped into fists that pushed hard into her hips. If Axl hadn't known better he'd have said Kate was doing her best to stop herself from shaking.

'She's ill.' It was as close as Kate had come to pleading and closer than she liked.

'I know.'

Mai was, too. Shakes like he'd never seen and night sweats that left her skin mottled and slick. The fever had come on immediately after the charnel ground and Axl was trying very hard to ignore the thought that she'd infected herself while tidying the corpses. Either that, or she'd caught some disease saying goodbye to her shadows when the wolves began to slobber all over her face.

'And she's a child,' Kate hissed at him. They'd been there before.

'That *child*,' said Axl, 'is a kinderwhore.' He flipped out his hand to grip Kate's wrist, stopping her from turning away. Here was somewhere they'd been as well.

'Sit down,' Axl snapped at Louis, then jerked his head at Tukten who'd dropped all the firewood he'd been collecting except for a large branch which he held like a club. 'You too.'

Neither moved.

'You can sit down,' said Axl, 'or I can kick seven shades of shit out of you, do it in public and sell tickets . . .' Both the boy and Louis sat down. And why not, thought Axl. Those were the words that always worked for Black Jack.

'The *child* was kidnapped, dumped in the middle of fucking nowhere and has spent the last month spreading her legs in the hope of getting out again. Don't even think of trying to guilt *me*.'

Axl left Kate standing there. He didn't need to look back to know she was really shaking now.

Mai was sitting in a huddle under a small oak tree, arranging the dried cups of last year's acorns into intricate mandalas. Axl tried to ignore her wet trousers as he dropped to a squat in front of her, much as he tried to ignore the puddle of urine that kept expanding around his boots into a fractal-edged map, darkening a slope crusted with acorn cups and rotted leaves.

The girl smelt of sweat and a sweetness that made Axl think of disease until he realised it was only the remains of a purple flower that lay stripped of its petals in her lap.

'People want to kill you,' Mai said softly. She might have been talking to Axl, but equally well her comment could have been to the flower dying in her lap. She glanced up and Axl realised she wasn't talking to the flower.

'Everyone has enemies.' Fortune cookie stuff and about as true. Some people had friends.

'Not enemies who intend to kill everyone around you too.'

Axl paused to wonder what they were actually talking about. 'Everyone?' He asked Mai.

'Ketzia, Louis, Tukten . . . Kate.'

'You too?' Axl asked quickly. Not wanting to think about the last name on her list.

'No, not me. But definitely you.' Mai concentrated on the PaxForce conscripts in the woods far below. The language they spoke was odd, a hill dialect not Spanish, but she had no trouble with what it meant. Its sense just fed through to her along with the pictures.

'That man,' Mai said.

'The Colonel.' Axl sighed. He'd been hoping he was wrong, that they weren't talking about the same thing but they were. 'All of the soldiers from the village?'

Mai paused, held up ten fingers and then her eyes glazed over and she was gone.

'Fuck it,' Axl said, standing up. He was going to have to talk to Kate after all.

'We've got problems.'

Kate looked up from stuffing twigs into a small fire. And as Axl watched her watching him, he tried not to think of all the others watching them. For someone meant to keep to the shadows he'd been doing a spectacularly bad job. She weighed up his words as she looked for the catch.

'Mai?' She asked at last.

'Yeah, that . . . And something else,' Axl gestured at the fire. He wasn't quite asking Kate's permission to sit but he wasn't far off. As close as he was likely to get to an apology anyway. And when Kate had finished looking surprised, she nodded.

Inside Axl's head, the soundtrack added strings which died abruptly as his adrenaline levels soared. He got steady drum and bass on their way down.

Part of him wanted to tell Kate that PaxForce were waiting in the woods. Somehow he never quite got round to it.

'Kate.' The single word was too hard, too abrupt.

She did that look, the half frightened/half aggressive one he was beginning to recognise.

'There was a mosquito,' said Axl, then stopped. Lost for his next line. Same as it ever was. There was enough room in the silence that followed for either of them to stand up and walk away. Neither one did.

Her frown was puzzled, her eyes watchful. Without knowing, she twisted her mouth and bit at the inside of her bottom lip. That was another tic of hers Axl recognised, the one that said, *Okay. I'm concentrating . . .*

'Look,' Axl said into the silence. 'You remember after . . . ?'

'After what?' Kate was about to say and then realised what Axl was talking about. She froze. 'Remember?' She couldn't forget and not from lack of trying. 'Yes,' she said carefully, 'I made a mistake. What about it?'

'The mosquito.' Reaching with clumsy fingers into the side pocket of his coat, Axl extracted a tiny tangled mess of chitin and gossamer-fine optic fibre. Even in the fading light and covered with grit its solar-powered wings were flecked with iridescence.

'PaxForce-issue,' Axl said. He held it out to her but Kate wouldn't take it.

'How do I know it isn't yours?'

'You don't.'

Very slowly Kate reached out for the bug, her shaking fingers closing around the tangled remains. They both knew she was trying to take the bug without touching his proffered hand.

Kate took the dead insect and squinted at it. Made by machines or once actually alive, she had no idea how to tell. Not her area of expertise. She used to have people to do that stuff for her. What the fuck do I actually know? Kate thought crossly, turning the tiny bug over in her hand.

She was meant to be considering what she'd revealed to him back then, doing grown-up things like working out the possible political impact of her indiscretions, Kate knew that: but what was really looping through her brain was the memory of Axl naked above her. That and the absolute certainty she'd been screaming by the end.

Well, if not actually screaming, then certainly not silent. And all the time . . .

'You told me about Mai, remember.' If Axl noticed Kate had gone red he didn't say anything, just waited.

'And Joan,' Kate said.

Axl nodded. 'Joan, the dreams, those memory beads.' He stopped, hesitated and told the truth anyway. 'I came here to get you. But after you told me about Mai, I knew she was key. The only question was, who'd get there first . . .'

'*Why did it have to be you*?' There was such upset in Kate's question that Axl winced, an actual physical flinch. And then he told her . . .

An hour was what it took, an hour Axl didn't have, while the others fidgeted and Mai hummed under her oak tree and PaxForce troops crouched in the woods below certain in their knowledge that there was only one trail down to the valley floor.

'That's the truth?'

'Yes.' Axl nodded. It wasn't, of course, not the whole of it. That would involve telling Kate facts he wasn't prepared to let go. Strange as it seemed, he trusted the woman and, now his decision was made, he had no intention of being responsible for her doing something stupidly noble . . . Like refusing to go home to Cocheforet.

Kate didn't need to know about the timecode, the soundtrack, the whole of Rinpoche's tatty little bag of tricks that locked him into the countdown for the Nuncio's cruiser. Any more than knowing about the Colonel's troops dug into the edge of the woods would be useful . . . In fact, Axl told Kate nothing that might complicate what he was about to do.

'I'm letting Mai go,' Axl said.

He expected shock, a flare of hope, outright suspicion . . . What he got was a slow nod of the head. It seemed Kate was ahead of him even in this.

'The Cardinal will kill you.' They both understood she meant it literally.

Axl shrugged. *No* would be a lie and *Yes* didn't bear thinking about. About the best he could hope for was *maybe*.

'You think you put her over the edge,' Kate said. 'But it was Father Sylvester who led her there. No,' Kate shook her head, 'he *dragged* her there, bound and with her lips sewn together – and I gave the order . . .'

Guilt, it was a wonderful thing.

'I'm going to tell Mai.' Axl pushed himself up off the ground. Both knees were locked from squatting by the fire and pins and needles threaded through both ankles but Axl felt none of it. In fact, he was working very hard at feeling nothing at all.

Kate didn't move. 'You coming?' Axl asked over his shoulder, and he walked off without looking back.

Chapter Forty-five

13.38.34

They heard the girl puking before they reached her.

'I'm scared she's dying.' Kate's voice was raw, as if she was the one who'd been vomiting over the tree roots.

'No,' Axl said firmly. 'Rinpoche wouldn't allow it.' Both Kate and he knelt in front of the girl and waited for her huge pupils to focus.

'13.38.34 . . .' She told Axl. Mai even did the dots between numbers.

He nodded. 'I'm looking for Rinpoche,' said Axl.

'Beloved?' She stared up at him, dark eyes as empty as the Big Black.

'The silver monkey . . . I need to talk to him. You know where he is?'

'Up.' The Japanese girl pointed directly into the night sky.

Yeah, thought Axl, surprise me . . .

'How do you know?' Kate demanded, voice uncertain.

'We're watching. You're small and suddenly whoosh . . .' Mai smacked her hand into the dirt, 'you're big.'

Radical focus shift, most vidSats came with it built-in except for the really cheap Italian ones. Watching not listening or he'd have been down already. Besides, Mai probably wasn't looking at them, not really, she'd spliced into some feed. Actually . . . Axl ran through what he knew about human optics and decided it amounted to the same.

'Tell Rinpoche I want to do a deal with Tsongkhapa.'

'You want *what* . . . ?'

'Tsongkhapa,' Axl stressed, ignoring Kate for a second, 'you got that?'

Mai had and within seconds so had Rinpoche . . . The silver monkey didn't so much drop as plummet. Not quite as fast as Mai's hand had hit the dirt but still swift.

Big beats crashed in Axl's head. One second there was blackness, then the silver monkey was landing, wings thrown wide and grown vast, its very own instant parachute.

Axl grinned and Rinpoche grinned back, wings already shrinking.

'So,' it said, folding the now small wings neatly across its back, 'you looking for extra muscle?'

'No, I'm changing the deal.'

'There is no deal,' said Rinpoche.

'As of now there is,' said Axl. 'Or there will be. And it's got to hold for Tsongkhapa too. Not just you.'

'No problem.' The silver monkey shuffled its feet. 'Hermetic hierarchy's hard to explain. Total autonomy within rigid limits, bit of an oxymoron really.' Rinpoche looked embarrassed, 'Soft intelligences have such a hang up on free will.'

Axl wondered what soft . . . then realised he was. You show me your guilt, I'll show you mine.

Digging his fingers into the inside pocket of his coat, Axl found the broken soulcatcher. It was wrapped in the anti-static cloth his biohazard chips had been in. 'Here,' Axl put the small bundle in the silver monkey's paw and watched as Rinpoche carefully unfolded the cloth, holding the matrix of wires, feather and beads up to the firelight so they glistened with an oily sheen.

'You want her mended before you take her back?' Rinpoche's voice was flat, uninflected.

'No,' Axl shook his head. 'I let her go and her safety becomes Tsongkhapa's responsibility. That's the deal.'

'Done.' Sharp canines sliced the web of wire criss-crossing the soulcatcher and Rinpoche caught the remaining beads as they dropped into its hand.

'You wanna get Mai's opinion before you fuck with her head?' Tukten demanded pushing ahead of the others.

'Mai doesn't have *an* opinion,' said the silver monkey, 'she's got three of the fuckers . . . None currently compatible.'

'Do it,' said Axl. He glanced at Kate, but it was Rinpoche he was talking to. 'She doesn't need to take responsibility, I will . . .' Axl sighed, picked up his snubPup from where it rested in the mud at his feet and stood. He didn't say *it's time I took responsibility for something*, he didn't need to.

The last thing Axl did before slipping away from the fire was pull the revolver from where it was stuck into his belt at the back and put it on the damp grass where Ketzia, Louis and Tukten had been sitting.

Rinpoche didn't need it. Nor would Mai if Axl's guess was accurate. The silver monkey wouldn't just follow her like a shadow, he would become her shadow – whether the kid liked it or not. Kate wouldn't touch the gun even if she did find it, but Tukten would and Axl's money was on Tukten to guard Mai for all he was worth. Always assuming Rinpoche let the boy get a look in . . .

In five minutes Axl would have exactly five hours before the SS *St Bernadotte* lifted off from Vajrayana and dropped through the first of the lock gates on its trip out into the big black. In thirty minutes the flowers out in the big black would open to catch and reflect the sun and Axl would be too late to spring anything, never mind a one-grunt ambush.

Colonel Emilio's conscripts were waiting below him. Not camped-out-on-the-forest below but directly, spit-and-it'll-mess-up-their-precious-hair below. From what Axl could tell, half of the conscripts were on this side of the road, the others across the road, also hidden. All any one of them had to do was look up and they'd see Axl glued to a rock face above, doing his best imitation of oversized gecko. Only they wouldn't look up, at least Axl sure as hell hoped not.

They'd be watching that path down from the slopes, wired up with infrared, waiting for him to lead the others straight into a killing zone. Well, he had a couple of reasons why it wasn't going to happen and the main one had a zytel butt and was cradled in his arms like a baby.

By the time Kate heard gunfire PaxForce would be excised, foreclosed, out of the loop. And if not there wouldn't be much Axl could do about it because he'd be dead. He was doing Kate a favour she hadn't asked for and would probably never even acknowledge to anyone. But hell, that was life.

The conscripts might be so ignorant, underpaid and brain-fried they didn't know their arse from their neighbour's elbow but the Colonel would report in on Mai's significance, if he hadn't already, that much was guaranteed. A little legalistic sleight of hand and WorldBank would be reclassifying the kid as Joan's clone and pulling her in for trial. Kate too, accessory before the fact . . .

Extraditing would be difficult, with luck. Taking her off Samsara now before the feeds got fed was a much softer option. That's what he'd have done if he was the Colonel. And Axl, as the Colonel, didn't even want to think about he'd do to Kate. And if the Colonel didn't, CySat would if she got returned for trial. It was humiliation and rape whichever way you looked at it, on screen or off, or both.

Blocks of wood banged slowly together echoed inside Axl's mind. No more than a basic click track. Somewhere far below it was melody, fractured like glass and soft as the footfall of rats in a dusty attic. *WarChild*, obviously. No gruff Latino voice was looped over the top but that was okay, Axl could do the rap from memory.

Read, Reconnoitre and – get dead or – get it Right.

The toughened twine he'd originally brought along to tie up Mai had cut raw strips into the centre of his palms. The rope was too thin to get a good grip and besides his hands were slick with sweat. Shaking, too.

Fear did that.

Always.

Axl didn't do fear, either, but recently his body seemed to have forgotten that.

'More light,' Rinpoche said and Tukten pushed another branch into the fire, then tossed two smaller ones on top, watched as sparks danced up into the pre-dawn.

'Beads,' demanded Rinpoche, then remembered he was already holding them. Small and lifeless, they looked as insignificant as bits from a child's necklace. They looked liked . . . small hard-spheres, really, which is what they were.

Rinpoche took the soulcatcher beads in his hands, thin lips pulling back over sharp canines as he stuffed them in like candy. And that was it. The silver monkey sucked hard, feeling memories slip between his teeth, releasing the sweetness of Joan seeing Kate for the first time, the sour taste of being a lonely child watching mist fill a deserted plaza, the angry slap of a teacher, the firm grip of a US president as she shook hands, the mew of a kitten trapped in a box hedge. Sex, darkness, death, love, power . . .

Mai was already empty of dreams, her own and Joan's taken from her head by Rinpoche who'd simply put his hands to her temples and kept them there until nothing was left to come screaming out of the dark.

Now holding Mai's hands Rinpoche fought to assimilate, making and breaking connections, getting it right less often than he got it wrong and had to start over again. Half the lamas in Samsara fugued as Rinpoche conscripted Tsongkhapa to distribute what had been Joan's senses into the lucid dreams of others before Rinpoche finally began to pull it back into a whole.

All this for something as transient as a single flawed identity, no wonder Tsongkhapa was amused.

'I'm me, aren't I?' It was Mai talking but the voice was way too knowing for Mai.

Kate burst into tears.

'Oh for fuck's sake . . .' It was Mai this time, staring at Kate in exasperation. 'I'd thought you'd be glad to get her back.'

'I am,' Kate protested.

Chapter Forty-six

Ammo Check/Check Ammo

The tiny sliver of basalt broke free from beneath his foot and Axl froze, flat to the rock face, the reptilian part of his brain kicking in with a reflex that pre-dated humanity. No one shot at him. In fact, none of the conscripts even looked up. They were busy watching a fire burn fiercely in the distance, near the flat stone that stood for a cairn making the final stretch of the path down from the high-plateau's foothills

Axl had been hanging above them for ten minutes longer than was wise. So he was now running late even by his own ludicrous timescale. He would have shrugged but he was kind of occupied counting heads. Four conscripts in each slit trench, all armed with squat Brownings like the model Axl carried and both their trenches were strung round with chameleon net, the kind that diffused heat and filtered out static. Not that Axl or anyone still up on that ridge had thermal imaging glasses any more than they carried comScanners.

Habit then, or the conscripts didn't have any dumb net.

The five-year-old kid who'd inherited the patent on chameleon netting from her grandfather had a house in Texas wrapped round with so much of the stuff that even her bodyguards had trouble refinding the place if they dropped out to get a beer. That was the urban myth, anyway.

Behind the netted-up trenches, dug into separate foxholes were a corporal and defMoma. The corporal was muttering into a throat mike, hands doing a ragged dance as he stressed and re-stressed some point to his unseen listener. Whoever was on the other end didn't seem to like what they were hearing.

defMoma was glued into a tiny romReader, trodes wired up to her temples and a pair of floating-focus CK wraprounds masking her podgy face. If she wasn't deep in some dyke N/Sim then Axl didn't know what she was doing. Samsara didn't do newsfeeds. Hell, even Vajrayana didn't have a decent backbone.

Officially, media fasting was part of the UN-agreed 'fugee rehabilitation process. Like simple living, no powered vehicles and one-way tickets only. Unofficially, Tsongkhapa flatly refused to waste processing capacity cross-monitoring 17,889 newsfeeds on the indisputable grounds that most were crap, few added to the total sum of human knowledge and lucid dreaming was better for you anyway.

The Colonel wasn't visible, but Axl intended to work on the basis that the man was dug-in further back and probably on the other end of that conversation the corporal was having. If he was wrong, then tough.

Axl grinned sourly. And if he didn't shift his ass off that rock face soonish he wouldn't be doing any dreaming, lucid or not. Daylight would see to that. Besides, there was nothing wrong with the snubPup's two clips, just with the fact he only *had* two of them.

Less than three hundred dumb-fuck bullets to take out eight grunts and three brass dug into slits set into a forest full of maturing oaklings that would take whole clips to chop off at the waist.

As his old sergeant would have said, tough call . . .

LockMart's finest smart munitions could tap dance round any object not soft, warm and sentient. Even semi-smart, self steering could nudge themselves a couple of degrees in either direction. But straight dumb ceramics . . . Enough already.

Bass got buried under heavy synth as Axl's shoulders tightened. And when electric fiddle screamed in over the top Axl knew his body was ready, even if he wasn't.

This was the plan.

Axl kicked off hard from the rock face.

And fell.

Guitar howled. Pain flamed in both hands as the sisal cut fresh track marks into his palms, the rope ripping under one arm and across his back until he tightened his grip and gravity slammed him back into the rock face. Kicking off again, Axl let the burning rope explode through his hands like fire and then it was gone and he was really falling, straight onto a conscript.

Axl snapped the boy's neck in a crash of drums, boots ripping down both sides of the conscript's flicked-up head to shatter breastbone on either side and rupture third and fourth vertebrae in a wet chord change of compacting bone. Breaking his fall by landing on some grunt's head was sheer luck, no matter how slick it looked.

The other three conscripts in the slit never stood a chance as Axl emptied his first clip in a single staccato four-second burst. Ceramics scythed through already-mangled flesh, snare drumming into the damp earth at the other end of the trench. No one did vocals, there wasn't time. Axl was bathed in blood, faeces and minced flesh as it splattered back to where he crouched on the floor of the trench.

Back to a single base line. Then that inevitable drum roll.

Ammo check.

Wiping flesh out of his eyes, Axl slammed the second clip into his snubPup, ripped free two clips from the leg of what had been a grunt, then scrabbled in the leg's blood-filled knee pockets, finding grenades.

Three grenades, static or crawling, retroAlessi. Featuring recessed legs and those clean chrome lines so fashionable ten years back, about the time some idiot at Harvard uploaded a paper on Art and the Aesthetics of Corporate Violence. The first one was even part primed, red diode primly blinking. It was also just smart enough to be irritating.

But not as annoying as the clips getting wasted in the other trench as conscripts fired in all directions, blasting scars in a dozen trees. Kids the lot of them, poor bastards. Not even properly trained.

'One second,' Axl told the grenade, snapping off a protective cover.

'Two?'

'One.'

He yanked the pin viciously, lobbed the grenade towards the foxhole behind him and hit the bottom of his own slurry pit in one easy move, face-first into the contents of someone else's stomach.

The little shit grenade still counted off two seconds before exploding. Not that it made much difference. Zero seconds after it landed in his dugout the corporal was beyond bagging.

Somewhere a mood layer fed in behind the bass line. It wasn't hard to get back in the swing of things.

Grabbing grenade number two, Axl got it to promise a three-second count, counted off one himself and threw the apple hard enough to arc up over the road.

Chord crashing backwards out of his trench, Axl had dumb fucks locking the other slit down and blind before his grenade fragged in a neatly controlled airburst between the slit and defMoma's foxhole. Sliced sushi.

What Axl had going for him . . . Hell, the only thing he had going for him was the chameleon net screening off the trench he'd just been in. Somewhere back in those trees the Colonel would know his shit had hit the proverbial, but not yet how. Another flip and roll took Axl to the edge of defMoma's foxhole and he dropped into it, breech ratcheted back and diodes doing the walk/don't walk dance.

'You.' defMoma was slumped at the bottom of her foxhole, staring at an arm twisted awkwardly in front of her. White bone glistened through a long gash in pink flesh and blood dripped from one ear. Other than that she was untouched. Axl's second grenade had fragged at least five paces in front of her foxhole, half filling it with earth, and it was only mischance that a sliver of chrome had opened her arm all the way from wrist to elbow, leaving red edges where the flesh used to meet.

She had her semi-smart hiPower holstered on a green webbing belt but her gun hand was useless. 'I surrender,' the woman said flatly and the music in Axl's head went into a holding loop.

'Surprise me.' Axl sat back against the edge of the foxhole, SnubPup on his knees, muzzle towards her gut. Digging casually into a pouch pocket for his last grenade, he snapped off the plastic cover and activated what passed for its intelligence.

'Okay,' said Axl, 'this is where you sit still, understand?'

The fat sergeant looked at the flecks of flesh matted into Axl's hair and the blood painted in splashes across his face and nodded. Yeah, she understood.

'I'm going to take out three threads,' Axl told the grenade. 'And then we'll go over to voice mode for detonation. So you can do a better job of helping me.'

'That's not advisable.'

Axl sighed. 'I'm going to do it anyway,' he said, 'so I'd be really grateful if you didn't do anything stupid. But first . . .' Axl glanced at defMoma, head cocked to one side. 'I need your sulphate . . .' The fat woman didn't move.

'Alternately,' said Axl, 'I can defuse the grenade with these.' He held up both hands, showing defMoma the rapid shakes that softened his fingertips to a snare-drum blur. 'Your choice.'

Axl caught the sealed packet she tossed him, ripping out the corner with his teeth and pushing his tongue through the gap, chemical cunnilingus.

'Better, much.' Axl twisted the grenade's base free from its chrome outer shell. Four little sticks of bioSemtex sat there on the base, oily and glistening, each wired to the intelligence with a spider's trace of optic fibre.

'I'm disconnecting the first one,' said Axl and yanked the connection, hard and fast. He didn't bother to tell the apple he was about to remove the other two tubes, the intelligence would be expecting it.

Soon done. Axl screwed the grenade shut and tossed the three dead tubes out onto the grass. He now had a grenade that could kill defMoma without killing him.

'We could use this as a suppository . . .' Axl told her. He'd seen that done, more than once, and so had she from the look on her face. Kolonics was a strictly equal-opportunities atrocity: the last time he'd watched it happen a Brazilian major paid the price for upsetting his own NCOs. There'd been barely enough left to scrape off the bunker walls.

'. . . but you're going to incubate it instead.' He waited while she shifted her vast buttocks and sat on the grenade. 'And we're going to keep this short.

'So,' Axl said, 'What is this really about?'

defMoma stayed silent, but only because she was trying to work out what to say. There wasn't much hope in her face, but it wasn't all despair. Somewhere inside the woman was telling herself this was survivable. She was wrong.

'I'll tell you what I think,' Axl said, cutting in just as she was about to speak. 'This isn't about Joan. It's about the Cardinal. WorldBank are trying to take him down.'

She didn't deny it.

'Well,' said Axl, 'they won't be able to . . .'

Blue eyes locked onto his, hard and spiteful. Lips thinned. 'If I were you,' defMoma said, 'I wouldn't place too much faith in tired old men. They die.'

Axl shot her. What he'd had in mind was something clever involving the grenade holding her prisoner here while he made his excuses, but it just happened . . . And by the time he realised what a fuck-wit idea shooting her was, the fat woman's heart had a third ventricle and blood was spreading across her vest. The soundtrack had gone silent.

It was the drugs, Axl told himself as a back beat started up again. Too much sulphate, not enough sleep. Or maybe it was just post-traumatic irony. defMoma certainly looked liked she couldn't believe anyone could be stupid enough to do what he'd done.

Check ammo.

Full clip in his Browning. Three fulls velcroed to his leg and now he had her hiPower too. More than enough to check out what was alive in the other slit and kill it.

Axl drum-rolled out of defMoma's foxhole. Common sense said approach the second slit trench silently from the back, but Axl wasn't doing common sense. Besides they'd already been fragged. And they were kids, scared and under-trained. Been there, survived that. Axl ratcheted back the breech on his SnubPup and . . .

Stood.

Like anyone could be that stupid and not be on camera. He went through his first clip without even realising his finger was on the trigger, hit silence and reloaded without being aware he'd done that, either. The second clip lasted the brief seconds it took him to scramble through the gaping hole he'd just gunned in the camoNet.

160, 180, 200 . . . The bpm were pushing hardcore, meth jungle even. In the trench up ahead a woman stood, snubPub rising, and Axl lifted the top off her skull without even thinking about it. He hosed out the trench with the rest of his clip, finishing off a grunt already wounded by his earlier grenade, splinters of bone stripping leaves from oaks as the grunt's head vanished as cleanly as if Axl had taken it off at the neck with a chainsaw.

Tempo change. Scratch violin chopping out a warning.

Four, plus one, plus three. Two left.

Behind him.

Axl hit the ground ahead of the empty snubPup that swung butt-first towards his skull, rolled sideways and came up onto his knees rough and fast, reversing his Pup and swinging it hard by its barrel straight into a conscript's knee, Babe Ruth style.

The grunt crumpled, eyes bulging and mouth wide, too shocked to scream. Instinctively, Axl put an elbow in his throat, silencing him anyway. Strapped to his ankle, the grunt had one of those quick-release glass blades, undetectable by ninety-nine percent of all airport scanners so Axl borrowed it.

The knife bit into flesh under the conscript's ear opening a wide bubbling grin. All Axl needed to do to make it a necktie was reach in and yank his tongue out through the slit. Not his style. Instead he put the blade into the kid's heart and closed his large brown eyes after he fell.

'Borja.'

Sudden silence. Not even a click track or heartbeat.

Skin crawled across Axl's back, hairs rising on his neck. And then he got a low tom-tom line, part goan/part Vou that kicked at his stomach and shrivelled his mind into a fetal ball. Someone had just called time.

Axl knew that when he turned round the Colonel's salt and pepper hair would still be brushed neatly back from a face that was handsome, despite too much food and not enough exercise. And beneath that full moustache the mouth would be grim but smug. Also, the man would have a gun, something expensive and it would be pointed straight at Axl's head.

Axl was right on all the points, especially the last. The gun was a lovingly retrofitted 1896 Broomhandle Mauser 7.63 machine pistol. The only other *kreigsmarine* Axl had seen was in a Potsdam museum, but that version wasn't converted for ceramics.

'Going somewhere?'

Axl nodded. 'Yeah, things to do . . .'

'. . . people to kill. Aren't you bit too old for all that Black Jack shit?' Colonel Emilio smiled sadly and his smile was every bit as supercilious as Axl had expected.

'It was just a kid's program, for God's sake. Cheap American v'Actors laid over a Jap backbone. It wasn't even good. Or didn't you notice no one bothered to made a second series?'

No, Axl could truly say he hadn't noticed that.

'I killed defMoma,' Axl said, more for something to say. He was watching the Colonel's trigger finger go white at the knuckle. Watching that happen saved having to stare into the black nothingness of the *kreigsmarine*'s barrel. Undoubtedly there was some way to turn this situation, Axl just couldn't remember what it was. Black Jack would have known, except Black Jack hadn't made it to a second series.

'Alone, friendless, disgraced . . .' Colonel Emilio smiled at Axl. 'You do know the Cardinal's finished, don't you?'

So everyone kept telling him. Axl felt he should have been glad. Maybe. Less than three hours left to get himself to the Nuncio's cruiser and apparently he didn't need to anymore.

'Still, life isn't all bad,' said Colonel Emilio. 'You killed my troops.' The Colonel didn't sound too disappointed. 'And I get to kill you. And you didn't even know what this was all about.'

'But you're going to tell me anyway . . .'

Colonel Emilio shrugged. 'What's the point . . . The rest of us are doing *realpolitik* and you're still running scripts from a kid's *novela*. I should have had you killed in *La Medicina* before this all started.'

Axl nodded. 'Yeah,' he said, 'you should have done.' He was staring past Colonel Emilio at a shiny object picking its way laboriously over twigs and splintered branches towards the Colonel's heel. Maybe that whole Alessi retro-chrome shtick hadn't been the design disaster he'd originally thought.

Chapter Forty-seven

Down Through Zero

The gyrobike ate up the road like Axl was in some advertisement for nanetic shaving dust, penis transplants, sperm-freezing facilities . . . Something typically macho but tender.

Gualagara's *The White Condor* ran as backing track, Axl wasn't big on reworked Dutch trance but he figured it was the Ludwig Van/Tierra del Fuego mix. Light and breezy like the new countryside.

Each tight curve came up to meet him in an easy blur of hedgerow and overhanging oaks, the straights opening out to zip past on either side. The curves getting less tight and the straights longer each klick the Honda got closer to Vajrayana.

'00.09.59,' read the Seiko timecode. It had been flashing deeper red, in ten minute bites, for the last fifty minutes. Had Axl had enough time, he'd have stopped and found some way to disconnect it. But the city was at least thirty minutes away and the airport was beyond.

Axl was going to make that cruiser. Without Kate, without Mai, but at least with himself. Some things you just did, no matter how stupid they appeared to others . . . He'd broken up one marriage procession, terrified more horses than he dared to remember and only just managed not to leave himself as a smear along the road when he flipped out of a curve and almost went under the wooden wheels of a cart.

Dutch to Deutsch, the trance choon changed gear and Axl instinctively blipped his throttle, grinning like a lunatic.

Up ahead brick, wood and stone waterfalled down a high

slope, the Potala. Only Vajrayana's famed palace was clearly visible this distance from the city, as impressive as being face-on to a glacier.

Vast windows that looked tiny were cut into walls that plummeted hundreds of feet before anchoring to granite below. Inside one of those rooms sat the Dalai Lama and behind the lower, windowless stretch of wall resided Tsongkhapa. At least, that was what half Samsara thought. The rest, including Rinpoche, believed Tsongkhapa was incorporate.

'Everywhere and nowhere,' insisted Rinpoche. And it wasn't until Axl was approaching the city he worked out that what the silver monkey had been talking about was widely distributed, infinitely parallel computing. Except that the rules of quantum processing meant most of the bit shuffling didn't actually take place in a sense anyone could understand. At least not in any place that actually existed.

All possible states just were, simultaneously.

No wonder the Dalai Lamas had always been such fans.

Lights flashed. Axl got a sudden drum fill. '*00.00.00.*' read the pulsing eye implant.

'Tell me about it.' Axl throttled back to flip into corner, flip out again and blip his accelerator. He was riding the Honda on dumb. The last thing he wanted was some military semiAI trying to second-guess what he had in mind, or just deciding Axl shouldn't be on the bike anyway.

Which, of course, he shouldn't. The gyro was strictly PaxForce issue. And quite probably the reason Axl hadn't been stopped was the large UN/PF hologram that lit bright above his front and rear mudguard. Though the little recognition chip tucked inside the pocket of his mud, blood and vomit-encrusted cargo pants might also have had something to do with it.

According to the chip, the man burning off other traffic on the road into Vajrayana was Colonel Emilio, personal envoy of the Emperor of Mexico. Which wasn't actually true. The real Colonel Emilio was face down in an oak wood with a ceramic through his brain. At least Axl hoped to hell he was, if only on humanitarian grounds, because the alternative was the guy was alive and legless.

Axl patted his trouser packet. There were three morphine crawlers clinging to his own leg, dug in by their claws. Another five were still asleep in the pocket.

Axl had watched as the grenade clawed its way up the side of a rotting branch and tumbled over the top to roll so close to the Colonel Emilio's boot that had he stepped backward the Colonel would have tripped on it. Giving grenades canine-based smarts made sense, no cat would have been that loyal.

Or that stupid.

'Explode,' Axl said simply and the grenade did. One tube only, yet the casing fragged exactly, a femtosecond burst of laser unzipping precisely defined-molecular chains along two horizontal and two shorter vertical axes just ahead of the bioSemtex exploding.

One second Colonel Emilio had feet, the next he didn't. Only confused and half-blind with flash, Axl didn't notice that at first, he was too busy trying to crawl across wet forest floor towards the Colonel's dropped Mauser.

Vocoder and theramin. It was as well the *WarChild* theme loaded direct inside his head, because Axl was too deafened to hear anything happen in the world outside. At first Axl wasn't sure why he wasn't moving faster, but then he glanced back and saw that a path of glistening bone below his knee was encrusted caddis-like with grit and dead leaves. Shrapnel had lifted a flap of flesh from his leg as cleanly as any butcher with a cleaver.

White noise roared in on a wave of sour adrenaline, dying away as Axl slowly realised that getting to the Mauser wasn't a race he could lose. Not with a slack-jawed Colonel Emilio still sitting where he'd landed, holding one of his own boots with his foot still inside. He was looking bemused, as if he'd never seen either of them before.

After he'd lifted the Colonel's identity chip, found six Hondas hidden under netting and crippled them all except the one he wanted, Axl broken open a packet of undertakers and sprinkled them into the f/holes and slits. And then he kicked the gyrobike to life and circled back between the trees to return the Mauser to the Colonel. Leaving it within crawling distance.

'Shoot yourself,' suggested Axl. 'You know it's what everyone wants.'

The timecode now read – 00.19.59 and flashed neon bright. And the ragged Elektrika mix feeding his aural nerves was wound so tight there was nowhere left for its step-fed chord changes to go . . .

Axl didn't need the special effects, he knew he was late.

Minutes later, tourists scattered in a fruit market built under the walls of a monastery as Axl slid into a skid turn on damp cobbles and gunned the Honda between two stalls, grabbing a green pear on his way past.

The bpm plummeted, temple bells echoed over chanting. Without needing a cue, he'd hit the human touch.

The pear was hard and unripe like the soil that produced it, blistered across its belly from grubs eating its skin, but the skin wasn't polymer and no Monsanto trademark ran down the inside of its core. The pear tasted sour and slightly woody, but Axl finished it anyway. There were people watching.

Weird as it might seem, he was going to miss Samsara. Seasons happened. Whichever way you looked at it, the place had USPs other destinations couldn't imagine. You didn't have to be rich to get in for a start. Though even the Dalai Lama would have trouble keeping the metaNational out once the atmosphere thickened and the temperature got hiked. Unless, of course, Tsongkhapa kept the place like it was. Axl could go for that . . .

Up ahead the market street split, two narrow lanes leading into shadow. Axl flipped right at random. No reason. Gunning the Honda, he ripped up the middle of a long incline steep enough to have pedestrians hunched forward as they walked. The walls either side were high and bare, windows beginning two floors above street level. The only breaks were sunken doorways that the peds stumbled back into as Axl raced past them.

And then the narrow street ended. Chopped off abruptly by a white wall at least five-feet thick if the depth of the open arch cut into it was anything to go by.

'−00.29.59,' read his timecode, but he'd been trying to ignore it since the readout flipped over to black fluoro, nine minutes, fifty-nine seconds ago.

Each tread in the stairway ahead dipped in the middle from centuries of constant use, except that was impossible and the steps had to have been cut or grown that way.

Axl could go on, or go back and try to find another route. For once instinct, conditioning and the backing track weren't feeding him any clues. Twin halogens lit automatically as Axl nudged the Honda through the arch, then blipped the throttle again until the gyrobike began to climb, monoshocks eating up the concussion of each step.

Under-trained conscripts, yeah. Dubious ethics, ditto doubled. You could say what you like about PaxForce, but they did source the best kit. Back in the jungle that had been one of the reasons Axl made a point of stealing it whenever possible.

Axl grinned sourly. He was shattered, his limbic system was in neuropeptide free fall, his mind trying to hang onto dopamine like it was some brat refusing to give up a dummy.

Chances were Axl was going to need a new leg, or at least a splice from the knee down. And when those morphine crawlers shrivelled up and died he was going to be in such pain he hadn't felt anything like it, at least not since last time.

And yet . . .

Axl blipped the Honda's throttle and bounced up over the last step, landed heavily and felt ABS and gyro cut in a split second after the back wheel started to slide on marble. He was upright and roaring down a darkened corridor before he'd even had time to worry about hitting the ground. Above him filigreed lamps hung on long brass chains from a high ceiling. Tapestries smothered both walls, flicking by so fast that Axl could get no sense of what they showed, only that red and gold predominated.

The steady thud of his engine should have roared off the walls but it was missing, swallowed to a low thud by the tapestries. Inside his head an African Sanctus soared into high chant and steady drums. *That* made no sense to Axl either. He just assumed the sound system he was running had nothing else suitable.

Every hundred paces a wild-eyed man or woman would appear, blue skinned with lips pulled back to show curved tusks that sprouted from a heavy bottom jaw. The figures were elaborately carved and painted. *Bon* was what Tukten called them back in the village, and for all Axl knew that was what people called them here too.

And wherever *here* was they employed monks to open doors for gyrobikes. At least, that's how it looked to Axl. Just as he began to hit his breaks – the wooden door embossed with an eight-spoked wheel rushing towards him too fast to ignore any longer – an old man in orange robes stood up from a three-legged stool to push half the door open just enough for Axl to ride through into freefall.

And he was juddering down a long flight of stone steps in a whine of synth and self-adjusting gyro, daylight blinding his eyes before he realised with shock that the monk had nodded to him.

The back of the Potala stood stark and quietly magnificent behind Axl. If not so awe-inspiring as when seen from the front then still impressive enough. But it was the sign to the airport that crashed chords and wrote a manic grin across Axl's tired face.

−00.37.00. No one could say it wasn't pushing the envelope,

but as yet the envelope wasn't ripped in two. Or the readout wouldn't have been happening because the SS *St Bernadotte* would have gone. That was how Axl read things anyway.

At the cargo gates to the airport was a human guard. Not just a token human, but the kind that actually flicked switches to lower a section of sonic fence. And as Axl came racing up, the man hit the switch *and waved*. Without thinking, Axl flipped a return wave and then he was past the perimeter, racing towards a vast yurt, constructed from a single transparent vat-grown sheet of goat's skin held taut by chromed metal guys as thick as a child's wrist.

The yurt was Samsara's Departure Hall and beyond it Axl saw the Nuncio's cruiser, already cleared for take-off, a group of saffron-robed lamas standing around it and staring in his direction.

Whatever Axl had been expecting, this wasn't it. One of the monks waved frantically and Axl realised that whatever the hell else was expected of him, neither sneaking or blasting his way aboard the austere, purple-lacquered cruiser was part of the menu. The Boeing had exclusive written all over it, from the near silence of its engines as they fired up to the elongated slow-glass bubble sat atop its nose like a freshwater pearl.

'Borja,' Axl said as he slid the Honda to a halt and dropped it where it stopped, back wheel still spinning. 'Axl Borja.' The Swiss Guard at the base of the moving walkway actually stepped back and saluted.

'You brought the girl?' The booming voice echoed from the cruiser's doorway, where an obese Namibian dressed entirely in purple stood staring down at Axl.

Axl was already shaking his head before he wondered, *which girl*, the kid or Kate? And what had happened to wanting Father Sylvester? Synth-loops looped, feeding on themselves. Didn't matter either way. He was into the signature tune.

'No,' Axl said, 'No girl, just me.'

Chapter Forty-eight

PoV Free

The first thing Axl noticed about the Nuncio's cabin was the mahogany panelling. Second he spotted Bronzino's painting 'Venus, Cupid, Folly and Time', commissioned by Cosimo de'Medici of Florence in 1545, though Axl just saw a naked boy with wings cupping the breast of an older woman. Finally, he realised the sound track was gone. He didn't know whether to be relieved or upset.

The Nuncio fed him while the engines finished firing up. Not nutrients, chelated vitamins or worse still, luke-warm plates of Tsampa and buttered tea, but a vast platter of beef, carved from the side of a huge joint that already sat steaming on a silver salver.

Maybe the Church really had streamlined itself into austerity but, if so, no one appeared to have told the Nuncio. Blood-dark Barolo came from a tall wine jug, hammered from silver and embossed with vine leaves that curled from its elegant base up through its round belly to a narrow fluted top which was closed by a single silver leaf that hinged at the stalk.

'The Two Sicilies, nineteenth-century, pre-Risorgimento,' the Nuncio told Axl, dropping crumbs from his mouth to his expansive lap. After the beef they ate syllabub and washed down slivers of basalt-like parmesan with a wine so sweet and thick it stuck to Axl's teeth.

Outside they were preparing for the Boeing to take off, but that was still ten minutes away. Time enough, the Nuncio said, to eat parmesan properly. And as Axl sipped the wine while sucking the slivers of hard cheese to soften them, he could feel spiders crawling over his leg. At least he assumed the mediCare box at his feet had got around to converting ants into spiders. The ants had gone in first, tiny metallic pincers stripping away dead flesh from the edge of the gash, then they'd excreted some kind of mite so small as to be invisible and so dedicated all it could do was repair cell walls and die. The spiders did the macro work, like stitching or spinning strips of new skin.

It was battlefield stuff, crude but reusable. Not what Axl would have expected the Nuncio to carry and undoubtedly not what he kept for his own use, assuming he paid as much attention to the Church's dislike of nanetics as he did to its exhortations to poverty.

Food, wine and the smallest of talk about who was doing what at the Vatican filled the time, the gossip as unreal to Axl as any newsfeed half seen on a feed across a crowded bar. But the Nuncio said nothing about Joan, soulcatchers or any coming conclave. Nothing about the Cardinal, either. And the only thing the Nuncio didn't offer Axl was new clothes or a shower.

Axl had a nasty feeling that lack of soundtrack and no shower fed back to a cryptic comment of the Nuncio's when Axl first clambered on board. The Nuncio's arm had gone round his shoulder, avuncular maybe, but still steering him away from the open doorway.

'This is dead space,' the Nuncio announced waving one arm at the ornate interior of his cruiser. 'Looped out/PoV-free.' Then he stopped, looked carefully at Axl.

'You don't have the faintest idea what I'm talking about, do you?'

Axl didn't, so he said he didn't and the Nuncio nodded, black eyes glittering in a face round and black as a total eclipse.

'Good.'

Chapter Forty-nine

Hollow Rooms

Villa Carlotta looked as it had the last time Axl had seen it. Purple bougainvillea still smothered the walls of the gatehouse, softening the hard lines of the reinforced titanium gate now shutting behind him. Squat palms like over-large pineapples edged the gravelled drive, fat trunks curved under the weight of waxed leaves as sharp as blades and as big as surfboards. And lush curling ferns buried the crested, baroque gates to the courtyard beneath an explosion of nature's pubic hair.

Arpeggios ran down his spine. The notes fuzzy, like a harpsichord sampled note for note and then damped. Perhaps that was because he couldn't see the Villa properly. Maybe, if he hadn't been squinting through the smoked glass windows of a vast Nexus stretch, the notes would have been clear as crystal.

Right back in Dey Effé, after the Nexus had asked him where he wanted to be taken, Axl told the stretch to wind down the window and it had suggested he use manual. So he'd hit the window's button himself and the window had suggested he ask the car. They'd been going round in the same circle ever since, with increasing bad temper.

So instead of watching open countryside, Axl had been forced to spend the trip looking at himself, since the inside of every car window was mirrored. And everywhere Axl had looked he'd seen his own haggard reflection staring back.

'We're here,' announced the Nexus, opening the door nearest Axl.

'Really?' Axl said, harpsichord and heartbeat syncopating.

It's my own choice, Axl told himself. No one could take that away from him. Everything else maybe, including his life, but not that. He slammed the car door, without giving the Nexus time to shut itself. Guaranteed to irritate the car, but Axl didn't care. Though no doubt it would whine to the Nuncio when it got back.

Grit crunching under his feet, Axl walked slowly across the huge courtyard towards the main doorway of the Villa Carlotta, watched silently by four guards. If they planned to arrest him now would be a good time.

No one moved.

'Fuck it.' The words weren't loud or directed at anyone except himself but that didn't mean Axl didn't mean them. He'd screwed up big time. God alone knew how Rinpoche was doing, or Kate, or Mai. And what upset Axl was the certainty at the base of his gut that he'd never get the chance to find out.

Straightening his back and pushing his chin in the air the way Kate did, Axl stamped over to door.

'Axl Borja,' he announced firmly. 'To see the Cardinal.'

'Is he expecting you?'

Axl looked at the door and shrugged. 'Who knows what His Excellency expects. I wouldn't presume . . .' Actually, he would and had, frequently. Now just didn't seem the time to mention it. Axl stepped through into the waiting hall.

It was empty. So was the long corridor.

The last time Axl had stood there, the corridor alone had been filled with a thousand petitioners, so full that bored ushers stood on plinths watching out for those who'd fainted in the crush. Now there was nobody at all in the echoing corridor but Axl, and the unexpected emptiness was at least as overpowering as the crowd had been.

It must have been the Villa's AI that opened the door at the end of the corridor for Axl because no human was there to do it, the doorkeeper's gilded stool was as empty as the plinths that once housed the ushers. Right then, Axl couldn't tell what was backing track and what was his own heartbeat. He had a feeling that was intentional.

Axl stepped in through the door and found himself again in the Cardinal's vast ante-room. Silence echoed off silk-covered walls and the only person reflected in the vast glass slabs of neo Venetian mirrors was him. Even the silver carts that dispensed hot chocolate were deserted and cold.

'Borja.' On the other side of the room, the Cardinal's major-domo stood proudly by the door to His Excellency's tiny octagonal study, but the man's face was grim and his smile troubled. Something was so wrong Axl couldn't even begin to imagine.

'Well,' growled a voice from behind the door. 'Who is it?'

'Axl Borja, Your Excellency.'

'Borja?' The voice was tired, gravel and glass. Older than Axl remembered and quietly angry. Yet still unmistakable enough to make Axl shiver.

'Borja, Your Excellency.'

'Well, send him in . . .'

And Axl walked past the empty benches and across the *impasto di gesso* floor, his steps echoing in the silence. Heartbeat filling his emptiness.

'Come to gloat?' The Cardinal pulled his top lip back into a sneer, revealing canines that were yellow with age. Yellow and cracked like old ivory. There was an edge to his voice, a cold disappointment that bordered on fury.

His in-tray was bare of paper and the only sign that he'd been working was a small screen angled up from the desk. Axl wanted to ask what disaster had happened but didn't know how. No matter what he achieved, how old he got he never had the right words when stood in front of this man.

'No,' said Axl simply. 'I've here to tell you I'm back from Samsara.'

'And you've brought me the soulcatcher?'

'No.' Axl shook his head. 'I brought only myself.'

From the look on the vampyre's face it didn't seen as if that was anything like enough. 'I'm not so powerless that I can't still have you shot,' the Cardinal said shortly.

Axl shrugged. 'No,' he said, 'I didn't imagine you were.' They both knew that was true.

'So why didn't you bring me what I asked?'

'It was needed.'

The Cardinal took off his dark glasses at that, and rested them neatly on his black glass desk. 'And who needed my soulcatcher?' The Cardinal's voice was low, his golden eyes fixed like sighting lasers on Axl's face.

Mai and Kate, Axl didn't know which one had needed it most. Mai for her sanity, Kate for her dead lover.

'Joan did,' said Axl.

When Axl had finished crying, the Cardinal ordered coffee, though there was only his major-domo to operate the coffee-maker and Axl ended up going to fetch the water himself. With the coffee they ate truffles dusted with pure cocoa powder. Or rather Axl ate the truffles while the Cardinal smoked a Partegas corona down to a damp stub.

'Joan was shot,' the Cardinal said suddenly, stubbing out his cigar. 'Her body was ripped apart by children. Do you deny that?'

Axl shook his head.

'So the Pope is dead?'

Axl shook his head.

'Surely,' said the Cardinal, 'Her Holiness is either alive or dead? All I require from you is that you tell me which it is . . .'

'I'm not qualified to answer.'

'No indeed,' the Cardinal gave a vulpine smile and lit another cigar, 'I'm not sure anybody is. We'll just have to see what the courts say.' He reached for the pop-up screen on his desk and swivelled it, so Axl could watch the frozen, tear-stained face of an ex-child star, ex-hitman, ex-burger flipper at McDonalds.

The date on the CySat copyright line was that day's, the time just gone. The blipvert moral expanding across the screen explained for the cognitively-challenged that Rome, WorldBank and the IMF had just been tied into a court case that would last decades, maybe longer.

The imminent, expected return to prominence of Cardinal Santo Ducque made first story on most newsfeeds that evening.

Epilogue

Points of Vision

On screen Axl swore on the Bible, the Koran, the Talmud and the works of Immanuel Kant. Then waited while the IMF, WorldBank and Rome read off his blood pressure, heartbeat and limbic pattern, took and matched MRI scans to already-prepared templates to confirm that Axl regarded Joan's being both alive and dead as a statement of fact not of faith, hope or belief. That statement would go on file until it was needed, several years from then.

Mostly, what happened after Axl's return to the Villa Carlotta were negatives. The Vatican didn't go into conclave to elect a new pope. Under a statute previously agreed by the UN, the Cardinal currently holding voting rights (which happened to be Cardinal Santo Ducque) kept both his proxy vote in the UN and control of the Vatican Bank. Interim audits were not issued. Nor would they be while the court case was running. Which could be forever, or at least as long as it took the Cardinal to replenish the accounts emptied by Joan shipping 'fugees to Samsara.

No matter how often Axl watched reruns, he was faced with the fact that he limped in through the door of Villa Carlotta, head jerking to some unheard soundtrack and looking so dirty you could practically smell him through the screen.

And the stuff shot though his own eyes shook so badly by the end that Axl was surprised CySat had been able to use it. But what Axl really remembered about that night were the calls which flooded in between the rolling of the credits and the breaking news of Cardinal Santo Ducque's comeback.

A thin man, utterly unmemorable except for the large pectoral cross hung round the neck of his black silk Armani jacket called from New York. He wanted to be the first to tell the Cardinal how audacious, how brilliant a move it had been to stream Axl's quest for Pope Joan live on CySat.

But others followed within seconds. Rome, Rio, even Beijing. Everyone thought the Cardinal was brilliant, none had ever doubted him . . . And sitting at his desk taking the calls, Cardinal Santo Ducque had looked up and seen Axl staring at him, with something between outrage and admiration in his eyes.

'Look,' said the Cardinal, 'I just wanted to run a dummy past WorldBank. The idea to run it live and reactivate your soundtrack came from that bloody gun of yours . . .'